Born in England, leaving school at the age of 14, founded three business selling the first two.

The third business became very successful with 600 employees and was sold in 1988 when Ian retired to Spain. Family wise married with six children all who have become successful in their own ways.

To my wife who has encouraged me over the years

Ian Leslie

THE LONELY MAN

AUSTIN MACAULEY PUBLISHERS™
LONDON • CAMBRIDGE • NEW YORK • SHARJAH

This is a work of fiction. Names, characters, businesses, places, events, locales, and incidents are either the products of the author's imagination or used in a fictitious manner. Any resemblance to actual persons, living or dead, or actual events is purely coincidental.

A CIP catalogue record for this title is available from the British Library.

ISBN 9781398408098 (Paperback)
ISBN 9781398408104 (ePub e-book)

www.austinmacauley.com

First Published 2022
Austin Macauley Publishers Ltd®
1 Canada Square
Canary Wharf
London
E14 5AA

The Lonely Man Conspiracy

It hadn't been a busy week in the CID office at Kilburn, small house robberies, two or three car thefts, six assaults and a dozen drunk and disorderly cases.

Ben Clark and Alex Quirk were in the CID office when a call came through.

'Safe blowing at a prominent building in Baker Street.'

Ben, Alex and Barrie Starnes from the CID squad travelled to investigate a rather simple routine robbery that turned out to be a nightmare. City Boys Security Company made the call, reporting that one of their contract buildings had been broken into, and a safe on the third floor of the building had been found blown open, the companies own investigating team were also on their way.

Charley Dawson stood six feet one, spotted face with brownish hair, in words of his employers a really nice chap. He had been employed as a Security Officer for about nine years, in those years nothing positive had happened. Charley felt really important that one of his buildings had been broken into, and some high flying CID officers were on their way.

The police were on site within ten minutes of the call; a further patrol car also arrived from the local police station.

Ben Clark asked Charley Dawson if he had seen anybody hanging around the office complex and was it correct the safes were on the third floor.

'That's correct, Sir, I have to check that floor twice a night but I didn't notice anybody around.'

'OK, let's take a look at the office on the third floor, if you two officers pointing at them could remain here preventing anybody entering or leaving the building.'

'Charley, is this the accounts department?' looking at the safe on the third floor.

'I have no idea, Sir.'

They looked at the next office which held two further safes that hadn't been touched, the robbers certainly knew what they were looking for.

As they returned to the ground floor the investigating team from Boys Security Company had arrived. 'I would appreciate if you all remain here until SOCO have finished their investigation,' said Ben Clark.

SOCO arrived led by Ken Tucky who had known Ben Clark for some I8 years, 'What have we got, Ben?'

'Safe blown on the third floor, the perpetrators got in through a window on the staircase.'

'I will take a look there first, Ben.'

'We better telephone the key holder,' said Ben, Alex sat with Charley taking his statement.

Alex, Ben and Barrie discussed the robbery, why would a security company only visit the third floor twice a night and not the rest of the building. Unless the third floor is the accounts department where large amounts of monies are kept in one particular safe, which means it must be an inside job.

Two safes not touched, so were the robbers frightened off or did they know exactly what they were looking for.

The senior investigating officer from Boys Security Company asked if he could interview Charley Dawson, Ben couldn't see why not, but asked them all not to leave the building without speaking with him first.

Ben pointed out, that soon as possible they would look at which safe blowing teams were active at that present time.

'Let's go and see how Ken's getting on.' As they arrived, SOCO were just finishing, 'Got anything, Ken?'

'No, Ben, clean as a whistle, a professional team without doubt.'

Returning to the front desk, one of the uniform boys was speaking with a tall man, early forties with dark eyes and rather large ears wearing a brown suit.

Charley came forward. 'Hallo, Mr Sainsbury, unfortunately there's been a break-in and one of your safes have been blown.'

'Christ no,' Sainsbury turned to go up the stairs.

'Hold on, Sir.'

'I must go up-stairs now. You don't understand it's a life or death situation.' Turning to one of the security company officials, 'That's your company finished here.'

Ben Clark stepped forward, 'What's going on here?'

Charley introduced Mr Sainsbury as the key holder.

'Nice to meet you, Mr Sainsbury, let's pop into this office and have a chat,' suggested Ben Clark.

'Who the hell are you telling me where I can go in my building, I insist on going immediately to the third floor.'

'Mr Sainsbury, we have an investigation taking place, we will be able to visit the third floor in five minutes, but first we require some details. One safe has been blown and two others not touched, are these safes part of your company's accounts department.

There was no reply from Sainsbury, other than 'O Christ, what am I going to do,' turning white and shaking and making a dash for the stairs.

Ben signalled Barrie and a uniformed officer to follow him while he and Alex took the lift to try and cut Sainsbury off.

Reaching his office Sainsbury shouted out 'O Christ, it's gone.'

'What's gone, Mr Sainsbury, is this the accounts office?' asked Barrie.

'No, it's not the accounts office, it's my bloody office and it's gone; my documents, maps and plans, and about three thousand pounds.'

'Steady yourself, Mr Sainsbury, sit down for a minute, and take some deep breaths.' Sainsbury pulled out a gun from inside his coat pocket. Barrie and the uniformed officer stepped back, 'Sir, please hand over the gun.'

Ben Clark and Alex Quirk where making their way to the office when Sainsbury appeared in the corridor with the gun.

Alex shouted to Sainsbury to put the gun down, Sainsbury just turned firing the gun hitting both Barrie and the uniformed officer.

Alex leaped at Sainsbury, but Sainsbury was able to get another shot off grazing the side of Alex's arm, which sent him flying, falling on top of Ben Clark both hitting the ground.

Sainsbury made for the staircase. The two other police officers and the security team made for the lift after hearing the shots telling Charley to remain at the front entrance.

SOCO also heard the shots and made their way down the back staircase to the third floor. Sainsbury arrived on the ground floor with Charley asking what was going on with the shooting.

Sainsbury just raised his gun shooting Charley, who slumped to the floor, Sainsbury jumped over Charley's body running out into the street and away.

Ken Tucky was the first to arrive, 'Christ, what the hell happened here.' Ben was removing himself from under Alex's body. Another officer was checking how bad Barrie Starnes and the uniformed officer were 'both were dead.

Ben checked Alex, 'You ok mate.'

Flesh wound Ben.

The lift doors opened with two police officers accompanied by the security investigators stepping out.

'We have two officers down,' and Sainsbury's made off down stairs.

'Christ, Charley, get back down to the ground floor,' yelled Ben.

Ken telephone Kilburn Police Station letting them know they had officer's down.

'Leave it to me, Ken, I'll get the ball rolling,' said Sergeant Weber.

Weber called Chief Inspector Bleasdale, along with the murder squad, letting them know they had officers down at Mallards Publishing House.'

Chief Inspector Bleasdale in turn called the Deputy Commissioner, 'Absolute awful news, Bleasdale, I'm on my way with Superintendent Parker.'

The two Security Investigators ran down stairs to the front office, 'Bloody hell, Charley's dead, the bullet had entered his throat and exited out the back of his head.'

Jack Towner called his own company explaining that at least four people had been shot dead, police cars were on site in minutes. Murder Squad Officers arrived along with Chief Inspector Bleasdale.

'Where are my men?' Bleasdale asked.

'Third floor, Sir.'

'Who's this poor fellow,' asked Bleasdale.

'The local security officer, Sir.'

'The Deputy Commissioner is on his way,' pointed out Bleasdale, checking his watch 22.35. The medics arrived and were directed to the third floor.

Chief Inspector Bleasdale was out of the lift and down the corridor 'Whose down, Clark?'

'Barrie Starnes and a uniformed officer, Sir, also the local security officer named Charley Dawson.'

'Yes, Clark, I have already seen him.'

'What about you, Quirk?'

'I'm fine, Sir, flesh wound.'

Ken Tucky placed coats over the faces of the two officers on the floor. The lift door opened and the medics were down the corridor looking at Quirk's arm.

Inspector Hales of the murder investigation team spoke with Sergeant Clark taking a brief statement before making his way back to the ground floor.

The Deputy Commissioner and Superintendent Parker walked through the front door.

'Hallo, Inspector Hales.'

'Good evening, Sir, three dead and one wounded.'

'Parker asked which officers were down.'

'Detective Barrie Starnes from Bravo Six and a uniformed officer from Baker Street, Nick. Also Mr Charley Dawson, the local security officer.'

'Who's this?'

'Mr Dawson's Supervisor, Sir, Jack Towner.'

'Have you informed your company of the incident, Mr Towner?'

'Yes, Sir, my Managing Director is on his way.'

'Let's visit the third floor, Superintendent.'

'Are you acquainted with any of the officers?'

'Yes, Sir, Sergeant Ben Clark, Alex Quirk, and of course, the unfortunate Barrie Starnes.'

'Hallo, Bleasdale.'

'This is Sergeant Clark, Sir.'

'Good evening, Sergeant, a bit of a mess.'

'Yes, Sir, and you are Ken Tucky, Sir.'

'SOCO, have you got anything so far?'

'Not really, Sir, a very professional job, no prints whatsoever.'

'So it's a safe blowing robbery,' suggested the Deputy Commissioner, looking at all the officers, saying, 'Superintendent Parker would be taking charge.'

'You better accompany me back down to the ground floor, Chief Inspector Bleasdale, as I am sure the newspapers will have heard all about the shootings.'

The telephone rang in a Madrid flat. 'Hallo.'

'Senior Moran, its Peter Sainsbury. The documents, they are gone.'

'What do you mean gone, you told us they were completely safe.'

'Somebody has blown the safe in my office and I've had to shoot some cops and a guard.'

'You did what, you fool.'

'You've got to get me out of here, Senior Moran, please.'

'Calm down, get down to Watford, Kuki's flat you've been there before, Alexander Road just off the Town Hall.'

'Yes, yes, where are the keys.'

'Around the side of the garage under a stone, I will send somebody over with passports to get you out of the country, you have certainly caused plenty of problems, Sainsbury.'

'I'm sorry, I panicked.'

'Ok get down to Watford.' Carlos Moran (known as fat Tony) was 5'8, rather fat with an oval face, with brown hair, Carlos was well known as an arms dealer.

Picking up the telephone, Carlos called Miguel Melgar, a thick set man, 5'9, always smartly dressed, living in Barcelona.

'Get over to England, Miguel, we have a serious problem, that fool Sainsbury has lost the documents and plans, and shot some cops, Make it look like an accident, Miguel, I've sent him to Kuki's flat in Watford.'

'Ok, Carlos, I'll be on the next flight to London.'

Ben Clark had made his statement to the murder squad detectives, with Superintendent Parker also making notes. Clark and Parker went back a long way, Ben knew he would be in deep shit, as Parker had no time for him or Alex Quirk whatsoever.

Ken Tucky was making his statement to another Murder Squad officer. Jack Towner was making a very critical statement about the handling of the whole affair.

The Deputy Commissioner overheard his comments and whispered to Bleasdale, 'Have we got a problem with Bravo Six?'

'I personally don't think so, Sir, Clark and Quirk are very good detectives hard but fair.'

'Very good, Chief Inspector, let's hope it turns out that way.'

The coroner arrived and one of the uniformed boys ushered them up to the third floor.

'Deputy Commissioner, can you give us a statement,' shouted a reporter from outside.

'I will be giving a statement in an hour,' was the reply.

'Who's that man speaking with the reporters.'

'The Managing Director from the security firm.'

'Christ sake, get him in here.'

'What the hell are you doing man, giving statements to reporters at this early stage of the crime,' the Deputy Commissioner shouted.

'I believe I have all the right in the world as one of my men has been shot.'

'You will not say another word until I instruct you. Are you clear? Now go and sit over there.'

Another reporter shouted, 'Deputy Commissioner, how many are dead?' This comment was ignored. 'Billy, run this story over to *the Sun* before any of the other newspapers gets the headlines.'

Alex Quirk had been patched up at the hospital, 'You were lucky by the sounds of it, Detective,'

'I guess so, Doctor. Can I get off now?'

'Yes, but I recommend you go home and rest.'

Alex returned to Baker Street in a taxi, listening to the driver telling him about the shootings 'They say about six are dead, and hundred thousand quid missing. Some Security Director has made a statement.'

Alex paid the taxi driver off, making his way along the street around the side of the building, showing his warrant card as he entered through the back door.

Chief Inspector Bleasdale was the first to see Alex, 'What are you doing back here, Quirk'.

The Deputy Commissioner turned around, 'Detective Quirk.'

'Right, Sir.'

The Deputy Commissioner wanted to know the ins and outs of the crimes.

'It appears, Sir, that some kind of documents and plans are missing along with some cash. This fellow Sainsbury pulled a gun on our boys and just started shooting. Sainsbury had been clearly asked at least four or five times, if the offices on the third floor were the accounts department and if cash was held in those safes.

'Bravo Six officers had asked Sainsbury to step into one of the offices on the ground floor and explain the situation, which Sainsbury reluctantly declined, running off in the direction of the third floor, with our boys chasing him. When they reached the office on the third floor, all Sainsbury would say 'they're gone'. He was again asked if there was money missing.

'Sainsbury replied saying about three thousand pounds, but important documents and plans were missing. He was asked what documents the reply was negative, this appears to be the time when the gun was produced from his pocket.'

'Thank you, Inspector Hales, I am sure you will furnish Superintendent Parker with all the written statements.'

'Ok, Superintendent, we better call the press conference, I notice we now have the television present.'

'I'm afraid so, Sir.'

Superintendent Parker made his way outside and informed the media that the Deputy Commissioner would be making a brief statement.

Chief Inspector Bleasdale came forward telling the Deputy Commissioner that Mr Charles Pidore, Managing Director of Mallards Publishing Company, had telephoned, after hearing the news on television.

'Call him back and have him come down to my office at the yard as soon as possible. Inform my secretary that we are expecting him.'

'Yes, Sir.'

The Deputy Commissioner went through the main entrance towards the media; 'I would like to say that unfortunately we have had two police officers shot dead along with a local security officer. A search has started for a man we believe can help us with our enquiries.'

'One of the newspaper men called out, 'is that the key holder Peter Sainsbury, and is it true that large amount money is missing from one of the upstairs safes.'

'I repeat a search is being made for a person we believe can help us with our enquirers, Superintendent Parker is heading the enquiry and further statements will be made at a later time.'

'Deputy Commissioner, Mr Shore of the City Boys Security Company suggested it was Peter Sainsbury who shot two policemen and his security guard, after removing one hundred thousand pounds.'

'Thank you ladies and gentleman, I have no further comments at this time.

'The media are going to try and get further interviews with Mr Shore and his investigator Towner, Have them taken to the yard, Superintendent.'

'Yes, Sir.'

'Inspector Bleasdale you will obviously keep some of your officers here until the murder squad and SOCO have completely finished.'

Peter Sainsbury rushed down to Baker Street tube station boarding a train destined for Watford, arriving forty-five minutes later. Walking smartly past Cassabury Park towards the Town Hall, he passed under the underpass and into

Alexandra road. Kuki's flat was on the ground floor next to the garage, looking around Sainsbury noticed the large stone with the key beneath.

Letting himself into the flat and drawing the curtains, looking at the drinks cabinet with a half a bottle of whisky and two bottles of dry ginger. Pouring himself a large scotch and sitting down tapping his feet on the floor, and wondering what the hell would happen to him. And who the dickens would have known about the documents and plans in the safe.

The Deputy Commissioner and Superintendent Parker were driven back to Scotland Yard through the darkened streets of London.

A further police vehicle left the back entrance of Mallards Publishing House headed for Scotland Yard with Mr Shore and Towner in the back seat with Chief Inspector Bleasdale in the passenger front seat. Shore was complaining to Bleasdale about their treatment. Bleasdale was 6 feet tall, greyish thinning hair, a long face, which didn't do him any favours as his glasses perched on his long nose. Many thought he looked like a creep and was only interested in his own wellbeing and promotion.

Ben Clark, Alex Quirk and Ken Tucky made their way back to Kilburn Police Station, one murder squad officer and one of SOCO's people remained at Mallards.

Television reports were made at half hour intervals, saying that the Deputy Commissioner of Scotland Yard had earlier made a statement to the fact that two police officers and one security officer had been shot dead; it was unclear at this time if any robbery had taken place.

However, the Managing Director of City Boys Security Company had suggested that three men were shot dead trying to prevent a man escaping with a large amount of money thought to be in the region 100,000 pounds, the police however have deigned this statement.

Murder Squad officers are still at Mallards Publishing House in Baker Street, we hope to be able to give further news through the night.

Sir John Bacon Police Commissioner, had arrived at the Yard and was waiting the arrival of his Deputy 'Bill, I have watched the news broadcast. Why on earth did this Security chap make a statement like that.'

'Sir John, unfortunately he arrived as we were investigating the shootings, the media grabbed him and he made this awful untrue statement.'

Superintendent Parker, having digested all of the statements, briefed the Commissioner and his Deputy.

The Commissioner looked stunned, why on earth would a man shoot three innocent people for some documents and three thousand pounds.

Sainsbury watched the news bulletins, where did this bloody I00,000 pounds come from. Clark, Quirk and Tucky also viewed the news; 'and it's our rotten luck having Parker heading the case. I can still remember the last time when we found the murderer and Parker claimed all the glory for our hard work and was promoted to Superintendent.'

'I think when this case is over, I'm retiring to Spain.'

'That sounds like a good idea, I'll come with you,' commented Ken Tucky.

Joe Bolt and Derrick Smallwood were sitting in the Boxers club at Brixton watching the newsflash "three shot dead in Baker Street". 'We were lucky getting out the area, possibly another thirty minutes and it would have been crawling with the Old bill, they would have been pulling everybody, that's for sure'.

'Joe, you know Jeff better than anybody, he didn't appear to unhappy when we only found three grand in the safe, instead of the ten grand promised, and those bloody documents Jeff took, what is that all about.'

'You know Jeff, he likes to read other people's documents, and then he burns them. Who cares, we got a grand each.'

'Yeah, but it's dangerous, Joe, those poxy documents could get us ten years and what about the snout who stuck the job up.'

'That's Jeff's problem'.

The Managing Director of Mallards Publishing House had arrived and was escorted to the conference room. Charles Pidore was in his late fifties with fair hair, adequately dressed and stood at 5'9.

Sir John Bacon came forward, 'Nice to meet you, Mr Pidore. Let me introduce my Deputy Bill Reading and Superintendent Parker who is in charge of the investigation.'

'Now what information can you furnish us on this fellow Peter Sainsbury?'

'I just don't know what to say Commissioner, Sainsbury has always been a very good employee.'

'Is he your company's accountant?' asked Parker.

'No, Superintendent, Peter is our international Manager for Spain and France looking after new business.'

'What sums of money would have been in his safe?'

'I would imagine no more than three or four thousand pounds.'

‘What about these documents and plans Mr Sainsbury has suggested are missing,’ asked Parker.

‘I have no idea whatsoever, Superintendent.’

‘Very strange,’ pointed out the Commissioner. ‘Has Sainsbury ever been, in your opinion, violent.’

‘No, far from it,’ commented Pidore,

‘Would he be involved in drugs,’ asked Bill Reading

‘Not far as I am aware, Deputy Commissioner.’

‘Mr Pidore, would it be possible to find out exactly the contents held in his safe?’

‘I believe so, Commissioner, I’ll certainly speak with his secretary, and let you know.’

Ben and Alex said goodnight as Ken Tucky left the building. ‘I’ll be in touch, Ben.’

‘Thanks, Ken. Alex, we better get on with checking names of known safe cracking teams.

Joe Bolt and Derrick Smallwood were still in the Boxing club when Jeff Mitchell walked through the door. ‘Have you heard the news two coppers and a security officer shot dead at Mallards.’

Jeff nodded. ‘Yeah, it’s been all over the television news, we better all be away on holiday for a short time.’

‘I’m married and can’t just bugger off,’ said Derrick.

‘I’m also married, Derrick, but Peggy knows the situation, I’ll be on my toes.’

‘What about you, Joe?’

‘I’m going down to Cornwall.’

‘Yeah that sounds good idea. I’ll come with you, don’t forget the Old bill will be putting their heads together reading all their dossiers on safe blowing teams.

Miguel Melgar booked onto a British Airways flight from Barcelona to Heathrow, if all went well he should be on his way home inside five days.

Tim Shore, 5’10, black hair and dark eyes, was escorted into the conference room.

‘Mr Shore, I am Sir John Bacon, Commissioner of Police. I am extremely disappointed to learn of the absurd statement you presented to the media suggesting one hundred thousand pounds had been taken. It is bad enough losing two police officers and one of your security officers, but to give a statement which is totally untrue is beyond limit.'

'I wanted to make my own company look good in the media.'

'I believe, Mr Shore, when this mess is all over, your company will find matters very difficult in securing contracts.'

'Are you threatening me, Commissioner?'

'Certainly not, Mr Shore, I am only advising you, to be very careful on future statements you make.

'Thank you for your advice and concern; may I go home now?'

'Yes, you may leave whenever you wish.'

Ben Clark was busy at his desk when Alex Quirk walked through the door, 'How's the arm, Alex?'

'Still stiff, it's going to be difficult to assist you with paper work.'

'No problem, Alex, I'll leave you to search the computer for known safe blowing teams.'

Miguel Melgar had arranged a British Airways Flight 5I70 (Barcelona-Heathrow) arriving at I0.50 am. Before leaving Barcelona, Miguel had telephoned Juan Riminez who lived in Barking East London, 'Juan, we have a job; can you pick me up at Heathrow at II.00 am?'

'Yes no problem.' Juan was a thick set guy, standing at 5'8, green eyes with very dark hair,

Miguel got into Juan's car at Terminal 2, and they pulled away. 'Carlos has given us a contract to bump off some idiot called Peter Sainsbury; we'll need another vehicle, and we must make it look like an accident.'

'No problem. I have this guy who sorts out any car problems; his name is Andres Lara.

Joe Bolt had been waiting for Jeff Mitchell for over an hour thinking back, 'I cannot imagine why Jeff has got the nick name 'Jet', he's always bloody late,' laughing to himself. Some years previous to the M1 motorway being built, a safe had been blown in a private house in Leicester, the robbers escaped with a complete case of jewellery. The police had always wanted to put Jeff Mitchell away but never seemed to manage the task, but this time they fitted him up.

They went along to Mitchell's house in Brixton. Jeff was out but his wife, Peggy, was in, and protested to the search. The police found nothing but unfortunately for Jeff, they planted some Gelignite in the fridge.

They left his apartment and waited nearby in an unmarked police car. Jeff returned home. Ten minutes later the police re-searched Jeff's apartment, finding the dangerous substance in the fridge. Jeff protested that the Gelignite was not his.

So the inspector in charge suggested that in that case 'It must be Peggy's, will nick her instead.' Jeff made a voluntary confession, was charged with the safe job in Leicester and received a sentence of ten years. Jeff's council protested stating it was impossible to travel from London to Leicester in three hours and blow a safe and return to London.

When Jeff was in prison, he actually met the safe blower who had pulled the robbery in Leicester. Jeff always pointed out that if you were a robber you must expect to get captured now and then, and was proud to be known as Jeff 'Jet Mitchell'. Jeff and Joe had spent some 25 years of their lives in prison.

Jeff was now two hours late, Joe telephoned Derrick explaining that Jeff hadn't turned up and he would be off to Cornwall on his own, 'I'll give you a call in five days.'

'Ok, Joe, stay lucky.'

Jeff Mitchell had received a call from Costa Esteve, a south American, who had employed Jeff's firm to pull the safe robbery at Mallards and wanted to meet at the Barbican Centre.

Costa hadn't been interested in the money in the safe, only the documents and plans.

Jeff had been promised a further three grand for the documents and plans, but had not mentioned that fact to Joe or Derrick, believing there was no honour among thieves.

Arriving at the Barbican Centre Costa was already waiting with another man 'by the way, Jeff, this is a mate Andres Lara.'

'Nice to meet you, Jeff.'

'You too.'

'Costa, have you got the money?'

'Have I ever let you down?'

'No, Costa 'as it happens you never have, these documents and plans must be bloody important to be mixed up with those shootings.'

Costa shrugged his shoulders. 'Yeah we have all seen the television news, anyway here is your money, Jeff, I will have something else for you in a few months.'

'That's what I like to hear, Costa.'

Andres opened the large envelope looking closely at the contents. 'Fantastic, Costa, all of them.'

'Once again, Jeff, thanks.' Costa had a quick look at Andres.

'Perhaps, Costa, Jeff and his mates who pulled the job at Mallards, should all take a short holiday in Spain as there is going to be a lot of police activity over those shootings and it will be only a matter of time before they get around to Jeff Mitchell,' said Andres.

They haled a taxi. 'Brighton hotel, please.'

'Maybe you are right, Andres; perhaps a permanent holiday for Jeff's whole team would be ideal.'

'By the way just before we met this afternoon, I received an interesting call from a Spanish friend of mine, Juan Riminez, he wants me to steal a car for him; he's always boasting being involved with the Spanish Mafia; our dear friend Carlos, fat Tony.'

'We must assist Juan Riminez with a nice car, I am sure it will help us with some of those stupid people, we've been introduced too in the last few months.'

In Madrid, Carlos Moran was meeting up with the rest of his circle in the Convention Hotel. 'It appears we have a problem, I want to know how anybody outside our firm, could have known about the documents and plans being held by this idiot Peter Sainsbury. Did any of you speak with anybody?' Nobody answered.

'Hold on a minute, Carlos, that friend of yours, the south American from Valencia.'

'Costa Esteve.'

'Yes, what about him.'

'He was in the restaurant having dinner with us. Vicente Prince introduced Esteve if you remember. Anyway Sainsbury came in and started to speak about the job. You asked Sainsbury to join you in the other room, to give him a rollicking.

'I remember Costa getting up and saying he was going to the toilet, say he didn't go to the toilet but listened at the door to what you were saying to Sainsbury.

'When Costa returned and sat down, a little later you returned with Sainsbury. Costa then asked Sainsbury how long he was staying in Madrid and invited Sainsbury to dinner, That's when Toni Alverez suggested he would go along too.'

'Bloody hell, get Toni on the phone and get him here.'

Toni Alverez arrived at the hotel twenty minutes later.

'Toni, I need to know the ins and outs of the conversation between Costa Esteve and Sainsbury.'

'Sure, Costa was interested where Peter Sainsbury worked and what business he was involved in with you. He told Costa he had some involvement in the publishing world and sometimes carried out business with your company, at that point I was called to the telephone, when I returned Costa asked to be excused.

'Sainsbury asked me where Costa fitted into our plan, as Costa was aware of the documents Sainsbury was holding at his office. I naturally thought he was on the firm. When Costa came back the conversation changed onto Vicente Prince and his connection with Freemasonry.'

'Why the hell didn't you tell me this before?'

'I didn't believe it was that important.'

Carlos fumed that bloody Costa has got to go.

Superintendent Parker and Sergeant Pierce were looking through the statements and were satisfied with the information they had collated.

'The report from the personal manager of Mallards, confirmed that Sainsbury was spending a lot of time in Spain. His secretary mentioned that on one occasion she visited a local bar. Sainsbury was with a number of Spanish guys, apparently he looked rather embarrassed.

'Her observation was these guys didn't really fit in with the publishing world. Later in the day she actually asked Sainsbury about those guys, 'he told her to forget she had ever seen them.'

'As you say, Superintendent, very peculiar, the whole business.'

'There's a little more behind Sainsbury and these Spaniards,' replied Parker. As his telephone rang it was Bleasdale, 'Just to let you know Clark and Quirk are working with different snouts collating the names of active safe blowing teams.'

'Jolly good, Chief Inspector; keep me informed of any developments.'

'Yes, Sir.'

Joe Bolt had driven down to Cornwall, booking himself into the East Looe Hotel, which overlooked the harbour. Joe was worrying about not hearing from Jeff Mitchell and the reports on television and newspapers.

Headlines

Safe crackers blow 'safe' and murder two policemen and a security guard at Mallards Publishing Company, London.

Joe couldn't stop thinking about the ten grand that had supposed to have been in the safe. Jeff didn't make mistakes when it came to money.

Then there were those bloody stupid documents and plans in the large envelope. 'Christ the old bill, are going to be seriously looking for safe robbers.'

Derrick Smallwood had also been looking at the newspapers and couldn't understand Why police officers had been shot; things weren't straightforward. 'Perhaps the wise move would be to tip off the old bill, that the safe blowers had nothing to do with the shootings. If all goes wrong and we get caught, we'll be going down for a twenty, however Joe wouldn't have anything to do with informing to the police.

To Joe that's not on, remembering when he first met Joe. Joe had told him the story of when he was twenty and worked with a very smart man called 'Mo the Toff. Mo would walk up and down the smart streets in the Kingston area, when the lady of the house was seen going out. He would signal Joe who would break in and take any money and jewellery that was lying about.

On one occasion, Mo received a tipoff about a large house in Kingston where there was a large amount of money and jewellery in a bedroom on the second floor. The inhabitants of the house would eat at I9.00 on the first floor. Joe and Mo put a ladder up to the second floor window and Joe was up in a flash, took the money and jewellery and was climbing down when the ladder snapped sending Joe through the first floor window.

The owner of the house was a rather large man, immediately jumped up from the table and laid across Joe, asking his wife to call the police.

Joe received his first prison sentence—ten years in Dartmoor, but never informed to the police that his accomplice was Mo, the Toff.

Andres Lara found the car he wanted to steal, a ford escort, after following two men from a pub. He watched them enter a house waited an hour broke into the car and away. Calling Juan Riminez, saying he could be with him within a couple of hours. Agreed to the price and obtaining the address where the car was to hidden, he drove to a garage in Escourt road, Watford.

Andres telephoned Costa saying he had the car and was meeting Riminez in a couple of hours in Watford. Costa told Andres about a call from Jeff Mitchell, he wants to come over to the hotel tonight.

'I've agreed to meet him.'

'Be careful, Costa.'

'Don't worry, I am ready for him, also I have arranged for Alonzo to be here. I'll finish in Watford and return to the hotel.'

Jeff Mitchell arrived at the Brighton Hotel, Euston road. Alonzo was watching from over the road, making his way into the hotel as Jeff was waiting for the lift to the fifth floor. Alonzo made his way to the stairs then up to the first floor watching the lift pass the first floor, pressing the lift button and waiting for the lift to return, he could see the lift stop at the fifth floor.

Jeff knocked on the door of room number 507. Costa opened the door, 'Hallo, Jeff, what a surprise.'

'Costa, I've been giving great thought to those documents and plans, they must be worth a lot more than the few grand you're paying me.'

'I reckon at least another ten grand, that's a lot of money, Jeff; and remember I'm only the middleman. In a few minutes, I'm expecting the man who will purchase the material. Perhaps I could squeeze another ten grand on the bill, and that's yours, Jeff, how's that sound.'

'I knew you would see it my way, Costa.'

There was a knock on the door. Costa greeted Alonzo like he had only met him for the second or third time, 'This is Mr Mitchell, an associate of mine who's helping me with this project.'

'Nice to meet you, Mr Mitchell.'

'Let's get down to business, Mr Esteve, how much are you asking for the documents and plans.'

'Thirty grand.'

'That's a little bit more than our conversation, how about twenty two grand.'

'Let's make it twenty five, Alonzo.'

'Ok deal.'

'It will take me two days to arrange for the money to be available. I suggest we meet at my place in Plaistow the day after tomorrow, say I9.30. We can all have dinner and then go our separate ways.'

'That sounds fine to me.'

'I look forward to seeing you in a couple of days,' the door closed.

'How about we travel together to Plaistow, Jeff, as I will feel a lot safer with you being with me.' Jeff was pleased with the outcome and arranged to meet Costa the day after tomorrow at I7.00.

Andres delivered the car to Juan, collected his money and travelled by train from Watford to Euston. Arriving back at the Brighton hotel, using the internal telephone Andres called room 507, just in case Jeff Mitchell was still there.

'Come on up, Andres, Mitchell's gone, it worked out a treat.'

Costa and Andres worked out the plan. Mitchell would arrive at I7.00, they would leave by car drive towards Plaistow, and have him killed.

Ben Clark and Alex Quirk were in the duty office at Kilburn CID when they received a call from Sergeant Pierce who was wondering how the collating of names of known safe crackers was proceeding.

'It's slow work as you could imagine, the only names we have so far are not known to be violent.'

Superintendent Parker walked into the office, 'We are off to Mallards Pierce. There's still something bothering me about this Spanish connection.'

Charles Pidore was standing looking out of the office window at the magnificent view. Turning around, he greeted both the superintendent and the sergeant, 'How can I help you, Superintendent.'

'I would like to know more about Sainsbury and his dealings in Spain.'

'As you are aware, Superintendent, Sainsbury was our International Manager and personal representative to the Colaboenos Publishing Company, which post he has held for the last five years.'

'I see. Have you been able to find out how much money was taken and what specific documents are missing from the safe.'

'We believe three to three and a half thousand pounds but cannot determine if anything else is missing.'

'Is there a possibility that some other person held keys to Mr Sainsbury safe?'

'No, but we do have an audit on all foreign dealings every six months, would you like me to check on the last audit?'

'That certainly would be helpful.' Pidore dialled 6789 'Westwood here. Would you be so kind enough to bring in the last audit you carried out on Peter Sainsbury.'

'Certainly, Sir.'

Mr Westwood brought up his books and ledges; he was a small man balding head with large ears and a pointed nose.

‘This is Superintendent Parker and Sergeant Pierce from Scotland Yard.’

Looking at this ledger the last audit indicated three thousand six hundred pound and one thousand euros, and some documents on wine; the next audit would have taken place next month.

‘Have you any idea what specific documents would have been stolen, Mr Westwood.’

‘I am afraid not, Superintendent, Peter Sainsbury had always carried out his work in an exemplary manner; we would never have problems with receipts.

‘However, saying that, when those Spanish gentlemen travelled to our office, I was concerned that they didn’t appear as being the publishing kind of people, they appeared very unsavoury.’

Both police officers looked at each other, ‘Most helpful Mr Westwood. That’s about all for the moment, Mr Pidore.’

‘By the way, Superintendent, City Boys Security Company have had their contract terminated.’

‘What do you make of that, Sergeant?’

‘Not a lot, Superintendent, there doesn’t appear to be anything of value in the safe. I can only imagine the safe crackers found what they were looking for, if not, they would have blown the remaining two safes.’

‘There is something more involved in this than meets the eye. Have we received any news regarding Peter Sainsbury?’

‘Nothing, Sir, he appears to have vanished from the face of the earth.’

‘Some bastard must be hiding him, Sergeant. What has Clark come up with on the safe crackers?’

‘Clark is still collating and it may take another day or two, as all the known safe crackers we have listed, are not known as being violent.’

‘I must agree with that, Sergeant; all of the safe blowers I have ever come across have not been the violent type unless there is a new young mob on the way up, however, there’s a connection here with Spain. I can smell it.’

‘I must say I agree, Superintendent.’

The fax machine bleeped and a number of names started to come through from Clark and Quirk.

‘George Spencer, too old, Sir, in his seventies.’

‘Yes, maybe but pull him in anyway.’

‘Freddie Smithers, only just come out from doing a Eleven, Sir.’

‘Needs money pull him in.’

'Thomas Prince, been out two years.'

'Pull him in.'

'Kenny Owen is for sure too old, seventy-eight.'

'Ok, pull him in anyway.'

'Jeff Mitchell, I know him; I was on the team that nicked him for the Gelignite in the fridge. Not very intelligent, but a good safe cracker. Definitely not violent.'

'Pull him in.'

'Joe Bolt, family friend of Mitchell, did time together, yes another good safecracker.'

'Pull him as well.'

'Ted Horn, probably the most likely; went down for ten, came out last year.'

'Pull him in.'

'Walter Brown was with Ted Horn on a safe job when Brown coshed the security officer. Brown received thirteen years for it.'

'Ok, is he out?'

'Yes, Sir, six months ago.'

'Pull him in. One of these villains knows something.'

Miguel Melgar and Juan Riminez arrived at Alexandra Road, Watford, after collecting the car from Escourt road. Peter Sainsbury opened the door. 'Hallo Peter, Carlos has sent us over to get you out of the country; this is your new passport in the name of John Taylor.'

'Why don't you two have a drink while I pack my clothes.'

'That's fine, Peter.'

Miguel made sure the glasses were clean and made sure the keys were placed back under the stone at the back of the garage. Peter was very talkative asking where he would be living in Spain.

Juan answered saying the Torrevieja area. 'Never been there,' said Peter.

They stopped just outside London, as Juan wanted some cigarettes; jumping back into the car, explaining that there was a News Flash that the Tunnel was closed.

'We better go through Ramsgate to France, which will be safer.' Their car was speeding along the M2, and onto the A249, Juan knew exactly where he was going, making his way to the Marshes.

Peter Sainsbury never noticed Miguel putting on his gloves. Juan was thinking to dump the car and Sainsbury into the Marshes, if nothing else the crabs would eat him.

Sainsbury asked, 'why are we here?' Peter was starting to worry. 'Miguel, it was not my fault losing those dam documents and plans. I didn't want to look after them anyway; I kept telling Carlos.'

'What's the problem, Peter, we are just going to take you over the water?'

'No, you're going to kill me, please don't.'

Miguel turned in his seat, hitting Sainsbury on the side of the head with his gun, but with such force as to make his head smack against the back window of the car. Pulling out his knife Miguel stuck it deeply into Sainsbury's ribs. Sainsbury was dead; his body slumping forward, hitting his head hard on the front seat.

Juan had been out to the Marshes two days previous; making sure their getaway car was well hidden. Having with him a fold up bicycle in the car, which he rode back to the village and stole a motorbike, driving out of town to the nearest railway station and catching a train back to London.

Miguel and Juan cleaned the steering wheel and other places where their fingerprints could be. Placing Peter Sainsbury's body in the driver's seat and pushing the car into the Marshes.

It went in a treat they thought. Juan had made one mistake he was under the impression that all the Marshes in the area were ten feet deep; unfortunately at this point they were only four feet deep.

Ben Clark and Alex Quirk pulled in the first of safe crackers, George Spencer, who kept protesting, 'I'm working these days as a cleaner, leave me out for God's sake, guv.'

'Look, Spence, we have to pull you in to eliminate you from our inquiries.' Now where were you Monday night?'

'O leave me out, guv, I was with the misses.'

'What do you know about the Mallards Job, George?'

'Nothing, guv, I swear nothing.'

'George, read my lips, what do you know about the Mallards job, you must know something; there must be something out on the streets.'

'Nothing honestly, guv, you know me, I would tell you.'

'George, you have never told us anything in your life, but this time it's not only robbery but murder too.'

'O for Christ sake, I have never been involved with violence you know that.'

'George, for your own good, tell us what you know.'

'Look the only information out on the streets, it was a team from Brixton, but no names have been mentioned.'

'All right, George, but if we find out you are holding out on us, we'll be back and perhaps, we might let the misses know about your trips around to number 82.'

'How do you know about that?'

'Never you mind. Alex, perhaps you better go around and tell Gloria anyway.'

'O please, don't do that, Sergeant Clark. Alright, alright, the word is Ted Horn, but that's not for sure.'

'We could have saved a lot of time, if only you had told us that in the first place.'

'You won't tell the misses about No 82, will you?'

'No, George, that is our little secret, now let's get you back home.'

'No, that's alright, Mr Clark; I can find my way home.'

Ben Clark and Alex Quirk sat in their car looking at the other names on their sheet to check out

'Ben, I fancy this Ted Horn, let's give him a pull.'

Miguel and Juan returned to London, calling Carlos Moran in Madrid and letting him know the contract was completed, after a little accident had taken place in a stolen car. The man concerned had a stolen passport in his pocket.

'Well done, Miguel. Make some more inquiries, find out where Costa Esteve is.'

Joe Bolt telephoned Derrick's house without success, 'That bloody Kelly, she's always on the phone, that's three times.'

'Bravo six, we have information that Ted Horn has done a runner.'

'Thanks central.'

Ben and Alex's next stop was Thomas Prince's house. The door was answered by his son who intimated that his dad was out and would not be back until tonight.

'Could you give your dad this card, and ask him to telephone me.'

'Who's that at the door, David?

'Two men looking for dad.'

'What do they want?'

‘It’s the police, Mrs Prince.’

‘What the fuck do you want with my Tommy, he’s done nothing.’

‘We only want a quick chat with Tommy.’

‘It’s that bloody Mallards job, you can forget that. Tommy was up at his mums in Manchester all day Monday and Monday night. He would have been home, but his car was stolen. You can telephone your bloody mates in Manchester to clear that up,

‘Thank you, Mrs Prince. We will ‘ask Tommy to telephone us when he returns, we don’t want to have to come looking.’

‘Shut the bloody door, David; it’s starting to stink of the filth.’

‘Lovely family, Alex. That poor kid seemed nice lad; I imagine he hasn’t much chance when he grows up. ‘Bravo Six to Central, would you put a call through to Manchester Central Police, asking if Thomas Prince reported his car stolen on Monday night and if so, what time was it reported missing.’

Looking down their sheet, ‘Freddie Smithers was next; we could be down in Clapham in about twenty minutes.’

‘Hold on, what about Kenny Owen, he only lives nearby.’

‘Hallo, Kenny, let’s have a quick chat in the car.’

‘Hold on, Mr Quirk, I can’t walk that fast anymore, me legs you know.’

‘Ok, Kenny, take your time, just sit in the car and talk.’

‘Kenny, what do you know about the Mallards job?’

‘Look, guv, my hands, they are no good for Gelignite and detonators these days.’

‘Sorry about that, Kenny, I mean your hands, not carrying out robberies. Now, Kenny, we need your help, what’s the news on the streets.’

‘The word is Ted Horn, but not murder. Ted Horn wouldn’t get involved in murder, he is very good at blowing safes but not murder.’

‘Who do you believe would get involved in that sort of caper?’

‘I just don’t know, everybody is talking about it.’

‘Have you seen or heard from Ted Horn.’

‘As it happens he telephoned me yesterday.’

‘What did he want?’

‘Asked me if any of the old bill had been around to see me. I told him no but I asked him outright if he had pulled the Mallards job, he laughed saying not me Kenny.’

‘Do you know where he’s disappeared to?’

'Not really, but the word is up north.'

'That wouldn't mean Manchester, Kenny, would it?'

'I'm not sure, he just said up north.'

'Kenny, it sounds to us that Horn has done a runner which puts him in the frame, and doesn't help him.'

'Do us a favour, if you hear anything or Ted Horn calls you again, telephone me, and ask Ted to call me. We only want to try and solve the situation.'

'Of course you do, Mr Quirk.'

'Now don't be silly, Kenny.'

'Mr Quirk, if anything comes up I'll give you a call.' Kenny got out of the car and walked over to the Nags Head pub and into the public bar where his mate sat in the corner.

'Hallo, Billy, the old bill just gave me a pull, wanted to know if I had anything to do with the Mallards Job, and have I seen Ted Horn.'

'What did you tell them?'

'I didn't know anything; they only had to look at my hands to see that I wasn't at it anymore.'

'What did you tell them about Horn?'

'I told them I haven't seen or heard from him for months?'

'Well done, Kenny, have a pint on me.'

'Thanks, Billy.'

Costa had been considering Jeff Mitchell's team-mates. 'Perhaps they should all be dealt with.' Remembering Jeff had given him, Derrick Smallwood's telephone number.

'Hallo, may I speak with Derrick please.'

'Derrick speaking, how can I help you.'

'I'm a friend of Jeff Mitchell, and have a small job for you. Would you meet me at the London Hilton in Park Lane.'

'Do leave off. I have no idea who you are.'

'No, Derrick, I'm not the old bill, just come and have a drink; that's all I'm asking.'

'Ok, how will I know you?'

'I have long white hair and I will be standing at the bar on the first floor.'

The Hilton was packed. 'Hallo, Derrick, I'm Costa.' As Derrick turned around, there was a man about 5'7, long white hair to his shoulders, standing with another chap about the same height but younger and smart looking.

'I don't think we have met.'

'No we haven't, Derrick, but we know all about you, don't we.' Andres just nodded.

'Listen I'm out of here, you're bloody police or something.'

'No, no, nothing like that, Derrick, come and sit down.'

Derrick thought bloody foreigners, what have they got that I am going to get excited about. 'What would you like to drink, Derrick.'

'Scotch and water.'

'Waiter, three scotch and waters.'

'Now, Derrick, as I told you, Jeff is away at the moment in France doing a little job for me. It was me who gave Jeff the Mallards job.'

'Nice but what happened to the ten grand that was supposed to be in the safe, we only found three grand.'

Costa shrugged his shoulder, 'That's the way it goes sometimes you know that.'

'Yeah but we all hope not too many times.'

'Of course, Derrick, that is why I used your firm.'

'Look, Costa about those murders, we had nothing to do with them.'

'Yes, I know, Jeff has already explained that to us. Derrick, we have a truckload of money being delivered to a Bank in Hayes. We want you on the firm.'

'No, sorry, I'm not into violence. Jeff must have told you our firm never gets involved in violence.'

'Yes, he told us. He also mentioned that if anything ever goes wrong, you're the youngest and would have to use a little violence if necessary, as Jeff and Joe are getting on.'

'Where is Joe by the way?'

'Down in Cornwall.'

'Have you heard from him?'

'No not yet.'

'I'm sure you will consider changing your mind, Derrick, for let's say three hundred thousand pounds, which would be your share.'

'Three hundred grand.'

'That's correct, Derrick, there will be six of you on the team, and hopefully there will be no violence.'

'Alright count me in, when do I meet the other members of the team.'

'Andres, telephone big Sam and arrange a time for Derrick to meet and have a drink.'

'Talking about drinks, would you like another scotch and water.'

'Yes, please.'

Andres re-appeared. 'Costa big Sam has suggested bringing Derrick around to his apartment in Battersea.'

'That's fine, Andres.' Finishing their drinks; they made their way to the car park and drove off to Battersea.

The door was opened by this big guy who seemed bigger than the door itself. Sam Davidson was 6'4, massive shoulders, his face was strong with blue eyes and brown hair.

'Hallo Costa, Andres, and you must be Derrick, come on in.'

'So, Derrick, you are considering joining us.'

'It appears that way; three hundred grand what an offer.'

'Well I can tell you, you will earn more money with us than blowing safes.'

'You are probably right, but there is less chance of being caught. So when will I meet the others.'

'Let's get one thing straight from the start, Derrick, I never piss around. I escaped from a prison van when being transferred from Pankhurst with three other prisoners. I was in for fifteen years and I'm not interested in going back. I met Costa through a friend and was determined to get away. Once we arrived in Portsmouth and knowing Costa had a safe flat in Guilford for me.

'We broke loose from the ferry. Costa had a car ready for me, I was driven down the A3 before the old bill had a chance of cordoning off the area. The other three were captured inside the day. I stayed in Guildford for two weeks before moving to another flat in Reading for a further four weeks, then onto here.

'Costa poked a bird into me in Reading which made the time go little bit faster. The firm we have at the moment has pulled a few jobs which has brought in a nice few grand.'

Costa and Andres decided they would be off and said their goodbyes.

'Ok, big Sam, you can count me in,' said Derrick.

'That's good. Let's go over the pub and have a drink.'

'Aren't you worried about being seen?'

'No, I've been out ten months, the old bill believe I am in France or Spain, the heats off. They walked off down the road to the Horse and Groom. 'Nice pub this, Derrick.'

'Do you come here often?'

'No I move about, less problems that way. Tomorrow, I will give the others a call, come and collect me at II.30. By then, I'll have it all sorted.'

'That sounds good to me. Well, big Sam, it's getting late. I better be off home, the misses will be doing here nut.'

Derrick pulled up outside his house just after II. Kelly came to the door

'Where the bloody hell have you been.'

'You know, I had a meeting with that foreign chap.'

'Joe telephoned twice; he said he will call you tomorrow at II.30.'

'It's impossible for me to be here, ask him for his number and I'll call him back.'

'I am not happy about this, Derrick, when you work with Joe. I know you will be safe, and now you want to go off and work with some foreigners.'

'No they're not all foreigners, and I'm in for some serious money which will set us up for moving down by the seaside, just as you've always wanted.'

Costa and Andres were now planning Jeff Mitchell's disappearance, Alonzo Ortuno was 5'7, a little fat with greying hair.

Jeff Mitchell arrived at the Brighton Hotel at I7.00 on the dot. Carlos and Andres were waiting for him in the reception. 'Hallo, Jeff, on time as usual.'

'Yeah, you know me, always on time. Let's get a move on as Plaistow is not the best places to get to at I7.00 in the evening, we'll have trouble getting there by I9.00 to meet this guy Alonzo.'

'Don't worry, Jeff. Alonzo will be waiting for us no matter what time we arrive. We have been thinking, Jeff, when we have received the money, perhaps it would be better if you and Andres shoot off to Spain. As the old bill will certainly be looking for safe cracking teams.'

'Yeah, you are right about that. The word is out on the streets, they have already started to pull in some of the known 'safe crackers'. So a nice holiday in the sun would be great.'

'Good, Andres has already picked up a dodgy passport for you. Once we have the money, you should both drive straight down the motorway out through the tunnel. The whole journey shouldn't take more than two days.'

Arriving in Plaistow; Alonzo was waiting in his apartment.

'Have you got the money, Alonzo?'

'Of course, Costa, and presumably you have the documents and plans.'

'Yes.'

'Good let's have a drink and complete our business. Scotch and water all around.'

Jeff and Costa were looking out of the window and didn't notice Alonzo put the powder in Jeff's drink. Jeff was telling Costa that he was looking forward to a great future in Spain.

'Here you are, lads.' Jeff walked across the room picking up his drink, returning back to the window. Costa gave a nod to Andres to follow Jeff and see he drinks his scotch.

'Cheers, Jeff,' said Andres.

'Cheers. How hot will it be in Spain?'

'Well in the 20's, Jeff, and plenty of scotch or Gin and Tonics sitting out in the sun.' Jeff drank greedily.

'I'll have another one, Alonzo.'

'Of course, Jeff. I like a man who can hold his drink.'

'Yeah, well I have never had a problem with drink.'

'I can see that, Jeff.'

Jeff walked back over to the window where Andres was standing.

'You're not drinking too fast Andres.'

'No, Jeff. I'm driving through France tonight, it would be unwise for me to drink and drive.'

'Yeah how right you are.' Jeff turned around to see Costa showing the documents to Alonzo. 'What about the money,' Jeff shouted.

'Don't worry, Jeff, these documents are not going anywhere without the money.'

Jeff felt a little wobbly. 'What the fuck,' and slumped to the floor.

'That took a little longer than I anticipated,' said Costa. 'Jeff was right he has no problem with drink.' Jeff was gazing up at the three men but couldn't speak.

His head was going around and around, 'what's happening to me?'

Costa looked down at Jeff's face. 'Don't worry, Jeff, you are going on you last ride very shortly. Surely you didn't think we were going to give you ten grand, you dumb fuck. You would have got us all nicked.'

'Ok, Alonzo, where is the other nicked car.'

'Down the road.'

'We'll give it another ten minutes.' Alonzo brought the car around to the front door, Costa and Andres held Jeff under the armpits, walking towards the car and pushing him in the back seat, with Andres slipping in beside him. If anyone had noticed, they would have imagined he was drunk.

Costa turning in his seat, saying, 'Now, Mr Mitchell, it's time for your last ride.'

They drove down to the farm on the Isle of Sheppy. Ken Delanny was waiting for them.

'Here's your five grand, Ken, and I'm sure the pigs will enjoy Jeff Mitchell.' They pulled up by a large shed and lifted Jeff out of the car, dragging him inside. The plastic sheeting was placed on the floor and up the sides of the four walls. 'Do you want any help Ken?'

'Only for the first two or three cuts?'

Jeff Mitchell could see what was going on but couldn't help himself. He tried to say something, but nothing came out. Ken started the electric saw. Jeff Mitchell fainted. There was blood everywhere. 'Ok lads, I can take it from here.'

Ken was laughing, 'I won't have to feed the pigs tomorrow, they will have enough tonight.'

'See you, Ken.' Costa shrugged his shoulders as the car sped off back towards London.

Andres turned to Costa, 'That's one sick bastard, that Delanny.'

'Yeah, and the amount of people he has fed to his pigs, bloody hell, what a way to go.'

'I want you to park the car, Alonzo, where the old bill can find it in three or four days.'

Ben Clark and Alex Quirk were sitting in the CID duty office when the telephone rang,

'Hallo, Mr Clark, Tommy Prince here; you wanted to see me.'

'Yes, Tommy, are you back in town.'

'I am, Mr Clark, I'm back home, arrived this morning.'

'You got your car back then.'

'No, it's still missing.'

'Ok, we'll come and to pick you up.'

'No thanks, guv, I'll make my own way down the nick.'

'Ok, Tommy, let's say I0.00 tomorrow morning.'

Big Sam introduced Derrick to the other members of the gang, and got straight down to business, pointing out the plan and the getaway. 'Once we are at the riverbank, we can either cut the bar across the bridge or walk over the bridge putting all monies into the getaway vehicle and away to Denham airfield, an ten-seated airplane will be waiting to take us out to France.

'However, we must be diligent, the old bill will be coming from all directions. Hayes, Southall, Uxbridge, that's where the regional crime squad is stationed. From now on, we will look at the job in two's.

'Starting tomorrow, Scotch Jack and Jimmy, you do the first run look for anything unusual. Next week, Derrick and I will carry out the run, the following week, John and Peter.

'After each run we will meet in different locations, the first meeting will be at Fulham Football Club at I3.30, the following week Covent Garden flower market 9.30; and the following week, Heathrow Airport terminal 2 at II.00. Other than these times we will not meet together, stay out of clubs. We do not want any shit grasses informing to the old bill. Everybody happy with those arrangements?'

'Yes, big Sam, we've all got the message.'

Joe Bolt telephoned Derricks house at II.30 as planned, 'Sorry Joe, Derricks gone on a meet with some Spanish chap. Joe give me your telephone number, I'll get Derrick to call you back.

'I'll be moving to a cheaper hotel, so it's best if I call you tonight.'

Tommy Prince walked into Kilburn police station, asking for Sergeant Clark, 'Who should I say is calling?'

'Mr Thomas Prince.'

'Would you like to take a seat for a moment?'

'Look at this fax, Ben, Northampton police have Ted Horn, best news today. I am sure Superintendent Parker and Chief Inspector Bleasdale will let us know of any further results.'

'Ok, let's pull up Tommy Prince.'

'Good morning, Mr Prince, thanks for coming in. Would you like a cup of tea?'

'Look, Mr Clark, I don't want any trouble, you know me.'

'That's right, Tommy, we know you. Now sit down and get comfy as we are going to be here for some time.'

'Mr Clark, I had nothing to do with the Mallards robbery.'

'Where were you on Monday night?'

'You already know, I was at my Mother's house in Manchester.'

'We don't know that, Tommy, that's the point.'

'Look my car was nicked; I reported the theft to the police.'

'Wrong again, Tommy. Your mother telephoned the local police.'

'Yeah but you were around at my house, my misses told you I was at my mother's.'

'Just because your wife says you're in Manchester at your mother's, doesn't mean you were.'

'You can ask my mother.'

'Tommy, let's put it this way, you drove down from Manchester, picked up Ted Horn in Northampton, pulled the robbery at Mallards, drove back, dropped off Ted Horn and back to Manchester, so simple Tommy.'

'Leave it out, guv. I'm telling you, I didn't pull the Mallards robbery, anyway I'm not into violence and definitely not murder.'

'Let's go back to your car; you can't really want us to believe that a villain like you goes up to Manchester and has his car nicked.'

'I know it looks silly but that is what happened.'

'What time did you arrive in Manchester?'

'I don't know probably about noon. I took my mother out for a drive had some lunch, we arrived home about 3.30, I went up to bed for a sleep. My mum told me when I woke up that she had reported the car stolen at 5.I5.

'I got up and went looking for the car locally.

'We think you and Ted carried out the robbery, you're up to your neck in trouble, Tommy. Even the word on the street, is putting you and Ted Horn in the frame for the robbery; and Ted Horn is in another police station talking away.

'No, no, Ted Horn doesn't grass on anyone.'

'So, Tommy, you did pull the robbery.'

'No I didn't. If Ted Horn is saying otherwise he's lying, he might have pulled the robbery, but I wasn't with him.'

'Start telling us about Ted Horn pulling the robbery.'

'I haven't any idea about Ted Horn carrying out the robbery.'

'You two are always drinking together, that's how you planned the robbery.'

'Look, guv, it's in my best interest to have a solicitor present.'

'Ok anyone in mind?'

'No.'

'Ok we'll arrange for a duty solicitor.'

In Madrid, Manual Corsino's telephone rang. 'Si.'

'Hallo, Mr Corsino, Charles Pidore here. How are you, Manual?'

'Fine thank you, Charles.'

'I've got some bad news, Manual, our representative Peter Sainsbury has been reported missing; and unfortunately he was involved in three murders.'

'What? Peter Sainsbury doesn't seem the type, Charles, to get involved in murder.'

'That was my own impression; however I wanted to know, Manual, if Sainsbury had any special assignment with your company, as all the records are missing from his office safe, along with some money.'

'Terrible, Charles, just terrible. No, he wasn't on any special assignment for us. Please keep me informed.'

'Yes, of course. The police required statements regarding accounts handled by Sainsbury, your company as well as others were given.'

'Charles, the damage may be devastating for my Publishing Company if we are brought into this connexion with Peter Sainsbury.'

The telephone went dead.

Manual immediately called Carlos Moran. 'Hallo, Carlos, I have had that fool 'Pidore on the telephone from England, speaking about Peter Sainsbury who has been reported missing after being involved in murder.'

'Hold on, Manual, you're getting all worked up over nothing. I'm sure you will be seeing Peter Sainsbury very soon; now we will meet tonight, have a nice bottle of wine and a good dinner.'

'Yes, thank you, Carlos, see you at the Las Salina at 22.00, bye for now.'

Later Manuel locked his office, walked down to the car park still upset with Pidore's telephone call.

He didn't take any notice that it was darker than usual. Manual was startled as out of the shadows came a thickset man who walked towards him.

'What do you want; this is a private car park. I will call the police.'

There were two muffled sounds, Manual fell to his knees clutching his chest, a further muffled sound, this time to Manual's head as he fell to the ground, dead in a pool of blood.

Pablo Llorens made his way over to the body, took Manual's wallet turned and made his way out into the street; walking to the local bus stop where he got onto the first bus that came along and within minutes he was in Madrid centre. Pablo walked into the Ola Bar picked up the telephone in the corner. 'Carlos, the contract is completed.

'Thank you, Pablo. I will be in touch.'

Joe Bolt made another call to Derrick. 'Hallo, Derrick, it's Joe.'

'Hallo, mate. How are you?'

'Running out of money. It's possible I will be on my way back by the weekend, heard anything from Jeff?'

'Nothing, Joe.'

'Kelly told me you have had a meeting with a new contact, anything interesting'

'Maybe, Joe, but I wouldn't believe you'll be interested. We'll speak on Monday.'

'Ok, I will call you as soon as I arrive back in Brixton.' As Joe put the phone down, he thought what's going on now.

Ben asked the desk Sergeant to call the duty solicitor.

'Hold on, Mr Clark, I had nothing to do with the Mallards robbery. You have to believe me, if I could help you, I would.'

'Tommy, let's get the duty solicitor here.'

'Please, Mr Clark, don't nick me, it will finish me.'

'That's not our problem, Tommy, you should have thought about that before carrying out another robbery.'

'I will tell you the truth.'

'That's better, Tommy.'

The telephone rang. 'Chief Inspector, Tommy Prince is just about to make a statement.'

'I will be right down.'

'Yes, Sir.'

'Mr Clark, you have got to help me.'

'Tommy, we can only help you if you tell us the truth.'

'I will, I will.'

The door opened and in walked Bleasdale, with a long face. 'Now let's get down to business, Tommy.'

'Some foreigner put up the Mallards robbery to Ted Horn some eight months ago.'

'Tommy, how did this foreigner know how to contact Ted Horn?'

'I don't know, Mr Bleasdale; he just telephoned out the blue. Ted Horn called me the next day asking me to meet him in the Kings head. He told me this foreigner wanted us to pull a robbery in London.

'I asked Ted how he got hold of his name, he just mentioned it was on recommendation and asked me if I was interested. I suggested meeting this foreign guy before making up my mind. We arranged a meeting in the Stag, in Brixton.'

'What did this foreigner look like and how old was he.'

'I would say he was 5'8, age about 56-57, and he was Spanish with long white hair.'

'Did he give a name?'

'Yeah, he said his name was Costa Esteve. Ted and I quizzed him on the job, he told us there was ten grand in a safe in a building in Baker Street.'

'I asked him where our names had come from. Costa mentioned that both our names had come up from the Spanish Mafia, who held a registrar on all known villains in England and which fields they were experts in.

'Ted asked Esteve what was in the safe for him. Esteve answered that he was interested in some documents and plans that were in the safe. Ted told Costa that we didn't go around blowing safes for unknown people, and how sure was he that there was ten grand in the safe.

'Esteve who was annoyed asked if we were interested or not, and if so we could meet again to discuss the plan. He gave us a week to make up our mind. Esteve just got up and walked out the pub.

'Once he had gone, Ted asked my opinion. I told him I liked the sound of ten grand but didn't like Costa very much. Ted agreed, saying let's see if Mr Costa calls us.'

'What happened next, Tommy?'

'Well as sure as eggs are eggs, one week later, this Costa chap was on the telephone. Asking if we had thought the matter over. Ted told him we fancied it. So we met up the following Thursday at the same pub at 2I.00.

'Dead on 2I.00, Costa walked in with another bloke who was introduced as Andres, an associate of his. Ted looked at me; and we both said we wouldn't be splitting the ten grand. Costa shook his head saying "no you have got it all wrong, we are not interested in the money, we just want the documents and plans in the safe".

'That sounded fine to us, but how do we know there is ten Grand in the safe and not just the documents. "Look Ted, I am assured there is ten Grand in the safe."

“Ok, Costa let’s make an agreement, you pay us ten Grand, and you keep the contents of the safe.”

“Ted I have no more time to waste, you and your mate are either in or out, what’s it to be?”

“Costa, we cannot be fairer, you pay us ten Grand, we’ll pull the job”. Costa just thanked us for our time, got up and walked out, that was the last we saw of them. Ted turned to me saying that if there was ten Grand in the safe, Costa would have paid us.

‘I believe the safe only holds those documents, which we haven’t a clue what they were all about, so why take a chance. We could have pulled the job, got nothing and got our collar felt at the same time by the old bill. Honestly, Mr Bleasdale, that’s what happened.’

‘Mr Prince, you will have to make a statement in writing, and I’m afraid we will have to keep you overnight to assist us with our enquiries. You are aware we have Mr Horn in another police station and must collate both your statements.’

‘Mr Bleasdale, please let me go. I won’t do a runner, that’s a promise.’

‘I’m sorry, Mr Prince, that would be impossible, let’s get your statement down on paper.’ Tommy Prince wrote out his statement and was taken to the duty sergeant.

‘Lock him up.’

‘What’s the charge.’

‘The Mallards robbery.’

Ben and Alex talked, both agreeing that something was not quite right regarding the Manchester connection. A fax from Superintendent Parker’s office came through. Northampton police were delivering Ted Horn to their custody the following day.

Superintendent Parker telephoned Ben Clark asking how’s the investigation was proceeding.

‘Tommy Prince has made his statement, so we are keeping him in custody for the time being. He gave us some interesting news, Ted Horn and Tommy actually met up with some foreign chaps who appear to be involved. The names given are Costa Esteve and a chap called Andres, we have no surname for this Andres.’

'That's interesting, as we have also received similar information, on a connection between Peter Sainsbury and Spain; it's possible that Peter Sainsbury has run off to Spain.'

The Deputy Commissioner read the reports and was extremely interested in the findings about the Spanish connexion. 'So, two foreign gentlemen approached Ted Horn and Tommy Prince regards the blowing of the safe at Mallards. On both occasions the figure of Ten Grand was mentioned with some documents and plans. That is very interesting.'

Ben and Alex looked for the next suspect, Freddie Smithers.

'Did you know, Ben, Sergeant Pierce was the officer who put Smithers away for eleven years.'

'No I didn't, Alex.'

As they drove into Elephant and Castle, they decided to frequent some of the drinking dens that Smithers patronised. After visiting five of the local pubs there was no sign of Smithers.

'I would have put money on, Smithers being in one of these pubs, Alex.'

'He must be hiding, Ben.'

'Quite possible. The word must be out that we are pulling known safe crackers for the Mallards job.'

'There's Freddie's house.' Alex knocked on the front door. 'Good afternoon, Madam, Kilburn CID, could we speak with Mr Freddie Smithers.'

'You just can't leave him alone; Freddie has only been out six weeks.'

'Freddie, it's the bloody old bill they want to speak with you,

'You better come in,' said Mrs Smithers. Ben and Alex made their way into the kitchen.

'Alex, it looks like Smithers is on his toes.'

'Bloody hell, he can't be far. Check the house, Alex. I'll check the garden. No, he's done a runner; get on the radio, while I go around the garage complex.'

'Bravo Six to Central. Central, can you put out a BOLO for Freddie Smithers who's done a runner. We are at 202 North Cross road, Elephant and Castle.'

Alex walked back into the house. 'My Freddie has done nothing,' implied Mrs Smithers.

'Where is he working at the moment, Mrs Smithers.'

'He's not working. How can he get work when everybody knows he has just come out of prison.'

Alex met Ben at the garage complex. 'We have BOLO out, so he won't be far, that's for sure. Let's take a ride around see what comes up.'

'Hold on a minute, Freddie had that friend of his; I remember giving him a pull when investigating a safe job in the city. Now what's his name. Yes, I remember, Kenny Raymond, he has a flat just around the corner of Great Queens Road, near Freemasons Hall.'

'Do you know, Alex; I've always fancied joining the Freemasons.'

'Yeah only inspectors, superintendents and upward get into the Freemasons. The nearest you'll have of joining is when you pass the door of Freemasons Hall in about fifteen minutes.'

'Honestly, Alex, I really do fancy joining one day. I've always wondered what they carry in those little cases.'

'Don't you know, Ben, Bleasdale's had his case open on his desk, when I was passing his door.'

'What was inside, Alex?'

'Oh I can't tell you, you're not a mason.'

'Oh bugger off, Alex, come on tell me.'

'There was a blue collar and apron. Bleasdale returned to the office and shut the case.'

'What did he say.'

'Nothing he just looked and smiled.'

'Stop over there, Alex, that's the address, 499 B Birdcall Street.' Ben and Alex walked up the stairs knocked on the apartment door, there was no reply, Ben pointed to a coffee shop on the corner. 'Let's have a coffee and pop back in thirty minutes or so.'

'The more you look at this case, Alex, nothing makes sense. On the one hand, we have the safe blowers, and on the other hand the murders. These documents and plans, what's that all about. If they were so important to this Costa Esteve, why on earth didn't he just pay Ted Horn the ten Grand.'

'I have no idea, Ben, but we must now focus on these foreigners as some agreement must have been made regards the documents and plans.'

'I'm sure once we know who pulled the job, it will start to make sense, and probably one of the gang members has been a traitor to his mates.'

'Yeah I can see your point, Alex, but I can't see Ted Horn being a traitor to his mates and he certainly wouldn't grass. That also goes for George Spencer,

Tommy Prince, Kenny Owen and even Freddie Smithers, so there must be another firm perhaps from up the north.'

'And why was Peter Sainsbury so frightened when he found those documents or plans missing, to then murder three people. He must have been working for some really heavy mob.'

'This Spanish connexion appears to be the more likely, Alex. Let's hope Sainsbury comes to light soon, there's enough policeman looking for him. Look at that newspaper that blokes holding on the corner table.

Front Page—*Mallards Murder, Man named.*

Peter Sainsbury foreign representative for Mallards is the suspect being sought by police for the murder of two police officers and a security guard.

'Bloody hell, Alex, the yard must have made a statement.'

'Looks like it.'

'Ok, let's have another look at Raymond's flat. Hay, Ben, look down that passage.'

'Bloody hell, it's Kenny Smithers.'

Walking up behind Smithers and tapping him on the shoulder. 'Hallo, Kenny.'

'Guv, I had nothing to do with the Mallards job. You know me, I'm not into violence especially murder.'

'Kenny, we are apprehending you to assist us with our enquiries.'

'Please, guv, I had nothing to do with the robbery.'

'Kenny, you can tell us your story down the nick.'

Two boys walking their dog by the Marshes and throwing stones and bits of wood into the water. Paul was watching Ian Pendale's dog. 'Look over there, Ian. There's a car in the Marshes.'

'Do you think it's been stolen and dumped?'

'Let's have a closer look, can't see much it must have got stuck in the mud. We better get off home and tell my Dad as he'll know what to do.'

Freddie Smithers sat at the table in the interview room at Kilburn Police station.

'When was the last time you were in touch with Ted Horn? asked Alex.

'Haven't seen Ted for years. I've been inside for the past eleven years, how could I have seen Ted Horn.'

'That's funny, Kenny, because we have information that you were drinking with Ted Horn only last week in the Nags head, Clapham.'

'Oh yeah, I remember now seeing Ted Horn in the pub, but I didn't speak with him. Look I had nothing to do with Mallards job.'

'Did Ted Horn offer you the chance of the ten grand?'

'Give Sergeant Pierce a call, Ben; he's interested in sitting in on this interview.'

'Look you pair of bastards, I had nothing to do with the Mallards job and only know what has been printed in the newspapers. I want a solicitor as I'm not happy with the way you are pushing me.'

'Freddie, we haven't even started pushing you. We already have Ted Horn and Tommy Prince in the cells and you will make the set. I'm not sure which one of you was involved with the murders, but you are a prime suspect after just coming out from doing an eleven, and then being seen drinking with Ted Horn, and blow me down, a safe is blown open on your patch.'

'You bastards are not going to fit me up; I want a fucking solicitor now.'

'Getting worried are we, Mr Smithers.'

'I'm not saying another word until my solicitor is present.' Kenny Smithers was escorted down to the cells, shouting as he was taken away, 'You two bastards are trying to fit me up for the Mallards robbery.'

Ben called Chief Inspector Bleasdale, letting him know they had Kenny Smithers in custody, he's asked for a solicitor. 'So the duty Solicitor has been called.'

'Keep me informed as I would like to be in on the interview.'

Ben and Alex were waiting for further developments, but decided to grab something to eat in the canteen before Smithers' solicitor appeared.

Sitting at one of the tables eating was Sergeant Terry Smith, who was disgruntled with Chief Inspector Bleasdale taking all the credit for their hard work.

'That's the way it goes, Terry, you know that.'

'Yeah, but you haven't got to agree with the system.'

'You have a point, Terry, but with Barrie Starnes being murdered, we really couldn't care who takes the credit as long as we get the bastards in the end.'

The canteen telephone rang. Sergeant Smith picked it up. 'There's a solicitor here for Mr Smithers.'

'What's the plan, Ben?'

'We'll carry on where we left off. Smithers will deny everything. I will ask you to telephone Sergeant Pierce, and that should start the ball rolling. We will casually bring into the conversation Kenny Raymond, and let's see where it all leads.'

The two boys were at home waiting for Ian's father to return from work, Ian's mother had cooked egg and chips for the boys, the front door opened and in walked Dick Pendale.

The boys jumped up with excitement running towards the front door. Penny Pendale shouted at the boys, 'Sit down and eat your food.'

'But mum,' called out Ian.

'Sit down at once,' called out Penny.

Dick Pendale asked what was going on, everybody started talking at once.

'Hold on, let's start at the beginning.' Penny outlined the finding of the car in the Marshes and told her husband that she had called Paul's father, who was coming over.

Sitting down the boys told the story in an excited fashion. After tea and when Frank Johnson arrived, the story was retold. Frank intimated there are always cars being abandoned in the Marshes.

'Yes, but Dad,' said Paul, 'this is a newish car.'

'Ok, Son. I am sure that Mr Pendale and myself will be able to determine and consider the possibilities once we have seen the car.' The two boys and their fathers walked off down towards the old mill across lover's lane. The excitement in the voices of the boys when they saw the car.

'Look, Dad, there it is.'

Frank Johnson turned to Dick Pendale. 'The boys are right, that car is no more than two or three years old, and look at the banks, there are no skid marks, it must have been pushed in.'

'They certainly were not locals as everybody around here knows the marshes are only four feet deep in this area, we better get off home, and give the police a call.'

Arriving home, Dick and Frank confirmed the boys' story was true, and called the police.

'I would like to report a car dumped in the Marshes down old lover's lane by the old mill.'

'Can I have your name and address and telephone number, Sir.'

'Yes, my name is Richard Pendale.' After giving his address and telephone number, he also gave details about the car, saying, 'It was a green ford escort.'

'Right, Sir.'

‘I am waiting for the sergeant to return, we will be in touch.’

The duty solicitor, James Carson, was sitting with Kenny Smithers. He advised Smithers to make no comment and he would attend to all the legalities.

Chief Inspector Bleasdale accompanied by Ben Clark entered the interview room; for the sake of the tape he introduced everybody.

James Carson mentioned that his client had no comment to make, and was not involved with the Mallards robbery and certainly was not involved with any murders.

‘That’s fine, Mr Carson, but we have a number of questions that need answering if we are to clear Mr Smithers from our inquires.’

‘Sergeant Clark also mentioned that Sergeant Pierce from Scotland Yard was also interested in talking with Mr Smithers.’

‘That bastard fitted me up and I got fucking eleven years. I’m not having this.’ As Smithers tried to stand up going red in the face and wobbling.

James Carson told Smithers to sit down and he would take care of the problem Smithers banged the table with his fist and collapsed to the floor. Bleasdale called for help and Clark and Carson knelt down by Smithers’ side.

‘I think he is having a heart attack,’ shouted Clark. An ambulance was called and Kenny Smithers was transferred to Lancelot Hospital.

Bleasdale immediately called Superintendent Parker letting him know about Smithers having a heart attack. Superintendent Parker sent Sergeant Pierce to Lancelot Hospital to sit and take notes of who came by to visit Kenny Smithers.

A WPC was sent to Smithers’ house to assist Mrs Smithers and take her to the hospital, as they arrived and walked towards the hospital room Kenny was in. Mrs Smithers noticed Sergeant Pierce.

‘What the fuck are you doing here, Pierce, you’re the one who fitted him up the last time. You got him eleven years and now Kenny’s here in hospital, you bastard, Pierce,’ as she ran at him, the WPC held Mrs Smithers back asking her to calm down.

‘Calm down? It’s my bloody husband lying in that bed and it’s all down to Sergeant Pierce,’ pointing at him, as he backed away asking the WPC to take over as he would call Superintendent Parker.

Sergeant Pierce called the office, reporting he was sick and going home. The WPC called Chief Inspector Bleasdale letting him know the situation at the hospital, it was agreed that the WPC would remain.

Sergeant Reg Moore and Det Rod Muir were in the duty office waiting for Ben Clark and Alex Quirk to arrive, so they could spilt up the inquires. Ben Clark was first in mentioning that he had received a fax from Northampton Police, saying they should be with us between I0.30 and II.00 with our old friend Ted Horn. 'I can't wait,' mentioned Reg Moore.

Clark agreed, but thought it was necessary to continue looking and interviewing the other safe blowing teams, the computer had come up with Jeff Mitchell and Joe Bolt, both from Brixton. It appeared Joe Bolt is the brother-in-law of Jeff Mitchell. The door opened and in walked Alex Quirk. 'Hallo, Alex, late night was it?'

'No, I have just been digging around on Sergeant Pierce as one of my snouts had a lot to say about him.'

'Come on then, let's all know,' said Reg.

'Not bloody likely, it wants looking into further,' replied Alex.

Alex and Ben made their way to interview Bolt and Mitchell. As they walked to their car, Ben asked Alex what he had found out about Sergeant Pierce.

'After yesterday's business in the interview room when Smithers said he had been fitted up by Sergeant Pierce. I spoke with one of my snouts and it appears that Pierce and his partner at that time, Detective David Shaw, took a bung of twenty grand and Pierce needed a scapegoat, so they set up Smithers to take the fall. Shaw retired from the force last year.'

'Are you sure it's true, Alex?'

'That's what my snout told me; also the only one who knows the truth is Peter Jones who's doing a ten at the moment.'

'What a bloody mess. We'll have to let Bleasdale know,' said Ben Clark. After returning to the CID office, Ben asked Reg Moore and Rod Muir to interview Bolt and Mitchell, as they had been called in by Chief Inspector Bleasdale. Once Reg and Rod had gone, Clark called Chief Inspector Bleasdale, saying something had come up which he should be aware of.

'Come up in fifteen minutes.'

Clark and Quirk knocked on chief inspector's door. 'Clark, I hope this is important as I am extremely busy.'

'Sir, we have some very disturbing news. Quirk has been speaking with one of his snouts about Kenny Smithers last prison sentence. It has been suggested that Sergeant Pierce and his partner Detective David Shaw where involved in setting Kenny Smithers up and also took a bung of twenty grand.'

'Clark, do you know what you are suggesting.'

'I'm afraid so, Sir, it appears that Mr Peter Jones who is doing a ten at the moment knows all the details, so shall Quirk and I follow up the information?'

'This is very serious, Clark, let me consider the matter. I will come back to you later.' Bleasdale pondered over the details he had just received, picked up the telephone calling Superintendent Parker.

'I have received some very disturbing news, Sir, Clark and Quirk have just been along and informed me that one of their snouts gave information suggesting that Sergeant Pierce and his partner at the time, David Shaw, fitted up Kenny Smithers and were involved with a twenty grand bung. We have reason to believe the person holding all this information is Mr Peter Jones, who is currently carrying out a sentence of ten years.'

'Thank you, Chief Inspector, please do nothing until I contact you.'

Bleasdale quickly telephoned Clark pointing out that the Superintendent did not wish them to follow up on the Pierce scandal until he had made some investigations of his own.

Superintendent Parker called Inspector Brown of the Serious Crime Squad, and after consulting Brown on the matter, they decided that first it would be better to travel down to Dartmoor Prison and interview Peter Jones, rather than first reporting to the Deputy Commissioner.

Peter Jones was a real hard case among the villains; he stood over six feet two with striking red hair, a broken nose and very thin lips.

'Why should I help you lot, I've only got five years left of my sentence. Anyway what's in it for me if I considered helping you,' as he walked across the interview room with his arms behind his back.

'I cannot promise anything, Peter, but if your information helps in my investigation, I will be able to have a word in the right places.'

'Not good enough,' giving a shrug. 'I want out now—if we can make an agreement. I'll make a full statement giving all the details about the job, and how Sergeant Pierce and his mate Shaw set up Kenny Smithers and took a bung of twenty grand.'

Inspector Brown looked Jones in the eye saying, 'Kenny Smithers couldn't have been very happy about your involvement getting him eleven years.'

'That's Smithers problem,' giving another shrug. 'Now have we got a deal or not.'

‘Ok, Peter, we will make arrangements to have you transferred to our care until the home secretary sorts out your release which should take about a week.’

‘That sounds ok to me.’ Making his way back to his seat with a great big grin on his face, ‘What’s a week to me, gentleman,’ laughing.

Once back in the car, Inspector Brown said, ‘What a nasty bastard that Jones is, he would sell his own grandmother.’

‘Unfortunately, Inspector, those are the type of people we have to deal with, however we now have to deal with Sergeant Pierce. What a silly chap. The Deputy Commissioner will suspend Sergeant Piece that’s for sure.’ The car telephone rang.

‘Bad news I’m afraid, Sir, Kenny Smithers died in hospital thirty minutes ago.’

Reporters from a number of the National Newspapers had gathered outside Kilburn Police Station waiting for Chief Inspector Bleasdale to make a statement on the handling of Kenny Smithers affair. Sergeant Terry Smith told the waiting newsmen that there would not be a statement as Chief Inspector Bleasdale had already left for Scotland Yard.

‘Ok, Sergeant, if that’s how your station wants to play it, but let me tell you Mrs Smithers has scheduled her statement for half an hour’s time.’

Mrs Smithers stood outside her house saying that her husband had been killed, and Sergeant Pierce and his partner, David Shaw, had set him up. Sending him to prison for eleven years, taking a twenty thousand bribe to make sure he was the scapegoat. ‘So when I saw Pierce sitting next to my poor sick husband in hospital. I told him outright I knew, and would make sure he paid for it.’

All the national newspapers made front line news of the story, it hit the television.

Sergeant Pierce was watching the news, ‘O Christ, I must make a move out of here.’ His telephone rang. Pierce picked it up.

‘Sergeant Pierce, this is the Deputy Commissioner Bill Reading. We appear to have a major problem, I would like you to make yourself available at my office inside the hour.’

‘I’m sorry, Sir, but I’m off sick at the moment.’

‘Never mind about that crap, get yourself down to Scotland Yard; do you understand me?’

‘Yes, Sir.’ Putting the phone down, picking up his coat and making his way to the front door. Walking slowly down the road towards the river Thames, knowing the newspapers would be trying to hunt him down. If he went to Scotland Yard, he would be arrested and would go to prison. Life would become a total misery as villains didn't like police officers.

He started to cry making his way to the side of the bridge. He climbed up onto a ledge and jumped into the swelling dark river below. Passers-by tried to grab him before he jumped but it was too late. There were screams from women.

The police were called but it was far too late. Pierce had disappeared under brown dirty water' the police suggested there was little chance of finding him alive.

The Deputy Commissioner made another call to Pierce's home, there was no reply. It left him little alternative but to call Inspector Brown. 'Sergeant Pierce has not responded to my telephone calls, please make arrangements to pull him in.'

Sergeant Reg Moore and Det Rod Muir arrived at Joe Bolt's apartment in Brixton. Joe lived with his sister Maggie and her husband, Tony, in a three bed roomed apartment. Maggie answered on the first knock.

'Yes, can I help you?'

'We are looking for Mr Joe Bolt; you are his sister I presume.'

'That's correct, but Joe's on holiday in Cornwall.'

'Would you be so kind enough to ask Joe to call us on his return from holiday, here's my card.'

Maggie closed the door hoping Joe called her that evening.

Making their way back to their vehicle Rod said, 'In my opinion, we are wasting our time with Joe Bolt, he's not involved.'

'Maybe you are right,' said Reg, 'but let's check out Jeff Mitchell, he's a different kettle of fish.'

'I remember Mitchell's house is on the left; yes, there it is. The one with the green door.

Reg pointed, 'O, no. There's Mrs Mitchell, she has seen us, and she's crossing the road.'

'What do you bloody lot want, I remember the last time you were here Sergeant Moore.'

'It's been a long time, Peggy.'

'Not bloody long enough for me.'

'Is Jeff around?'

'No, he is on holiday.'

'What without you, Peggy?'

'I don't like holidays.'

'So where has he gone? Cornwall?'

'Yeah somewhere like that.'

The detectives walked away towards their car. 'We better give the Plymouth Regional Crime squad a call, letting them know they have two well-known safe blowers on their patch.'

'I'm a little disappointed in Joe Bolt. If it's true, Joe never crossed any of his mates and took his porridge; in the war Joe was out blowing bridges stopping the Germans getting at our men and that's where he learnt all about Jelly and detonators. If he is messing around, he's going to land up behind bars for an awful long time and let's face it, he's not a young man anymore.'

'Sergeant, I do believe you're getting sentimental.'

'You must be joking, Rod, let's have a drink in the Red Lion, we might learn about some useful information while we'll there.' Walking through the front door of the pub, the first person they came across. 'Hallo, Billy, how are you?'

'Mr Moore, nice seeing you. I thought you were working on the other side of London.'

'I was, Billy, but I've been transferred back.'

'Can I offer you a drink, Mr Moore?'

'That's kind of you, Billy, two pints, and by the way this is Rod Muir.'

'Nice to meet you, Mr Muir,' Rod just nodded.

'Look at the television news is not good for your lot.'

They all looked at the television where Mrs Smithers was being interviewed.

The presenter stated Mr Smithers died in hospital after being interviewed at Kilburn Police Station by detectives investigating the murders and robbery at Mallards. A detective from Scotland Yard has been accused of setting up Mr Smithers and also of bribery. The presenter turned to Mrs Smithers.

'Has Scotland Yard been in touch with you over this matter?'

'No, they haven't. We tried for a long time to have the case re-opened against Sergeant Pierce and his partner, David Shaw, as a large amount of money changed hands between different policemen.'

'How much are we talking about Mrs Smithers.'

'Twenty thousand pounds.'

'Christ, Sergeant, the shit is going to hit the fan.'

'No doubt, Rod, we'll keep our head down for a few hours.' Billy walked away from the detectives to talk with another chap having a drink.

'Rod, look over your shoulder, there's Kenny Owen.'

'Yeah, but he's already been pulled by Ben Clark.'

'Sure he has, but it's always better to give these villains another pull, just in case they change their story.' Walking over towards Kenny Owens table.

'Hallo, Kenny, how are you?'

'O, Mr Moore, never saw you over there. I'm just on my way home.'

'Now, Kenny, you just sit down and have a Gin and Tonic on us.'

'That's kind of you but I don't want people thinking I'm a grass.'

'Now you know better than that, Kenny, now tell us what's going on.'

'Mr Moore, the word is Ted Horn.'

'Kenny we all know that, now give me something that nobody knows'

'The word on the street…its some foreign firm moved in. This foreign firm were looking for a safe cracker and spoke with a number of little firms, including me.'

'Why on earth didn't you tell Mr Clark about this, it would have saved us so much time.'

'Mr Moore, I didn't want to get involved.'

'I met them at the Swan at Stockwell, but once they saw the state of my hands they brought me a drink and told me to forget ever seeing them, slipping me I00 nicker. I tried to find out some more details, but they said to me isn't I00 pound enough to mind your own business, so I told them—guv, I've never seen you in my life.'

'Kenny, what did these foreigners look like, could you give us a description.'

'One was older than the other, with long white hair down to his shoulders, the other chap was younger and a smart dresser.'

'Kenny, did you hear any names mentioned.'

'The younger one called his mate with the white hair Costa; if I saw them again I'd recognise them. I'm sorry I never told Mr Clark the whole story.'

'Ok, Kenny, don't worry about that. I will clear it with Mr Clark for you.'

Sergeant Moore and Rod Muir made their way back to the bar. Billy came over. 'I couldn't help overhearing old Kenny telling you about the foreign firm, unfortunately, everyone who comes in and buys him a drink, he tells them the story. He still believes in his heart he's still a big time villain as he was twenty years ago.'

'I'm sure you're right, Billy.'

'We better be off back to the nick, I would imagine it's getting lively today. I've learnt a lot today, Sergeant. I wouldn't have thought about re-interviewing a villain, that information will be a great help to Ben Clark.'

'Yeah, but first we are going to make further enquiries of our own, this could be promotion for us both, never mind about Ben Clark.' Sergeant Moore was thinking to himself, with this information he could get straight into Bleasdale's good books.

The Northampton police delivered Ted Horn to Kilburn Police Station. 'Well here we are, Ted, in your own back yard.'

'Yeah I could well do without this,' curling up his lip.

'Not to worry, Ted, the newspapers will give your story. Don't forget we are the ones that nicked you, not the Met.'

The big electric gate closed behind the police car. The three policemen accompanying Ted Horn got out, one handcuffed to Horn.

Ben Clark and Alex Quirk were in the yard to welcome Horn, 'Good journey, was it?'

'O, piss off, Mr Clark.'

'Don't worry, Ted, we are going to have plenty of time to get used to each other. Let's get Mr Horn booked in, then the Met boys are going to treat you lads to a good London breakfast.'

The desk sergeant, looked up, 'Mr Edward Horn, we have been looking forward to seeing you. Cell number 3.'

'You won't be keeping me for long.'

'Don't kid yourself, Ted. Murder has got a lot of clout, along with safe blowing of course.'

'I want a solicitor.'

'Of course, Mr Horn.'

Sergeant Richard Hill was on his way towards Dick Pendale's house, thinking sadly, 'All we get out in my area is stolen vehicles and a few house breakings, all petty stuff.' Penny Pendale was looking out of her window watching the police car pull up, letting the curtain fall back in place

'Dick, the police have arrived.'

'Mr Pendale?' the Sergeant asked.

'Yes, Sir, that's me, please come and have some tea.'

‘Now tell me, Mr Pendale, about the vehicle you have found.’ Taking out his pocketbook and pen from his tunic.

‘Actually, Sergeant, it was my son and his friend, Paul Johnson, who were out walking the dog along the Marshes when they noticed a car sticking out of the mud. They ran home telling my wife and I. Paul’s father was coming around to pick his lad up, so we decided to take a look. The boys continued saying that car was not that old which intrigued me a little, usually when cars are stolen and dumped, they appear to be older vehicles.’

‘What type of car is it, Mr Pendale?’

‘It’s a green four door Escort, no more than three years old by looking at the number plate. The funny thing is there are no skid marks, so it was obviously pushed in.’

‘Well lets go and take a look.’ Sergeant Hill and Dick Pendale made their way across the road into the small dirt road each side covered by trees.

‘You can see why they call it Lover’s Lane, Mr Pendale; it’s so peaceful and totally concealed.’

‘Yes, there are plenty of cars coming down this way after dark.’ They walked on towards the old Mill, commenting on the wildlife and the beautiful trees and bushes.

‘Over there, Sergeant,’ said Dick Pendale, pointing towards the car.

Sergeant Hill wrote down the number of the car. ‘Doesn’t look like there is anything inside the windows are so dirty. Ok, I’ll call it in and have a tow truck come out.’

As he walked back towards Mr Pendale’s house, he asked if he had seen anything strange. As it would have taken two people to push the car into the Marshes, and they would certainly have had another vehicle to get away from the area. Dick Pendale scratched his head saying he hadn’t noticed anything strange.

Back at Pendale’s house, the sergeant received a call on his handset, letting him know. ‘The car had been stolen four nights ago in London, another job solved for the Met police. The annoying part is the paperwork it gives us locally.’

As the sergeant left the Pendale’s house, Dick felt a little sorry for the local police especially that young sergeant. What chance has he got being promoted to a big town job?

Costa Esteve knew that Carlos Moran would be trying to figure out who would have known the contents of Peter Sainsbury’s safe. Andres had picked up a copy of the EL Paris, and was reading the article on Manual Corsino Garcia being murdered. Turning to Costa he said, 'Somebody has bumped off Manual Corsino in Madrid.'

'That doesn't want too much working out, it must be our friend Carlos Moran. This is all connected to the Peter Sainsbury affair.'

'There isn't any trace back to us, is there, Costa?'

'No, how could there be. Carlos is no fool and will be trying to figure out everything at his end. Our names won't even come up.'

Juan Riminez was checking out the sightings of Costa Esteve. Juan had been tipped off that Esteve was staying in the Brighton Hotel in London. After stopping at a telephone box, he made a call to the hotel. 'May I speak with Mr Esteve please.'

'I'm sorry, Sir, but Mr Esteve and Mr Lara checked out yesterday.'

'Did they happen to leave a forwarding address?'

'I am afraid not, Sir.'

'Thank you.' Deciding to check out flights back to Spain in the last two days, after going through the lists there was no Costa Esteve or a Mr Lara flying out. Hopefully, they were still in England. Juan called Carlos Moran explaining the situation.

'Juan, you have done well. Esteve and his friend are involved with our missing documents and plans, get onto all our contacts. I want them found quickly.'

Dick Pendale was sitting reading the local newspaper when the telephone rang. It was the local tow truck company asking if he could meet Mr Pendale near the site of the dumped car.

'That's no problem. I'll walk down to where the road bends into Lover's Lane.'

'Yeah I know the place, see you there in about thirty minutes.'

Dick called out to Penny. 'I'm off to meet the truck driver, see you in a couple of hours.'

'Ok, don't forget to put your top coat on, as it will be cold down at the Marshes.'

The truck driver was on time as Dick Pendale jumped into the cab of the truck and pointed the way down lover's lane to the old mill. As the truck jumped and went side to side as it hit the ruts of the hard ground. 'It's a pity we cannot just push the car further into the Marshes, it would save us a lot of time and effort,' said the driver, who was a big guy, broad shoulders not that tall but had arms and hands like tree trunks. Dick pointed over there on the left.

'Yeah I see it. I'll reverse into that corner, put those planks of wood on the Marshes, and hopefully get the chain on the back of the car and trust the car is not stuck too far into the mud.'

'That's very dangerous,' said Dick.

'All part of the bloody job, mate,' said the driver, putting the planks of wood steadily across the Marshes, inching his way along the planks even though he was a big guy, you would have thought he was a ballerina. He attached the chain to the back of the car and returned to safe ground. 'That's the easy part,' said the driver. 'Now we have to pull the car in very slowly. If I give it full throttle it would probably pull the back off the car.'

The driver started the motor. The chain tensed up and slowly the car started to move. 'Look at that, sweet as a nut,' said the driver.

Dick just nodded, as the car came closer to the bank, then horror showed on Dick's face, he shouted at the driver. 'There's a bloody body in the car.'

The driver looked. 'O Christ, the poor chap must have driven in the Marshes by mistake.' Stopping the engine of the truck. 'You better get back to your house and call the police.'

Dick nodded, turned around and rushed off back up lover's lane, slipping on the wet grass as he ran. As he reached his house, he was shaking and pale in the face.

When Penny saw him her hands went up to her face, 'Whatever has happened Dick?'

'We found a body in the car, it's awful.' Dick picked up the telephone and called Sergeant Hill.

'Sergeant, there's been a problem at the old mill, that stolen car has a body inside.'

'A body? Are you sure?'

'Most certainly, Sergeant.'

'Ok return to the vehicle; but whatever you do, don't open the car doors, just wait until we get there.'

'No problem, Sergeant.' Dick made his way back to the truck driver.

Sergeant Hill reported the find to Inspector Medows at Sittingbourne headquarters. 'Have one of your constables meet the CID car at Iwade turnoff 6 and lead them to the crime scene.'

Inspector Medows spoke to his duty Sergeant, 'Rice, we have a body reported in a stolen car at Chetney Marshes, the car was reported missing some four days ago.'

'I'll get detective Willis and we'll be off, Sir.'

Making his own way to the crime scene, Sergeant Hill arrived just as the car was pulled onto hard ground. 'Ok, lads, we'll have to wait until the CID officers arrive, we don't want to contaminate the surrounding ground to much.'

Twenty minutes later the two police cars turned into Lover's lane. The CID officers jumped out of their car. Dick thought the truck driver was big. But Sergeant Rice was well over six feet tall, wide shoulders and long arms. Detective Willis was smaller but also had rather large shoulders with dark hair.

'How are you, Sergeant Hill, haven't seen you for a while.'

'Fine thanks. Really pleased I have a bit of excitement going on in my area.'

D.C. Willis had made his way to the stolen car, pointing to the car windows. 'Looks like blood to me.'

Sergeant Rice after meeting and greeting Dick Pendale and the truck driver, turned back walking towards the stolen car, looking at the ground. 'No way was this driven into the Marshes, there's no skid marks, and if that's blood on the back window. Why is the driver sitting in the front seat, or maybe there's another body in the back of the car.'

Inspector Medows was at the crime scene forty minutes later. 'I was just about to give you a call, Inspector. It looks to me like a murder scene.' The inspector nodded to everybody present and made his way to the stolen car.

'Look at the ground, Sir, there are no skid marks, this car was deliberately pushed into the Marshes. The body is in the front of the car but the blood is all over the rear windows, unless we have a further body in the back.'

'I would say it's a murder. Have you called SOCO?'

'Yes, Sir, they should be here shortly; thirty minutes tops.'

'We need more men, ropes and sheeting. Willis, get onto Sittingboume and have another ten officers down here ASAP.'

D.I. Medows, asked the name of the truck driver.

'Sid Parris, Sir.'

'Are you ok as you look a little nervous.'

'I'm ok, but I have never seen a dead body before.'

'Perhaps you should call your company as I'm afraid you're going to be here some time.'

'Sergeant Hill, would you take full statements from Mr Pendale and Mr Parris.' D.I. Medows called Chief Superintendent Roger Greedy, letting him know the situation and asking if he would let Barking police know that the car which they reported stolen had been found, with at least one dead body inside.

Chief Superintendent Greedy called Barking CID letting them know about the stolen car and the dead body.

Inspector Cavendish promised to follow up their own inquirers on the theft of the car and send down the file to Sittingboume.

Inspector Cavendish read the file which was very simple; two lads had been out for a drink, returned home locked the car and played music. The following morning the car had disappeared. He told Detective Jenkins to follow up on the boy's statements of the missing car and make sure they were not involved.

The SOCO team had arrived with another van full of police officers, and were dispatched to duties of cordoning off the area and placing plastic sheeting over the vehicle. 'Nasty business, Inspector.'

'Yes, it is.'

Dick Pendale was told he could go home, but they would wish to interview Dick's son and his friend Paul Johnson later.

One police officer was stationed at the end of the lane, stopping any traffic that came along. D.I. Medows had his officers searching the surrounding area for evidence of any disturbance of bushes or small trees knocked down or trodden where another vehicle might have been hidden.

Sergeant Rice was assisting the SOCO team clearing mud from the car, after opening the rear car door, there were no further bodies. The body in the front was a little decomposed. The coroner's ambulance arrived and removed the body.

Medows asked how long it would be before they received the toxicology report.

'As soon as possible, Inspector.'

The fingerprint boys from SOCO were all over the car.

Sergeant Rice intimated to the D.I. that in his opinion it was highly unlikely that prints would be found as it smelled of a hit.

'You are probably right, Sergeant, there seems to be something really strange and not quite right about this case. The perpetrators obviously didn't know the area, as if they had only gone around the corner. The car would have sunk in fifteen feet of mud and probably would never have been found. So was the car stolen or did the owners drive down themselves, place the body in the car and push the vehicle into the Marshes.'

Sergeant Hill who was standing near the D.I. shrugged his shoulders in reply.

Ian Pendale and Paul Johnson were walking towards home, when they noticed all the police activity. 'Cor what's going on, Ian.'

'No idea.' Running the last few yards home, Dick Pendale and another man appeared at the front gate. 'What's going on, Dad?'

'Nothing to worry about, Son. this is Detective Willis and he would like to ask you both some questions.' Five minutes later, Paul's father arrived; after introductions they all sat down. Both Ian Pendale and Paul Johnson made statements, along with Paul's father. Detective Willis thanked them all and returned to the crime scene.

D.C. Jenkins returned to Barking CID reporting to Inspector Cavendish. 'The boy's statement appears to be solid; they returned home and found the vehicle missing in the morning. In my opinion, the vehicle must have been stolen between midnight and 06.I5 the following morning.'

'I am sure the boys are telling the truth without doubt.' Cavendish put a call through to Chief Inspector Greedy letting him know that his officers had interviewed both the boys concerned and there statements appeared to be solid, the files would be with him by special currier.

Sergeant More and Reg Muir were back at CID Kilburn office, speaking with the Plymouth Regional Crime Squad, explaining that they had two known safe blowers on their patch, giving the names of Jeffrey Mitchell and Joseph Bolt. 'We have contacted their homes and their relatives who have intimated that both are holidaying in Cornwall.'

'Thank you for the information, Sergeant More. We will put the information out and call you if anything comes up.'

Reg called out to Ben Clark, 'We stopped off at the Red Lion and bumped into Kenny Owen, he told us you interviewed him early on.'

'That's right.'

'Well he didn't give you the whole story. Apparently, he also met up with some foreign chaps, one was called Costa and other one he was not sure about.'

'Why the bloody hell didn't he tell me.'

'He was worried about getting involved.'

'Silly old bugger, it appears this Costa guy is coming up everywhere.'

Ted Horn after a few hours of interviewing admitted that this Costa fellow propositioned him to blow a safe along with Tommy Prince; however both denied carrying out the job.

The Deputy Commissioner sat at his walnut coloured desk waiting for Inspector Brown to bring in Sergeant Pierce for interview. When he received a call from Inspector Hilton from river police. 'Sir, we have just identified a jumper which was found washed up at Newham, it is the body of Sergeant Pierce.'

'O dear, thank you for the call.' Pressing the intercom to reach Superintendent Parker, 'Parker, the body of Inspector Pierce has just been recovered from the river Thames.'

'I see, that just leaves the newspapers to contend with, Sir.'

'That's what worries me, Parker, once they get hold of the news they will be on us like a pack of wolves. Perhaps, we should hold a press conference at 20.00.'

The Conference room on ground floor was packed with newspaper people and television reporters. The Deputy Commissioner and Superintendent Parker sat with the police News consultant on the top table.

'Ladies and Gentleman, unfortunately, a body was washed up at Newham earlier today. It had been reported that a person had jumped off the Chelsea Bridge. Unfortunately, the body has been identified as Sergeant Pierce. It is a tragic affair all together. We had just started an investigation over the Freddie Smithers affair.'

'Will the investigation continue?' Deputy Commissioner. 'Most certainly and will be headed by Superintendent Williams.'

'Thank you all for being here and trust we can count on your discretion.'

A number of news people were talking among themselves saying it's a cover up, this is a hot story for the front pages.

At Kilburn Police Station, Chief Inspector Bleasdale was reading the report from Sergeant More. 'We proceeded to the home of Joseph Bolt, but according to Bolt's sister, he was on holiday in Cornwall; working as a painter and decorator and wouldn't be returning for at least three weeks. We then proceeded to Mr Jeffery Mitchell's house and were told by Mrs Peggy Mitchell that Mitchell was also on holiday in Cornwall, and could be working as a painter and decorator.

'We have contacted the Plymouth Regional Crime Squad letting them know that they could have two known safe blowers on their patch; they will inform us if either suspect is sight.'

Joe Bolt called his sister. 'Joe, I've had the police around asking for you. I told them you were on holiday in Cornwall for three weeks, they left their card asking for you to contact them on your return.'

'Which police station are they from?'

'Kilburn, it is a Sergeant More.'

'Ok don't worry too much. I know him. I'm going to be staying down here for a few more weeks, if they come back just say you haven't heard from me.'

Joe called Derrick Smallwood. 'Listen, had the old bill around wanting to know where I am, my sister told them I was on holiday. Has Jeff been in contact with you?'

'No, Joe, I haven't heard from him and nobody has seen him.'

'That's really strange, Derrick, look would you pop around and see Peggy ask her where he is.'

'No problem, Joe, I'll pop around in the morning, give me a call tomorrow night.'

In Madrid at the headquarters of the Guardia Civil, Captain Sifre had received via Interpol, information on Peter Sainsbury. 'Three murders at the Mallards Publishing House and another here; coincidence, I don't think so.'

Sergeant Gillispe came into his office, finding the captain looking out the small window at the square below. 'Sergeant, I want you to find out how many times Peter Sainsbury entered Spain, check with all the airlines that fly from UK to Spain. I'm sure they will be able to give us information on dates and times.

'Has Officer Gloria Egido returned from Colaboenos Publishing House yet?'

'I will find out, Sir.'

Officer Egido reported to Captain Sifre. Gloria had a slender figure. She stood 5'6, with her brown hair swept back into a bun, so that her Guardia hat fitted.

'You wanted to see me, Sir.'

'Yes, Gloria, were you able to find out any more details regarding Peter Sainsbury?'

'Some, Sir, it appears that he came on a regular basis with a number of proposals for publishing, he also attended a number of exhibitions around Spain.

In particular Alicante, Valencia, Barcelona and Madrid. When he visited Madrid he stayed at the Hotel Convention.'

'Ok let's start there. Find out what the hotel knows about Sainsbury.'

Captain Sifre looking once again through his window at the square below with people sitting at the bars drinking coffee or beers, thought for a moment about the paper money changing hands. Was Sainsbury into counterfeiting?

Sifre put a call through to Scotland Yard. 'I would like to speak to the officer in charge of the investigation of Mr Peter Sainsbury.'

'May I ask whose calling?'

'Captain Sifre from the Guardia Civil Headquarters in Madrid.'

'Good Morning, Captain. My name is Superintendent Parker, I am heading the Peter Sainsbury investigation. How can I help you?'

'We had a murder of the Managing Director of Colaboenos Publishing House here in Madrid, and it appears Peter Sainsbury was also involved with this company. Interpol has informed us that Peter Sainsbury was involved in three murders at a London Publishing house.'

'That's correct, Captain, do you think Sainsbury could be in Spain at this present time.'

'We are checking that possibility.'

Captain Sifre gave Parker the ins and outs of the case in Madrid. Parker asked if it was possible to track down two names that had come forward in the investigation, Costa Esteve and a senior Andres. 'We are unable to substantiate whether it is his surname or Christian name.'

'No problem, Superintendent, I'll have these names checked and come back to you.'

Parker called the Deputy Commissioner informing him of the connexion with the Guardia Civil in Madrid and the two publishing houses.

'Surely not a coincidence, Parker, another shooting of the managing Director, Manual Corsino Garcia, being shot dead.'

'The Guardia have not ruled out the possibility that Sainsbury maybe be in Spain. I have also passed on the two names we are interested in, Costa Esteve and this Andres person, they are checking and will get back to us, Sir.'

Parker next called DCI Bleasdale regarding the conversation with the Guardia Civil. 'Is there any more developments regarding the two foreigners?'

'Not as yet, but all the information coming through continually points to this Costa Esteve and Andres fellow.'

‘Has Ted Horn come up with anything new?’

‘No, Sir, nothing.’

‘Ok, Bleasdale, keep me posted as the Deputy Commissioner is on my back and with the ongoing problem of Sergeant Pierce, I’m really stuck in the middle.’

‘I appreciate the problem. We will be doing all we can to help.’

Bleasdale was thinking Parker must be right up to his neck in trouble, if I can get this case cracked, I’m in line for his job.

Ben Clark was wondering if they should have another go at Ted Horn and Tommy Prince. When Alex Quirk shouted over his desk, ‘Take a look at the newspapers. The Deputy Commissioner has appointed Superintendent Williams to investigate.’

‘Sergeant Pierce and the Freddy Smithers affair, then there’s another load on why Pierce was never investigated before Mrs Smithers made her complaint.’

‘By the way, Walter Brown hasn’t been pulled in yet, we better leave a note for Sergeant More, he can follow that up.’

Billy Chambers was known as a nasty dangerous villain using violence whenever he could, Billy had been tipped off that Kenny Owen was talking to the police and had been pulled in. Billy was a big guy 6’2, in his thirties with black hair and dark eyes. He had been in prison on a number of occasions.

The grapevine was speculating that Kenny was talking again to the old bill in Clapham, ‘Silly old fool, now he has to go,’ thought Billy.

Kenny Owen was on his way home walking slowly down a nice old street with old type London house’s either side, with a few trees here and there, when a car pulled up beside him.

‘Hallo, Kenny, do you fancy a pint,’ called Billy Chambers,

‘Yeah that would be great.’ Getting into Billy’s car.

‘I hear the old bill gave you another tug, Kenny.’

‘Yeah they never leave you alone; such a bloody inconvenience.’

‘What you tell them?’

‘Nothing really, just crap.’

‘Kenny, people are talking, saying you’re giving information to the old bill. You should be keeping your mouth shut,’ pulling out a gun.

‘No, Billy, please, don’t hurt me. I won’t say another word honest.’

There were two muffled shots from the silenced gun. Kenny slumped to the side with his head on the passenger window. Billy drove into Battersea Park pulled over to the side where there were some small bushes and trees. Looking around there wasn't anybody around, he opened the passenger door and pushed Kenny Owen's body out of the car and drove off, thinking if somebody came along seeing him lying on the floor, they would just think some old drunk and pay no attention.

Two hours later, a jogger running along the path noticed a body and saw blood on his clothes. Battersea Police sent a squad car and an ambulance to the site. CID turned up in minutes of the call. Looking down at the body, one of them recognised it was Kenny Owen. 'Poor old bugger.'

Derrick Smallwood drove into Kingston road, Brixton, parking between some cars. Walking over the road to Peggy Mitchell's house.

'Hallo, Derrick, how are you and Kelly.'

'She's fine, Peggy. Joe called me last night after speaking with Maggie. Apparently, the old bill had been around her place looking for Joe.'

'They were around here too, Derrick, looking for Jeff. I told them he was on holiday.'

'Have you heard from Jeff, Peggy?'

'Not since the other night when he left here for a meet with some foreign chaps to collect some money, Jeff told me he would keep his head down for a week. But you know Jeff; once he's got a few quid in his pocket, he'll be out a flutter on the horses or whatever.'

'Yeah, Peggy, you are probable right. When you see Jeff ask him to give me a call.'

Derrick drove off for his own meeting with Big Sam Davidson at Fulham Football club. They met for a drink in the Hare and Rabbit before meeting the others. At I.30, all the team was assembled. Scotch Jack and Jimmy gave there reports, saying the security van picked up the money as scheduled, then drove through the old factory and onto the airport.

The only problem they encountered was the riverbank and crossing the bridge. If they cut the chain, they could possibly be spotted by people drinking in the pub, and that information passed onto the old bill.

Big Sam walked back and forward nodding, he agreed the bridge was the only danger point. It was agreed to have another meeting the following Wednesday at Covent Garden where Derrick and Joe would give their reports 'And don't forget keep your heads down and don't be seen together.' The team went their separate ways in two's.

Big Sam was telling Derrick, 'That bridge is going to be there problem.'

Jimmy mentioned to Scotch Jack, 'circumstances are different for Big Sam he's already on the run after escaping from that prison van, so he hasn't anything to lose. If we get caught, we'll be done not only for the robbery but also for harbouring an escaped prisoner. It's only another three weeks until the robbery.'

Reg More and Rod Muir were in the office early looking at the work load. Reg picked up a fax. 'Bloody hell somebody's knocked off old Kenny Owen, poor old bugger, in Battersea Park.'

'You know, Rod, when that landlord of the Red Lion told us that Kenny was shouting his mouth off whenever somebody brought him a drink, it worried me.

'If we're realistic, there must be someone in the Red Lion in the middle giving information and are involved with the foreigners. The boundaries are changing; we need surveillance at the Red Lion knowing whose going in and out. Let Ben Clark interview Walter Brown, we'll pop upstairs and see Chief Inspector Bleasdale and put our idea to him.

'Morning Sir, I am sure you have heard about the murder yesterday of poor Old Kenny Owen in Battersea park.' Bleasdale nodded.

'Well, Sir, DC Rod Muir and myself were at the Red Lion talking to the landlord and Kenny Owen, so maybe it would be a good idea to put surveillance on the Red lion. Potentially we would then monitor which faces are seen going in and out which may lead us to these foreigners, and whoever may be involved in bumping off Kenny Owen.'

'I think you have a good idea, Sergeant, it certainly would be a feather in our cap if we found both the murderer and the foreigners through the surveillance. Sergeant Weber and Constable Taylor would be ideal for those duties.'

Ben Clark, Alex Quirk, D.S More and Det Muir along with Sergeant Weber and Constable Taylor where in the CID office discussing the idea of the surveillance vehicle.

Ben Clark was sad about the news of Kenny Owens' murder. Reg More and Rod Muir made their way towards the Red Lion as did Sergeant Weber and Constable Taylor in the surveillance vehicle. Parking the vehicle in position across the road on a vacant building plot; both the front and the side entrance to the Red Lion could be viewed. D.S. More and Det Muir entered the front door of the pub. 'Morning, Billy.'

'Not a very good morning, Mr More, with the news of poor old Kenny Owen being murdered not to long after you two had been speaking with him.'

'That's right, Billy, so who was in the other bar at the time we were here.'

'Quite a number of people but once they knew the old bill were in here, they buggered off.'

'Give us some names, Billy.'

'Mr More, you know I don't have any names, do I.' Billy Fleming was another big guy well over six feet, hands like shovels being a former bare knuckle boxer who continued to keep his hand in the illegal fights around the London area.

'Billy, come on now, your licence is due up soon, funny if somebody objected to your licence giving wrong information. Isn't that right, Mr Muir.'

'Most certainly, Mr More.'

'Look, you two if anything comes up, I would most certainly let you know.'

'I hope so, Billy, we'll be off now, hear from you soon.'

Billy said his goodbye thinking 'what bastards you two are.'

Ben Clark and Alex Quirk made their way to Lewisham to interview Walter Brown as they drove up to Brown's house. Walter was looking through his curtained window of his smart three bedroom house with a wonderful bowed front window both on first and ground floors.

Walter called out to his misses, 'The old bill are here. It's bound to be about the Mallards job. They have been pulling in everyone.'

Jelly Brown answered the front door after the second knock.

'Yes, can I help you?'

'Is Walter in please,' showing their warrant cards. 'Mr Brown I am D.S. Clark and this is D.C. Quirk. We would like to ask you a few questions. Where were you last Monday night?'

'I was with the misses and twenty other friends at a sixtieth birthday party at the Whitely club, everybody can confirm I was there.'

'When was the last time you spoke with Ted Horn or Tommy Prince?'

'At least two years ago.'

'Have you heard anything about the Mallards job?'

'Not really, only what I have read in the newspapers.'

'Come on, Walter, you must have heard some of the names being bleated about.'

'Look, you two, if names were being thrown up, frankly speaking, you would have picked them up by now, and so if you haven't anything better to do, I would like you to leave.'

'Good day, Mrs Brown.' As they walked down the path to the front gate Alex looked back noticing Walter Brown behind the curtain watching them.

Barking police found another stolen car and after checking the number plate. Found it belonged to Mr Thomas Prince with an address in London, but had been reported stolen in Manchester. The desk sergeant had the vehicle towed into their police pound and asked the young police constable if the car had been examined.

'No, Sir.'

The young constable called Manchester police reporting, the MET had found the stolen car. The traffic division from Manchester replied saying there had been a red flag on the car from Kilburn CID. Returning to the desk sergeant and relating the story.

'Have you called Kilburn?'

'No, Sir.'

'Honestly, have I got to do everything for you, lad. All right you attend to the front desk and I'll sort the vehicle out.' Walking into the collator's office and running the number plate, the red flag from Kilburn came up showing Mr Thomas Prince who had plenty of form for safe blowing.

Sergeant Murphy ran up the stairs knocking on Inspector Cavendish's door. 'Sorry to bother you, Sir, but one of my chaps found a stolen car in Stall Street. Apparently, it had been there for some days. The vehicle is registered to a Mr Thomas Prince who has a red flag against his name, from the CID Kilburn.'

'That's interesting, Sergeant, as Kilburn are looking into the Mallards publishing, safe blowing and murders affair. I will give Kilburn a call. Thank you, Sergeant, well done.'

'Jenkins, are you there?'

'Yes, Sir.'

'There's a dodgy vehicle in the pound belonging to a known villain; give the vehicle a good search.'

'Right away, Sir.'

Cavendish tapping his fingers on his desk picked up the telephone calling Chief Inspector Bleasdale. 'Hallo, Chief Inspector. It's Inspector Cavendish from Barking CID, we've picked up a stolen car belonging to Mr Thomas Prince; reported stolen in Manchester. It's in our pound. I'm just about to have the car searched.'

'Thank you, Inspector, that's great news. Please keep in touch if anything is found in the vehicle.' Bleasdale thought about the situation, perhaps Prince did drive the car down to London, pulled the Mallards job with Horn and then travelled back by train.

'Hallo Clark, I want to interview Prince in twenty minutes.'

'Sir, we were just about to interview Ted Horn.'

'Clark, I have received new information so I want to interview Prince.'

'Alex, Bleasdale wants to interview Prince, as he has picked up some new evidence.'

The crime site at the Marshes had been thoroughly searched. Sergeant Rice was stamping his feet to keep out the cold damp feeling you get when standing on wet and muddy grounds. He was thinking it was a professional hit job without a doubt. D.I. Medows made his way through the damp grass and mud towards Sergeant Rice.

'Anything?'

'Nothing of interest. We have started the house to house, Sir, just in case anybody noticed anything suspicious.'

'Ok, Sergeant, I'm off back to Sittingboume. We'll speak later.'

'Yes, Sir.'

Detective Willis returned to the crime scene. 'I've been speaking with Mrs Deacon from number 45, she apparently noticed two men walking from Lover's lane. Unfortunately, it was too dark for her to give a description of the men's faces. They disappeared some fifty yards up the other lane.

'About twenty minutes later, she noticed lights of a car making its way out of the turning. The car sped off in the direction of London.'

'Ok, Willis, let's go and take a look. It might be the break we are looking for.' They made their way up Lover's Lane over the rumps in the ground and slippery wet patches, chatting about the case in general. Turning onto the main road, they could see the other lane some fifty yards up ahead on the right. Turning into the lane. 'Visible tyre marks,' pointed out Sergeant Rice.

As they walked further on, working out the timing of when the lights of the car were seen by Mrs Deacon, they came across the tyre tracks turning into the bushes.

'There you are. The car must have been well hidden by the looks of it. The villains had a hard time freeing the car from the mud. Look at the branches, they used under the wheels,' pointed out the Sergeant. 'We better get SOCO to carry out another thorough search, we may yet come up with fingerprints.'

D.I. Medows received a call from the Coroner Peter Powell. 'What have you got for me, Peter?'

'Well the face was unrecognisable. Fingerprints and the dental condition of the victim have been taken, and are being checked at this moment. I would say the victim had his head bashed against the window, and then hitting the front seat with great force which probably made him dazed but didn't kill him.

'He has stab wounds in the side just under the heart, which caused him to bleed to death. That's all I have at the moment, Barrie, hopefully I will have a name later today for you.'

Sergeant Rice had the new search area cordoned off. SOCO had found some fingerprints, branches and greenery were being examined. One of the team shouted to Sergeant Rice that the two men couldn't have been large as the footprints measured were only size eight. They wore leather souls with a particular marking, definitely not farmers.

Sergeant Rice put through a call to D.I. Medows giving him the up-to-date news from the crime site. Medows was tapping his feet on the office floor. 'The car was obviously hidden down there some days before the crime took place. Get Willis to contact all the local taxi firms, find out if anybody was picked up or dropped off at the railway station or taken and dropped elsewhere nearby.'

'Yes, Sir.'

Willis contacted the two local taxi companies and received a negative answer from both.

Sergeant Rice scratched his head. 'I just don't understand how they drove the car down here and nobody saw them. If a taxi didn't pick them up, they had to have another vehicle. Ok let's backtrack, we'll re-interview Mrs Deacon.'

Mrs Deacon opened the front door. 'Hallo, Mr Willis, back again?'

'Yes, I am sorry to bother you, this is Sergeant Rice.'

'We just have a couple of questions. You told Mr Willis that you saw two men come up Lover's Lane turn right and disappear into that turning over there,' pointing with his arm.

'That's correct, Sergeant, they walked down that lane and then some twenty minutes later, I noticed car lights coming from the lane.'

'Would you recognise the car again?'

'Yes, Sergeant, I would. As the car turned into the main road, it was forced to stop as a fox ran in front of the car, you can see by the skid-marks. The car was a red Mazda; my cousin has the exact same car. I couldn't see the passengers clearly because it was dark, and they looked to be of dark complexion.'

The two police officers walked over to the skid marks, looking and decided that they better have the marks checked for tyre print. SOCO were just about finishing up. 'You're in luck, Sergeant, we have some clear fingerprints and some flaks of paint from the car which is red on that silver birch tree,' pointing to the tree. 'The perpetrators must have had difficulty moving the car as it skidded on the back wheels and hit the tree.'

'Is there a possibility you'll be able to give us the make of car from the flaks of paint.'

'Most certainly, it may take a couple of days.'

'That's great,' said Sergeant Rice.

'We are still no further forward on how they got here, let's go and see the Pendale family again and see if we can't jog their memories.'

'Mr Pendale, sorry to bother you again, we just need to ask a couple more questions.'

'Come on in and have some tea,' as Penny Pendale entered the front room with a tray of tea.

'Thanks, Mrs Pendale, this will go down a treat. Did you notice any other strange vehicles in the area over the last week or so?'

'As you know, Sergeant, we get a number of cars going down Lover's lane for a few hours.'

'Yes, we understand that, however we are puzzled about how the perpetrators got out of the area without anybody noticing them.' Ian and Paul came through the door.

'Hallo, Ian and Paul, how was school today?'

'Great thanks, Sergeant, we noticed a policeman checking some skid marks across from Mrs Deacon's house.'

'We were asking your mum and dad, Ian, if there was any chance you noticed any other suspicious vehicles in this area in the last week.'

Paul looked at Ian. 'Yeah I remember we saw that red car if you remember, Ian, we thought it was going into Lover's Lane but it didn't and turned into the next lane'

'Did you notice the passengers?'

'I thought there was one guy of dark completion.'

'I think that about clears up the matter, if anything crosses your mind, give us a call.' He passed over his business card to Dick Pendale.

Walking back to their car and chatting about the red Mazda, 'We've checked the taxi companies. There's nothing and there couldn't have had another vehicle hidden, as they would have been spotted by Mrs Deacon or the boys come to that. So how did they get away after leaving the Mazda?'

'Let's check for any thefts that have been reported.' After requesting the information they received a call saying that the only report of a vehicle theft was that of a motorbike from a Mr Christopher Billinson of I23 High Street, Whitstable.

'Has Mr Billson been interviewed?'

'Yes, but only routine questions, such as the bike's documents, it has been thought it was joy-riders.'

'Willis, I have a hunch, let's head for Whitstable and interview Mr Billinson.'

'I'm Sergeant Rice and this is D.C. Willis. We are just carrying out routine questions about your missing motorbike, would you show us where the bike was kept at night.'

Mr Billinson pointed to the side wall. 'I park it there all the time, when I got up in the morning to go to work, it was gone.'

'Did you see anybody hanging around?'

'No, Sir, I've asked all over town, we checked everywhere even down to Chetney Marshes.'

'Thank you, Sir, we will be in touch if we have any news,' said the Sergeant. As they walked back to their car, Sergeant Rice turned to Willis and said, 'I have a funny feeling about this motorbike. It could be the getaway vehicle, it's something we will have to consider. Let's get back to the office and see what D.I. Medows has come up with.'

The interview room felt cold as Ben Clark and Chief Inspector Bleasdale interviewed Tommy Prince.

'Look, Chief Inspector, I've told you everything I know. I had nothing to do with the Mallards job and I was certainly not with Ted Horn.'

'Mr Prince, we are not happy with your report of your stolen car. By the way, it's been found in London. So why would it be in London when you say it was stolen in Manchester. What I suspect is you drove down to London to pick up

Ted Horn, went along to Mallards Publishing House, blew the safe and made off with the money and documents.'

'I haven't a clue what you are talking about and you're not going to pin this on me, I want a solicitor,' jumping up and knocking over a chair. Bleasdale hit the alarm and two police officers rushed in and held Prince, who was shouting and kicking.

'Take him down,' shouted Bleasdale.

In the police car compound at Barking police station, D.C. Jenkins was checking the inside of the stolen car. He found nothing under the seats in the clove compartment under the carpets. He opened the boot, it appeared clean. Pulling up the carpet and checking under the spare wheel, he found a flat black bag which contained three detonators. Jenkins immediately called Inspector Cavendish.

'What have you found, Jenkins?'

'A flat black bag containing three detonators, Sir.'

'Ok, Jenkins, be careful just in case you come across some gelignite.'

Cavendish quickly called Chief Inspector Bleasdale. 'We have found a black bag containing three detonators in the boot of Tommy Prince's car.'

'Now we are getting somewhere at last. Thank you, Inspector.'

'Clark, Barking CID have found three detonators in the boot of Tommy Prince's car.'

'Surely, Sir, that puts Prince completely in the frame. What an idiot carrying detonators in his car boot.'

'I am sure you are right, Clark, let's interview Ted Horn.' Horn was already in the interview room when Bleasdale and Clark entered.

'Before we go any further, I want a solicitor, and you both can piss off as I am not speaking another word without one.'

'Have you anyone in mind, Mr Horn?' There was no answer.

'Ok, I will make sure a duty solicitor is called.' Horn was lead back to the cells.

The Coroner's office having the fingerprints analysed along with the dental records, had the information on the victim. Peter Powell telephoned Inspector Medows.

'Hi, Barrie, I had hoped to catch you before you went home. We have the information on the victim, I'm faxing the paper work as we speak. You'll be astonished when you know who it is. It's Peter Sainsbury who's wanted in connexion with those murders over at Mallards Publishing House.'

Sergeant Bobby Rice was sitting opposite Medows, 'Did I hear right, Sir, that body in the car at the Marshes is Peter Sainsbury?'

'That's correct, Sergeant.' Picking up the telephone and calling Chief Inspector Greedy.

'Sir, we have the identification of the victim in the car at the Marshes, it's the wanted man Peter Sainsbury.'

'Well that's a turn up, Inspector. I'll call Scotland Yard and let them know of the discovery.' After furnishing Superintendent Parker with the story, it was arranged that they would all meet at the crime scene. Parker who was sitting with Inspector Brown told him the news that the body of Peter Sainsbury had been found.

Parker then called Chief Inspector Bleasdale letting him know of the situation of the body of Peter Sainsbury. Before Parker could put the phone down, Bleasdale gave him the news of Prince's car having three detonators being found in the boot of the car.

'Wonderful news, Bleasdale, the case is unfolding at last.'

Parker and Brown were speaking in the back of the car about Tommy Prince and Ted Horn. It appeared they both fitted nicely into the case of Mallards Publishing House.

Brown asked the Superintendent where he thought the foreigners fitted into the crimes. 'I am not sure; however everything appears to point to them, and as the case opens up further more information will come to light I am sure.'

Chief Inspector Greedy, Inspector Medow and Sergeant Rice made their way to Chetney Marshes, with Chief Inspector Greedy acquainting himself with the statements in the back of his car.

Sergeant Richard Hill made his way to the Marshes. He was over the moon with the importance of a very big murder taking place on his patch. He had arranged for three extra constables to be on duty to be stationed around the crime scene and at the top of Lover's lane to direct the important visitors. Another police motorcycle was waiting for the superintendent's car, so to direct him to the crime scene.

'Hallo, Sergeant Hill, I've been hearing very good reports about you. Now lead the way, I would like to look at the crime scene before the Met gets here, Sergeant,' as they walked off through the mushy ground.

Inspector Medow's and Sergeant Rice walked slowly behind letting Sergeant Hill have his day. C.I. Greedy commented how nice the area must be in the summer months. Walking further into the mushy ground, Sergeant Hill pointed out how the car was found by the two boys, and that in his opinion the perpetrators couldn't have known the area, as if they had, they would have selected pushing the car in the Marshes where it is at least fifteen feet deep.

'Yes, I agree, Sergeant,' as they arrived at the crime scene. They turned making their way through the trees to where the getaway car had been parked. C.I. Greedy turning his head towards Inspector Medows, 'Very interesting Barrie.'

The branches and bushes were still lying down on the floor. 'It was evident SOCO were able to identify the vehicle as being red. With two witnesses saying the car was a red Mazda. We believe the driver of the getaway car must have walked to Whitstable where we believe, he stole a motorbike.'

'I see, Scotland Yard will be with us shortly, gentleman. They of course were looking for Peter Sainsbury for the murders of at least three people.'

Superintendent Parker's car lead by the police motorcycle made their way to the crime scene where C.I. Greedy, Inspector Medow and the two Sergeants were waiting.

C.I. Greedy came forward to greet the Superintendent. After pleasantries were made, they all moved off through the mushy ground to the actual crime scene. After discussing the whys and wherefores of the depth of the Marshes, it was agreed that the killing of Peter Sainsbury was a hit. They wandered through the trees and mushy greenery towards the place of the hidden getaway car.

Superintendent Parker was pleased the way the Kent police had dealt with the discovery of the car containing the body. After thanking them all, it was agreed to send all copies of the findings to Scotland Yard.

Chief Inspector Bleasdale and Sergeant Ben Clark were informed by Sergeant Smith that the duty solicitor had arrived. They made their way to the interview room and met Miss Kerry Dickson, who stood at least three inches taller than both Bleasdale and Clark. She was wearing a blue trouser suit with a blue folder held under her left arm.

'I would like to speak with my client first before we proceed with the official interview,' pointed out Miss Dickson. Ted Horn was brought into the interview room. Miss Dickson introduced herself. After agreeing on the procedure, she opened the door, letting the constable know they were ready to be interviewed.

Bleasdale and Clark entered the room, sat down and switched on the tape, gave all the names of those present and started the proceedings. 'We are led to believe that Tommy Prince and yourself met with two foreign gentleman, named Costa and Andres, in a public house in London. You were propositioned with a large amount of money, ten grand, to blow a safe at Mallards Publishing House in Baker street.'

'Chief Inspector, my client has no comment to make at this particular time.' Horn sat at the table with his crocked smile, tapping his fingers on the table.

'Mr Horn, you agreed with this Costa fellow to carry out the safe blowing job. Tommy Prince on his part travelled to his mother's house in Manchester. Reported his car stolen, drove back to London picked you up and together pulled the job. You then decided to go back to Northampton and Tommy Prince travelled on to Manchester.'

'Chief Inspector, my client has no comment to make.'

'Mr Horn, you then tried to sell the documents to Peter Sainsbury, but you couldn't get an agreement so you and others decided to kill him dumping his body in the Marshes at Chetney.'

'I'm being fitted up with a load of crap, you bastards.'

'Please calm yourself, Mr Horn,' pointed out Miss Dickson. 'Chief Inspector, this is pure hearsay and you haven't any evidence.'

'Miss Dickson, we have lots of evidence against your client.'

'Then I suggest you either charge Mr Horn or let him go home.'

'Mr Edward Horn, I am charging you with breaking and entering of Mallards Publishing House, Baker Street, using an explosive substance to blow open a safe and then removing documents and money. I am also cautioning you that at a future time, a further charge of conspiracy to murder may be brought against you after further investigations have been completed.'

'I never had anything to do with the fucking Mallards job,' jumping out of his seat banging the table and trying to punch the Chief Inspector.

'Sit down, Mr Horn,' said Bleasdale'

'You fucking liar, Bleasdale, you're not fitting me up,' Horn shouted.

Ben Clark turned and hit the alarm button; two constables entered and led Horn back to the cells.

Kerry Dickson who was startled, walked away turning her head. 'I'll be seeing my client later,' shouted Miss Dickson.

'Blasted woman,' said Bleasdale. 'We better interview Tommy Prince.'

'For the benefit of the tape, Tommy, we have a lot of evidence now. Your friend Ted Horn has been charged with the safe blowing and robbery, and could be charged with murder. I suggest you answer carefully. Tell us what happened when you drove down from Manchester and picked Ted Horn up.'

'I didn't drive down from Manchester and picked Ted Horn up.'

'Look, Tommy, we are trying to help you here. Your car has been found in London and in the boot of your car we found detonators. Your car is now being searched for traces of gelignite.'

'No, no, you are trying to fit me up. I had nothing to do with the Mallards job.'

'This is becoming tedious, Tommy—start telling us the truth as it could save you quite a lot of time in prison.'

'I'm being set up.'

'Don't be silly, Tommy, a known safe cracker with detonators in the boot of his car, who on earth is going to believe you for one minute. Now you need to start telling the truth, we are convinced you had nothing to do with the murders.'

'O Christ, what's happening. I've told the truth, Mr Bleasdale. I told you Ted Horn and I met the two foreigners but we had nothing to do with the Mallards job. I'm not stupid, I wouldn't be driving around with detonators in my car.'

'Tommy, this is your last chance, tell us the truth or I'm going to charge you.'

'I had nothing to do with the Mallards job, Mr Bleasdale.'

'Mr Thomas Prince, I am charging you with the breaking and entering of Mallards Publishing House, Baker Street, and using an explosive substance to blow open a safe, removing documents and money. I must also caution you that you could be charged at a future time with conspiracy to murder after further investigations have been completed.'

The Police Commissioner, Sir John Bacon, reported to the home Secretary, saying that the investigation was proceeding nicely and he was led to believe the case would be tied up in the next few weeks.

Superintendent Parker called Chief Inspector Bleasdale congratulating him on the arrests of Ted Horn and Tommy Prince. However, it was imperative that the foreigners be found quickly.

Reg More and Rod Muir made their way to the Red Lion to pick up the surveillance tape, meeting up with Sergeant Weber in the police van.

'How's it going, Sergeant?'

'Fine, plenty of activity. A few known villains but mainly small time.'

'No sign of any foreigners?'

'Not that we can see, Reg.'

The newspaper media besieged Kilburn police Station, asking for a statement. Chief Inspector Bleasdale made a short statement informing the media that two men had been charged with the safe blowing at Mallards Publishing house.

'Can you give us the names, Chief Inspector?'

'You all know better than that, gentleman.'

'Can you confirm the body found at Chetney Marshes is that of Peter Sainsbury?'

'Yes the body is that of Peter Sainsbury.'

'Are the two men arrested for the Mallards crime, also involved with the murders?'

'Let's say they are assisting us with our enquiries. Thank you, Ladies and gentleman.'

The newspaper people were shouting for more answers, but Bleasdale was having none of it. In the CID office, the team were sitting in easy chairs watching the surveillance tape.

'Hay look there, its Tony Roberts with Ronny Graham. I wonder what those two are up to.' said Ben Clark. 'And there its Bob Warden; what would he be doing over this part of the waters,' said Reg More. 'We'll have to be checking that little lot out.'

Chief Inspector Bleasdale walked in to the CID office.

Reg More spoke up saying they were watching the surveillance tape from the Red Lion.

'See anything interesting?'

'Yes, Sir, a few villains that we will be checking on. By the way, Sir, it will be necessary to keep the surveillance vehicle for another week.'

Bleasdale went a little red pushing out his lips.

'Let's hope you crack the case then, Sergeant More,' walking to the door. 'Clark, you will be with me tomorrow at the court appearance of Ted Horn and Tommy Prince.'

It was decided that Clark and Quirk would take a look at Bob Warden while More and Muir would look at Tony Roberts and Ronny Graham.

In Whitstable, everybody was talking about the murder in the Marshes and the missing motorbike. The local pub was full of locals and reporters continuing with their questions, promising the locals money for any information that could be headline news. They found out about Mrs Deacon and her statement, and Mr Pendale and his son who actually found the car.

Then there was Mr Billinson and the theft of his motorbike thought to have been used as a getaway vehicle. The reporters rushed around to Billinson's house.

'Did you see anybody?'

'O yes, I chased the thief up the road, but unfortunately he got away. However, I would be able to identify him. The police are coming around with an identity kit,' walking back inside his house laughing his head off.

Other reporters pestered Mrs Deacon, asking about the identity of the people she had seen in the car.

'I've already explained all to the police, now be off with you.' The reporters got the same explanation from Dick Pendale, who slammed the front door in their faces.

All the newspapers reported that the body of murderer Peter Sainsbury had been found in Chetney Marshes, and two men were appearing in court charged with the safe blowing at Mallards Publishing house and could be involved with the murders.

Also printed,

Mr Billinson, who had his motorbike stolen, had actually chased one man up the road who was thought to be involved with Peter Sainsbury's body being found inside a vehicle.

Chetney Marshes.

In Spain, Captain Sifre was perturbed over different statements he had received and what was so important in the safe at Mallards publishing house in London that caused three people to be murdered in England and one in Spain so far. He decided perhaps it would be better to travel to London and speak with Superintendent Parker at Scotland Yard.

At Baker Street Magistrates court, the case against Mr Edward Horn and Thomas Prince was called. Chief Inspector Bleasdale gave evidence, Mr Horn and Mr Prince were asked how they pleaded. 'Not guilty.'

Miss Kerry Dickson, solicitor for both, asked under the circumstances both men be allowed bail. The prosecuting inspector suggested that under the seriousness of the crime and impending investigation into murders that had taken place at Mallards Publishing House, both men were therefore assisting the police in their inquiries.

The Magistrates conferred and agreed with the police that the two men should remain in custody.

The newspapers and the television had the information of the two named men. The evening news gave the first report of the two named men involved in the Mallards Publishing House safe blowing.

The television gave the news at 9.00 saying that Mr Edward Horn and Thomas Prince had been charged with unlawfully entering and using an explosive substance to open a safe and remove monies and other documents. They were not given bail, as there was an impending investigation into murders that had taken place at Mallards Publishing House.

Joe Bolt watched the TV news. 'Those two poor buggers are being framed for the Mallards job.' He thought about Jeff and wondered where he was. What was going on with Derrick, and how had he got involved with a heavy mob, nothing was making sense. Joe called Maggie, 'Has anybody been around?'

'No. Joe. Did you know the police have arrested two men for the Mallards job, you could come home now.'

'No, Maggie, I must keep away from London, I will call another time.'

John and Peter Shephard popped into the Red Lion for a drink, they occasionally received tips from some of the villains drinking their regards any robberies going down.

'Hallo, Billy, how are you?'

'Hallo, John, Peter, haven't seen you two around lately, you missed the send-off for poor old Kenny Owen.'

'Yeah we heard about his murder. The word is he was telling everybody about how he was approached for that safe blowing job at Mallards.'

'Yes, that's correct, but the old bugger didn't deserve being bumped off, John.'

'No you're right,' as they walked back to their car chatting about Kenny Owen. 'I can't see the foreigners being involved with bumping off Kenny Owen, still we better get Big Sam to check it out.'

Sergeant Weber pointed at the surveillance camera.

'Well looky here, 'John and Peter Shephard; a couple of heavies, things are looking up.'

With Ben Clark being in court with the Chief Inspector Bleasdale, Reg More and Rod Muir took it on themselves to visit Bob Warden. Pulling up outside his flat where he lived and taking the lift up to the sixth floor, knocking on number 68. The door opened and standing with his legs apart, virtually covering the whole of the door frame with his black curly hair, touching the top of the door was Bob Warden, his right hand on the door frame.

'What do you two want?'

'Hallo, Bob, we thought we would come around and have a chat.'

'What about?'

'We were wondering what you were doing on the Southside of the water.'

'Is it a new law to drive from the north side to the Southside of the river?'

'No, Bob, not at all.'

'Well, go away and help somebody else,' shutting the door in their face.

'Bob Warden wouldn't go over the water just for a drink in the Red Lion, he's a nasty piece of work when he's riled up and he is rather handy with his fists, believe me,' said Reg.

Sergeant Richard Hill had read the newspaper reports, when he received a call from D.I. Medows. 'Yes, Sir, I have read newspaper reports. I'm really surprised that Billinson is shouting his mouth off saying he could identify the perpetrators who stole his motorbike. It's a big mistake on his part.'

'You better pop round and see Billinson and Mrs Deacon, as they could be in danger.'

Sergeant Hill noticed reporters were everywhere sniffing for stories in Whitstable. One reporter came over to his police car as he pulled up.

'Morning, Sergeant, have you anything for us.'

'No.' Making his way to Billinson's house, being followed at some distance by the reporter.

Billinson came to the front door. 'I know why you're here, Sergeant, they made me give those reports handing me hundred pounds for my story.'

'Mr Billinson, if that villain who stole your motorbike is also involved with the murder, and he believes you recognised him, you may be in serious danger. I would suggest you refrain from telling untruths to members of the press.'

'I'm sorry, Sergeant Hill, it won't happen again.'

Sergeant Hill drove off towards Mrs Deacon's house. 'Morning, Mrs Deacon, I hope you are all right.'

‘Thank you so much, Sergeant Hill. I’ve been besieged by those reporters all last night, they offered money for my story. They wanted me to say I had seen a number of men in cars on the night of the murder. I wasn’t having any of it, but they kept on trying.’

‘That’s ok, Mrs Deacon, if they continue to pester you, give us a call and I will get one of the constables around.’

As Sergeant Hill drove back to his station, he noticed a car following. Stopping and jumping out of his patrol car, he stood in the middle of the road holding his hand up indicating to the car to pull over to the curb. As the car stopped, Sergeant Hill made his way to the open window.

‘Good Morning, Sir.’ Noticing the same reporter driving as he had seen in Whitstable just before talking with Mr Billinson.

‘May I ask why you are following me’

‘I’m only doing my job, Sergeant, trying to get a story.’

‘Sir I must caution you, if you continue to follow me around, I will pinch you for obstruction. Is that clear?’

‘Yes, Sergeant.’

Miguel Melgar and Juan Riminez had also been monitoring the stories in the newspapers.

‘They’ve found that bloody car with Sainsbury’s body inside. We’ve made a bad mistake. You told me the Marshes were at least ten feet deep. At least the car is clean. They won’t find any prints and what about this Billinson chap saying he can identify you, Juan. He will have to be taken care as of today.’

‘Ok, Miguel, I’ll take care of him.’

Juan departed London driving towards Whitstable, stopping only at Iwade service station for some coffee and work out his plans. It would be getting dark soon and Billinson would be getting home from work. Parking his car in a space in the main road. It was getting dark and damp.

Reaching over to the back seat for his camera and placing it around his neck. Walking out of the main road and noticing a telephone box on the corner of Mr Billinson’s road. He looked up Billinson’s telephone number in the yellow pages, and made the call. Billinson answered.

‘Good evening, Mr Billinson. I’ve got some good news for you, we’ve found your motorbike.’

‘Are you the police?’

'No, I'm with one of the newspapers. We received a tip about your stolen motorbike and where it was hidden. Could you meet me in the next ten minutes?'

'That would be great. I'll just get my coat. Where shall I meet you.'

'There's a telephone box just down on the corner of your road, I'll meet you there.'

Billinson told his mum he was popping out to meet a reporter who had found his bike and should be back inside the hour. He walked down to the telephone box where he noticed a man of dark completion.

'Are you the reporter who called me?'

That's right, Mr Billinson.'

'You sound foreign.'

'Yes, I am Spanish and work as an agent for a number of newspapers. Before I take you to your motorbike, have you any more news on this chap you can identify stealing your motorbike.'

'I didn't see anybody really. One of your colleagues from the newspapers gave me hundred pounds to say that.'

'Yes of course they would do, let's go and get your bike.'

'Where was it found?'

'It's in the woods.'

'That's strange; we searched all over the woods and didn't find a thing.'

'It was probably dumped later when all the news came out.'

Turning right up that dirt path pointing the way. The path had become slippery through the wet and damp weather. Billinson was a few feet in front of Juan Riminez, who had already fitted the suppressor to his gun which he had under his jacket.

As Billinson turned around, it was too late. Two shots to the head. Billinson didn't even have chance to cry out as he fell to the wet ground. Riminez pulled the body into the undergrowth and walked away.

He was annoyed as he returned to his car, noticing that it was boxed in with a van double parked; looking around for the owner, he couldn't see anybody. He certainly didn't want to go in any of the shops asking about the van. He decided to remain cool and stand just down the road.

Ten minutes, then further twenty minutes passed by. He didn't want to panic and was thinking he probably had another thirty minutes before Billinson should have returned home. Another ten minutes crept by and no sign of the driver of the van. A police car turned the corner slowly making its way down the high road. Juan ducked into a cake shop.

'Can I help you young man,' said a rather plump lady dressed in the cake shop smock with the shops logo sawn on the upper part?.

'Yes, I will have a cream bun. By the way, you wouldn't know whose van that is out there, would you?'

'Yes, it's our delivery driver.'

'Unfortunately he's blocking me in.'

'O dear, is that your nice red car?'

'Yes, it is.'

'He shouldn't be long as he has just delivered some fresh pies to the Blue Boar.'

Making his way to the Blue Boar, Juan noticed a chap in the baker's overall, coming out of the Blue Boar Inn.

'Hallo, mate, your van is blocking me in.'

'Sorry about that. I was longer than I anticipated waiting to be paid.' They walked back together. As they reached the shop, the bakery chap got into the van and pulled up twenty feet.

Most of the reporters had left Whitstable except for Tony Humpreys who was going to stay a further night at the Blue Boar. Ordering a pint of the best he sat down at the corner table, opened his notebook. Reading his last few pages, he laughed to himself after reading the bit about following Sergeant Hill until he was stopped and warned.

'I'll have another couple of pints and then I'll be off to Reads Restaurant for a late dinner and a nice bottle of red wine.'

After his second pint, the pub door opened with Mrs Billinson pocking her head inside. 'George, is there any of those reporters about?' George pointed over to Tony Humpreys' table.

'Are you the reporter who telephoned my son about his missing motorbike two hours ago?'

George, the landlord, who was listening to the conversation mentioned, 'Mr Humpreys is the only newspaper person left since early afternoon, perhaps your boy is around at the Ducks Head.'

'No, George, he doesn't like the beer there.'

'I would go and have a look,' said George Cobum, who had been the landlord of the Blue Boar for thirty eight years, nothing exciting has happened here in

Whitstable since 1966 World Cup, when some of the squad came here for a drink. Tony Humpreys could smell a story and asked Mrs Billinson if she would like him to accompany her.

'That would be nice, thank you.' Walking along the road to the next corner, all the houses were the same as you see in all towns—two up two down, different coloured painted doors some with flower boxes on the downstairs window stills. As they reached the Ducks Head, Mrs Billinson opened the door stepping up two steps. Tony nearly bumped his head on the second step, the pub had no atmosphere and there were only three locals in the bar.

'Has my Bruce been in here tonight, Stuart?'

'No, Mrs Billinson, you know Bruce doesn't like my beer, he's told enough people that over the years.'

'He could have gone home by now, Mrs Billinson.' Making their way back to her house, opening the front door and calling out his name, there was no answer.

'Perhaps he's taken his bike out for a spin.'

'Not without telling me first.'

'Maybe it's broken down and he's taken it to the garage.'

'No, he does all his own repairs.' Two and a half hours passed and no sign of Bruce Billinson. They gave a call to the Blue Boar just in case he popped in, there was a negative answer there too.

'Mrs Billinson, perhaps we should give Sergeant Hill a call.'

'Why, do you think something has happened to Bruce?'

'I'm not sure if anything has happened to Bruce, but it would be a good idea to report the fact.'

'O my God, you think somebody has done harm to my Bruce. He's all I've got.' as she started to cry.

'Sit yourself down and I'll give Sergeant Hill a call.

'I'm sorry but Sergeant Hill has gone home for the night. Can I help?'

'I really need to speak with the Sergeant, it's about Bruce Billinson.'

'May I have your name, Sir?'

'Tony Humphrey from the Daily Scribe.'

'O yes, the reporter who followed the Sergeant around all day. Believe me, Sir, just call it a day,' putting the telephone down. Tony's next call was to the Daily Scribe, 'Roy Smith please.'

'Hallo, Tony, you're not still sniffing around down there, are you?'

'You bet, I think I'm on to something. Young Bruce Billinson is missing after receiving a call from a chap saying he was a reporter and had found his motorbike, since then Bruce hasn't been seen. I tried calling the local police station but they just put the telephone down on me.

'When we spoke yesterday, you mentioned that you had a friend at Sittingboume police, a D.I. Medows. I was wondering if you could give him a call.

'Ok, Tony, I'll call him, stay at Mrs Billinsons until the police or I contact you.'

'Hallo, Inspector Medows, Roy Smith, Daily Scribe.'

'Hallo, Roy, what can I do for you.'

'One of my boys is still sniffing around the area. The lad Bruce Billinson has gone missing after receiving a call from a guy saying he was a reporter and had found his motorbike. My reporter is worried that this so called guy, could be the person Billinson suggested he chased up the road and could identify.'

'Where is your man?'

'At Mrs Billinson's.'

'Ok, Roy, we will take it from here, thanks for the call.'

'Barry, if anything comes up remember who tipped you off.'

'If anything comes up your newspaper will be the first to know.'

D.I. Medows called Chetney sub-station asking for Sergeant Hill.

'Sorry Sir, he's gone home for the night.'

'Get the sergeant on the phone and tell him I'm on my way to Whitstable as Bruce Billinson has gone missing.'

Calling Sergeant Hill the constable explained why he hadn't taken any notice of Tony Humpreys when he called. 'No worries these things happen,' said the Sergeant.

Sergeant Hill looked out his window. It was raining. Getting his topcoat from the peg, thinking just what we need a search in the rain. As he drove off towards Whitstable, he thought about his conversation with D.I. Medows regarding Bruce Billinson.

D.I. Medows and Sergeant Rice made their way to Whitstable, Sergeant Rice saying perhaps young Bruce isn't missing but just gone out for a spin on his motorbike.

'Let's hope you're right, Sergeant, but I have this awful feeling about this case. There have already been four murders connected so far according to Superintendent Parker. I just hope this is not another, Sergeant.'

'Yes, Sir.' Arriving at Mrs Billinson's house, Sergeant Hill was already interviewing Tony Humphreys and Mrs Billinson.

'Good evening, Inspector. What have we so far?' Tony Humphreys explained the situation with Mrs Billinson agreeing.

'Ok, Mrs Billinson, when was the last time you saw your lad?'

'It must be four hours ago now. Mr Humphreys and I have been all over town searching for him.'

'Are you sure it was a reporter that spoke with Bruce about his motorbike.'

'Yes, Inspector, the chap said he was a reporter and would meet Bruce down by the telephone box on the corner of the road.'

Sergeant Rice telephoned Sittingboume asking for ten more constables with Sergeant Hill requesting four of his own constables.

D.I. Medows told both Sergeants, 'When your officers arrive have them search the town from top to bottom, every pub, cafe, video store, you name it. I want it checked. And when the town has been searched, start a search of the woods.'

Mrs Billinson broke down saying, 'Bruce, is all I've got.'

'We'll find him,' said Medows The local police car arrived with the four constables. Sergeant Hill detailed them to search the town.

D.I. Medows and Sergeant Rice where making plans to collate the search in the woods. Tony Humphreys offered to assist in the search.

The police vehicle arrived from Sittingboume with a dozen police officers, D.I. Medows lined them up explaining that they would be searching the woods behind the house, pointing in that direction, 'Make sure you all have flashlights. The rain was really pouring down and with the darkness visibility would be nearly zero.'

Everybody lined up no more than two feet apart, they would move off until they reached the top of the hill, returning down the next stretch. It was going to take hours we need more men thought the inspector.

Sergeant Hill's men had been in every pub, coffee bar and shops, nobody had seen Bruce Billinson. Making their way back to the main party, they joined the line-up.

In the Blue Boar, the conversation was about Bruce Billinson going missing, the pub door opened and in walked Tom Bale. 'What's going on?'

'Haven't you heard Bruce Billinsons missing?'

'But I saw him about four hours ago talking with some dark looking chap near the telephone box on the corner of his road.'

'You better get over to the woods and let the police know,' said George Cobum.

Making his way to the entrance of the woods, he could see the flashlights but they were too far up the hill, and wouldn't hear him shout until they came back down which by the looks of it would be another thirty minutes. Tom made his way to the telephone box, getting inside to keep warm and keep out the rain.

He stamped his feet, pushing his hands in his raincoat pockets. Forty minutes later, he could see the flashlights coming down the next stretch, he estimated they were near enough to see him. Making his way over the soaked road and into the woods which had become mushy, 'Hi there.'

'Yes, Sir, what can I do for you?'

'I have some information about Bruce Billinson.'

'Hold on a minute, Sir.' Inspector Medow told his officers to start the next stretch, making his way over to the gentleman.

'I understand you have some information on Bruce Billinson.'

'That's correct, Inspector. I was passing the end of the road near the telephone box about four hours ago, when I noticed Bruce speaking to a man aged about 42, dark complexion, about 5,8 tall, wearing a green jacket.'

'Did you see where they went?'

'Afraid not, Inspector. I was on my way to the corner shop for some cat food, when I came back they were gone.'

'Let's sit in the car and get a statement.' Tom commented that it was better in the car than outside. D.I. Medows said, 'Yes, it's a nasty night.'

Tom gave his name as Tom Bale, of 64 St Johns Street. 'It's just around the corner, ten houses down on the left.'

'Thank you, Mr Bale, we will be in touch.'

D.I. Medows made his way back through the wet undergrowth to the police line, explaining to Sergeant Rice, 'It doesn't sound good for the boy, Sergeant.' The rain was pouring down in sheets, visibility was nil. D.I. Medows called off the search until daybreak.

Dry cloths had been sent for, all trudging around to the Blue Boar Pub. George Cobum offered to put any of the officers up if they didn't mind sharing, that was great news to the inspector. Sergeant Rice asked George Cobum if it was possible to arrange for any local men to assist in the search which would commence at 7.30. A WPC was requested to sit with Mrs Billinson until Bruce had been found.

Medows put a call through to C.I. Roger Greedy at home, giving him the bad news. Greedy suggested he would be in Whitstable at 7.30 and would authorise another dozen officers.

'That's great, Sir.'

At 7.I5, forty eight men were outside the Blue Boar. George Cobum had coffee arranged. Inspector Medows was overwhelmed with the response of the local people to help in the search. They all stood around with hot coffee cups in their hands while Inspector Medows explained how the search would proceed.

'Sergeant Hill, will you start questioning everybody in shops, coffee bars, pubs and offices in the roads and streets around the town. We want to know about a man in the age bracket in his fortes, 5'8 tall with a dark complexion wearing a green jacket.'

Chief Inspector Greedy's car pulled up outside the Blue Boar. It was agreed that they could have a downstairs room as a coordination point for the investigation, where C.I. Greedy would be stationed, the rain eased off a little.

The temperature was down, with the ground of the woods sodden with wet branches and trees dripping water. With the extra men, it meant the search would take six hours to complete.

Sergeant Hill and his officers started door to door, stopping everybody they came across asking if they had seen Bruce Billinson or a man in his forties, 5'8 tall with dark completion. Two hours went by and they had drawn a blank Sergeant Hill looked through the window of the Kent High Bakery shop seeing Mrs Branton and decided to enter.

'Hallo, Sergeant, sorry to hear about young Bruce going missing.'

'Yes, awful business. You didn't happen to see Bruce Billinson last evening.'

'No, Sergeant, afraid not.'

'What about a man of dark complexion about 5'8, wearing a green jacket.'

'Yes, Sergeant. He was quite rude to our van driver, as the man was complaining about being blocked in by David's van.'

'What sort of car was it?'

'It was a red car, Sergeant. I didn't know the make, but David would know as he is very knowledgeable about cars.'

'Where can I find David, Mrs Branton.'

'He is on his rounds delivering cakes and pies.'

'Is there any way we can get in touch with him.'

'I could telephone Mr Kent, he would be able to find out for you.'

'Please do that, Mrs Branton, it's urgent.' After speaking with Mr Kent they found David at Leysdown-on-sea who would be waiting at the local shop. Sergeant Hill flagged down a passing police car and drove off to Leysdown. The weather wasn't holding up and would hinder the search. Reaching Leysdown they found David waiting outside the shop, he was able to give a complete description of the man and his car which was a red Mazda.

'Thank you, David. I will need you to pop in the Blue Boar and make a statement later.'

C.I. Greedy was looking at the statements when Sergeant Hill arrived giving his report on the description of the man and the red Mazda starting with the Registration of T4. 'That's good work, Sergeant. It certainly confirms our witness statements regarding a red Mazda.' He immediately called the collator's office giving the details.

Chief Inspector Greedy's radio clicked in. 'We've found a body which has a couple of bullet wounds.'

'O dear.'

'I'm going to cordon off the area, ready for SOCO and the coroner.'

'Thank you, Inspector. I'll see you shortly.'

Peter Powell and his team arrived; the chequered blue and white crime scene tape was already in place along with a tent erected covering the body.

'Hallo, Barry, not a nice day for a search.'

'Hi, Peter, you can say that again. We are all drenched to the skin, so if you don't need us for a while, I'll get away and get some dry cloths,' shifting from one foot to the other.

'No problem, Barry, I'll take it from here, and call you if I need you.' SOCO started there part of the investigation. Photographs were taken of the body from all different angles. The surrounding area and pathways leading to the different roads and entrances were also searched and photographed.

Chief Inspector Greedy was in his temporary Ops room in the Blue Boar Pub; D.I. Medows changed his soaking wet clothes, taken a hot bath and entered the

Ops room. 'If only Billinson hadn't made the mistake of telling the newspapers that silly story, he probably would be alive today.'

'I've informed Superintendent Parker of the bad news. He also agrees with our theory, at least we have part of the car registration number, the collator's office is working on it as we speak.'

Superintendent Parker suggested, 'a general meeting of everybody involved together from the different stations, maybe we would be able to collate all the information they have, and something may crop up that we hadn't considered.'

'Well get on with it, Superintendent, stop dithering about.'

'Yes, Sir.' Superintendent Parker faxed all concerned with details of the meeting to Chief Inspectors Bleasdale and Greedy, Inspector Brown of the Serious crime squad and D.I. Medows from Sittingboume, Inspector Cavendish from Barking, Sergeants Ben Clark-Reg More from Kilburn, Sergeant Rice and Sergeant Hill from Sittingboume, Captain Sifre of the Guardia Civil in Madrid.

John Shephard gave Big Sam a call, 'Something has come up, I think you should know about.'

'Ok let's meet at the Barbican Centre say 8.30 tonight.' Big Sam Davidson took the train to the Barbican, sitting down looking at the day's programme and watching the cleaning company carry out the massive duty of keeping the centre clean. All the cleaners looked smart in there overalls with HDH cleaners printed on the breast pocket.

The centre was packed. John and Peter Shephard made their way towards Big Sam who sat on a bar stool in the first floor bar.

'Peter and I had a quick pint in the Red Lion. The landlord Billy Fleming, a really nice block told us about the murder of Kenny Owen, a former safe blower in his day. Billy told us that Kenny had been approached by two foreigner guys to pull a job. As we are doing business with this Costa fellow and his mate, surely it wouldn't be them who killed poor old Kenny Owen.'

'Definitely not, but its good information. I'll have a word with Costa anyway.'

'That's great, Sam. We wouldn't want to work with somebody who murders a guy like poor old Kenny Owen.'

'Don't worry, lads, I'll check it out and get back to you.' Travelling back home on the train Big Sam was thinking over the conversation he had with John and Peter Shephard. There was no way any of gang would want to be associated with a murder of Kenny Owen. Once at home, Big Sam called Derrick asking about Billy Fleming, the landlord of the Red Lion.

'I don't know much about him, Sam. Jeff and Joe Bolt used to use the Red Lion to gather tips on jobs from different villains. Fleming himself always seemed to be a stand up nice guy, tough bastard. He was into all that illegal boxing. Why, what's up?'

'Nothing to worry about, it may be necessary at some point to pay a visit to the Red Lion.' Making his second call, which was answered on the second ring. 'Hallo, Costa, its Big Sam. Two of my lads are very upset as somebody has bumped off one of their friends, old guy named Kenny Owen, a former safe cracker. I just wanted insurances from you that your firm had nothing to do with it.'

'Sam, what on earth would we want some old guy bumped off.'

'That's fine, Costa; I just wanted to hear you say it.'

'By the way, Sam, is everything on schedule?'

'We have one more meeting and then it's a go.'

'Super, Sam, be hearing from you shortly.' Putting the telephone down in its cradle.

'What's that all about, Costa,' asked Andres.

'Nothing to worry about, the big job is on schedule.'

Chief Inspector Greedy made his way from the temporary Ops room to the crime scene. The weather was still "hit and miss", raining one moment, stopping the next. The temperature was still low and cold. Looking up at the clouds he could see the temperature falling even further. Spotting Peter Powell, Greedy made his way across the wet undergrowth towards him.

Peter seeing Greedy approaching, shrugged his shoulders saying, 'Terrible waste of life. Two gunshots to the head.'

Greedy moaned, 'Another bloody contract killing.'

Sergeant Rice who was standing by the side of the C.I. pointed at the body 'This lad was murdered because of that silly statement he made to the newspapers.'

C.I. Greedy placed his fat hand on his chin, pouting his lips and nodding his head. 'It certainly looks that way. How long for the toxicology report, Peter?'

'It's going to be some time, as I cannot see us clearing up the crime scene for a few hours.'

‘Ok, Peter as soon as possible.’ Walking away with Sergeant Rice back towards the Ops room when he bumped into the local doctor who was about to see Mrs Billinson.

‘You know, Doctor, this is one of the worst parts of my job, having to let somebody know that one of their family members is dead.’

‘I know the feeling too well, Chief Inspector,’ pushing his right hand into his raincoat pocket further, his left hand holding his briefcase. As they arrived at Mrs Billinson’s house, the WPC opened the front door to let them in. Mrs Billinson was sitting on her easy chair.

‘I’m afraid I have some bad news, Mrs Billinson. A body has been found which we believe is that of your son.’

‘O no, no, he’s all I’ve got!’ The doctor held Mrs Billinson’s hand, the WPC held her shoulder. The doctor asked Mrs Billinson if she would like something to calm her down.

C.I. Greedy asked if there was anyone that he could contact, a relative maybe who would come and stay. ‘I have a sister in Ramsgate.’

‘Give me her address and we will have her collected and brought over here.’

C.I. Greedy telephoned Inspector Waters at Ramsgate police, giving him the information. ‘That’s not a problem, Chief Inspector, I know Mrs Beech very well. She’s on the local police safety committee.’

Greedy called the collator’s office, asking for any further news on that red Mazda registration.

‘Not yet, Sir.’

‘Make it a propriety, I want to catch these bastards.’

D.I. Medows, Sergeants Rice and Hill were busy in the temporary Ops room, carefully going through each of the statements taken from different witnesses, hoping they may pick up one little item that had been overlooked. Chief Inspector Greedy said the word will be out among the newspapers, the town will be flooded once again with reporters, ready to pay and even make up stories which place other witnesses in danger.

Big Sam and Derrick arrived at the Red Lion. The conversation in the car had been after the forthcoming robbery. Sam mentioned that he would be retiring to Spain with his share of the money, and Derrick intimated he would be purchasing a little house on the coast, probably in West Sussex and start a small business.

Walking towards the front door of the pub, Sergeant Weber had the two of them on the surveillance tape. 'Look there, Derrick Smallwood, a small time villain that we have never caught as he has always been on his toes. However, that big fellow with Smallwood, I've seen him somewhere but cannot put a name to the face.'

Big Sam ordered two pints of the best. As Billy Fleming pulled the two pints, he looked at Derrick, 'Don't I know you?'

'Yeah, Billy, I used to come in with Joe Bolt.'

'That's right, how is Joe?'

'He's on holiday down in Cornwall.'

'What with Jeff Mitchell?' looking Derrick straight in the face.

'I'm not sure about that, Billy. We heard about poor old Kenny Owen.'

'Yeah, Derrick, a real shock,' putting the two pints on the counter.

'The problem was poor old Kenny after a couple of drinks would start talking about the two foreigners who offered him the safe job at Mallards.'

'Really?'

'Yeah, Kenny was adamant about it. He always finished his story by saying that he gave the foreigners names of other safe blowing teams. In my opinion, Derrick, he told the story once too often. Somebody overheard him and had him bumped off, as Kenny was no grass as you know, Derrick.'

'Yeah you're right there, Billy.' Big Sam nodded to Derrick to sit at one of the side tables near the windows.

'Derrick, there's no way Costa is involved with the murder of Kenny Owen, as Billy Fleming just pointed out. Somebody must have been listening to poor old Kenny's story which had become dangerous to them.'

'Yeah you're right there, Sam. We should say clear of this as the old bill will be all over this Kenny Owen business like a rash.'

Bob Warden was looking out of his window thinking about the murder of Kenny Owen. He knew it wasn't a mugging and nobody really knew that Kenny Owen was Bob's uncle.

Sitting in his chair one leg crossed over the other, then shifting his legs and tapping his big hand on the side of his chair, wondering how he was going to get information from the old bill about Kenny Owen's murder/mugging. He knew the only fair and trustworthy police officer was Sergeant Ben Clark. 'I'll give him a call.'

'Sergeant Ben Clark please'

'Listen, Sergeant, its Bob Warden. It's about Kenny Owen's murder. I might have some information, but I would like some information in return. Could you meet me tonight at the Prince Albert say 8.30.'

'That's fine, I'll be there,' putting the telephone down and turning towards Alex Quirk. 'We might be getting some information on the murder of Kenny Owen, tonight at 8.30.'

In the Guardia Civil headquarters in Madrid, Captain Sifre was collating all the information they had received from Scotland Yard. Officer Gloria Egido was excited being involved in a big murder and robbery crime. Life had been quite dull at the headquarters. Most of the crimes she had been involved in were small time robbery of shops and some awful car accidents.

Looking at her computer were the names of suspects sent over from Scotland Yard. Gloria walked down the corridor to Sergeant Gillispe's office. Chatted about the list of suspects and the case in general. Finishing up, Gloria made her way along to the captain's office, knocking and entering.

'Sir, I have all the information on the names we received from Scotland Yard. first of all this Costa Esteve is a South American. He is known to us on forgery charges along with Andres Lara Ferrer. Both Esteve and Ferrer served five years in prison at Alicante. I have already put a call through to Alicante to have their addresses checked out.'

'Well done, Gloria.'

Ben Clark made his way to the Prince Albert pub. Sitting at the bar in the far corner was Bob Warden. They shook hands and Bob asked what Ben was drinking. Picking up there drinks, they moved to a table near the window away from the door and the bar.

'Ok, Bob, what's on your mind?

'Sergeant, my uncle was Kenny Owen. The poor old bugger never hurt anyone in his life and he never grassed on anybody either. What I am about to tell you remains between us.'

'Bob, if the information you give me leads to some villains committing murder, it would be difficult to leave you out.'

'Ok, Sergeant, we'll have to get over that problem when the time comes. I've been nosing around here and there regarding this Mallards caper, right down to Kenny's murder. It is in my opinion, your lot have nicked the wrong men in Ted Horn and Tommy Prince.

'However, saying that, I can't prove it as yet, but I'm close to finding out who it was. There are two foreign guys involved, they are the ringleaders. When I last spoke with Kenny, he told me these two guys had another very big robbery on the go.

'Kenny was nosy like that. He also told me the heavies being selected for this big job, were from the Brixton area. I'm not a grass, Sergeant, so please don't ask me for their names. Later perhaps I will help you out.

'I would be able to work underground and get information you wouldn't get a sniff at. Kenny also told me the leader of the heavy's was on the run.'

'What, from us?'

'So I was told.'

'Ok, Bob, what do you want?'

'Information. I need to know who gets pulled in on Kenny's murder and what information they give.'

'Bob, that's a lot to ask, in some cases I wouldn't be able to get that information, and if I'm not careful somebody may believe I'm on the take, and that's not my way.'

'Sergeant, I know that, that's why I'm talking with you. Please think it over.'

'Bob, for a start, I would have to bring my partner in on any further meetings.'

'Who's that?'

'Alex Quirk, he's a good guy. Let me give it some thought.'

'Ok, Sergeant, when will I hear from you?'

'I'll meet you here tomorrow night, same time; probably with my partner.'

'Ok tomorrow night.'

Ben finished his drink walked out of the bar back to his car. Driving away he thought about the meeting with Bob and decided to give Alex a call and meet with him in the Fox and hounds, giving a detailed explanation of the meeting with Bob Warden.

'Ben, that's a difficult situation to be in. Giving villains information on a murder case, even if it is his uncle. However, maybe it's the only way forward so let's go for it and see where it leads us, but Bob gets nothing in writing as we will have to be on our guard.'

Miguel Melgar and Juan Riminez were having dinner in the La Salana Restaurant in Cobham. The conversation was being unable to find Costa Esteve and his associate; all their contacts were drawing a blank. Maybe Costa has driven out through the tunnel into France on his way back to Spain. If that's correct then it will be much easier for Carlos Moran to deal with.

Captain Sifre was ready with all his investigation. He had decided to take Gloria Egido with him as she spoke perfect English, and would be able to take notes on the proceedings. Flights had been arranged for I0.00, Madrid to Heathrow. A Detective from Superintendent Parker's office would be meeting them at Heathrow.

The Captain had a nagging feeling about this case. There was more to come regards this investigation, perhaps all the murders had in common "forgery". Both Costa Esteve and Andres Lara Ferrer had spent time in prison for forgery. Both these publishing house's, the one in London and the other here in Madrid have to be connected.

Forged hundred and five hundred euro notes have been distributed in Alicante, Valencia, Madrid, Barcelona and Malaga. Sergeant Gillispe had been given the task to investigate the forgery part.

Alicante Guardia civil had arrested two suspects in Elche after searching their homes and finding a number of forged euro notes.

Sergeant Reg More had his feet on his desk reading a memo from Superintendent Parker's office giving the precise time of a special meeting to be held the following day at Scotland Yard. He and Ben Clark had been selected to attend with a number of very distinguished officers not only from the Met, but also from Kent and even the Guardia Civil from Spain, headed by the Deputy Commissioner.

'Am I invited?' asked Alex Quirk.

'No sorry, mate, it's only Sergeants upwards. Anyway you wouldn't have liked those horrible paste sandwiches.' Ben inquired if anything exciting had happened overnight.

'No not really. A couple of shop break-ins, a taxi mugging. Rod Muir is out now taking statements.'

D.I. Roger Rimmer was waiting in Terminal 2 special security office at Heathrow airport for the arrival of flight IB 293I from Madrid. Looking at his watch, then up to the flight screen, IB 293I had landed. Special arrangements had been made for both Captain Sifre and Officer Egido to be met and taken out of the airport as VIP guests.

Captain Sifre was over six feet tall, large shoulders and dressed very smartly in a dark suit. Officer Egido who stood next to him looked like she was in her twenties, very smartly dressed in a dark trouser suit with a white blouse.

'Good Morning, Captain. I am Detective Inspector Roger Rimmer, and will be looking after you.'

'We are both pleased to meet you,' was the reply'

'I suggest we get you booked into your hotel where you can rest, and then I will collect you this evening for dinner with Superintendent Parker at 20.00.' They drove towards the Melia Hotel at Piccadilly. D.I. Rimmer apologised for the fact the weather was rather wet and cloudy, and not like the warm weather of Spain.

Checking in the hotel had been especially quick. They were staying on the sixth floor in rooms 650 and 620. 'We will meet in the bar at I9.I5,' said the Captain.

D.I. Rimmer seeing them safely into the hotel lift, used the hotel telephone to call Superintendent Parker, letting him know that his guests were safely in the hotel and he had arranged to collect them at I9.30, and bring them along to the Horse-Guards Hotel restaurant.

'Unfortunately, your Sergeant Thomson has called in sick, so I am arranging with Chief Inspector Bleasdale for a reliable replacement for the next few days.'

Bleasdale called Clark and Quirk up to his office asking which one of them would like to take on special duties with Superintendent's Office for a few days. As Clark was on the special meeting, Alex Quirk was selected. Before leaving Bleasdale's office, Ben was asked if he had all the paperwork/statements collated for the meeting at Scotland Yard.

'Yes, Sir, Sergeant More is collecting all the items this very moment.'

'Very good, Clark.' Bleasdale was thinking to himself if all goes well, I'm in for promotion.

Returning to the CID office, Ben explained that Alex had been transferred to special duties at Superintendent Parker's office. Which leaves Rod Muir on his own, so let's hope there's not too much crime happening in the area. Ben and Alex walked down to the canteen speaking about Battersea CID, and the information on the mugging/murder of Kenny Owen.

'As they've promised to have a copy of the file with us this afternoon, that's good news.' Finishing their coffee, they agreed to meet that evening at the Prince Albert at 20.00.

Returning to the CID office, they overheard Reg More and Rod Muir agreeing with each other that Ted Horn and Tommy Prince were guilty of the Mallards safe blowing but probably not involved with any murders.

Big Sam and Derrick made their way to Hayes. Standing in the Woolworths store opposite the bank; they watched the security van pull up. 'That's the van, Derrick, and it's on time,' looking at his watch. 'Let's make our way to the factory units so that we can monitor the time it takes the van to arrive, then we'll take a look at the bloody bridge.'

Their car was parked just around the corner from Woolworths, driving slowly past the bank along the main road, turned right towards the factory units and then hit the temporary traffic lights caused by road works.

'Look at that, Derrick, those traffic lights appear to stay red for ages.'

'Yeah I know what you mean, Sam.' The traffic lights changed to green and they slowly crossed over the metal covering placed across the road which had been dug up for pipe work.

They parked their car behind unit No I2, walking over to the side of the railway line. Big Sam pointed to where Scotch Jack and Jimmy would have their vehicle. 'John and Peter will have their vehicle parked here. We'll be parked on that road going out towards the bridge. When the security van enters the units over there, and reaches that point opposite No 8 unit.'

'Jack and Jimmy will pull out behind the security van. John and Peter will drive their vehicle towards the security van here at No 22 unit. We'll have monitored the situation of the security van entering the road, making our way towards the security van blocking it against the wall. Bingo we have them jammed in. We'll knock out their radio link on top of the roof of the van and do the business with the gas, pull the money out of the security van and away.'

'Sounds good, Sam.' Big Sam looked at his watch, the security van should be coming into vision in five minutes.

'Do you think any of those new factory units will be open before we hit the security van?'

'I hope not, Derrick, I drive up here twice a week. Look at the bridge, drive around to the record factory, have a sandwich at the takeaway van and in the eight weeks I've been looking, I haven't seen a soul.'

'There you are, Derrick, the security van is on time. Bloody hell, those temporary traffic lights have stopped them as well, and that means another five minutes on their journey.'

'What will that mean to us, Sam?'

'Nothing to worry about. Their head office won't worry about their van for at least thirty minutes after their designated time. If they haven't reached the record factory and they cannot contact their security van. They wait between ten and fifteen minutes before alerting the local Hayes police.

'I have estimated that our raid on the security van will take no longer than twelve minutes max, that will give us another fifteen minutes to get to the bridge remove the money from our vehicles, swapping it to our getaway vehicle and away. The Hayes police will take another eight to ten minutes to respond and find the security van.

'By which time we will be well on our way to Denham airport, taking us no more than thirty minutes. Costa has arranged for another large four wheeler backup vehicle in North Street Uxbridge. If anything should go wrong, so all we would do is swap vehicles.

'Waiting for us at Denham airfield will be a ten seated aircraft which will fly us and the money to France. Another of Costa's men will pick up our getaway vehicles take them to Watford clean them and dump them.'

'Sam, it sounds so easy.'

'That's the way I like it, Derrick. Ok here come the security van and there it goes. Now let's go and take another look at the bridge which we all believe is the dodgy part of the raid, driving the three minutes journey towards the bridge.' Derrick looked at the bridge.

'I can't see the problem, Sam; we just cut the chain on the barrier and drive off.'

'That's the way I see it too, Derrick, but Jack believes that if somebody walks by or looks out the window of the pub over there—they could take the number of the vehicle and call the police.' Both looking around and only noticing two cars, one car parked outside the pub and another some distance away, there was nobody down the side road by the water.

'Is there another way, Sam?'

'Derrick, I've checked all the roads. One way goes to the Great Weston road and the other takes you towards Heathrow airport. If we went towards the Great Weston road we are boxed in, and if we go towards Heathrow, we have to go over the Hayes Bridge past the record factories, so that's a no go.'

'Ok let's put it to the others at tomorrow's meeting.' Derrick drove back towards London, dropping Big Sam off and agreeing to pick him up the next morning. On the way home, Derrick was deep in thought regarding the robbery when he decided to pop into the Red Lion for a late drink, parking his car and walking around the corner to the Red Lion.

Sergeant Weber had him on the surveillance tape. 'Derrick Smallwood again and Billy Chambers is already in the bar. Perhaps they are doing business together, Sergeant.'

'Maybe you are right.'

Derrick ordered a pint of the best. Billy asked him how he was and walked off to serve another customer. Derrick walked across the bar to a small table by the window, when he heard his name being called, turning his head he saw Billy Chambers.

'Hallo. Billy, how's it going?'

'Not bad, Derrick, it could be better.'

'Yeah I know what you mean. Joe's away on holiday down in Cornwall for a few weeks, so I'm just bumming around.'

'Well maybe I could put something your way, Derrick. I know you don't like the heavy stuff, but there could be five grand in it for you.'

'Thanks for the offer, Billy, but hopefully Joe's returning next week.'

'No problem, Derrick, here's my card give me a call.' Derrick drained his glass and said his goodbyes making his way to the door. Billy Chambers followed him. They stood out on the street talking for ten minutes and then made their separate ways home.

Sergeant Weber suggested it be great if we had one of those voice detectors, that way we would know exactly what robbery they were organising.

Captain Sifre was ready and in the hotel bar, having spoken with Sergeant Gillispe earlier about the two suspects concerned in the forged banknotes from Elche. Gillispe told him that they had confessed to a conspiracy naming a number of villains. Three living in Alicante, one from Torrevieja, two from Benidorm, two from Valencia and two from Barcelona, but no mention of publishing company or Peter Sainsbury.

Captain Sifre sat at his table pondering over the forged banknotes and what connexion they might have with the Madrid Publishing Company. Gloria Egido walked into the bar, she was wearing a long black silk dress, black high heels and her hair swung about her shoulders. As she reached Captain Sifre's table he asked what she would like to drink.

‘Gin and Tonic please.’ Gloria sat down and spoke about how excited she was being involved in an international crime meeting. Captain Sifre asked Gloria’s opinion on the forged banknotes and what connexion these villains from Elche could have with the Madrid Publishing house or Peter Sainsbury.

Inspector Rimmer arrived halfway through their discussion, driving them to Horse Guards Restaurant which was situated along the River Thames. Both commenting how beautiful the river Thames looked at night with the boats and buildings lit up.

Superintendent Parker and his wife, Helga, were sitting at a corner table by the far wall, as Captain Sifre and Gloria Egido joined them. Picking up their menus, they all chose prawn cocktail to start with. Roast duck as their main meal.

Superintendent Parker and Captain Sifre spoke about the forged banknotes indicating there could be a connexion between Peter Sainsbury and the Madrid Publishing House, agreeing it would be another avenue to investigate. Helga Parker was deep in discussion with Gloria about her Guardia Civil duties.

Driving back to the hotel, Parker informed Captain Sifre that another driver would be at his disposal. The officer was a CID Detective who was involved in the Mallards crime and was one of the first on the scene.

Ben Clark and Alex Quirk were sitting at a window table away from the bar area with Bob Warden, explaining that once the investigation was finished there would be no comebacks on either side. Ben pointed out that Battersea CID thought the murder was just a mugging gone wrong. The bar area was getting packed out, so they decided to move to another location.

The best spot would be Cricklewood Race track, finishing their beers they made for the door. Just at that moment, the door opened and in walked Rod Muir, saying good evening to Ben and Alex and only nodding to Bob Walden. Ben turned to Bob Warden thanking him for the chat and left.

Bob Warden walked into the other bar and made small talk to a market trader he knew. Rod Muir ordered his drink and sat at the bar, looking over at Bob Warden. Ten minutes later, Bob was able to slip away, meeting up with Ben and Alex at the racing track.

‘Did Rod Muir say anything to you, Bob?’

‘No, I saw somebody I knew and started speaking with him and then slipped away.’

'Ok now this is what we have. Battersea have pulled in three known muggers, Terry Peachy, Ralf Graham and Paul Bailey, all have drug problems. Graham has done time for murder and Peachy and Bailey have done time for mugging.

'We know from the report that your uncle frequented a number of different pubs, telling people that he was a well-known villain and had plenty of money saved. Thereby, Battersea believe one of these muggers followed him into the park, shot him, took his money and house keys.

Alex pointed out that Battersea may have Kenny's flat under surveillance.

'Bob, have you entered Kenny's flat since he was killed?'

'No but it's on my list to take a look around, as I have a spare key.'

'Ok, Bob, now it's your turn what have you for us.'

'I've being around different establishments listening to the gossip. There are two lots of foreigners involved, but they are not working together. I haven't received all the evidence yet, but Ted Horn and Tommy Prince are not the guys who pulled the Mallards job.

'I hope to have the names of who did carry out the job shortly. The mobs running out of Brixton are getting ready to pull a heavy job. Six heavies have already been recruited and are connected to one of those foreign firms I have mentioned, and again I hope to have their names shortly. They agreed to meet in two days' time at 20.30.' Ben and Alex drove off talking about tonight's episode.

'Alex, Bob does receive the information we need. Certainly if he's correct about the two foreign firms and about this big job going down. If its six heavies and two foreign guys involved, it's got to be a sizable job and what's it to do with the Mallards robbery. And why does Bob keep saying Ted Horn and Tommy Prince aren't the safe blowers involved with Mallards?'

'I've no idea, Ben. It makes tomorrow's meeting at Scotland Yard even more exciting and interesting. Let's hope somebody from the meeting will be able to give information to put this puzzle together.'

The large conference room on the first floor of Scotland Yard was prepared. Name plates of those individuals who had been invited were laid out on tables. A further table by the windows was laid out with coffee and biscuits. The Deputy Commissioner, Bill Reading, and Superintendent Parker entered the committee room.

Parker had already informed the Deputy Commissioner on the information from the Guardia Civil in Spain. 'They have a very interesting theory on a forgery aspect of the crimes.'

Chief Inspector Bleasdale and Inspector Brown entered, with Sergeant Richard Hill from Chetney, and Inspector Medows and Sergeant Rice from Sittingboume. Chief Inspector Roger Greedy from Maidstone and Inspector Cavendish from Barking were speaking with Sergeants Ben Clark and Reg More. Last to arrive was Captain Sifre and Officer Gloria Egido from the Guardia Civil Madrid.

The Deputy Commissioner rose, saying how pleased he was to see all concerned in the investigation to be able to be present at today's meeting and special reference was made to Captain Sifre and Officer Egido from Spain.

'The seriousness of these crimes must be our prime object and collating the information will be highly important to this investigation. I now hand you over to Superintendent Parker. Lastly lunch will be served at I3.I5, it is hoped that the Commissioner Sir John Bacon will be able to join us.'

Superintendent Parker pointed out, 'The first murders took place at Mallards Publishing House. We are still unsure of the contents of Peter Sainsbury's safe. We understand from information received that there were certain documents, plans and maps with some cash valuable enough for him to be murdered by unknown persons.

'The motive why Sainsbury gunned down two police officers and a security guard is totally unknown. We are aware Sainsbury was involved with another publishing house in Madrid, Spain, where the Managing director of that company was also murdered; again by unknown persons. Two safe crackers, Mr Ted Horn and Tommy Prince have been arrested and charged with the safe blowing at Mallards and are involved with two Spanish gentleman who apparently paid them for the documents, plans and maps.

'The two Spanish gentlemen have not as yet been found. Whether or not Horn and Prince were involved with the murder of Peter Sainsbury is as yet unclear. We have two stolen vehicles; one found with the body of Peter Sainsbury inside and the other belonging to Tommy Prince, which was found to have detonators hidden in the boot of his car.

'We then come to the murder of Mr Billinson, who unfortunately made statements to the press, saying that he had actually witnessed the murderer and chased him down the street at Whitstable. Later he was lured from his house and shot in the woods behind his house.

'In a number of the statements received from witnesses, a red Mazda car has been seen; scraps of paint of a red Mazda have been found by good police detective work at the murder scene of Peter Sainsbury. I would now ask each of you in turn to furnish us with any further information or developments you might have on this case.'

'Chief Inspector Bleasdale, would you care to start.'

'Yes, Sir. As you have already stated, we have two safe crackers charged for the Mallards Publishing House crime. It is believed they had been employed by a Mr Costa Esteve and his associate Andres, who offered ten thousand pounds for the contents of the safe, except for the cash which the safe blowers could keep. We have received information from a number of other safe crackers that they had been offered a similar deal by Costa Esteve.

'Sergeant Clark perhaps you would like to add further information.'

'Over the past few days, my partner and I have been following certain leads. We have received concrete evidence that there are actually two sets of foreign firms working, but at this moment, we are unaware of how they fit in together. One of these firms has employed six heavies for a large aimed robbery to take place.

'Again we are awaiting further information and details. We are also investigating the murder of Mr Kenny Owen and where he fits into these crimes. Battersea police have suggested it is a mugging gone wrong, but information received points to murder.

'Sergeant More have you anything to add?'

'Yes, Sir, although Horn and Prince have been charged for the Mallards job, I am a little worried that Tommy Prince wouldn't drive around with detonators in the boot of his car. He is a professional villain and would remove evidence such as detonators, however it could be a mistake on his part.

'Regarding the Kenny Owen murder, we have set up a video surveillance outside the Red Lion public house, where Mr Owen drank and was contacted by Mr Costa Esteve and Andres. It is imperative that the surveillance continues so we gain knowledge of the entire suspected villains frequenting that premise.

'Chief Inspector Greedy, have you anything to add on the Kent side of the matter?'

'Mr Billinson's murder is still ongoing, and therefore we have nothing further to add.

'Inspector Cavendish?'

'We have thoroughly investigated the two stolen vehicles. First the one that was used for the murder of Peter Sainsbury, this vehicle was stolen after two lads returned home. The second vehicle which is owned by Mr Thomas Prince was removed or stolen from Manchester.

'One of my officers has been up to Manchester and is convinced it was stolen from outside Mr Prince's mother's house. We have had the vehicle thoroughly searched for any other substances, all we found were lots of pig's hairs indicating this vehicle must have been on a pigs farm.'

'I see that could be interesting.'

Captain Sifre said, 'First of all I have carefully listened to the statements made by learned officers. May I say that Costa Esteve is South American and his associate is Andres Lara Ferrer, a Spaniard from Alicante. We are investigating other gangs who could possibly be involved.

'The information we have received will I am sure help us in our own inquires in Spain. The murder of Peter Sainsbury at the Mallards Publishing House and the murder of Manual Corsinos Garcia, Managing Director of Colaboenos Publishing House, Madrid, appear to be too much of a coincidence. We have been looking into forged banknotes in the Alicante area. Maybe in the safe at Mallards were forgery plates. That is all I have at the moment.'

The Deputy Commissioner suggested they retire for lunch, walking towards the private dining area which had been arranged, Chief Inspector Bleasdale caught hold of Sergeant Mores arm.

'That was a silly comment you made about Horn and Prince. You looked like you were undermining my authority. If you have any other comments like that please consult me first. I'm disappointed in you, More.' Bleasdale walked off leaving Reg More startled.

As they all entered the dining area, Superintendent Parker was standing with the Deputy Commissioner chatting, when he spotted Ben Clark and called him over. 'We were very interested in your report on the six heavy's being assembled for an armed robbery. As soon as you gather the names and information, report to me immediately'

'Of course, Superintendent. Also what's this about Sergeant More worrying about Prince and detonators in the boot of his car.'

'Sir, our informant who gave us the information on the six heavy's also mentioned that Horn and Prince were not involved in the blowing of the safe at Mallards, but we haven't been able to substantiate this at this time.'

'I see, Sergeant, let's hope your informant is wrong on that score. I'll speak with Chief Inspector Bleasdale myself.'

The Deputy Commissioner sat chatting with Captain Sifre inquiring about police work in Spain. Officer Egido had already received many offers of dinner dates, but turned them all down.

Sergeant Hill walked over to Ben Clark and Reg More, congratulating them on their nerve to have spoken up about the possibility of a villain driving around with detonators in the boot of his car. 'Obviously you received information from your informants and you have used good old detective work.'

Sergeant Hill explained he was stuck in a small village type sub-station and was hoping that with these murders, he would be able to do well and receive a promotion to another police station.

After lunch, they all returned to the conference room, the rest of the meeting went very quickly and smoothly with some good points being raised.

Ben Clark and Reg More made their way out of the room, bumping into Alex Quirk. 'Hallo, Ben, you won't believe the duties the Superintendent's office has given me, driving two bloody Guardia Civil officers about.'

'Alex, believe me you might be pleasantly surprised. One of the officers is a woman a real stunner so it could be a big bonus. I'll call you after the meeting we had arranged.'

The Deputy Commissioner standing with Superintendent Parker introduced Detective Alex Quirk to Captain Sifre and Officer Egido. 'D.C. Quirk will be looking after you tonight and tomorrow. Captain Sifre you have been invited to a dinner party with the police Commissioner planned for the following evening.'

Captain Sifre inquired if it were possible to visit the site of the murdered Peter Sainsbury in the Kent Village.

'Yes, that won't be a problem. I'll have a word with Chief Inspector Greedy.' Leaving officer Egido chatting with D.C. Quirk.

'So how are you finding England?'

'Fine thank you, Detective.'

'Please call me, Alex.'

'Ok, Alex, my name is Gloria. I understand that you have been on this case from the start.'

'Yes, that's correct. I was there when Peter Sainsbury shot our two officers.'

'How awful, Alex. Your partner explained at the meeting that you had come across new evidence from an informant. I thought that your Chief Inspector Bleasdale looked unhappy with the comment made by Sergeant More.'

'We have heard from a number of informants that the two villains we have in custody are not responsible for the safe blowing. But unfortunately, it puts Chief Inspector Bleasdale in a very difficult position, as it was him who wanted to arrest Horn and Prince. Anyway what's police work like in Spain?'

'Probable just the same as here, forged banknotes, drugs, robberies, murders and traffic accidents.'

Captain Sifre re-joined. 'Detective Quirk and Gloria, I have made arrangements to meet Sergeant Hill at Chetney at I0.30 in the morning. What time will it be necessary for you to collect us.'

'I would say 9.00, Sir.'

Parking the car and walking into the hotel, Captain Sifre turned to Officer Egido, saying as he would be dining out with Inspector Brown of the Serious Crime squad that evening. It would be best if she made her own arrangements for dinner. Turning and walking away to collect his hotel key.

'If you haven't arranged anything for dinner, I know a wonderful Italian restaurant in the West End,' said Alex

'Alex, are you married?'

'No, Gloria, I'm single.'

'I'm also single, Alex.'

'That's it then, let's have dinner together.' Alex waited in the bar area of the hotel for Gloria to change. They enjoyed the Italian restaurant talking over different areas of Spain. With Alex mentioning that he had an uncle in Palmer in the Balearic Islands, who wanted him to retire from the Police Force and go over and work with him.

'It's a lovely island, Alex, a lot different from the mainland.' It was agreed that as Captain Sifre would be at a cocktail party the following evening, they would meet again.

Bob Warden had been all over London seeking information from old friends. He was determined to get to the bottom of poor old Kenny Owens's murder. He was convinced he had a better chance than the police.

After speaking with the Italians, Greeks, Turks and many of the known villains in the East end of London, two names had come to light, Alonzo Ortuno and Ken Delanny. Bob knew Ken Delanny, a right bastard who couldn't be trusted. But if he was paid his asking price, he would carry out his business and that was feeding a body to the pigs.

Bob thought about the two names he had been given and decided that it would be pointless to try and get information out of Delanny. So it had to be Alonzo Ortuno first, who was living in Eastham.

Bob drove over to Eastham to see his old friend called Liam. He was a real hard nut, not a tall guy 5'8 with dark curly hair, large shoulders and the biggest hands Bob had ever seen in his life. Bob found him in the cock and sparrow. 'How are you, Liam?'

'By Jesus, its Bob Warden, come on now and have a pint,' Liam banged the bar top and ordered two more pints.

'Well stranger, what brings you over to my manner?'

'Liam, I need your help to find somebody. My uncle Kenny Owen was murdered.'

'The fuckers. Bob, count me in.'

'Thanks, Liam, I knew I could count on you.'

'Who's the guy you are interested in?'

'He's a Spanish guy called Alonzo Ortuno. I'm unaware what he looks like only that he lives around here and I need to have a chat with him.'

'You think he killed Kenny?'

'I don't know, Liam, but he's mixed up in something big. Also he may have something to do with the murder of Peter Sainsbury. The other person who has been named is Ken Delanny.'

'Bob, that's one nasty piece of work, however I haven't heard of anybody going missing lately. I'll look into that as well. Now let's enjoy ourselves tonight, we'll have a few pints and drink to poor old Kenny Owen. And tomorrow, I'll have this Spanish man found for you.'

'That's great, Liam, I owe you.'

'That's what friends are for, Bob.'

Ending the night and thinking he shouldn't really be driving home; Bob made his way to Kenny Owens flat, after looking around the streets to make sure the old bill weren't hidden away watching the flat. He removed the spare flat key from his glove compartment of his car and let himself in. The place had been ransacked. Bob had no choice but to switch on the lights.

Two minutes later, there was a knock on the door. Bob immediately thought it was the old bill and hadn't a clue on what answer he was going to give. Opening the door he was relieved to find Mrs Norman from next door standing there.

'Hallo, Bob.' putting her hand to her throat. 'I didn't know who it was. I've been checking ever since you called me, looking around Bob's body and seeing the mess. O my god, what a mess,' making her way inside the flat.

'Unfortunately, it appears someone has beaten me here. Whoever murdered poor old Kenny took his keys and arrived here before I called you.'

Bob I made notes of all the people who called here. Just at that moment, Mrs Carol from the other side poked her head around the door.

'I thought I heard voices. Hallo, Bob. Sorry to hear about Kenny. What a mess, Bob. I questioned one man who came here and let himself into the flat.

'What did he look like, Doris?'

'Big guy, I've seen him before.'

'What, with Kenny?'

'No, but when I was up at the Red Lion with my old man for New year, Kenny was talking with him. The funny thing is when I asked him what he was doing here. He said, "don't you recognise me; I'm Kenny's mate from the Red Lion".

'He told me that Kenny had given him his key to pick up some letters that had been delivered by mistake. There was also two policeman came on separate occasions, then there was some foreign man, he wouldn't give me his name and just said Spanish.

'That's very helpful. Look if I give you thirty pounds, would you tidy the place up. Put any good cloths in a bag and give them to charity and any of the old cloths in another bag which can be dumped.'

'That's very fair of you, Bob.'

Bob told both Mrs Norman and Mrs Carol, he would just stay a moment on his own and reflect on poor old Kenny. 'I'll pop around just before I go.' Bob looked around and in a small cupboard he found the telephone numbers of both Joe Bolt and Jeff Mitchell. Bob knew them both as he had spent time in prison with Joe Bolt and even had to give another prisoner a slap because he was giving Joe a hard time.

Jeff Mitchell was a good safe blower but not as trustworthy as Joe. Checking the other papers, he found an old diary which he also slipped into his pocket. There was nothing of value in the flat and after having a last look around left, knocking on Mrs Norman's door and giving her the key.

Reg More and Rod Muir were in a coffee shop just off Cricklewood high street. Rod was asking how the meeting at Scotland Yard had gone. Reg outlined the different statements made by the various police officers present Also that Chief Inspector Bleasdale was annoyed with Reg because he had commented that it was difficult to see Tommy Prince driving around with detonators in the boot of his car, as a good defence lawyer would pull the evidence apart.

'Reg, that was taking a chance saying that in front of Bleasdale.'

'But it's true, Rod, we've heard it and so has Ben Clark.'

'It's funny you mention that. I was in my local the other evening when I bumped into Ben Clark, Alex Quirk with Bob Warden.'

'Yeah, but Rod, Bob Warden is no grass. He wouldn't piss on you if you were on fire. But it was Clark who informed us that there were two foreign gangs working and one such gang had recruited six heavies to pull an armed robbery, All of this is just after me seeing Clark with Bob Warden.'

As More and Muir drove into the Kilburn police yard, Reg More noticed Ben Clark walking towards his car. Opening his car window, he shouted over to Ben Clark, 'Hay, Ben, have you got a minute?' Ben turned and walked back across the yard towards Reg More's car.

'Those comments you were making at the meeting about the six heavies and the two foreign gangs working, did that information come from Bob Warden?'

'O, I see your partner Rod Muir was in a pub the other evening when Alex Quirk and I were looking for Sam Kelly.'

'Earlier in the day, we had received a telephone call informing us that a big robbery with six heavies was taking place and Sam Kelly's name was put forward. We couldn't find Sam Kelly but bumped into Bob Warden, who was as unhelpful as usual.'

Reg thought to himself I could have told you that.

'So what about Kelly?'

'It's difficult, Reg. As you know I am working on my own for a few days.'

Reg More walked into the CID room telling Rod Muir the story he had gained from Ben Clark. 'Anyway its dog eat dog. I'm off to see the Chief Inspector and do some creeping.' Knocking on the Chief Inspectors door and entering. Bleasdale looked up. 'I'm pleased you have come to see me, as my wife told me you actually tried to contact me before I left for the meeting at Scotland Yard.'

'That's correct, Sir. I wanted to let you know about the information received from informants and I thought you might be interested to know that Sam Kelly's name was put forward.'

'Well, Sergeant, what are you waiting for, go and find this Sam Kelly.'

‘Thank you, Sir. I was just about to suggest that to you.’ Turning around and making his way back to the CID room to collect Rod Muir.

Ben Clark anticipated exactly what Reg More would do, so he telephoned Bob Warden letting him know the score.

‘Thanks, Ben, see you tonight.’

Alex Quirk arrived at the Hotel to collect Captain Sifre and Officer Egido at 8.55, both were waiting in the hotel coffee bar. Gloria’s eyes sparkled when she saw Alex.

‘Good morning all. Are we ready to go?’

Sergeant Hill had informed his constables that he was expecting a VIP visit, from two high ranking officers from the Guardia Civil from Spain and wanted to give a good impression about policing in Kent, as they were part of the overall crime team looking into the murders and safe blowing.

Alex drove towards Kent as Captain Sifre and Gloria Egido were commenting on the beautiful countryside. Alex explained that they would be on the B roads shortly where they would view lots of wildlife and much greenery Gloria was thinking how romantic. Arriving at the police station, Sergeant Hill came outside to greet them, showing them around his very small police station explaining that the station was a sub-station but with today’s computers and emails, they could easily connect with major networks.

‘Yes, Sergeant, I understand perfectly.’ Alex only had eyes for Gloria.

Sergeant Hill mentioned that they had no detectives working from this police station. Their main duties were patrolling the nearby villages and any traffic accidents or house break-ins.

All major crimes were dealt with by Sittingboume main police station where Inspector Medows gets involved. Sergeant Hill suggested that they should all travel in his police car to the different crime scenes, as he had arranged for lunch in the Blue Boar inn, where the temporary Ops room for the Billinson murder had been held.

‘That sounds great, Sergeant, lunch in an old English Pub.’ Captain Sifre chose to sit in the front of the car with Alex and Gloria sitting in the back. It only took ten minutes to get to Lover’s lane. ‘It’s so pretty here,’ commented officer Egido, ‘look at those trees, they are so green’. Sergeant Hill parked his car.

The area was still roped off as they walked off down the lane towards the Marshes, with Sergeant Hill pointing out the tyre marks which were still visible and had been edged into the bank while the car was being pulled out. ‘Over here,’ pointing to the area, 'is where the car was pushed into the marshes. The perpetrators thought that the marshes were at least fifteen feet deep at this point. If you look over there,' pointing in that direction, 'towards those two large trees the marshes are between twelve and fifteen feet deep.'

'Yes I get the picture, Sergeant.'

'If we walk over this way, Sir, through the small bushes and scrubs on to that pathway you can see where the getaway red Mazda car was parked. 'Over there,' pointing to a tree, 'we found scrapings of red paint, which our SOCO team have been able to diagnose coming from a Mazda car.'

'Very good police work.' Sergeant Hill's shoulders pushed up with the compliment, 'So the villains have made a few mistakes, Sergeant.'

'Yes, Sir, let's hope their mistakes have them apprehended. We will now make our way to Whitstable to where Mr Billinson was murdered.'

Sergeant Hill parked his car in the high street of Whitstable. Captain Sifre kept up with Sergeant Hill with Alex and Gloria walking behind. 'Over there is Mr Billinson's house and on the corner, here the perpetrator we believe called Mr Billinson and lured him away from his house on the pretence of finding his motorbike. Walking him into the woods and shooting him in the head. The area as you can see is still cordoned off.

'Is there anything else you would like to see, or we could make our way to the Blue Boar.'

'You have shown us the complete picture, Sergeant, so let's go along to the English Pub.'

'By the way, Sir, that is the bakery shop,' pointing at the shop, 'where we were able to get information on the red Mazda registration number.' A table had been reserved by the window and the Landlord George Cobum was there to greet them.

'I hope you enjoy your meal. Not on the menu is Steak and Kidney pie or Wild Duck with mash potatoes and fresh greens.'

Captain Sifre had only heard of Steak and Kidney pie and decided to plumb for the pie as did Hill and Quirk. Gloria went for the wild duck. Twenty minutes later, they were tucking into their meals. Captain Sifre ordered a pint of bitter; the others chose soft drinks.

'This is magnificent,' indicted Captain Sifre with suitable replies from the others. 'Sergeant Hill, this has been a memorable day and I will be passing on my gratitude to the Commissioner this evening.'

‘Thank you, Sir, it’s been a pleasure having you here in Kent.’

At the Melia Hotel, D.C. Quirk asked Captain Sifre what time he wanted collecting that evening.

‘Don’t worry yourself, the Deputy Commissioner is collecting me, so take good care of Officer Egido. I’m not blind you know. See you both tomorrow,’ laughing as he walked away to collect his hotel key.

‘Yes, Sir, that will be my pleasure.’

‘Alex, the best thing is to come up to my room, I’ll change and then we can go to your home and you can freshen up.’

‘Sounds good to me. I better call Ben Clark while you’re getting ready Gloria.’

‘Hi, Ben, I’m still on duty.’

‘Don’t worry, Alex; I can manage without you for one night.’

Gloria returned looking stunning. They made their way to Alex’s house where Gloria would have the opportunity to have a look round, as she didn’t want to get involved with a married man. The house was clean but you could see it didn’t have a woman’s touch.

When Alex came out of his bedroom, Gloria mentioned that she wasn’t that hungry, so they decided just go to the cinema and have a hamburger before returning her to the hotel.

Ben Clark had met up with Bob Warden as planned at 20.00. Bob told him that Sergeant More and his partner had picked up Sam Kelly down at the Medway cafe.

‘I guessed that would happen. He’s a real bastard, however if I hadn’t suggested that I received a tip from Sam Kelly, they would have come looking for you, Bob,’ explained Ben.

‘Ben, I have been in touch with some friends in the East end, and they have come up with a few names which could be connected with Costa Esteve. I’ve also been around to Kenny’s flat which had been turned over. The Ladies living next-door reported that not only did two police officers call, but on separate occasions, a foreign chap turned up but wouldn’t give his name and only said Spanish.

‘The second guy to appear actually went into Kenny’s flat. Mrs Carol saw him and spoke with him. He told her that he had met her at the New Year’s party at the Red Lion, and was only doing Kenny a favour by picking up some letters that had been incorrectly delivered.’

'Listen, Bob, be careful if you return to the Red Lion as the pub is under surveillance.'

'Thanks I will remember that, Ben. The two names I have are Alonzo Ortuno and Ken Delanny.' Ben scribbled down the names,

'Bob, that information on two sets of foreign gangs are already in the hands of Scotland Yard. Captain Sifre of the Guardia Civil, at the high powered meeting yesterday pointed out that after checking through their computer files of known Spanish or South American villains arrested or having been involved with corruption of any kind who might be living in the UK.

'Two names actually came out of the computer, a Mr Alonzo Ortuno and Mr Jose Ordofioz. Ortuno had been involved with heavy armed robbery and Ordofioz car theft and minor crimes.'

'Ben, this Ortuno guy, he's bad news. My friends are looking into his whereabouts.'

Bob made his way towards Eastham after receiving a call from Liam Murphy. Arriving at the pub, he noticed that Liam had with him two big guys

'Hallo, Bob, this is Mike and Paul.'

'Hallo, Mike, and you, Paul.' Bob just got a nod back from them both.

'Don't worry about them, Bob, they are two of my most trusted. We have found your Alonzo Ortuno. My boys have been following him around for the last three hours and I have been told he's a real handful. So we are going four handed, also I've been told he is unbreakable and keeps his mouth closed.

'This is what I propose we do, we take him to a safe house, truss him up and go from there. Mike is going to his apartment and hopefully we will be able to drug him. He will give us a signal if all is well, we'll come around in the van and whisk him away.

'We are well aware of his friendship with Jerry Thomas, so on the prefix of Thomas's name we'll get entry into his apartment, which gives us time, Bob, for a few pints.'

Making their way to Ortuno's apartment; parking the van on the corner of the street which was filled with trees and had the usual two up to down old houses. A few house had flower boxes and plants, and some had a small gardens. Ortuno's apartment was located on the first floor of one of these houses.

Mike who had walked down the street, made his way to the apartment knocking on the door. The door opened and there stood Alonzo Ortuno, six feet tall, a beer belly but big arms and legs, a bald head and nasty looking eyes.

I'm a friend of Jerry Thomas, my name is Mike O'Reilly. Perhaps Jerry has spoken of me. I've a little job that might be of interest to you.'

'Stop there, pal. Jerry Thomas hasn't spoken about you and I'm not interested in any work with you,' trying to shut the door in Mike's face.

'Hold on, friend, don't be too hasty. Just give me a couple of minutes of your time.' Pulling out a small bottle of scotch, 'Let's have a drink and let me explain.'

Alonzo thought for a minute, this Irish guy cannot be the police. 'Ok, you've got ten minutes.' Alonzo went to a small cupboard and produced two glasses. Mike poured out the scotch asking if he had any ice. Alonzo nodded and walked into his kitchen, as soon as Alonzo was out of sight, Mike poured some liquid drug into his glass.

After returning with the ice, Alonzo put two pierces of ice into both glasses.

Mike commented, 'You have a lovely apartment, my friend.'

Alonzo nodded, 'Now, my Irish friend, what's this little job you have in mind.' Mike sat down next to Alonzo at a small table, clinking glasses and saying cheers. They downed the first glass and Mike poured another.

'I had this friend who did the dirty on me, Alonzo. He has a factory down Locks lane and collects the wages on Fridays for his factory personal. We would park around the corner from the bank, when he returns to his car, we attack him and put him in the boot of the car. Take him to a lockup I know, and shoot off with the cash.'

'How…much…is…there?'

'What's up mate, are you ok?' asked Mike as Alonzo slumped to the floor. Mike was up at the window signalling Liam.

'Mike has him,; said Liam. 'Pull the van up to the front door.'

Bob and Liam leaped out of the van walking towards the apartment; Mike opened the door and lifted Ortuno up under the armpits. Liam and Bob got hold of one arm apiece and walked him towards the side door of the van which was open.

They bundled him in, driving off towards the underground garages of the safe house. Arriving at the garage, they again took hold of an arm apiece and half carried him up to the flat, putting him in a back room chained to the floor. Bob asked how long would it take for the drug to wear off.

'About an hour, so he should be coming around in about twenty minutes.' Paul poured four beers and they sat down chatting about old times. Half an hour later, they could hear Ortuno trying to move about. They all walked into the back room. Ortuno looked up. 'You four Irish bastards are dead.' With that Liam walked over to him and punched him in the face.

'Now let's have a bit of respect, do you get my meaning,' said Liam.

'What the fuck do you Irish want with me?' Bob thought, don't open your mouth and let Ortuno think I'm Irish as well. Liam looked at Ortuno.

'We want to know about the death of Kenny Owen and your friend Ken Delanny's connexion to the death.'

'I don't grass on anyone.'

'Ok let me tell you what's going to happen. You can piss and shit yourself, scream to your heart's content but nobody's going to hear you. You're not getting anything to drink or eat,' pointed out Liam.

'You Irish pigs, do you think I'm worried about you. We have real tough guys in Spain and they would worry me.'. Mike walked over to the windows and started pulling the shutters down.

'What you doing?' asked Ortuno.

'I forgot to mention, we are leaving you in the dark for a couple of days. Nobody can hear you, as you can see the chair you are in is bolted to the floor and I think it will smell nice and ripe when we return.'

'You Irish bastards, you'll all be dead.' Liam walked over and gave Ortuno another smack. 'I told you before we like a little respect,' switching the lights out as he reached the door.

'Wait a minute.'

'Yeah,' asked Liam as he put his head around the door.

'I didn't have anything to do with the murder of Kenny Owen. I just heard a word.'

'Well who was it then.' asked Liam.

'Look, I have never grassed in my life and the bunch I work with would kill me.'

'Fuck this; are you going to tell us or not?'

'His name is Billy Chambers.'

'Ok now what about Ken Delanny.'

'No way.'

'Please yourself, see you soon,' shutting the door and locking it.

'Did you hear that, Bob, it was Billy Chambers.'

'Yeah I heard, so what are we going to do with Ortuno?'

'Leave him for a few days. When we return, he'll talk his head off that's for sure.' Having checked around making sure all the windows and doors were locked they made their way to the club for a few pints.

Bob drove home after having a serious drink at Liam's club, thinking of all the loose ends to clear up, especially this Billy Chambers and how he was going to kill or set the bastard up.

Costa Esteve was just about getting into bed when his telephone rang. 'Hallo.'

'Costa, it's Alberto Carda. I thought you should know I had some business with Alonzo Ortuno tonight. As I pulled into his street, I noticed Alonzo being bundled into a van. I tried to follow but lost them at some traffic lights. I went back to Alonzo apartment. Its tidy and no sight of a fight, there was a couple of glasses with drains of whisky in them.'

'Alberto, don't worry too much about Alonzo, he can look after himself, He'll be ok.'

Costa turned to Andres Lara telling him about Alonzo being bundled into a van. 'It must be Carlos Moran's people. We better pack and be on the move, as his people will break Alonzo by tomorrow night. I'll make reservations at a hotel near Heathrow.'

'We'll telephone big Sam in the morning and find out exactly how far away he is from pulling the robbery, 'then we'll disappear to France and plan for the treasure.'

'Sounds good to me, Costa.'

Captain Sifre had enjoyed himself with the Commissioner and his Deputy. They had been able to speak freely about their different methods of policing and their own feelings on this particular case. Captain Sifre pointed out that he had hoped that by Friday he would have received the names of all Spanish and South American villains working in England.

Gloria and Alex woke at 6.00. Gloria thought to herself that this was the guy she was looking for and would spend the rest of her life with. Alex turned over and kissed her.

'O, Alex, I've never been so happy.'

'I better have a shower and get going before the Captain wakes up, as I have to be back to collect you both at 9.30.'

Alex was totally in love. Driving off to meet Ben Clark at Tom's café, just off Kilburn high street. Ben was waiting at a small table near the window.

'Ben, I'm in love.'

'I'm really pleased for you both. Now it's down to business I'm afraid. Bob has given me a couple of names, one in particular a Spanish guy name Alonzo Ortuno. Whose name happened to come up at the special meeting at Scotland Yard on known Spanish villains, so I am sure the Serious Crime squad will be looking at Ortuno.

'Bob has his own methods and we must be careful not to get caught in the middle of a very nasty situation. What duties are you on today, Alex?'

'I'm collecting Captain Sifre and Officer Egido at 9.30. They are expected at Kilburn Police Station for a tour. What about you, Ben?'

'I'm off to meet Sergeant Weber and his video surveillance tapes.'

'I thought Sergeant More was covering the tapes.'

'That's correct, Alex, but I want to know the comings and goings first-hand.'

Captain Sifre and Officer Egido had finished breakfast and were talking about the information on known Spanish villains who were known to be in England. Miguel Melgar and Juan Riminez both were believed to be extremely dangerous. Others were Costa Esteve and Andres Lara Ferrer and Alonzo Ortuno.

'We know for sure that Melgar, Riminez and Ortuno are connected with Carlos Moran. So where does Carlos Moran fit into the puzzle of Peter Sainsbury.'

Alex had parked his car and walked into the hotel restaurant. 'Good morning all.'

'I've been speaking with Superintendent Parker this morning; he tells me that both Mr Horn and Mr Prince are in court this morning. I would be very interested to see the proceedings.'

D.C. Quirk took both Captain Sifre and Officer Egido into Bleasdale's office.

'Good morning,' said Bleasdale, 'would you like some coffee or would you like to take the tour of my station first,' looking at his watch.

The Captain replied that he would like the tour first, but asked if they would be able to monitor the court proceedings.

'Not a problem, Captain. Quirk will give you the tour while I prepare for the court, we can all travel together to the court.'

Alex led the way to the CID office and introduced everybody. Sergeant Clark and More both said it was nice seeing both the Captain and Officer Egido again. They were then led into the adjoining room where photos were pinned on the large board, Alex pointed at the photo of Ted Horn and Tommy Prince. 'These are the two you will be seeing in court this morning.'

Alex then pointed to the photo of Peter Sainsbury, looking over to the surveillance equipment he asked Sergeant More if it would be a good idea to show the Captain the villains being monitored at the Red Lion.

'Yes that's a good idea,' puffing out his chest. As the video played, Sergeant More gave names to the faces on the screen. 'This is Billy Chambers a nasty piece of work, this is Bob Warden a really hard nut and this is a petty villain Derrick Smallwood. Now this chap here, I've seen him before but, just cannot place him. Both Ben and Alex said he's wanted.

Alex went into the other room, the next photo came up and Captain Sifre asked could that photo be frozen. Reg More froze the photo.

'That's Alonzo Ortuno,' said the Captain, 'well known as a heavy villain in Madrid.'

'That's interesting, Captain,' Ben Clark said. 'I wonder who he was meeting.' Moving onto the next photo which showed more petty Villains who came in and out of the Red Lion. Then came Billy Chambers with Alonzo Ortuno who entered the pub.

'Well, well so that's the tie up between the foreigners and our known villains.' explained Ben.

'Quite possible, Sergeant.'

Alex who had been going through the wanted posters returned to the CID office. 'Got him,' he shouted coming back into the room with the poster in his hand. 'Mr Samuel Davidson, he escaped from a prison van with three other prisoners; all were recaptured except Davidson who has never been heard of since his escape. The only information mentioned here, was a possible sighting of Davidson in France, he was carrying out a fifteen year sentence.'

'I wonder if there is any connexion with Billy Chambers or this Alonzo Ortuno,' exclaimed Ben. 'That's really marvellous being able to put all the names to the photos.' Finishing their coffees and cakes that D.C. Muir had brought in.

The CID office door opened and in walked Chief Inspector Bleasdale. 'Captain, I hope my officers have been able to enlighten you on the police work we cover here.'

'Chief Inspector, I am very impressed and with all the additional information your officers have shown me. It won't be long until this investigation is completed with favourable results.' The Captain thanked all the officers present for their time putting his coat back on and followed the Chief Inspector, Alex and Officer Egido out of the CID room.

In the small courtroom, Miss Kerry Dickson, solicitor for both Ted Horn and Tommy Prince, was sitting at her table going through the bundle of papers concerning the case.

The police lawyer was Mr Jonathan Crisp. 'Good morning, Chief Inspector.' Bleasdale introduced Captain Sifre and Officer Egido from the Guardia Civil Spain.

'Nice to meet you both. Have you a connexion with this case, Captain?'

'Yes in a way. We've had murders committed in Spain which we are lead to believe maybe connected with Peter Sainsbury and the Mallards Publishing House.'

'Interesting. We should all take our seats if you Captain and officer Egido would care to sit over there with Detective Quirk. I will be able to see you all after the hearing.'

'All rise, Commissioner of Police verses Edward Horn and Thomas Prince.'

Mr Jonathan Crisp stood and gave his case against the defendants. Miss Kerry Dickson suggested that the evidence against Mr Horn and Mr Prince was so flimsy that the case should be dropped. Mr Crisp pointed out that the evidence against the two defendants was very serious indeed, having highly explosive equipment in one's boot of a car should not be taken lightly.

After further two's and throws, Mr Edward Horn and Mr Thomas Prince were committed to appear for another hearing. Chief Inspector Bleasdale invited Jonathan Crisp to lunch back at his station. 'That's very kind of you, Chief Inspector, but I have another court appcarance in an hour.'

They all returned to the Police Station where Bleasdale whisked Captain Sifre and Officer Egido to the officer's mess for lunch.

Alex made his way to the CID office, letting his fellow CID officers know that Horn and Prince had been committed to another hearing, but thought after listening to the evidence, it was flimsy and in his opinion not that convincing.

Sergeant More told Alex that they had been working on a system to trace this Samuel Davidson. Alex asked how many times Davidson had been seen in the Red Lion. The reply was once.

'So it's no good chasing around the area and what about Derrick Smallwood.'

'Three times,' was the reply.

'It would be more sensible to put a tail on Smallwood,' prompted D.C. Muir

'That's going to be costly,' replied Ben.

'Reg and I could tail Smallwood from his house,' said Rod.

Ben turned to Alex. 'How many more days are you on duty with Superintendent Parker's office?'

'Until Friday, when they return to Spain.'

Ben suggested that 'They wait until Alex returned from his duties at Scotland Yard, and in the meantime we continue to monitor the surveillance at the Red Lion. That way they might be able to gather more information on this big job going down.'

'I agree,' replied Reg. 'This Davidson fellow along with Smallwood and Chambers must be involved somewhere along the line.'

'Looks that way to me,' said Rod Muir. The next video will be with us tonight.'

'That's fine then we can sit down tomorrow and decide on our next move,' said Ben.

Over lunch, Chief Inspector Bleasdale inquired about the Captains schedule.

'I'm off to Scotland Yard at I4.30 as I have a meeting with the Serious Crime Squad.'

'And this evening?'

'Nothing planned.'

'I would be delighted for you both to have dinner with my wife and I.'

'That's very kind of you, Chief Inspector.'

'Let's say I'll collect you at 20.00 from your hotel.' Officer Egido asked if she could be excused as she had planned to go to the cinema with a friend.

'Yes of course, my dear,' said the Chief Inspector.

Alex was waiting in the car as the Captain and Officer Egido came down from Bleasdale's office, driving them off to Scotland Yard.

Captain Sifre implied 'Look you two; why don't you both go off and have a good time. I'm sure you would rather be with Alex than sitting down with a bunch of men talking about murders. I'll see you both in the morning.'

'Thank you, Sir.'

'By the way, Alex, give me your opinion about the court case this morning.'

'Sir, I thought our case was flimsy. I really couldn't see a well-known safe blower like Tommy Prince driving around with detonators in the boot of his car.

If he had been stopped by the traffic police or by CID, and they found the detonators, Prince would have got ten years, I just can't see it.'

'So somebody has gone to great lengths to set this Mr Prince up, but why,' said the Captain.

'That's all in this large puzzle we are all looking at, Captain.'

As the Captain got out of the car, he nodded saying, 'I think we all have a lot to think about.'

Ben telephoned Bob Warden making arrangements for their meeting. The surveillance tape was checked for all the comings and goings at the Red Lion. Billy Chambers and Alonzo Ortuno were spotted together, also another heavy Sam Davidson,

'I've heard of him, Ben. Isn't he the guy who escaped from the prison van?'

'That's him. Was he with the other two?'

'No, Bob. I wouldn't have thought so, as he visited the Red Lion on another occasion with Derrick Smallwood.'

'I know him as well but he's not a heavy.'

'That's our opinion too.'

'Ben, I have to meet with my friends tomorrow, so hopefully I will receive further information for you. Can we meet the day after tomorrow same place and time?'

'That's fine, Bob. See you then.'

Joe Bolt had been calling Derrick Smallwood for days and was getting no replies. I'll give it another hour and then I'll try again.

'Hallo, Derrick, it's Joe.'

'Hallo, mate, how are you?'

'I've been trying to contact you for days.'

'Sorry about that, I've been busy, Joe. I've got something on which I spoke to you about.'

'Derrick, I'm on the way back home tomorrow.'

'That's fine, Joe. I'll look forward to seeing you,' putting the telephone down and thinking he would speak with big Sam about trying to find some work for Joe Bolt.

Joe was disappointed with Derrick's attitude. Joe thought Derrick had acted a bit flash and was sure Derrick had made a huge mistake in getting involved with a heavy gang.

Big Sam and Derrick made arrangements to meet in Battersea and explore several car parks to steal cars for their robbery in Hayes. They wanted sizable high powered cars, maybe a couple of BMW's or a big Ford. Big Sam had already monitored four such cars in different car parks, which they selected they would steal. Big Sam pulled out a special key from his trouser pocket which he knew would fit the BMW.

The colour suited him as it was dark grey. Inside fifteen minutes Big Sam was at the wheel of the BMW driving down towards his rented garage, where he changed the number plates. Derrick who had been following him back to the garage suggested they went for a drink.

Over drinks, Derrick explained to Big Sam that he had received a call from Joe Bolt who was returning from holiday in Cornwall and was it possible that we could fix something up for Joe Bolt.

'There's nothing I can offer him you must realise that, however I'll meet him with you at some point.'

Captain Sifre over dinner with the Chief Inspector and his wife spoke of the differences of dealing with murders cases in Spain, both realising something big was about to go off either in the UK or Spain.

'I've been checking the possibility of a big job being pulled in Spain. Our intelligence people are looking at buildings holding diamonds, gold or even silver. The days of robbing armoured trucks are well past there sell by date.

'As the guards are armed and once the alarm goes off our Guardia Civil officers are there in minutes. It was explained to me today by your Serious crime squad that they are looking into all sorts of possibilities.'

'That's correct, Captain, I'm positive we will get results but unfortunately it all takes time. Let's hope we can prevent any more murders taking place.'

'Yes we both agree on that,' said the Captain.

Bob Warden telephoned Liam Murphy. 'I've received information today that Alonzo Ortuno was with Billy Chambers so they must have been involved with Kenny Owen's murder.'

'Don't worry, Bob, when we see Alonzo, he won't be able to tell us quickly enough on what happened.'

'Ok, Liam, see you later.'

Alex and Gloria were totally in love. 'Alex, I have enjoyed myself so much over the past few days. I just do not want it to end, I really do not wish to go back to Spain without you.'

'Gloria, I feel the same. I've been thinking it over. I think I'm going to retire from the police and move over Palmer and work for my uncle.'

'If you do, Alex, I could transfer from Madrid to Palmer.'

Joe Bolt called his sister asking if the police had been around and had Jeff Mitchell appeared.

'Joe, the police haven't been near or by, but Jeff hasn't been in touch with Peggy at all. He never leaves it this long before calling home. What on earth could have happened to him.'

'Don't worry, I'm returning home tomorrow morning.' Secretly Joe was worried sick something was seriously wrong. 'Derrick wasn't any good as he was working with a heavy gang, so I'm on my own.' Joe just dozed on the bed not sleeping just worrying about Jeff Mitchell.

What the hell could have happened to him. Then there was Ted Horn and Tommy Prince being set up for the Mallards safe job. Then having his car stolen from outside his house. It has to be set up.

Joe felt awful about Horn and Prince being sent for another hearing especially as it was Jeff Mitchell, Derrick Smallwood and himself who had pulled the Mallards job. Joe packed his suitcase paid his bill and travelled back towards London.

Sergeant Gillispe had been checking on the known villains associated with Miguel Melgar and Juan Riminez. He and officer Gabriel Bello had been seeking information around the different clubs in Madrid, stopping off at El Turn club. Standing at the bar area was Francisco Avails, who promptly told them of a hit contract on a number of people, at least two or three of those were situated in England.

'Have you any names, Francisco,' asked Garial Bello.

'No not as yet but hopefully I'll receive the information by tomorrow.'

'Alright, Francisco, we will meet you here.'

'Have you any idea who put up the hit?'

'Yes it was Carlos Moran.'

'Ok, Francisco, be careful but remember to meet us.'

'Yes, yes, I'll be here.'

Sergeant Gillispe and Officer Garial Bello walked away and down by the Cus Cus Hotel. 'Look at all those girls, Garial, something should be done about these street walkers and their pimps.'

'How do you stop it, Sergeant, when there are so many guys wanting to pay for the girls.'

'Garial, Francisco has never proved wrong before. I am sure he will gather the names for us,' as they walked on and down to their headquarters. 'I'll contact Captain Sifre in England and I'll see you in the morning, Garial.'

'Sorry to call you so late, Captain, but I thought it was too urgent to wait. Garial Bello and I met up with an informant, Francisco Avails, who gave us the name of Carlos Moran. It appears he is behind a number of contract hits in the UK. The name of those hits I will receive tomorrow night.'

'Sergeant, Carlos Moran has his hands in many pockets in Spain, so the news doesn't surprise me. What have you found on the computer regards his business ventures.'

'Other than being a bent lawyer with an associate in Valencia, he has his hands in the travel business.'

'Very good, Sergeant.'

'How's London, Captain?'

'I'm very impressed with the developments so far especially the way they handle crimes. I was able to visit two of their large police stations and at one, we were able to sit down and watch surveillance tapes of those believed to be involved and connected to the Mallards robbery and murders. Which could lead to crimes in Spain, so all in all we are moving in the right direction, and maybe the bonus could be the arrest of Carlos Moran.'

'Excellent news, Captain.'

After joining Officer Egido and D.C. Quirk for breakfast, Captain Sifre explained the information he had received from Sergeant Gillispe the previous evening. 'So it is possible we may have to delay returning to Spain for a few days.' Gloria was all smiles with the news and Alex could have jumped up to the ceiling he was so pleased.

'I'll contact Superintendent Parker this morning asking if you can remain as my driver for some extra days, Alex. I would also like to revisit Kilburn Police Station and look at the surveillance video. Now if you will excuse me, I'll call Superintendent Parker,' as he walked off towards the lift.

Gloria said, 'O, Alex what wonderful news,' as they held hands.

'Superintendent, I've received certain information from Spain which I believe will keep me here for a further few days and could unravel some of the crimes here in the UK.' All being agreed he walked back into the restaurant letting both Alex and Gloria know that the Superintendent was very happy for them to remain for a few more days.

Tomas Sanchez telephoned Miguel Melgar. 'I've some information on Costa Esteve. He and his associates are in the Ilford or Eastham area.'

'Very good, Tomas, keep looking; find out all you can about the gang.'

Miguel called Juan Riminez, 'We have information on the whereabouts of Costa Esteve; he's in Ilford or Eastham area. Come over and pick me up, we'll take a drive over there and see what we can find.'

Bob Warden also received a call from Liam Murphy. 'Bob, we'll be going over to see Mr Ortuno. Do you want to be present?'

'You bet, I'm on my way.'

Big Sam Davidson and Derrick were meeting up with the team to report on their findings. Big Sam was getting edgy, he wanted to pull the job, pointing out that tomorrow he wanted to see the Dutchman and get the teargas and hardware.

'I thought we didn't need any hardware on this job, Sam.'

'Derrick, it's just in case. it's a big job we can't take any risks.'

John and Peter Shephard along with Scotch Jack and Jimmy Simmons were sitting on the stone wall by the river watching the river run by.

'Hallo, lads. We've looked at the bridge. On the morning of the raid, we'll take the vehicle down the lane, cut the bolt of the chain over the bridge, put the chain back on without a new bolt Then back to the factory units and wait for the security van. We stole the first of the cars last night; a BMW, the other vehicle's we will have over the next couple of days.

'We raid the security van, pile the money into our cars and drive down to the bridge. Put the money in the getaway vehicle, leave two of the stolen cars blocking the bridge and road and away to Denham Airport. Everybody happy with the plan?'

'Yes,' was the reply.

'Tomorrow, Derrick and I will meet the Dutchman and purchase the gear. He wants five grand which Costa has already given us. That leaves Peter and John to carry out the last check on the factory units and the security van. The only problem noticeable was coming from the bank to the factory units.

There are some temporary traffic signals at roadwork's which will hold us up for ten minutes.'

Sam asked are there any more comments.

'Just one,' said John Simmons, 'there's a lot of talk going around on the grapevine about the murder of Kenny Owen. They're saying its Billy Chambers. He's a real nasty piece of work. Peter and I pulled a job with him some years back down the Wembley area. The manager had the safe number and the staff swore blind they didn't know the number.

'Jack and I collected all the ready monies lying about. Chambers wasn't having any of it, smacking one of the girls in the face with the butt of the gun; he then pushed the shotgun into the mouth of her boss, who shit himself signalling he would open the safe. Not being satisfied, after the guy opened the safe, Billy smacked him in the face with the gun.

'Jack went mad, shouting there was no need for that violence. Chambers just turned and said "we got the money didn't we", smiling all over his face.'

'What did you get?'

'Twelve and a half grand.'

'Chambers also wanted to knock the guy who put up the job. Jack went ballistic. In the end, Chambers gave the fellow who put up the job a monkey. I can tell you the fellow was not a happy bunny so if Chambers is responsible for the murder of Kenny Owen he deserves everything that come his way.'

Ben Clark, Reg More, Rod Muir, Captain Sifre, Gloria Egido and Alex Quirk were in the CID office. Rod Muir collected the coffees and sticky buns. Thinking to himself this is like Saturday morning pictures. Reg placed the last surveillance tape into the video.

Turning it on, first came Billy Chambers, then Derrick Smallwood, then Terry Peachy. 'The notes from Battersea CID say he was picked up and interviewed over the Kenny Owen mugging/murder,' said Reg More.

'That's very interesting put him on the list for a pull, Rod.' There were a few more petty villains but nothing to interest or wet their appetite. Reg More and Rod Muir were going to follow up some of the Red Lion suspects.

Captain Sifre asked D.C. Quirk to take him over to Scotland Yard to see Inspector Brown himself. As they walked out of the door, Reg More suggested you see that Guardia Civil guy he is going to grass us up at the Yard saying we are at a dead end.

'That might be the case, Reg, but we don't answer to Captain Sifre,' said Ben Clark.

Bob Warden made his way to meet Liam Murphy in the Bulls head pub. Liam, Mick and Paul were already drinking their beers at the bar when Bob walked in.

'We've moved Ortuno as he stunk the flat out with his shit and piss and we didn't want to be spotted coming and going too often. He's now safe in a small empty factory unit.'

Finishing their beers, they made their way to the factory unit down by the cannel. The factory was surrounded by small trees and scrubs with other unused factories. The pavements had grass and weeds growing out of the floor, and the roads looked dirty.

Unlocking the outside door of the factory they walked on the concrete floor that led to the small set of stairs and the upstairs office. As they unlocked the door, the smell whiffed out.

'O Jesus, he's shit himself again,' said Liam. 'Paul, open that window and leave the door open, Mick.'

Alonzo shouted out, 'Let me go. I'll talk what do you want to know.'

'Now that's better, Alonzo, now start talking.'

'It was Billy Chambers who killed Kenny Owen. Chambers told some petty villain named Terry Peachy that Kenny Owen had a considerable amount of cash hidden in his flat.'

'Why did Chambers tell him that?'

'He wanted Peachy to go around and be seen by Kenny's neighbours.'

'Now what about Ken Delanny.'

'Please they will kill me, the people behind all this are very dangerous.'

'What the fuck do you think we are, Disneyland?'

'Ok, Ok. Ken Delanny was given the job of feeding Jeff Mitchell to the pigs.'

'What on earth did Jeff Mitchell do,' asked Bob.

'He was involved in the safe blowing at Mallards; he got greedy and wanted more money, so Costa Esteve paid Delanny to kill him.'

'Was Jeff Mitchell alive when they fed him to the pigs.'

'No, Delanny cut him up first while he was alive.'

Bob Warden couldn't keep still. 'What was in this bloody safe,' asked Bob.

'There were plans and a treasure map for gold and diamonds and some cash.'

'How much treasure are we talking about?'

'10 million pounds at least.'

‘Bloody hell, Bob, perhaps we should find this Costa Esteve and his mate first. What’s his address,’ asked Liam.

‘220 Docks road. Now please let me have water.’

‘Ok, Alonzo, water you want and water you will get. Paul, tape the fucker’s mouth up.’

Bob asked Liam what he was going to do with Alonzo.

‘The fucker wants water so we will put him into the canal, there’s enough water for him there.’

‘Mick, get the concrete boots.’ Alonzo went white and fainted as they put his feet into the concrete. The four of them carried him downstairs putting him into the van and drove the short distance to the bridge of the canal.

Looking around to make sure nobody was around. They removed Alonzo’s body from the van carried him onto the bridge and drooped him over the side into the water.

Joe Bolt returned home had a bit of lunch with his sister, told her he was going around first to see Derrick and then onto see Peggy.

Kelly opened the door. ‘Hallo, Joe, I’m so pleased to see you. I’m so worried about these guys Derricks mixed up with, he should be home in twenty minutes, please have a beer.’

Ten minutes later, Derrick walked through the back door. ‘Hallo, Joe, I hope you had a good holiday in Cornwall.’

‘Fine, Derrick, nice and quiet.’ Kelly said she was going to the shops and left.

‘Joe, I’m pleased you’re back as I wanted to tell you face to face. I’m working with a heavy gang and my cut in the robbery will be 300 grand.

‘Derrick, please don’t get involved, it’s not worth it. If anything goes wrong you’ll go away for a long time.’

‘Joe, you told me you wanted to retire, this is my big chance. I’ll be able purchase a nice property down at the coast, start a little business and just keep my head down.’

‘I’m sorry to hear that, Derrick. I’ll wish you the best of luck and I’ll see my own way out.’ Joe walked down the path jumped into his car and away towards Brixton road. Two minutes later he pulled up outside Jeff Mitchell’s house. Peggy answered the door and looked around hoping Jeff was with Joe. ‘I haven’t seen Jeff since we got on our toe’s, Peggy.’

‘Where has he gone, Joe?’

'I haven't a clue, Peggy, but I'll make it my business to find out.'

'Be careful, Joe, you don't want the old bill around.'

'Don't worry, I'll be careful, how are you off for money.'

'No problems there, Joe. Jeff left me with plenty before he went off.'

Bob Warden, Liam Murphy, Mick and Paul sat around a table in the Thames Tavern speaking about Ken Delanny and Costa Esteve and the amount of valuables taken from the safe at Mallards. Liam decided to call a girl he knew on the telephone exchange to verify Costa Esteves address.

'Hallo, Phyllis, can you do me a favour and check out this address for me it's a Mr Costa Esteve of 220 Docks road, Eastham.'

'Ok, Liam, I'll call you back.'

'Ok lads, we have time for another drink and it's your shout, Bob.' Four pints came over and Liam received his call.

'Hi, Liam, Costa Esteve is registered at I89 Queens Road, Eastham.'

'I owe you, Phyllis,' putting his mobile away.

'Ok lads, we can have another few drinks and then go and pick up Mr Costa Esteve,' said Liam.

The CID at Plaistow police station received a call from Mr Eric Proud, who mentioned that while looking for somewhere to fish he had seen four large men carry, and then throw into the canal something that looked like a body at Pigeon Farm.

'Could you hold on for a minute, Mr Proud' D.C. Macman called over Inspector Ward, after telling him the subject of conversation.

'Hallo, Mr Proud sorry about the delay, I'm Inspector Ward. I understand you witnessed what looked like somebody being thrown into the canal at Pigeons farm by four large men.'

'That's correct, Inspector.'

'May I have your address, Mr Proud?'

'25 Euston Street.'

'Are you still in the area of the canal and are the four men still in sight?'

'Yes, Inspector, I'm at the telephone box on the corner of Pigeons farm, but I'm afraid the four men disappeared.'

'Mr Proud, I'm on my way. Is it possible you could remain there until I arrive?'

'No problem at all.'

Inspector Ward left a message for the Chief Inspector informing him of the details so far. He also put through a call to the river police requesting a couple of frogman. Twenty minutes later, everybody was on site. Inspector Ward asked D.C. Glen to take a statement from Mr Proud, where exactly where the men when they through something like a body into the canal.

'Over there,' pointing.

Inspector Ward asked the frogman what they thought.

'If the body was thrown into the canal, it could have floated down-stream a bit, but we'll take a look.' After only ten minutes in the canal, they gave the thumbs up sign; attaching a rope around the body and with assistance of the other CID officers pulled the body to the bank.

Climbing out of the canal one of the frogmen said, 'This guy has got concrete attached to his legs.'

'Get SOCO down immediately.' Calling Chief Inspector Phillips, letting him know the situation.

The Chief Inspector picked up some papers from his desk reading a memo from Superintendent Parker. He immediately contacted Inspector Brown at Scotland Yard letting him know that a possible contract hit had been carried out at Pigeons farm by four men throwing a man into the canal with concrete attached to his feet. The incident had been witnessed by a local fisherman.

Inspector Brown called his Sergeant. 'Let's move we have another murder which could be connected with our ongoing inquiry.' Looking over at another Detective asking him to let Superintendent Parker know where he had gone.

At Pigeon Farm, Inspector Brown was greeted by Inspector Ward who introduced him to Mr Proud, who has already given a witness statement.

'Ok let's run through the crime scene.' Looking at the body which lay on the canal bank. SOCO were already photographing the body and surrounds, a cover was placed around the body.

'Those factories over there,' pointing towards the units. 'Are they occupied by any chance,' asked Inspector Brown'

'I'm afraid not but I have men searching that area.'

'Without doubt, it's a contract hit,' said Inspector Brown, the leader of the SOCO team Detective Mike Veal had gone through the pockets of the deceased and found some ID.

'Inspector Brown, we have ID, the deceased is Alonzo Ortuno.'

'I can't believe it. He is a person of interest we had hoped to interview regards the ongoing crime at Mallards,' replied Inspector Brown.

The officers searching the factory areas were flagging.

'It looks like my men may have found something over at that factory unit, Inspector Brown.'

Making their way over towards the factory they noticed tyre marks on the dirt road. As they moved closer to the factory they could see clear footprints. 'Let's get this area cordoned off, Inspector Ward.'

Detective Veal who had finished his work of the body made his way to the factory area. Entering the factory they could see clear footprints on the concrete floor leading towards a set of stairs which led to what looked like offices. Making their way up the metal stairs, an awful smell overwhelmed them.

'Somebody has been here that's for sure.' Reaching the office they could see a chair that had been bolted to the floor with chains and ropes laying across the chair. The smell was overwhelming and it was obvious the person who had been imprisoned had shit and pissed himself and probably may have been imprisoned for days. There was no sign of any water or food stains on the floor.

'Fingerprint the whole area from the front door to the office.' Photographs were taken. Inspector Brown stood outside the office on the mizzen floor looking down on the concrete floor, watching the officers carrying out a search of every inch of the factory. The search was completed, the factory and all the surrounding areas.

Inspector Brown called Superintendent Parker letting him know of the death and killing of Alonzo Ortuno

Superintendent Parker passed on the information to both the Deputy Commissioner and Chief Inspector Bleasdale.

Bob Warden, Liam Murphy, Mick and Paul finished their drinks making their way to I89 Queens Road. Paul walked down one side of the street and Bob and Liam the other, reaching the house where Costa Esteve lived. Mick drove slowly down the street, parking outside the house. Bob knocked on the door which was answered by a lady in a cleaning smock.

'Hallo, may I speak with Mr Costa Esteve please.'

'I'm sorry, Mr Esteve has left and will not be returning.'

'Did he by any chance leave a forwarding address as it is very urgent that I contact him.'

'No love,' said the lady, 'the owner told me Mr Esteve travelled over towards Heathrow Airport.'

'Thank you, Miss.' Bob walked back towards the car.

'It appears that Costa Esteve was tipped off and decided to do a runner, over towards Heathrow area, but that could be a red heron.'

Returning to the pub and after a small beer, Bob made his apologies saying he was going to find Terry Peachy and give him a pull.

Liam asked Bob, 'What are we are going to do about this Costa Esteve guy?'

'We can only try and find out where he has gone. You make enquires over this side and I will make enquirers over my side of London. I'll give you a call tomorrow, Liam.'

Bob drove back towards Brixton, thinking about giving Derrick Smallwood and Joe Bolt a call. Bob called Derrick Smallwood's home number. 'May I speak with Derrick please.'

'I'm sorry but Derrick's not home at the moment, if you give me your phone number, I will get him to call you on his return.'

'I'll call back, thank you.'

Next, Bob called Joe Bolt, 'Hallo may I speak with Joe Bolt please.'

'Speaking.'

'Hallo, Joe, it's Bob Warden; we need to meet and speak about Jeff Mitchell.'

'Ok, Bob, lets meet at the Prince of Wales at Stockwell in an hour.'

'That's fine, Joe, see you there.'

Bob sat at a side table near the window of the salon bar with a pint of beer on the table. Joe walked into the bar saw Bob, nodded and made his way to Bob's table.

'It's been a long time, Bob.

'Yes it has, Joe. You're looking well I might say.'

'I'll get straight to the point. I received information that you Jeff and Derrick Smallwood pulled the safe job at Mallards.'

'Now hold on, Bob, I'm not here to talk about who did what jobs.'

'I understand, Joe, but let me finish. Jeff Mitchell did the dirty on you and Derrick.'

'Bob, Jeff would never do the dirty. I think it's time for me to say goodbye.'

'Joe, please let me finish, it's for your own benefit and it's bad news. Jeff's dead, he was cut up and fed to the pigs by a guy called Ken Delanny. You were all set up by a foreign guy called Costa Esteve. Whatever this guy promised you all, was never going to happen.'

'How do you know all these facts, Bob?'

'It all started with my uncle Kenny Owen being murdered, by Billy Chambers. I need your help, Joe. I want to set the bastards up.'

'Bob, I'm sick as a parrot over this information about Jeff, he was a relative of mine. How on earth am I going to tell Peggy about Jeff's death.' Joe shook his head looking down at the table. 'It's unbelievable to imagine Jeff doing the dirty. When we opened the safe there was only three grand instead of the ten grand promised, Jeff took the papers and bits as he always liked to read the crap of other people's business from the safe.'

'Joe, those papers are more valuable and worth quite a few grand. I was only told that news today, which leads me to the point, that you and Derrick are in danger, as this Costa Esteve believes you may also know about the paperwork inside the safe.'

'Ok, Bob, count me in for whatever help you require, give me a call when you want to meet.'

Joe called Derrick, they spoke about the three grand instead of the ten grand promised in the safe, and both didn't want to believe that Jeff had done the dirty on them. But now they knew the truth.

Chief Inspector Bleasdale popped down to the CID office, briefing all on the murder of Alonzo Ortuno. 'These murders are getting out of hand; we need more information so put the squeeze on your snouts and push harder.'

Captain Sifre spent most of the day with Superintendent Parker and the Deputy Commissioner, afterwards a meeting was arranged with Inspector Brown over the murder of Alonzo Ortuno. Inspector Brown was convinced that something much bigger was behind all these murders, making Costa Esteve and his partner Andres Lara number one proprietary.

Inspector Ward of the Plaistow CID had been given the task of finding the whereabouts of Costa Esteve and Andres Lara as it was believed they lived in that area.

Information from Spain, some big time villain called Carlos Moran was also looking for both Costa Esteve and Andres Lara, and has probably put a hit on them both.

Alex called Ben Clark filling him in on all the information. 'Maybe these other villains from Spain will catch up with Costa Esteve before we do.'

'It's a possibility Alex. I'm meeting with Bob Warden tonight so we will see what information comes out.'

'So how's the lovely Officer Egido.'

'Great, Ben, we are so in love.'

'She's a beautiful woman, Alex, you couldn't do better.'

Ben Clark made his way to meet with Bob Warden. He was sitting at his usual table by the window in the corner and had two pints on the table. 'Had a good day, Bob?'

'Usual, Ben, nothing exciting.'

'There's been another murder, Bob, a guy named Alonzo Ortuno, a Spaniard.'

'How was he murdered?

Ben looked at Bob straight in the eyes. 'Concrete around his legs and thrown into a canal, which fortunately was witnessed by a local fisherman.'

'Have they pulled in the villains?'

'No but the Serious Crime squad are looking into the matter and they are confident of an early arrest.'

'Bloody hell, Ben, it's getting unsafe to be about these days; we were only talking about Alonzo Ortuno the other day.'

'That's been bothering me, Bob. I trust you were not involved.'

'No way, Ben.'

'Ok, what have you been able to find out, Bob?'

'Not a great deal, it appears the word is Billy Chambers is connected with the big robbery but as yet I have no other names or where the robbery is going to take place, but something will crack soon.'

'I hope so, Bob, you'll just have to put pressure on those people of yours for information. It doesn't surprise me Billy Chambers is involved.'

'Where's your partner, Alex.'

'Working at Scotland Yard for a few days he's been given special duties of driving around a member of the Guardia Civil from Spain. It appears the murder of Peter Sainsbury is somehow connected with murders that have taken place in Spain. One of the big time villains in Spain is also looking for Costa Esteve and his mate.'

'Really getting hot then, Ben.'

'Yes it seems that way, see you in a couple of days, Bob.'

Bob sat at the table for a few minutes wondering what to do, 'I better get hold of Liam and let him know about the old bill finding the body of Alonzo Ortuno. After trying a few telephone numbers to contact Liam, there was no reply. The best bet was to drive over to Eastham.

Sergeant Weber had another surveillance tape ready. Many of the regular petty villains along with Billy Chambers and a surprise Jimmy Simmons known to work with heavies with a lot of violence had arrived and in some cases gone after thirty minutes or so.

Bob Warden drove over to Eastham. He was on his guard just in case the old bill where visiting all the pubs and clubs. Bob eventually found Paul, whispering in his ear letting him know about the information he had received.

Bob and Paul made their way to the Otterman club where Liam was chatting with a very stunning black girl. After noticing Bob and Paul enter, he ordered a bottle of Champaign telling the girl he would be back in a few minutes.

'Hallo, Bob, didn't know I would be seeing you so soon.'

'Liam, the old bill have found the body of Alonzo Ortuno. Some local fisherman witnessed us throw the body into the canal.'

'You're joking.'

'No, Liam, the Serious Crime squad are involved; also another big firm from Spain are also looking for this Costa Esteve.' Liam nodded.

'It's time to be on our toes, lads. Have you seen Mick?'

'No, Liam, I haven't seen him for some hours,' said Paul.

'Ok we better disappear but first we must set the factory on fire. Bob, it's no good you hanging around. You get back to your side of the river. This is my mobile number if anything comes up, call me.'

'Sure thing, Liam, see you both.'

'Paul, you go and find Mick, as I've some unfinished business,' nodding over to where the girl was waiting.

Bob made his way back to his car and away. Paul visited pub after pub but was unable to find Mick. Walking back towards his car, Paul spotted an unmarked police car with four CID officers holding Mick McRight.

Paul stepped back into the shadows, thinking what's happening surely they haven't found fingerprints at the factory. Paul made his way back to the Otterman club. Liam was already upstairs with his girl and wouldn't want to be disturbed.

The CID car pulled into Plaistow police station. 'You better have a good look around, Mick, as its going to be a long time before you see daylight again.'

'I haven't a clue what you're talking about,' answered McRight.

'Book him in, Keith,' said Inspector Ward, 'while I give the serious Crime squad a call.'

Returning to the interview room, Inspector Ward looked at Mick McRight.

'Ok, Mick, let's start. We found your fingerprints in the factory unit at Pigeons farm where you kept Alonzo Ortuno chained up in the first floor office of the factory. We have a witness who will be identifying you and the others, throwing the body into the canal.'

'Inspector Ward, I have nothing to say. I know nothing of any murder and I know nothing of this chap you have mentioned.'

'Mick, you're looking at life in prison.'

'What for going fishing in the canal. The witness you have would only have seen me fishing and throwing my bait in the water.'

'Alright, Mick, have it your way. We'll be taking you over to the Serious Crime squad at Scotland Yard, as they are now in charge of this murder and really you should know, Mick, they'll just throw the keys away.'

'I want a lawyer.'

'Sorry, Mick, I don't understand you. Get him out of here, take him over to Scotland yard.'

'You bastards, you can't do this to me,' jumping up and trying to get to the door. All four CID officers jumped on top of McRight who had to be restrained and taken and bundled into the police van and driven away.

Liam came downstairs with his black beauty on his arm. 'Are we going to have more Champaign, Liam?'

'Maybe a bit later, Denise. I need to speak with my mate over there.' After listening to Paul, they decided to burn down the factory unit immediately

'What if the old bills watching the factory, Liam?'

'I can't see the old bill watching the factory in the dark, but we'll keep a good look out.' They drove slowly towards the factory not noticing anybody.

'Not a soul, Paul.' They parked up and removed the petrol cans from the boot of the car. Walking over the few feet to the factory, Liam pulled the keys out of his pocket went to put the key into the lock when the door burst open.

With police and dogs coming out running, other police and dogs came out of hiding around the area. Liam and Paul threw their petrol cans at the police pulling out from their trousers coshes, which they immediately got stuck in putting down at least five police officers. The dogs came running in and Liam tried to hit out at the dogs, giving time for other police officers to move in with their batons pushing Liam to the floor.

Paul tried to escape but was brought down by a police dog and held by other police officers. More police vehicles arrived with more officers. Liam Murphy and Paul McCathy were handcuffed and bundled into the police van.

Sergeant Rogers called Inspector Ward letting him know they had Liam Murphy and Paul McCathy in custody.

'Ok, Sergeant, get them over to Scotland Yard, the Serious Crime Squad can have them.'

Derrick Smallwood had met up with Big Sam letting him know of the conversation he had with Joe Bolt.

'Derrick, I just cannot see Costa Esteve wanting Jeff Mitchell fed to the pigs, what for; and if this Bob Warden has evidence why hasn't he put it up.'

'I haven't a clue, Sam.'

'Derrick, just keep away from Joe Bolt until after the job has been pulled. I cannot afford any problems and hindrance from anybody and I don't want this Joe Bolt poking around.'

'Ok, Sam.'

'At our next meeting, I'll ask the others if they have heard or spoken to anybody regards Jeff Mitchell disappearance. We must be on top of our game, Derrick, we just can't take any chances.'

'Sorry, Sam, you're right.'

Inspector Brown was delighted to hear that two other suspects had been arrested, this maybe the first piece of the puzzle we are looking for. As he walked down to the holding cells, he met up with Inspector Ward.

'Good work, Inspector. We now have three out of the four villains, so I'm confidant by tomorrow morning we will be charging them all with murder of Alonzo Ortuno. Let's have McRight up into the interview room.' McRight was put into the interview room yelling he wanted a lawyer.

'I'm not saying another word.'

'I'm trying to help you, Mr McRight, nobody is aware you are here and that is how it's going to remain at the moment. So let's start from the beginning. You Liam Murphy and Paul McCathy held Alonzo Ortuno against his will at the factory at Pigeons farm.

'Your fingerprints are everywhere even on the cement on Ortuno's feet, they are all over the van used to transport Alonzo Ortuno. You and others then murdered Ortuno by having his body thrown into the canal with cement attached to his legs.

'You'll be going down for a twenty-five years. So help yourself and talk before one of the others talks his head off. Then it's goodbye for a very long stretch.'

'I have nothing to say, Inspector.'

'Ok take him down.;

The internal telephone rang to let Inspector Brown know that Murphy and McCathy were in the holding cells. 'Let's have McCathy up next.' McCathy was grilled in the same manner as McRight, even down to the point where Inspector Brown suggested that McRight had already given information.

'I don't believe a fucking word of it,' said McCathy.

'Ok take him down.'

Liam Murphy was next up and grilled in the same manner as the other two and given the same opportunities, He said, 'I have nothing to say.'

'Liam, think very carefully you are at least five years older than your two mates. Twenty-five years to life, you'll probably never see the light of day again.'

'I'll take my chance, Inspector.'

'Ok take him down.'

Inspector Brown turned to Inspector Ward, 'Murphy is acting tough but believe me he'll be the one that cracks.'

Superintendent Parker made his way to the interview room.

'How did it go, Brown?'

'It's early days, we need time.'

'What about this forth person involved?'

'We have purposely left that out at the moment, as it is quite possible one of these three will grass.'

'Maybe you could be right, but I want results quickly, Inspector.

The telephone rang in Parker's office.

'Superintendent, I have some very good news. In my report, I spoke about one of the stolen cars had been on a pig farm.'

'Yes, Chief Inspector, I remember your report.'

'Our technical boys after testing soil samples on a number of pig farms in our area, we found one belonging to Mr Ken Delanny which matched the soil samples on the stolen car.'

'Are you picking Mr Delanny up, Chief Inspector?'

‘Not as yet, I was wondering if the Serious Crime squad wanted that pleasure.’

‘Chief Inspector, I’ll have my lads down to you. Could you send me a copy of the forensic files.’

‘Inspector Brown, it would appear our day is getting better. Chief Inspector Greedy has just received evidence we were waiting for. You are able to confront Murphy, McRight and McCathy with that fact that it has now been proved that Ken Delanny, fed unfortunate criminals to his pigs.

‘And evidence has come forward placing them as being involved with Delanny. So let’s have them brought up one at a time and put the new evidence to them.’

McRight was the first to be brought up.

‘I’ve told you, Inspector, I have nothing to say.’

‘We have just obtained new evidence which involves you with Mr Ken Delanny who if paid the correct amount of money, fed unfortunate villains to the pigs.’

‘I don’t know anybody called Delanny and the nearest I have come to pigs, is a bacon sandwich.’

‘Very funny, Mr McRight, do you realise the seriousness of the crimes which you are going to be charged with.’

‘I’ve had enough of this shit. I want a lawyer now or charge me.’

The Superintendent who had been listening from the adjacent room pointed out that it was necessary for each of the prisoners to have lawyers. otherwise they could find themselves in trouble and the whole lot could be thrown out of court.

McCathy was next into the interview room, the same procedure was used, McCathy had nothing to say other than he wanted a lawyer.

Murphy was next up and when he was given the news about Ken Delanny, he pointed out he wanted a lawyer.

‘Have you anybody in mind, Liam?’

‘Yes Terry Cornish; his telephone number is 05893 2267790.’

‘Would you please get a telephone in here Detective Howell.’ The telephone was connected and Murphy spoke with Terry Cornish who told Liam not to say another word until he arrived.

Superintendent Parker asked Liam if he wanted anything to eat.

Steak and Chips, which was ordered and Murphy was lead to a special cell away from the other prisoners.

'Let McRight and McCathy sweat it out for the time being, once Murphy's lawyer has completed his business, we will let the other two make their calls.'

Superintendent Parker briefed the Deputy Commissioner on the case so far, the Deputy Commissioner was delighted with the progress.

Terry Cornish arrived and was met by Inspector Brown who after a short chat escorted Mr Cornish to the interview room where Liam Murphy was waiting. After thirty-five minutes Superintendent Parker and Inspector Brown were called.

'What can we do for you, Mr Cornish?' My client wishes to make a statement, but first of all if he makes that statement he wants a deal and will turn queen's evidence.'

'I see,' said the Superintendent. 'I will have to get authority from the top but before I go and get that authority, I want some evidence worthy of getting you queens evidence.'

Liam looked at his lawyer who nodded. 'I was with McRight and McCathy when we murdered Alonzo Ortuno in the factory at pigeon's farm. We placed him in a concrete jacket and throw him in the canal. The reason for his murder, he was involved with Billy Chambers in the murder of Kenny Owen, however I had nothing to do with Ken Delanny, although I knew he fed villains to the pigs for a price.'

'Why did Chambers and Ortuno murder Kenny Owen?'

'Owen apparently couldn't keep his mouth closed. Kenny Owen was approached to carry out the safe blowing at Mallards Publishing House. But when the foreigners turned up to meet Kenny Owen, they took one look at his hands and knew he was well passed blowing safes.'

'Who are the foreigners and what are their names?'

'One is called Costa Esteve and the other Andres Lara. They gave Kenny a few bob to keep quite. In exchange, Kenny gave them names of other safe blowers, Ted Horn, Tommy Prince and Jeff Mitchell. However, Kenny kept telling everybody who brought him a drink that he was the main man behind the robbery and he could identify the foreigners.'

'Who pulled the Mallards Robbery?'

'I'm not sure but somewhere down the line Jeff Mitchell was involved. He removed the papers, plans and maps or something from the safe. Apparently, Jeff Mitchell got greedy and was taken down to Ken Delanny's farm where he was cut up and fed to the pigs.'

'Who was the fourth person involved with you on the murder of Alonzo Ortuno?'

'There was no forth person.'

'But we have a witness who is saying there were four of you.'

'Then your witness is mistaken. Now what about my deal, Superintendent, as I have much more to say.

'I'll go and make the call.' Parker and Brown left the interview room.

'Bloody hell, Brown, what a scoop. We'll be able to pick up quite a few villains here, especially Billy Chambers. Parker spoke with the Deputy Commissioner who in turn spoke with Commissioner. After an hour, the home Secretary agreed to the deal. Superintendent Parker and Inspector Brown returned to the interview room where coffee and sandwiches were ordered.

'Ok, Liam, you have a deal and you'll be moved to a safe house. Your life will be in danger is that understood?'

'Yes, I understand perfectly.'

'Now we need more information. Have you any idea where Costa Esteve and his mate, Andres Lara, are?'

'Costa Esteve was living at I89 Queens Road, but before we could get to him, Esteve must have been tipped off, as he's landlady told us that he had moved somewhere towards Heathrow airport.'

'Have you any idea where this other big robbery is going to take place?'

'No, but everybody knows it's going down.'

'We need a written statement to these facts and you will sign it.'

'Yes, that is not a problem,' indicated Liam.

More coffee and sandwiches were brought in. Superintendent Parker and Inspector Brown removed the tapes and left the interview room, with Inspector Ward staying with Liam Murphy and Terry Cornish in the interview room.

The Deputy Commissioner being briefed by Superintendent Parker, thought that it would be a good idea to have an extra meeting with all concerned because of the new evidence received which it was hoped would escalate the findings of Costa Esteve and probably bring fresh news regarding the big robbery.

Superintendent Parker agreed and would make all the arrangements for the following day at I7.00. He had also moved another squad of special police to the Heathrow area focused on sightings of Costa Esteve and Andres Lara. Emails and faxes had been forwarded to Chief Inspectors Greedy and Bleasdale, Inspectors Brown, Cavendish, Medows and Ward, Sergeants Ben Clark, Reg

More and Hill along with Captain Sifre and Officer Egido, if they hadn't flown home.

Inspector Brown having Liam Murphy's statement typed, walked down to the interview room where Liam signed the necessary papers. Liam was moved to a safe house and was informed that under no circumstances was he to leave the safe house, where he would have the company of two Serious crime officers. Terry Cornish was informed and agreed that he would not know the whereabouts of Mr Murphy, and when it was time for him to meet with his client, arrangements would be made for a suitable location.

McRight and McCathy were brought up to the interview room separately and given the chance to make statements which both refused, they were informed that duty lawyers would be appointed for them.

Captain Sifre finishing dinner with Officer Egido and Alex Quirk received a sealed envelope, which after reading the contents. Looked up saying that they would have to delay their return to Spain as new evidence and developments had come to light, and a further meeting was arranged for I7.00 the following day.

Ben Clark received his message, as did Reg More for the meeting scheduled at Scotland Yard at I7.00.

Costa Esteve and Andres Lara moved into their new three bedroom flat at Heston. Sitting down and enjoying a glass of red wine, discussing their next move on how to dispose of Big Sam's gang after the robbery. 'I'm going to indicate to Big Sam that it would be a better idea if you, Andres, drive a getaway vehicle with the monies.'

'He won't like the idea, Costa.'

'I'm sure he won't, but this is where my leadership skills will suffice. We need a scheme to get his gang caught by the police as we need the monies to finance our treasure hunt with the maps we have.'

Ben Clark arrived at Kilburn CID office at 8.30. Reg More was already working away.

'Hi, Reg, we have to be up in Bleasdale's office at 9.I5 as important developments have come to light.'

'Great news, as plodding through these blasted tapes is getting on my nerves. I'm not getting anywhere. Many of these small time villains wouldn't work with each other if you paid them, and I cannot see Billy Chambers lowering his standards working with them either.

'Let's hope that the next surveillance tapes that Sergeant Weber brings in will shed some light on the big robbery, Ben.'

Rod Muir entered the CID office with coffee and buns.

'You are a life saver, Rod.'

Ben and Reg finished their coffee and made their way up to Bleasdale's office. Sitting down, Bleasdale came straight to the point, 'We have this meeting this afternoon and I do not want any outbursts of Horn and Prince are not guilty. Plaistow CID have arrested the murderers of Alonzo Ortuno who have been transferred to the Serious Crime squad at Scotland Yard. Late last night one of those arrested turned queen's evidence and has given a lot of information such as one of our known villains on our patch was chopped up and fed to the pigs by Ken Delanny.'

'May we ask who the villain was?'

'Yes of course, it was Jeff Mitchell,'

'My God, what a way to go,' exclaimed Ben Clark.

'That's right, Clark; anyway I'll leave the rest of the information to Superintendent Parker this afternoon.' As they arrived back in the CID office, Sergeant Weber was just about ready with the surveillance tape. Rod Muir asked Reg about his meeting with Bleasdale.

'Red hot information, the Serious Crime Squad have arrested three men for the murder of Alonzo Ortuno. One of them has turned Queen's evidence giving details that Jeff Mitchell was chopped up and fed to the pigs.'

'Bloody hell, poor bastard,' said Sergeant Weber.

'The meeting this afternoon is to give us further information. The Chief Inspector doesn't want this latest information to leave the CID office. Is that understood?'

'Of course, Reg.'

The video tape started to play as they sat down drinking coffee and laughing, the usual suspects came and went. Billy Chambers entered with Terry Peachy.

'That Peachy needs a pull,' Ben Clark said. Then in walked Jimmy Simmons. 'Well, well,' said Reg, 'does that mean Jimmy Simmons is working with Billy Chambers and where does Terry Peachy fit in.'

The lawyers representing Mick McRight and Paul McCathy arrived at Scotland Yard. Inspector Brown and Inspector Ward met with them both, leading them to interview room's numbers I and 2. After explaining the seriousness of the crimes and telling both lawyers that their clients would be charged with kidnap and murder along with trying to set fire to a factory unit at Pigeon's farm.

Inspector Ward would sit in to interview Paul McCathy with his Lawyer Sidney Williams in attendance and Inspector Brown would sit in on the interview of Mick McRight with his lawyer Reginald Garnett in attendance. Both lawyers where given time with their clients and when ready the interviews would commence.

Sidney Williams indicated that his client was ready to be interviewed. Inspector Ward entered and sat down, turned the tape on giving the date and time and who was present.

Mr McCathy, I am led to believe that you and two others kidnapped and held Mr Alonzo Ortuno on the 26 June of this year in a factory unit No 22 at Pigeon's farm, and later murdered him.'

'I have no idea what you are talking about. I had nothing to do with any kidnap or murder.'

'We have a witness to the murder, Mr McCathy.'

'So I have been told, some bloody fisherman. I know nothing about any of this nonsense you are talking about.'

'It is my duty to inform you that one of your members to the crime has turned queen's evidence, therefore it would be in your own interest to focus on your own statement'

'There's no way Mick McRight would grass, so I have nothing further to say.'

Inspector Ward turning towards Sidney Williams, shrugged his shoulders.

'Mr Paul McCathy, I am charging you on the 26 day of June you and others murdered Mr Alonzo Ortuno, after holding him in captivity for at least two days at a Factory Unit No 22 at Pigeons farm Plaistow. You and others carried the body to a vehicle, drove to the canal where you and others having attached concrete to his legs, threw the body from the bridge into the canal.

'At a later date, you and one other tried to enter factory unit No 22 and set fire to that factory. Police arrested you on the spot.' Inspector Ward asked the two constables present to remove Paul McCathy to the cells.

Inspector Brown had been called and told that Mick McRight was ready to be interviewed. Entering the interview room Inspector Brown sat down switched on the tape indicating the day, month and who was present.

'Mr McRight, I am led to believe that you and two others kidnapped and held Mr Alonzo Ortuno on the 26 June of this year in a factory unit No 22 at Pigeon's farm, Plaistow, and later murdered him.'

'I have nothing to say.'

'We have a witness to the murder, Mr McRight.'

'Yeah some bloody fisherman. I was fishing down at the canal, so that's that.'

'Mr McRight, it is my duty to inform you that one of your members to the crime has turned Queens's evidence.'

'Paul McCathy wouldn't grass on me. I have no more to say.'

'Mr Michael McRight, I am charging you on the 26 day of June, you and others murdered Mr Alonzo Ortuno after holding him in captivity for at least two days at a Factory Unit No 22 at Pigeons farm Plaistow. You and others then carried the body to a vehicle, drove to the canal where you and others attached concrete to his legs, threw the body from the bridge into the canal.'

Inspector Brown asked the two constables present to remove Michael McRight to the cells.

Both Inspector Brown and Ward made their way back to the Duty room inquiring if there was any news of the capture of Ken Delanny or any sightings of Costa Esteve and his mate, Andres Lara. Sergeant Skelton reported that Ken Delanny wasn't at his pig farm when the officers had called, and unfortunately, there had been no sightings of Costa Esteve or his partner.

Bob Warden had driven over to take a look at Terry Peachy. Parking his car in the street, he noticed Detectives More and Muir leading Peachy away to their own police car. I bet it's that bloody video at the Red Lion, Bob thought, watching as they drove away.

He drove off to Brixton to meet Joe Bolt. Thirty minutes later pulling onto a roundabout at Stockwell, he noticed a prison van and out of the top part of the window he noticed Mick McRight waving and pointing. My God what's going on Bob thought. At the next window appeared Paul McCathy.

Bob pulled up a little to look at the next window just in case Liam Murphy was within, no he wasn't. Bob made signs indicating did they want anything. But the prison van turned towards Brixton Hill and Bob was moving in the other direction. Bob stopped his car at a telephone box calling Liam Murphy's mobile, it had been disconnected.

Bob got back in his car and made for Leigham court road, where he was meeting Joe Bolt. Joe was just pulling up in his car as Bob arrived. They made their way up to the bar, ordering their drinks and moving to a table by the window which overlooked a splendid flowered garden.

'Joe, I have just seen two of my mates in a prison van obviously off to Brixton remand centre. I can't believe they've been nicked I was only with them two nights ago.'

'That's the way it goes, Bob,' Joe said.

'Yeah I know, but before I was coming over to meet you I thought of going over and giving Terry Peachy a pull as I received information that he was involved with the murder of Kenny Owen. When I arrived at his street, there were two Detectives More and Muir taking Peachy away obviously to Kilburn CID. The other night when I explained to you about Jeff Mitchell being fed to the pigs, it was my two friends who had told me, now there nicked.'

'Coincidence, Bob.'

'Maybe, Joe, but it doesn't smell right,' putting his big hands on the table. 'Billy Chambers, he's the one behind so much of the trouble; he must be sorted out one way or the other.'

'Bob, if Chambers is behind Jeff Mitchell being murdered then I'm with you.' A waiter walked over to their table and asked if they were staying for lunch, Bob looked at Joe. 'That sounds good to me, this way, gentleman.'

Terry Peachy was in the interview room of Kilburn police station. 'I have nothing to say to you, Mr More.'

'Terry, Kenny Owen was murdered.'

'I had nothing to do with that. I've been cleared by Battersea CID,' exclaimed Peachy.

'No you haven't, Terry, you are still in the frame for the murder. We have information that a big robbery is going down and you're involved with Billy Chambers. Also on the day of the murder, you were seen at Kenny Owen's flat, so you are right in it up to your neck, so unless you want to go down for fifteen year stretch, you better start talking to us.'

'I've got nothing to say.'

'O dear, Rod, we'll just have to charge Terry with conspiracy to commit murder and then there's Terry going into a dead man's flat. That's going to look really good for Terry.'

Rod Muir shrugged his shoulders looked at Terry Peachy and said, 'You are really going down for this.'

‘Look I had nothing to do with the murder of Kenny Owen,’ said Terry. ‘It is true I went around to Kenny Owen’s flat because I had been tipped off there was a few thousand pounds hidden inside the flat.’

‘Who tipped you off, Terry.’

‘I can’t say, he’ll kill me.’

‘Terry, you have just admitted burglary to steal money from a dead person’s flat, now tell us who it was.’

‘I want a deal if I tell you.’

‘What sort of deal, Terry?’

‘You drop any charges of the burglary.’

‘Ok we might be able to help out there, so who was it.’

‘Billy Chambers.’

‘Now that wasn’t too hard, Terry, was it, so what do you know about this big robbery going down?’

‘Nothing.’

‘Terry, you have been seen in the Red Lion at least four times with Billy Chambers, so that’s not a coincidence and we have it on good authority that you have been in the presence of other villains, so if you want us to help you must start talking.’

‘Alright, alright. All I know is some foreigners have lined up a big robbery. If you let me out I’ll find out where the robbery is taking place and also all the names of those taking part.’

‘So you’re saying you’ll become an informer?’

‘Yes, yes. I promise.’

‘What do you think, Rod, shall we nick Terry for the burglary and then let it slip on the streets that Terry Peachy has been very helpful. Or shall we trust him and hope he keeps his word and we receive good information.’

‘Reg, I believe we should give Terry the benefit of doubt and let him slip around getting useful information for us.’

‘Terry, if you fuck us about I’ll nick you. Is that clear enough for you?’

‘Yes, Mr More, you won’t be disappointed, I promise.’

‘Ok, Terry, do you want a lift back home.’

‘No, no. I’ll walk or get a bus, thank you both.’

Reg and Rod called Ben Clark over letting him know of the new evidence gained from Terry Peachy which fitted into the murder of Kenny Owen.

‘So Billy Chambers is up to his neck in all of the capers which we are investigating,’ Ben said.

As Ben Clark and Reg More made their way out of the CID office, ‘Are we travelling with the Chief Inspector,’ asked Reg

‘No he’s gone ahead. I would imagine he was hoping to catch lunch with the Deputy Commissioner, to explain what a wonderful chap he is.’

‘Yeah that’s Bleasdale alright,’ said Reg. As they made their way to the London Tube Station catching the train across London and reaching Scotland Yard fifteen minutes before the scheduled meeting. Sergeant Hill had saved two empty seats for both Ben and Reg.

The door opened and in walked the Deputy Commissioner with Superintendent Parker.

‘Good afternoon, Ladies and Gentleman. Thank you so much for being able to be present on such short notice. I thought it would be an excellent opportunity to give you an up-to-date idea of the case so far, I now call upon Superintendent Parker.’

‘Yesterday we were very fortunate to be able to apprehend three known villains for the murder of Alonzo Ortuno. One of those apprehended has now turned queen’s evidence, giving us much insight into the pieces of the puzzle that were missing in our investigation. If you can recall at our last meeting, Chief Inspector Greedy explained that one of the stolen cars which he and his team were processing, had been found to have dirt and hairs from a pig farm.

‘Part of the evidence given from our informer was that Mr Jeffrey Mitchell who was involved with Costa Esteve and Andres Lara in the safe blowing of Mallards Publishing House was driven down to the pig farm owned by Mr Kenneth Delanny, where he was cut up and fed to the pigs.’

Gasps were heard from all the way around the room. ‘Yes, it is absolutely awful that is why these villains must be apprehended. We have a squad from the Serious Crime unit and a squad of CID officers from the Kent police searching for Kenneth Delanny.

‘And another Squad from the Serious Crime unit based at Heathrow police station searching for Costa Esteve and Andres Lara. With this new evidence of Jeffrey Mitchell being involved with the safe blowing at Mallards Publishing House, it does put doubt in the case of Ted Horn and Tommy Prince being involved with the safe blowing at Mallards Publishing House. However that is being investigated again by the Serious Crime Squad.’

'Are there any questions?'

'Yes, Sir, now we have more information about the different crimes which have been committed, are we looking to arrest Billy Chambers who appears to be in the middle of our investigations,' asked Reg More.

'Sergeant, we are dealing with the problem of Mr Chambers as we speak, hopefully in the next few days and once we have arrested Kenneth Delanny, Chambers will be arrested.'

Sergeant Hill inquired if there was any more information on the contents of the safe at Mallards. 'We are led to believe that there were in fact some treasure maps and plans pointing to the whereabouts of gold and diamonds, along with three grand.

Captain Sifre thanked all present for the wonderful way Officer Egido and himself had been treated. 'We have without doubt learnt a lot about British policing and we are positive that once back in Spain one of our top criminals Carlos Moran who we believe is mixed up in these terrible crimes, will come to justice.'

The Deputy Commissioner rose and thanked everybody for attending and their inputs into the crimes. 'Refreshments will be served in the adjacent room.'

Ben Clark and Reg More made their way back to Kilburn CID office, where Rod Muir was waiting to be briefed on the meeting. After being told that it was now believed that Ted Horn and Tommy Prince may not be involved with the Mallards safe blowing, because of new evidence received by the informer, who had indicated it was Jeff Mitchell and for his part was cut up and fed to the pigs.

'How did Bleasdale take that information?' asked Rod.

'We are unsure as he was very quiet and never looked over at us or made any comments after the meeting,' replied Ben. 'However, our main objective is this big robbery going down. We must push for information from our snouts, with Alex hopefully back with us tomorrow, we will be at full strength.'

Ben Clark made his way to meet up with Bob Warden and hopefully receive some more information. Bob was already seated at the corner table by the window as Ben walked in. Ben's pint was on the table waiting for him.

'Cheers mate,' said Ben, 'you don't look so happy today, Bob. What's up?'

'Every avenue I've taken today just hasn't worked out for me.'

'That's the way it goes sometimes, Bob.'

'My day hasn't been that bad, there's been a break through. Plaistow CID, apprehended and later arrested and charged three villains for the murder of

Alonzo Ortuno, fortunately one of them has turned queen's evidence. And has been placed in a safe house, he has already started to give information. The other two are in remand at Brixton Prison.

'There was confirmation that Jeff Mitchell was definitely fed to the pigs by Ken Delanny, a warrant has been issued for Delanny's arrest and it looks like Jeff Mitchell carried out the safe blowing at Mallards with unnamed persons. If that is proved Ted Horn and Tommy Prince will be free just as you had mentioned, Bob.

'This Terry Peachy was picked up today by Reg More and Rod Muir. Peachy told them both that he had definitely gone to Kenny Owen's flat because he had been tipped off by Billy Chambers that Kenny kept a great deal of money hidden. Lastly, a large search in the Heathrow area is on its way to apprehend Costa Esteve and Andres Lara, as we are focusing on this big robbery going down'

'Your team, Ben, must be very proud of themselves.'

'Not really, Bob, mainly it is the Serious Crime Squad who managed to have the villain turn queen's evidence.'

'That's a great achievement, Ben. What's the supergrass's name?'

'You know better than that Bob. Would you like another pint, Bob?'

'Ben, if you don't mind I'm going to get an early night.'

'Ok, see you in a couple of days, Bob.'

Bob made his way to the woodpecker arms to meet Joe Bolt thinking as he drove which of his three mates had turned queen's evidence, which ultimately would put himself at great risk.

He needed to speak with Liam, Mick or Paul but they were inside the prison. Bob couldn't go along and visit them as all visitors were policed.

Joe had a table in the salon bar with a pint of the best for Bob which was on the table, and a Gin and Tonic for himself. Walking into the bar, he sat down picked up his pint and said cheers.

'Joe, the info I received tonight definitely puts Jeff Mitchell as the safe blower at Mallards with unnamed persons. The old bill have got themselves a supergrass, and I need help contacting somebody in the remand wing at Brixton.'

'Leave that to me, Bob, I'll have a word around tonight. Where can I contact you.'

'I'll be at home, Joe.' Finishing their drinks they made off in different directions.

Costa Esteve and Andres Lara had met up with Big Sam.

'How's it all going, Sam?'

'We are nearly there, Costa, just one more meeting this week for the final planning. We've had a small problem with the bridge over the river and its chain, but it's all go.'

'That's good news, Sam. I have been thinking of the robbery. What if I give you Andres here,' looking sideways at him, 'in another car to help get some of the gang and money away.'

Sam looked at Andres, 'Nothing against you Andres but we like people we know and trust as it's our liberty at stake.'

'I can understand, Sam, but you need another car and driver really.'

'We've already discussed that, Costa. I'll give it some thought and talk it over with the lads.'

'I'll leave it to you, Sam, give me a call.'

Driving off Sam was thinking the matter over perhaps another car and driver would be useful. I'll see what the lads have to say.

Costa and Andres entered the Elevated Club and ordered a bottle of red wine 'I told you, Andres, Sam will think about the situation, and sure as eggs are eggs, you will be driving the getaway car with the money inside.'

'That's fine, but how are we going to get the money away from Big Sam's gang'

'That's going to be my master stroke, Andres. Billy Chambers will be waiting with his friends they'll shoot the villains in your car. Then you'll drive the car back to our place, we will keep our head down for a week and then catch the private aircraft out to Spain.'

'What about Billy Chambers?

'He will carry out the job for five hundred thousand pound, which is less than we are paying each member of Sam's gang, so we save a fortune.'

'Big Sam will come after us.'

'No I don't think so. I have a nasty surprise for Big Sam. Billy Chambers will let the police know where Sam Davidson is living and all the names of his gang.'

'We are taking a big risk, Costa.'

'Andres, I have collated the risk,' with a big smile on his face, 'Drink up, my friend.'

Captain Sifre had arranged dinner inviting Gloria and Alex. 'Alex, this is our last night in London, it's been a great pleasure having you with us. We are going to celebrate with a bottle of Champaign. Finishing their dinner, Captain Sifre mentioned that he was going to have an early night and reminded Alex that he was to collect them at 7.00.

'No problem, Sir.' Alex and Gloria decided that it would be better if they also returned to the hotel. 'Let's have one more drink, Gloria, as I have something to say,' ordering another half bottle of Champaign.

'Gloria, what would you do if I went to work for my uncle in Majorca.'

'I would hope to come over and see you as much as I could.'

'What if I suggested we got married?'

'Are you serious, Alex?'

'Yes, deadly serious.'

'I would certainly consider your proposal. I could transfer to Palmer.'

'Ok, Gloria, tomorrow I'll call my uncle, and perhaps we could fly over to Palmer and look around.'

'That sounds wonderful, Alex.' Drinking there glasses dry, they made their way back through the streets of London to their hotel.

Alex drove Captain Sifre and Gloria to Heathrow airport arriving at terminal 2 at 9.I0, after seeing them both to the departure lounge. The Captain turned to Alex saying, 'I am sure I'll be seeing you in Madrid.' Turning to Gloria and winking. Alex watched as they disappeared through the lounge, thinking to himself if it hadn't been for those murders, I would have never met Gloria.

Reg More and Rod Muir were talking to Ben Clark about pulling in Billy Chambers.

'Reg, you heard Superintendent Parker, the Serious Crime squad are looking into Chambers and Ken Delanny, so we must wait,' answered Ben Clark.

The CID door opened with Chief Inspector Bleasdale stomping in and looking directly at Reg More. 'I suppose you are full of yourself, Sergeant, over the information that Horn and Prince may not be guilty, but let me tell you, Sergeant, that unless this informer of the Serious Crime Squad comes across with evidence supporting his theory, Horn and Prince remain in prison.'

'Yes, Sir. By the way Chief Inspector we were just talking about Billy Chambers.'

'Why are you talking about him. It was made thoroughly clear at yesterday's meeting that the Serious Crime squad are looking into Mr Chambers. So get on with getting results on this big robbery.' Turning on his heals and stomping back out of the door. They all looked at each other. 'Obviously, Bleasdale got a rocket stuck up his backside from Scotland Yard yesterday,' said Ben Clark.

Sergeant Abrahams from the Serious Crime Squad telephoned Inspector Brown. 'We have found Kenneth Delanny. He's hiding out in a house in Maidstone.'

'I'll give Chief Inspector Greedy a call and have him liaise with you near the house concerned.'

Unfortunately, it took some time for Chief Inspector Greedy to arrive, the Serious Crime Squad knocked on the door. There was no answer. A couple of the officers walked around to the back entrance where they found the door open. Searching the house, it was found to be empty, but cups of warm coffee were on the table.

'We must have just missed him, Sergeant.' Abrahams called Inspector Brown, explaining that Ken Delanny had slipped through their net.

'Any ideas, Sergeant?'

'Not as yet, Sir. I'll call you as soon as possible,' putting the telephone down.

Chief Inspector Greedy received information from his technical people, that the fingerprints found on Peter Sainsbury's passport belonged to Mr Terrance Churchill. C.I. Greedy sent the file over to Superintendent Parker's office.

Superintendent Parker walked along the corridor, down the stairs and into the Serious Crime office. Seeing Inspector Brown and Inspector Ward, he placed a file on Inspector Browns desk. 'It appears that fingerprints found on Peter Sainsbury's passport are those of an old friend of ours, Terry Churchill.'

'I remember Churchill. I put him away for five years for forgery,' said Brown.

'Then he's at it again.'

Inspector Brown checked his computer for the address of Terrance Churchill, Norwood road.

D.C. Hirani and DC Smithy drove down to Norwood road. Looking out of their car window at the park, that park looks great for a nice hot day just lazing about on the grass.

Knocking on the front door which had a grained wood stained door. The door was opened by a small fat guy, his shirt wide open showing a little hairy chest.

'Mr Churchill please.'

'He's not here.'

'Then we'll wait for him.'

‘Not possible,’ at the same time trying to shut the door.

DC Hirani stuck his foot in the door preventing the door to close

‘Take your foot away Mr or its going to get hurt.’ Both Detectives pushed hard on the door, pushing the fat man up against the wall.

‘Serious Crime Squad,’ they shouted. ‘What’s your name and where is Terry Churchill?’

‘Terry, run it’s the old bill,’ he shouted.

‘Hold him Smithy.’ As Hirani rushed up the stairs he could smell burning. As he reached the first floor, looking up further he could see a person trying to get out of the window. Hirani was up the next flight of stairs in a flash grabbing the person by the arm and pulling him back inside pushing him onto the green cord carpet.

‘Mr Churchill I presume.’

‘I’ve done nothing.’

‘Then why run off.’

‘Smithy, bring the fat guy upstairs and take a look around the first floor.’ Smithy with one hand on the fat man’s arm, he poked his head in the first room on the left which was a bathroom. There in the bath were smouldering passports. Smithy pushed the fat guy into the bathroom further, pulled a vase off the window ledge and poured the contents onto the bundle of smouldering passports.

Smithy shouted up at Hirani, ‘Bring Terry Churchill down stairs.’

‘Well, well, Terry. What have we here. Passports, so you’re at your old game.’

‘I’m not saying a word.’

‘You don’t have to, Terry, we’ve got the evidence right here. Terrance Churchill, I am arresting you on forgery charges. What you do say might be taken down and used in evidence. Handcuff them together, Smithy, while I put a call through to the yard and get some more officers down here.’

Ten minutes later two police cars arrived outside. Officers jumped out of the cars and into the flat. D.C. Hirani told them to search the flat from top to bottom. The technical boys were next to arrive, who found printing press equipment for printing euro notes and passports.

D.C. Hirani told the technical boys that there was a bundle of burnt passports in the bathroom on the first floor. D.C. Smithy in the meantime had asked the fat guy for some identification, ‘Ok what’s your name?’,

‘I haven’t anything to say.’

'Ok fat man, forgery and defrauding, the crown are enough to send you down for ten years at least.'

'Don't say a word,' shouted Churchill, as they were lead away.

'Terry, you're in enough trouble. You'll be going down for at least a fifteen with your form. We already have a supergrass who is talking his head off. How do you think we found you.'

'My life is more important than talking to you, Mr Brown, they would kill me and that's for sure.'

'Nobody would be able to reach you, Terry, while you with us'

'You're joking, Mr Brown. These people are really a heavy mob, they would be able to reach anybody at any time.'

'Terry, what age are you now; 49, 50?'

'I'm 5I.'

'In normal circumstances, you would get out when your 65, but being an accessory to murder and not giving up any information, I'll make sure you go for a twenty, that way you wouldn't be coming out until you were 7I. I'm going to leave you for ten minutes, so you can have a good think about your future. D.C. Hirani will remain here with you.' Inspector Brown left the interview room.

'Mr Hirani, help me. I'll make it worth your while.'

'What on earth could you possible offer me?'

'A million euros.'

'A million euros; Terry, you won't have that money for long, your flat's being pulled apart.'

'They're never find it and don't expect Keylock to know where it is, 'he hasn't a clue; now be a good cop and let me go.'

'Terry, if I were you, I would start talking fast if you want help.' Thc door of the interview room opened and in walked Inspector Brown.

'Ok, Terry, I can't mess about with you anymore. The situation is this, your fingerprints were found on the passport of Peter Sainsbury who was murdered, so I can only imagine that you were involved in his murder.'

'No, Mr Brown I had nothing to do with the murder of Peter Sainsbury. I'll admit I made his passport, that's why it has my fingerprints. But murder, no way that's not my style.'

'You have one chance, Terry, tell us who ordered the passports and what you know about the murder of Peter Sainsbury.'

'I'm sorry, Mr Brown, my family will be killed.'

'Terry, what's it going to be fifteen to twenty?'

'Alright, Mr Brown, I was approached by Billy Chambers who asked me if I would be interested in preparing a number of passports for some foreigners. Chambers told me they would pay over the odds for the merchandise. A week went by when I was introduced to Costa Esteve and Andres Lara by Billy Chambers.

'They ordered seven passports at an agreed price of thirty thousand pounds. Some weeks later, another foreigner approached me saying he was a friend of Billy Chambers and asked me to prepare another passport for a further ten thousand pounds. I was warned by this Miguel Melgar guy, that if I mentioned any of this to a soul, I would be cut up and fed to the pigs. I told him he had no worries of me informing. The following day, Miguel Melgar and Juan Riminez brought me the photograph of the person they wanted the passport for.'

'Did you know who this person was?'

'Not at the time, it wasn't until some two weeks later that I noticed his photo in the newspapers.'

'What did you do?'

'Nothing. I was so frightened to do anything.'

'The six new passports, do you know the names of the people?'

'No, Mr Brown, I haven't got a clue as the photographs aren't being delivered to me until next Friday, and they want to collect the passports by the following Friday.'

'What do you know about this big robbery going down?'

'I have no idea about any robbery, Mr Brown.'

'Ok, Terry, that will do for now, we will speak later when I have had a chance to speak with Superintendent Parker about your situation.'

'You'll put in a good word for me, won't you as I will be very helpful.'

Inspector Brown walked next door to interview room 4. 'How's Mr Keylock performing, Inspector Ward'

'Oscar is being very helpful at the moment; he was present at Norwood Road when Billy Chambers brought Costa Esteve and Andres Lara to meet Terry Churchill and talked about preparing seven passports. Oscar also tells us that a vast amount of euros were ordered by Costa Esteve to be taken to Spain.'

'What have you heard about a big robbery going down, Oscar?'

‘I haven’t heard anything about a robbery and nothing was spoken about a robbery to Terry while he was in my presence, they only spoke about passports and euros.’

‘Oscar, you are facing a long jail time for your part in this caper, probably twelve years, however I have an idea that if you agree and you help catch these villains; we will make sure you get off with a suspended sentence.’

‘I don’t want to go to prison, Mr Brown. I’ll do anything you want.’

‘Remember, Oscar, if you do a runner, we’ll find you and send you to prison and let people know you informed on them. Do you understand?’

‘Yes, Mr Brown.’

‘Ok this is what I want you to do, we’ll take you back to Norwood Road. You will wait for somebody to contact you asking for Terry Churchill. You will indicate Terry is away on business but has left instructions to collect the photographs, and the new passports will be prepared for collection by the following Friday. Now this is our contact telephone number it will operate twenty-four hours a day seven days a week. You will call us as soon as contact has been made. Is that understood?’

‘Yes, Mr Brown.’

‘Lastly, you will tell nobody that your flat in Norwood road was searched by the police.’

‘Yes, Mr Brown, you can rely on me.’

‘D.C, Smithy will have your statement typed out and you will then sign it and remember not a word to anybody.’

As the two inspectors walked down the corridor, Inspector Ward turned to Inspector Brown saying, ‘Don’t you think we are taking a huge chance on Oscar Keylock?’

‘No he’s a weasel and will work for the highest bidder; in this case us. he’ll inform and turn his back on friends when it suits him.’

‘That’s what worries me.’

‘We’ll monitor the telephones at his flat twenty-four hours a day, that way we will know if he is giving us a load of bollocks.’

‘Let’s take a look at those burnt passports then we will interview Terry Churchill again.’ Looking over to the other side of the squad office, Inspector Brown shouted over to Detective Facer. ‘Get our special black cab ready. I want you to drop Oscar Keylock back at his flat in thirty minutes.’ Next Inspector Brown telephoned his specialist team.

'Have you finished at the flat?'

'Yes, Inspector, but we were unable to find any more passports or monies.'

'Have you fitted our gear to all the telephones?'

'All connected and ready, Inspector.'

'Billy Chambers name is cropping up everywhere; he is obviously at the centre of all these crimes. It's time to bring him in for an interview, shall we pull him or let Kilburn CID have the pleasure.'

'Let Kilburn have him.'

'Chief Inspector Bleasdale, I wonder if we could ask a favour. Would it be possible for your CID officers to pull in Billy Chambers for an interview,' asked Inspector Brown.

'Yes that would be our pleasure.'

Bleasdale with a big smile on his face trotted off down stairs to the CID office. 'Reg, I have considered your opinion to pull in Billy Chambers for interview, so go ahead let's have him in.'

Detective Facer was waiting with his cab as D.C. Hirani brought Oscar Keylock out of the Yard putting him into the black cab. 'Oscar, you know what to do,' shutting the cab door and walking away. D.C. Facer drove off towards Norwood Road.

The traffic was light for this time of day and shouldn't take long to reach Norwood Road. Keylock sat in the back of the cab as it went over Westminster Bridge turned right along the embankment. Twenty minutes later, he pulled up outside his flat in Norwood Road. Oscar Keylock jumped out of the cab like nothing had happened and walked to the front door opened the door and walked in.

Inspector Brown and Ward stood in the corridor speaking with D.C. Hirani and Smithy, 'Ok you two go and give it the works.'

As they sat in the interview room with Terry Churchill, D.C. Hirani suggested that he was about to remove the tapes so they would be able to speak openly.

'I have been thinking about the offer you spoke about,' Churchill looked at DC Smithy. 'Don't worry about him he's with me if the offer is right.'

'Can you get me out of here?'

'We think so. It's going to be difficult but we have a plan.'

'Well my offer still stands one million euros, split between yourselves, if you get me out.'

'Ok where's the money?'

No, no you get me out first, the money and passports are well hidden.'

'Terry, you'll do a runner on us and we'll be in the shit.'

'If you get me out, I would slip away to France on one of my passports and then the worlds easy from there.'

'Sure, Terry, we can see you'll be ok, but it's our careers that are on the line.'

'I promise you you'll get your money.'

'Promises do not pay the bills, Terry. Ok Smithy I'm going to replace the tape and carry on with the interview.' Smithy nodded.

'Hold on a minute,' Terry said. 'I've got the money hidden in the flat.'

'Terry, your flat's been searched top to bottom, there's no money or passports.'

'Don't make me laugh. Your people couldn't find cookie in a candy store. I'll have to show you'

'Of course you want out, Terry, and then you're on your toes and Smithy and I have egg all over our faces. No Terry, you go back to the cells overnight and think it over, we'll make sure we are the officers who interview you tomorrow.'

'No wait, I want a lawyer.'

'Don't be silly, Terry, nobody knows you are here.' Hirani pressed the button and the burly constable returned and led Churchill away back to the cells, both Inspector Brown and Ward walked into the interview room.

'That sounded great lads well done. I think he'll crack at the next interview.'

Alex Quirk walked into the CID office at Kilburn. Reg and Rod both spoke at the same time.

'Look who's here, the holiday maker.'

'Yeah, yeah very funny,' replied Alex. 'So what's happening?

'Reg looked up saying all we seem to-do is look at Sergeant Weber's surveillance tapes, however we have been given the green light to pull in Billy Chambers so that should be fun.'

Ben Clark looked up and waved with his hand for Alex to come closer whispering, 'Don't forget we have a meeting with Bob Warden tomorrow night.' Alex nodded and gave the thumbs up sign. The CID office door opened and Chief Inspector Bleasdale poked his head around the door.

'Clark, tomorrow morning Horn and Prince are in court. I would like you to accompany me, as I shall be opposing any attempts of a release by their Lawyer Kerry Dickson, so meet me at I0.30.

Billy Chambers had heard about Terry Peachy being pulled in by Kilburn CID after making his way to Peachy's flat and looking around in case any of the old bill were hanging around. Billy walked up to the front door and rang the doorbell.

'Hallo, Billy, what are you doing over this way.'

'I had to see a couple of friends, so knowing you lived here, I thought I'd pop in and have a chat.'

'Come on in, would you like a beer or something.'

'No I'll come straight to the point, Terry. I've been told you were pulled in by the old bill.'

'Yeah, that's right. They wanted to know about people in the Red Lion and what was I doing at Kenny Owens's flat.'

'Now that's interesting, Terry, why would they ask you that?'

'I'm not sure really. I told them the Red Lion was my local.'

'Did they ask you who was in the pub, like me for instance?'

'Yeah funny enough. I told them that I occasionally saw you and would have a pint with you and many other friends. As for the Kenny Owen business, I told them that I visited him from time to time.'

'You made a bad mistake Terry. The old bill know you were already pulled in by Battersea CID. Now tell me you prat, you grassed on me, didn't you?'

'No, Billy, I wouldn't do that.'

Terry hadn't noticed that Billy Chambers was wearing gloves.

'No Billy, please I haven't grassed honestly.'

It was far too late Billy Chambers pulled out his gun which had a silencer attached and pulled the trigger twice. There was just muffled shots. Terry just stared at Billy Chambers as he fell to the ground. Billy looked around checking there was nothing to connect him with Peachy.

Walking over to the back window, looking out, all he could see was an overgrown garden path leading to a rotten gate. Billy walked down the path through the gate which wouldn't close and walked smartly down the road towards his car.

Thinking the old bill must have followed Peachy to the Red Lion seen him drinking with me and put two and two together, so I wonder what information Peachy gave the old bill.

Billy drove back to the Red Lion, parking his car and walked inside. Sergeant Weber muttered into his tape, 'Billy Chambers has entered the Red Lion.'

Captain Sifre was looking out the window of his corner office, when Sergeant Gillispe entered holding a number of files. The captain turned and looked over to him.

'I see we have a lot of work ahead of us, Sergeant.'

'I afraid so, Sir,' planting the files on the Captain's desk for his perusal. The door opened and in walked officer Egido, pointing out that there was nothing new on the forgery angle.

'What about Carlos Moran?'

'We have him under twenty-four hour surveillance.'

The Captain having quickly finished examining the files, looked at the two officers. 'We must be overlooking something.'

The three of them sat down around the table going through the files. After an hour all getting tired, Officer Egido looked up. 'Captain, I may have found something here.'

'Pablo Llorens worked with Carlos Moran who employed him as a hit man. Llorens served six years in prison and Moran was his lawyer at the time.'

'My God, how did we miss that?'

'Get everything we have on Pablo Llorens.'

'Four years ago, Llorens was mixed up with Carlos Moran on a property scam in Palmer Majorca,' said Sergeant Gillispe.

'Captain, do you think the information received about a second gang working in the UK, is actually Carlos Moran.'

'Quite possible; this is going to be a long day and night, so settle in we must find out more about any associates of Llorens and Moran.'

Ben Clark was in the CID office, knowing that he had to accompany Chief Inspector Bleasdale to the court hearing of Ted Horn and Tommy Prince. He wasn't looking forward to be present as he was sure that both Horn and Prince were innocent of the Mallards Safe blowing. Realising that if Jeff Mitchell had carried out the Safe blowing, he wouldn't have been working with Horn and Prince according to the information received from Bob Warden.

Bleasdale was hoping for promotion if he could get Horn and Prince convicted which would be a big plus for Bleasdale at Scotland Yard.

The CID office door opened and in walked Alex, Reg and Rod.

'Morning, Ben,' shouted Reg More. 'Anything new in?'

'Somebody robbed a cleaning company of their wages.'

'How much was stolen,' inquired Reg.

‘Six grand, nice for a mornings work,’ said Ben.

‘D.C. THornson and Cattrict are over there; the information passed back so far is that there are a number of iffy window cleaners working for the company. I’ve already put some of the names through the computer and left the others for you to do while I’m at court with Bleasdale.’

The door opened and in walked the Chief Inspector, ‘Are you ready, Clark.’

All in the CID office started laughing. ‘Who would want to have to suffer Chief Inspector Bleasdale for the day.’

Ben Clark pulled up outside the court and Bleasdale rushed inside, while Ben parked the car. Bleasdale found Jonathon Crisp standing over a desk reading the documents.

‘Good morning, Jonathon.’

‘Morning, Chief Inspector. I’ve been going through these documents on Horn and Prince. I believe we might be in for a rough ride from Miss Kerry Dickson. She is bound to go for dismissal and ask us to drop the charges.’

‘Jonathon, Miss Dickson is going to be very disappointed as I want those two kept on remand. We have several murders connected to this Mallards robbery and the Serious Crime Squad are looking at connexions between not only Horn and Prince but other well-known villains.’

‘That may be so, Chief Inspector, but the case is a little shaky. We will have to tread carefully and hope the court sees it our way.’ The door opened and in walked Ben Clark. Jonathon looked up. ‘Good morning, Sergeant Clark.’ There was a further knock on the door and in walked Miss Kerry Dickson. ‘Well if only the Devil could cast his net now.’

‘Good morning, Kerry,’ said Jonathon.

‘Morning, Jonathon. I’m pleased you are all hear, as I shall be going for dismissal of all charges for my clients Mr Horn and Mr Prince.’

Chief Inspector Bleasdale cleared his throat. ‘Miss Dickson we will have to see about that.’

The Court was called to order. Bleasdale sat with Ben Clark and Jonathon Crisp. Miss Kerry Dickson stood and asked that all charges to be dropped against her clients, Mr Edward Horn and Mr Thomas Prince, as she believed there was not enough evidence to convict them for the safe blowing at Mallards Publishing House. Jonathon Crisp smartly rose saying that unfortunately the Mallards safe job was only the tip of the iceberg, as a number of very serious crimes had been committed.

Mr Horn and Mr Prince are very high on the agenda which as we speak are being investigated by the Serious Crime Squad from Scotland Yard. As you will have read in the newspapers, one of the murderers has now turned queen's evidence. The Serious Crime Squad with this new evidence are looking further into many different crimes including this one. Therefore, on behalf of the Commissioner of police, I ask that Mr Edward Horn and Mr Thomas Prince be committed and remanded.

Miss Dickson tried to overcome the supergrass part but was shouted down by the Judge, who agreed with Jonathon Crisp that Mr Horn and Mr Prince should be committed and remanded to the Old Bailey.

Horn stood up and shouted, 'This is a bloody setup we're innocent.'

'Take them down,' said the Judge.

Jonathon turned to the Chief Inspector. 'Let's hope your supergrass has more information as we may not be so lucky at the next appearance of Mr Horn and Prince.

As the Chief Inspector and Ben Clark made their way from the court to their parked car. Miss Kerry Dickson was holding court with at least three newspapers, who looked over catching sight of Chief Inspector Bleasdale, they made a move towards him.

'Would you give us more details of this supergrass, Chief Inspector?'

'I have no comment.' As Bleasdale climbed into the car, the newspaper photographers were taking photos of both Bleasdale and Ben Clark as they pulled away.

'I told you, Clark, bloody lawyers.'

'Yes, Sir.'

'How did it go, Ben,' asked Reg More. 'Jonathon Crisp believes we need more evidence against Horn and Prince. However, the supergrass bit went well. The newspapers were outside the court and were all over us like a rash, taking photos of us leaving.'

Inspector Brown was on his way back to Scotland Yard after speaking with Liam Murphy. Murphy had given the Inspector more information on the whereabouts of Ken Delanny. Inspector Brown was worrying about the safety of Liam Murphy once that his mates found out he was the supergrass. Murphy had already given up many criminals who had carried out robberies and other criminal activities which would clear up many of the outstanding case files.

As Inspector Brown walked into his office, Inspector Ward gave him the up-to-date agenda. Oscar Keylock was safely back at his flat in Norwood Road. There had been no contact made from the outside, the telephone was bugged and working. Inspector Brown told Ward about the possible whereabouts of Ken Delanny, also mentioning he had received information on another ten robberies, with the names of those who had been involved.

So Liam Murphy is earning his keep. Brown called D.C. Facer to collate the names against those robberies and have the villains picked up. 'Inspector Ward, take a team to this address and hopefully we'll pick up Ken Delanny, take no chances. Delanny is dangerous and is probably armed.'

Inspector Brown entered Superintendent Parker's office. 'I received a call from the duty inspector from Westend Magistrates Court telling me that at least three newspapers interviewed Horn and Prince's lawyer, Miss Kerry Dickson. Who complained that her clients had been set up by the police and that a new supergrass had been giving information regarding a number of murders relating to the Mallards publishing house robbery.

'The information I received from Liam Murphy, Superintendent, defiantly points to Jeffrey Mitchell and unknown accomplices carrying out the safe blowing at Mallards, so we need to follow up that lead.'

'I'm going to see the Deputy Commissioner, so I will leave it to you to follow up the business of Jeffery Mitchell and who may be his accomplices.' Inspector Brown headed back to his office making the first call to Ben Clark asking his opinion on Jeffery Mitchell and who could his accomplices be, if Mitchell had pulled the Mallards job.

'Mitchell has worked with a number of known villains Sir, I will have their names faxed over to you'.

Superintendent Parker had spent a couple of hours with the Deputy Commissioner running over the complete case. It was becoming blatantly obvious that the information received from Liam Murphy that Jeffrey Mitchell had carried out the safe blowing and not Horn and Prince, so it must be investigated very quickly without a lot of fuss.

It was agreed that Chief Inspector Bleasdale should be given the chance to have the matter investigated at his end. the Deputy Commissioner lifted his telephone and spoke with Chief Inspector Bleasdale.

Ben Clark was summoned to Bleasdale's office. 'Scotland Yard want us to follow up on the information that Jeffrey Mitchell carried out the safe blowing and who were his accomplices' on the robbery, so you and Alex Quirk will look into the affair without causing fuss in the CID office.'

'Yes, Sir.'

Ben returned to the CID office. 'Where's Reg and Rod?'

'They received a tip-off on that cleaning company robbery, so they have gone to interview Paul Bailey.'

'Bleasdale received the green light for us to follow up on the Jeff Mitchell part of the Mallards safe blowing; we need to know who might have been with Mitchell.'

Reg More walked across the road towards Paul Bailey's flat. Rod Muir had parked the car when he looked over, seeing Billy Chambers standing on the corner of the road watching Reg Muir knocking on the door of the flat. Chambers hadn't noticed Rod Muir walking towards him, until Muir was in the middle of the road.

Chambers ducked around the corner jumped over a small wall and ran along the path and into the shopping centre. Rod reached the corner of the road looking up and down the street but couldn't see Chambers anywhere. He continued looking along the road over small hedges and walls.

'Nothing. Chambers had vanished.' Rod walked back to the front of Paul Baileys flat.

'Where have you been, Rod?'

'Billy Chambers was standing on the corner of the road watching you. I walked across towards him, when he saw me and vanished.'

Reg knocked again on the door and this time Paul Bailey opened the door.

'cor blimey, what do you two want?'

'A chat Paul. Are you going to invite us in?'

'Get fucked.'

'Thank you, Mr Bailey, you better get your coat as you will be accompanying us to Kilburn Police Station to enable us to eliminate you from our inquires.'

'What inquires? Betty, the old bill are taking me down to Kilburn police Station.' Betty Bailey ran from the kitchen to the front door.

'Why don't you bastards leave us alone. Paul's done nothing.'

'Thank you, Mrs Bailey, for your concern.' Reg on one side of Paul Bailey and Rod on the other side walked across the road putting Paul Bailey in the back of the car. As they drove towards Kilburn Police Station, Reg turned towards

Rod Muir saying, 'I wonder what Billy Chambers was doing on the corner of the road watching Paul's flat.'

'Now you listen to me, you pair of bustards, I have nothing to do with Billy Chambers.'

'O dear Paul, we have it on reliable information that you and Billy Chambers along with two other villains held up and robbed a cleaning company in the West End.'

'Not me. I didn't have anything to do with a cleaning company robbery.'

'Have it your way, Bailey,' said Rod. Pulling their car into the police yard, they made their way to interview room 6.

'Wait a minute, you two, I want to make a statement to the desk sergeant.' The Sergeant shrugged his shoulders, retrieved a piece of police paper and looked at Paul Bailey.

'Full name, date of Birth and address.' Paul Bailey gave his details.

'Sergeant, I have no idea why I am here. I had nothing to do with any cleaning company robbery in the West End, and had nothing to do with Billy Chambers, now I want my solicitor here.'

'Have you anyone in mind, Mr Bailey,' asked the desk sergeant.

'Yes I want John Garret,' giving the telephone number'

'Fine, Mr Bailey, we will give him a call, in the meantime you can cool off in cell No 15.'

'Now wait a minute, I want to go to the interview room.'

'Sorry, Mr Bailey, but as you are a suspect on a robbery, you will wait in the cells.'

As Paul Bailey was led away he turned to see both Reg More and Rod Muir smiling.

'You won't get away with this set up, you two pair of bastards,' shouted Paul Bailey.

Reg and Rod made their way back to the CID office where Ben Clark and Alex Quirk were tiding their papers on their desks.

'How did it go, Reg?'

'We pulled Paul Bailey in for questioning, but when we arrived at the front desk he shouted he wanted to make a statement to the Desk Sergeant. Which he did saying he knew nothing about any robbery and wanted his solicitor present'

'Anybody we know?'

'O yes, John Garret.'

'That's Billy Chambers solicitor. I've just seen his name on the computer. Yes he defended Billy Chambers 5 and 8 years ago; he was successful both times and now he's Bailey's solicitor as well,' said Alex.

'The funny thing is, Rod noticed Billy Chambers standing on the corner of Paul Bailey's road but as Rod approached Chambers did a quick vanishing trick.'

'Reg, you better give Inspector Brown a call, as he is looking for any details on Billy Chambers, especially if he might be connected to a robbery this morning.'

'See you both in the morning; we've got a snout to interview.'

Reg More telephoned Inspector Brown, telling him all about Billy Chambers being seen on the corner of Paul Bailey's road and that Bailey had requested a solicitor named John Garret who also happened to be Billy Chambers solicitor.

'Do you believe that Chambers might be connected to this cleaning company robbery?'

'It's quite possible, Inspector.'

'Then as soon as Bailey's solicitor arrives put the pressure on Bailey, if he cracks about Chambers, let me know immediately.'

Inspector Brown put the telephone down in its cradle. 'D.C. Hirani, has Inspector Ward called in?'

'No, Sir.'

Ben Clark and Alex Quirk were sitting in the Horse and Groom salon bar waiting for Bob Warden and chatting about the day's events. 'Billy Chambers seems to be involved with everything going on. It's a wonder that the Serious Crime Squad haven't picked Chambers up already,' said Alex.

'I believe they have enough on their hands, they want Chambers all right and when we pick Chambers up, the Serious Crime Squad will appear very quickly.'

'Yes you're probably right there, Ben.' At that moment the salon bar door opened and in walked Bob Warden.

'What you drinking guys?'

'Pints please. Bob.' Paying for the drinks Bob put them on a tray and brought them over to the table in the corner.

'Had a good day, lads?' asked Bob'

'Yeah not too bad.'

'Well let's hope I can make your day. There was a robbery in the West End at a Cleaning Company, four people were involved Billy Chambers, Paul Bailey, Ken Harvey and Michael Staler. Harvey was nicked for car thefts and Staler for some fraud at some post offices. However, on the robbery Staler was the driver and Chambers, Bailey and Harvey carried out the robbery. I really hope this information helps you put Billy Chambers in prison as I have many friends of Kenny Owen inside, who would love to make life very unconformable for Mr Chambers. So what you got for me?'

'Bob, not a lot. The Serious Crime Squad has decided that the information received on the safe blowing at Mallards is defiantly correct and Jeff Mitchell was the one involved. Therefore, they are looking for Jeff Mitchell accomplices; they are also arresting many villains on the evidence of this supergrass, clearing up a long list of unsolved robberies.'

'That's certainly great for the Serious Crime Squad. What about the Irish gang from the other side of the water?'

'I already told you before, Bob, one of them has turned queen's evidence and is giving lots of information.'

'Well, chaps, if there's nothing else, I'm off as I have a date tonight.'

'Ok Bob, have a great night; we'll see you in three days.'

'Fine, see you both.' As Bob walked out the door Alex said, 'I don't trust that guy why's he giving us information'

'Alex, I'm of the same opinion. I'm unsure why he continues asking about the Irish gang. The other day, I noticed the witness statement saying that there was four members involved in throwing Alonzo Ortuno's body in the canal, so perhaps Bob Warden was the fourth member of that gang, Alex.'

'It sounds a bit iffy to say the least, Ben. We better get back to Kilburn and let Reg and Rod know about our tip-off.

Returning to the CID office, Reg and Rod were already interviewing Paul Bailey; they walked along to the interview room knocked on the door. Ben poked his head around the door, 'May I have a word please.'

Reg and Rod came into the corridor.

'I just received information from our snout on your Cleaning Company robbery. The four involved are Bailey, Chambers and Ken Harvey who carried out the robbery and Michael Staler, who was the driver.'

'That's great info, Ben; we'll put the pressure on Bailey now.'

'I'll call Inspector Brown letting him know about Billy Chambers.'

'Ok, Ben.'

Returning to the interview room, Reg More sat tapping his hand on the table, looked up at Paul Bailey and his solicitor. 'Further information has been received on the robbery at the cleaning company. Your accomplices were Billy Chambers, Ken Harvey and Michael Staler who acted as the getaway driver.'

'My client hasn't anything to say at the present time,' said John Garret.

'Mr Paul Bailey, I am arresting you in connection with the robbery at Day's Cleaning Company at 228 Devonshire way, West End. Anything you say will be recorded and could be used in evidence,' said Reg More.

'My client hasn't anything further to add, however I would like some time with my client'

'That's fine, Mr Garret, there will be a constable outside the door.'

Ben Clark called Inspector Brown, laying out all the information received from his snout; also Reg More and Rod Muir were interviewing Paul Bailey at this present time.

'Really good news, Ben, well done. We'll have Billy Chambers picked up and brought to Kilburn. I want to see John Garret's face when he realises that Chambers has been nicked and we'll let Chambers believe that Paul Bailey has grassed.'

A warrant was issued and Inspector Brown along with D.C. Hirani and Smithy travelled to Chambers known address, without success, 'they made their way to the Red Lion.

Billy Chambers was standing at the bar with a pint of bitter in his hand laughing and joking with other known villains. Chambers noticed the Serious Crime Squad come through the door of the pub walking towards him. The laughing and joking stopped as Inspector Brown neared the bar.

Chambers had his elbow on the bar. 'Look lads, it's the heavy mob from the yard, slumming it tonight, are you, Inspector Brown,' laughed Billy Chambers.

'We never slum it, Mr Chambers. Mr William Chambers, I'm arresting you for the robbery at Day's Cleaning Company in the West End, also you are to be questioned on the disappearance of Jeffrey Mitchell.'

Chambers throw his pint of beer at the Inspector and tried to make a run for it, but D.C. Hirani and D.C. Smithy brought Chambers down to the ground handcuffed him and bundled him out of the pub to the waiting police car and driven off to Kilburn police station.

'Mr Chambers, we've received a lot of information on you. As far as we can see you've made lots of mistakes on selecting your accomplices for robberies. We have Paul Bailey helping us with our inquires at Kilburn.

'But let's be fair you already have that information as you were on the corner of Bailey's road when he was picked up. Other officers are also picking up Ken Harvie and Michael Staler the other two members of your robbery team.'

'That bastard Bailey, what a fucking grass, you better keep him away from me,' said Chambers.

'We also have Mr Ken Delanny and it would appear you were an accomplice of the murder of Jeffrey Mitchell.'

'I didn't murder Jeff Mitchell, and Delanny would never grass on me.'

'O, dear, Mr Chambers, it's funny what people will say when facing twenty years. Then we have you down as instigator with Costa Esteve and Andres Lara'

'How do you know all that?'

'Mr Chambers, that's our job getting information.'

'I want my solicitor.'

'You mean Mr John Garret.'

'Yes that's correct.'

'No problem, Billy, he'll be so pleased to see you at Kilburn, won't he, D.C. Hirani.'

'Yes indeed, Inspector.'

At Kilburn police station Inspector Brown had Billy Chambers booked in.

'Is Sergeant Clark still here?'

'Yes, Sir, he's in the CID office.'

'Would you call Chief Inspector Bleasdale letting him know that I am here and will be interviewing Mr William Chambers.'

'Yes. Sir.'

Inspector Brown poked his head through the open CID office. 'Good evening lads, it's going to be a busy night. We have arrested Billy Chambers and will commence to interview him.'

'Chambers believes Paul Bailey has informed on him, which is very convenient.'

Ben Clark and Alex Quirk pointed out they had arranged to pick up Michael Staler and Reg More and Rod Muir would pick up Ken Harvey.

'Great news lads, well done,' said Inspector Brown.

The four Detectives made their way to the different addresses. Reg More knocked on the door of Ken Harvey's home. Harvey was home with his wife. 'Mr Kenneth Harvey, I am arresting you for your part in the Days Cleaning Company robbery at Devonshire Way, West End.'

Harvey's wife ran to the door shouting, 'You promised me you wouldn't get into any more trouble.' As they drove Harvey away in their car, Harvey asked who had grassed him up.

'Let's just say we have Paul Bailey and Billy Chambers down at Kilburn.'

'Ok Ok. I put my hands up, I will help you.'

'Ken, you'll have your chance back at Kilburn when you make a statement'.

Clark and Quirk arrived at Stoler's flat, as the door was opened, Ben Clark said, 'Mr Michael Stoler, I'm arresting you for your part in the robbery at Days Cleaning Company in Devonshire way, West End.'

'I don't know anything about a robbery.'

'Mr Stoler, you were the driver. We already have the other three members of the gang at Kilburn—Billy Chambers, Paul Bailey and Ken Harvey.'

'Which one grassed?'

'Never mind about that, if I was you I would have my story right.'

'Look I only drove the van. I didn't know they were going to commit a robbery.'

'Please, Michael, leave it for your interview, but get your facts right as the others are telling their side of the robbery. How do you think we knew you were the getaway driver.' Stoler fell back against the back seat putting his head in his hands saying the bloody grasses.

Inspector Brown had got stuck into Billy Chambers. 'Come on Billy you might as well come clean. We have all the information on what you've been mixed up in. If you want help from us, we must know where Costa Esteve and Andres Lara are living.

'At the moment, you are down for the robbery at Days Cleaning Company, then there is the conspiracy to murder Jeffrey Mitchell with Ken Delanny. And somebody else has suggested that you were the fourth member of the Irish gang who murdered Alonzo Ortuno.'

'Look, Mr Brown, I had nothing to do with the murders of Mitchell or Ortuno.'

'Ok, Billy, we are going to arrest you on two murders and armed robbery, so that to me looks like life, and lets be fair, at your age you are unlikely ever get out.'

'You bastards are setting me up for those murders.'

'Really, Billy, you are in trouble right up to your neck. Don't you think so, D.C. Hirani?'

'Looks that way to me, Inspector.' Just then Inspector Brown who had a small buzzer strapped to his right leg, felt it vibrate.

'Just one minute, Mr Chambers,' getting up out of his chair and making his way to the door.

Opening the door, there was Paul Bailey being led away and in tow was John Garret.

'Hallo, Mr Garret, what a pleasant surprise seeing you here,' said Brown. Billy Chambers hearing their voices tried to get up out of his chair but was restrained by D.C. Hirani, so he shouted

'You fucking grass, Bailey, you're dead. Do you hear me, you're fucking dead.'

John Garret immediately recognised the voice of Billy Chambers, turning to Inspector Brown, 'You have my client William Chambers in there?' pointing to the room.

'That's correct, Mr Garret, if you like to wait in the reception area. I will call you.'

'This is not correct, Inspector. I will have to report this to your superior.'

'Yes of course, Mr Garret, here is Superintendent Parker's number,' giving him a card. 'Now go and wait in the reception area.'

'This is not correct, Inspector,' walking off towards the reception area moaning.

Inspector Brown re-entered the interview room, 'Well fancy your solicitor, John Garret, being next door with Paul Bailey.'

'That grassing bastard,' said Chambers.

'Now let's get down to facts, you put your hands up for the Days Cleaning Company robbery.'

Chambers made his statement leaving nothing out.

'Now how about telling us the whereabouts of Costa Esteve and Andres Lara.'

'I really haven't the faintest idea where they could be.'

'Ok Billy, we'll get your solicitor up here for you.'

John Garret arrived at the interview room and was told that Billy Chambers had made a statement to the fact that he had carried out the robbery on the Days Cleaning Company.

'I would like to see a copy of the statement.' Reading Chambers statement, he said, 'I would like some time with my client.'

'Most certainly, Mr Garret. Billy has been very helpful,' said Inspector Brown as the detectives retired from the room.

Inspector Brown, D.C. Hirani and Smithy made their way to the canteen, as Chief Inspector Bleasdale arrived and sat down with the other Detectives.

'I have a plan, Chief Inspector, Chambers has put his hand up for the Cleaning Company robbery, but he is not going to cough for any of the murders. Chambers and his solicitor will be trying very hard to work something out. I'm prepared to let Chambers out on bail.'

'Bail?' said the Chief Inspector.

'Yes, I believe it will be the only way we are going to find Costa Esteve and his partner.'

'Chambers will contact Churchill, once we have the information we'll be able to pounce on the lot of them.'

Bleasdale pointed out, 'It's a massive risk you are taking, Inspector.'

'It may be a risk, Chief Inspector, but I believe it will pay off.'

'I just hope you're right, Inspector, however it's your case.'

Ken Harvey and Michael Staler were both charged with the robbery at Days Cleaning Company, and placed in the cells.

John Garret had worked out a plan with Billy Chambers and was hoping that Inspector Brown would fall for it. He asked the constable to call Inspector Brown as his client would like to make further statement.

Inspector Brown receiving the news, turned to the Chief Inspector and DC Hirani and Smithy saying, 'Here we go, they've made their plan.'

Re-entering the interview room, John Garret informed the Inspector that his client wanted to make a further statement.

'That's fine, let's get it down on the tape.'

'First of all, Inspector Brown, I had nothing to do with the murders of Jeffrey Mitchell or Alonzo Ortuno. Like everybody else, I heard on the grapevine that Jeffrey Mitchell and this Spanish guy, Alonzo Ortuno, had been murdered. I've already admitted to my involvement in the Days Cleaning Company robbery and will help in any way I can.

'As to these two foreign gentleman you are interested in, Mr Costa Esteve and Andres Lara, they contacted me but I couldn't come to any satisfactory agreement and had nothing further to do with them. It's possible I may be able to find out where they can be found.'

'I see, well that's it then we'll pack you off to the remand prison and go from there,' said Inspector Brown.

'One minute, Inspector, my client has been helpful and wishes to help you further. He appreciates that the robbery at the cleaning company is serious, but he is not a flight risk and he would be prepared if you granted bail to report daily to a police station.'

'Mr Garret, the robbery is a very serious offence, and Mr Chambers is a very dangerous person but our prisons are full, so maybe on this occasion I'll agree. Although, Billy, if you do a runner we will find you and throw the book at you.'

'I appreciate that, Inspector Brown, and I will report daily if you want me too.'

'Yes that will be condition.' Inspector Brown got up and walked out of the door back to the CID office where the Chief Inspector and all the others waited for the news. 'Ok we are going to bail Chambers and he must report to a police station daily. However, I would imagine that by tomorrow, Chambers will contact Costa Esteve and Churchill, as Chambers needs a passport for himself.'

Paul Bailey, Ken Harvey and Michael Staler hearing that Billy Chambers had received bail, also applied, but were turned down. Sitting in their cells, they all thought what a shitbag Chambers was he obviously was the grass.

Forty minutes later, Bailey, Harvey and Staler were transferred to Brixton remand prison, they shouted to each other on the way saying 'Make sure you let everybody know that Billy Chambers is a grass.'

In Putney Walk, some of the neighbours had been complaining to the Town Hall about the awful smell coming from a ground floor flat. Council officers had been around but couldn't raise anybody and decided to report the matter to the police. Two police Officers arrived.

'We're from Putney Police Station investigating a complaint of a bad smell coming from one of the flats.'

'I'm Colin Sapsford and this is Mrs Ward, we made the complaint. The awful smell is coming from that flat over there,' pointing at the door.

'Who lives in the flat?'

'Mr Peachy.'

'Does Mr Peachy work away or go on holiday?'

'O, no he doesn't work and he doesn't take holidays, he always says he is too busy.'

'I see.'

'I noticed this big chap come to the front entrance. Mr Peachy let him enter. However this big chap didn't leave by the front entrance, he left by walking out by the back garden. I must say we have both noticed lots of shady characters coming and going.

'What do you mean shady characters?'

'Colin Sapsford butted in, 'Marisa means unsavoury people.'

One of the police officers knocked the door and then bent down and looked through the letterbox, 'Awful terrible smell, Bert, like dead dogs.'

'Did Mr Peachy keep animals?'

'No Sir, he didn't like animals.'

'Bert, you better call the Sergeant and tell him we will have to break-in.' Thirty minutes later, two CID officers arrived. 'Hallo lads, what have we got then?' After explaining the situation and looking at the door.

'Mr Peachy was very security conscious, three locks, one deadlock and two yale's.'

'You say Mr Sapsford has a back door.'

'Yes come this way.' They all traipsed down a small passage Sapsford opened a door which lead to a small garden. 'That's Mr Peachy's back door,' pointing at the yellow painted door

'I see. Peachy has another three locks on the back door.' Constable John Bruton put his hand on the door handle and found it open. Both officers made their way into the flat, the smell was awful. 'No wonder there were complaints.' turning on the kitchen lights, there was nothing in the kitchen. Making their way further into the flat, checking different rooms as they passed, nothing was found. 'cor the smell it's bloody terrible,' reaching the front room.

'Over there,' pointing to the dead body on the floor, taking a closer look. 'This guy has been shot twice. Cordon off the area and call SOCO,' as they made their way back out into the fresh air,

'What happened officer, is there a dead body?'

'It would be better if you returned to your homes as this area will be cordoned off.'

'What do you think, Colin,' asked Mrs Ward'

'It's murder, Melisa, just like you see on the films.'

Ben Clark received a call, looking at the others, he mouthed another murder, 'Thank you for letting us know.'

'Terry Peachy has been murdered, this has to be connected. You and Rod only recently interviewed Peachy. We better call Inspector Brown.'

'There's been another murder, Sir. Terry Peachy, he was under surveillance at the Red Lion and had recently been interviewed by Sergeant More and DC Muir.'

'Where did this happen?'

'At his home, Sir.'

'Who's looking after the case?'

'D.C. Bill Richards'

'Do you know him, Ben.'

'No, Sir.'

'Ok I'll have somebody call him and get over there.'

Reg looked at his notes, every time there's a murder, who comes up, Billy Chambers. Chambers had been with Peachy on a number of occasions at the Red Lion, that's why we gave Peachy the pull.

Joe Bolt had visited a good friend of his who was on remand at Brixton remand prison. Joe had never liked visiting the remand prison, as he was aware that all visitors were policed. Wynn was a great guy; a Welshman who came from Cardiff, he only stood 5'6 and was thin as a rack, with his red hair, he stood out and was easily picked out on any identification parades.

'Hallo, Wynn, sorry to see you in these circumstances.'

'My fault, Joe. I'm getting old and silly carried out a stupid robbery and with my form my solicitor believes I will probably get eight to ten years. I'm sixty-six, Joe, and with my bad health, I'm not going to make it. If by any chance I do get off with the robbery, I'm retiring as the missus is not going to stand by me going inside again.'

'That's why I have never married, Wynn,' said Joe. 'Who would stand by me?'

'Joe, I'm so pleased you gave up your time to visit me. I've got some monies that I've hidden under the garden shed washing machine. If anything does go wrong for me, would you pop around the house and make sure the missus gets the money.'

'You have no worries there, Wynn, count it as done, my friend.'

'I knew I could count on you, Joe.'

'By the way, there are some terrible rumours here inside. There are two Irish lads on remand accursed of the murder of Alonzo Ortuno. They are saying Liam

Murphy has turned queen's evidence, and so far at least twenty villains have been picked up by the Serious Crime Squad on this supergrass say so.'

'Really he must be a marked man, Wynn.'

'Not only that, Joe, but these two Irish guys are saying there were four guys on the murder and the fourth member was Bob Warden.'

'You're joking, Wynn.'

'No, Joe, those Irish guys are really pissed off. They believe that Liam Murphy will sooner or later inform the old bill that Bob Warden was the fourth member on the murder.'

'When are these two Irish guys in court?'

'Next Monday, also Joe, do you remember Paul Bailey, the mugger?

'Just about, Wynn.'

'Well he's on remand with his two mates, Ken Harvey and Michael Stoler. They carried out the robbery of the Days Cleaning Company, and apparently Billy Chambers grassed them, and he was granted bail because he assisted the police. So I ask you, Joe, is there no honour and loyalty among thieves anymore?'

'Wynn, it's gone I'm afraid.'

'Joe, will you come and see me again.'

'Wynn, you can count on it.'

'Thanks, mate, you are one of the last genuine criminals.'

As Joe left the remand prison he was thinking if Warden was involved with the murder of Alonzo Ortuno, that's the end of our relationship. He stopped at the first telephone box he came across and called Bob Warden.

'Hallo Bob, we need to meet ASAP'

'Ok Joe, what about thirty minutes at the Nags Head?'

'I'll be there.'

Bob was already sitting at a corner table with a pint of beer for himself and a gin and tonic for Joe. Joe parked his car in the large car park with trees and a small wall surrounding the car park, thinking to himself where could you find such a beautiful setting inside London.

Walking inside the pub, Joe found Bob at a corner table.

'What's so urgent, Joe, that couldn't wait until this evening?'

'Bob, I've just visited my old mate Wynn Trail at Brixton remand prison, there's a lot of rumours going around inside the prison. One of those rumours concerns you, Bob. Two Irish guys on remand are saying Liam Murphy has become a supergrass. The Serious Crime Squad have already arrested twenty or so villains on the word of Liam Murphy. Also they have mentioned you Bob, as the fourth member on the murder of Alonzo Ortuno. They are concerned that Murphy will give up your name to the old bill. Now, Bob, I must know if this information is true.'

'Joe, that's not my style, however I was present when they bumped Alonzo off.

'Bob, this is where I say my goodbyes. I cannot at my age be involved.'

'I understand, Joe, and I thank you for the help you have given me. I will disappear on holiday for a little while.'

'That I would recommend, Bob. Now one other matter, which will please you no doubt, three guys Paul Bailey, Ken Harvey and Michael Stoler are on remand for their part in the Days Cleaning Company robbery the fourth member was Billy Chambers who grassed on the other three, getting himself bail for his helping the police.'

'I can't believe it, Joe, what on earth are the old bill thinking about?'

'Perhaps they have taken a back hander.' Bob smashed his hand on the table. Joe drank up his drink as fast as he could and said his goodbyes.

Bob ordered another pint and sat there smouldering. Did Ben Clark and Alex Quirk know of the rumours that he was the fourth member of the Irish gang. He would call them letting them know he was going on holiday to Greece.

Billy Chambers had placed an advert in the evening newspaper which had been arranged by Costa Esteve, if Billy wanted to meet urgently.

Billy was sitting down at a garden seat at the Barbican centre, with his vodka and tonic. Costa Esteve and Andres Lara walked over the concrete path by the waterfall towards where Billy was sitting. They had been upstairs in the foyer watching through the glass, just in case Billy had betrayed them.

'Hallo, Billy, how are you?'

'Hi, Costa, Andres.' Billy's voice sounded edgy.

'What's up, my friend?' said Costa.

'Bits and pieces, Costa. I believe it's time to get our passports ready, when is the job taking place?'

'Soon, Billy. Andres and I will be meeting up with Big Sam on Friday. He will let us know the final arrangements. 'that is when our own plan comes into action, when we take the money.'

'Costa, don't underestimate Big Sam; he is a real handful and has nothing to lose.'

'Billy, stop worrying, we will be ready. Now for these passports, get in touch with Mr Churchill, give him these photos and say we want the passports ready by Sunday. Also let him know the remaining photographs for the other passports will be with him at the same time and we would like the new passports ready for the following Friday.

'He will receive extra cash if he completes his job on time. We will meet you here on Sunday morning, Billy, with the photos and the extra cash that way we should have everything in place.

'So my friend, don't worry about Big Sam, if he becomes a nuisance, we'll shoot him.' Costa and Andres got up from there seat and made their way out.

Billy finished his drink and made his way to the car park on the lower level. Worrying about the time factor and knowing he needed money to skip the country, he made his way to the Red Lion. Sergeant Weber had him on the surveillance tape entering the pub.

Billy walked up to the bar ordering a pint, turning and putting his elbows on the bar. He noticed John Carr, who promptly said, 'I thought you were inside, Billy.'

'Yeah I was but I have a good lawyer so they couldn't hold me for long, but I was grassed by that bastard Paul Bailey.'

'I am sure that Bailey will get his just dues inside, Billy.'

'I hope so John,' said Billy. Billy slid a note over the counter for John Simmons winking to Billy Fleming, who just nodded.

'Constable Walters nobody knows you in the Red Lion go and take a look around and let's see who's who in there,' said Sergeant Weber.

Entering the pub, the Constable noticed Jimmy Simmons and John Carr sitting at a table in the far corner. Ordering a half a beer, Billy Fleming asked, 'I haven't seen you in hear before.'

'No I work for the underground working as many hours as I can. I've just moved into Tooting street and I was thirsty so decided to pop in for a beer as it looks like your pubs going to be my local.'

'Sorry, mate, about the questions but we get a lot of old bill in here, so we can't be too careful.'

'Yeah I understand,' finishing his beer and walking out and back to the surveillance van. 'Bloody den of thieves in there. Jimmy Simmons is sitting with John Carr.'

'Well done, David. That's funny about Simmons and Carr we haven't got them entering the Red Lion, they must have entered around the back somehow.'

John Carr finished his discussion with Jimmy Simmons, walked over to the bar nodded to the barman who lifted the hatch to the bar passing through the kitchen and out of the back door. Ten minutes later, Jimmy Simmons carried out the same procedure, first collecting his note from Billy Chambers. Sergeant Weber suggested they stay in the van until closing time.

The pub lights went out down stairs and went on in the first floor bedroom.

'That's unusual, David. Jimmy Simmons hasn't come through the front entrance, they must have left by a back door, and perhaps they have become wise to us, Sergeant.

'I'll have to report this in the morning.' They drove their van around the back of the pub noticing a back door they hadn't seen before. 'There,' pointing, 'that's how they are getting in and out without us knowing.'

Jimmy Simmons arrived home reading the note from Billy Chambers 'We will meet next Monday at the Red Lion and plan the final score. We must know which car you are travelling in. I have told Costa not to take Big Sam lightly as he has nothing to lose, find out what you can.

Oscar Keylock had been sitting in Terry Churchill's flat. There hadn't been any contact whatsoever. Had somebody be driving by when the police cars pulled up and seen Terry Churchill and himself being led away. Just then the telephone rang which made Oscar jump.

'Hallo.'

'Put Terry on the phone.'

'Who's speaking.'

'Never mind all the crap, put Terry on the phone.'

'I'm sorry but I must know who's speaking.'

'Listen to me, you silly bastard, get Terry on the phone now.'

'I'm sorry but I have no idea who you are, so I'm putting the phone down.'

'Wait a minute, its Billy Chambers; now get Terry on the phone.'

'Mr Chambers, sorry about that, but you can't be too careful. Terry has been called away on family matters but he has left instruction for me. Have you the photographs?'

'Yes, I have three which need processing quickly we want the passports for Sunday. Will that be a problem?'

'No, Mr Chambers, I'll have them ready for you.'

'Good. The other six photographs you will have by Sunday night and you can tell Terry that there will be extra cash for him if the passports are ready for the following Friday.'

'Mr Chambers, that will be fine and I'm sure the extra cash will go down a treat.'

'By the way, your security was good, mate.'

'Thanks, Mr Chambers, we have to be careful if you know what I mean.' Putting the telephone down on its cradle, Oscar was wet with sweat; at the other end the police had recorded the call. Sergeant Miller walked into Inspector Brown's office with a copy of the tape.

After listening to the tape, Brown turned to the Sergeant saying, 'We will know if Keylock is straight, or not very shortly.'

Billy Chambers put his telephone down, poured himself a beer, sitting there in his easy chair, thinking that the passports would be ready, so if the worst came to the worst he could be off. He pressed the television remote sitting back thinking to himself, I only hope nothing goes wrong, as I can't hang around too long. The television news flashed up, '*another murder in London, Mr Terry Peachy had been found with gun-shot wounds inside his flat, police believed it could be a gangland hit.*

They showed a photo of Terry Peachy's flat in Putney, stationed outside the flat was Constable John Bruton. The newspapers fired questions at the constable. Bruton pointed out there was no comment at this time, and future questions should be addressed to the Serious Crime Squad. The television presenter then claimed, '*it was believed from a sauce at Scotland Yard that this murder was connected with a number of people helping the police with their inquirers.* Chambers switched channels putting on the sport. After finishing his beer he went off to bed.

Inspector Brown sat at his desk reading the evening news. Inspector Ward entered his office. 'This murder of Mr Terry Peachy has the hand marks of Billy Chambers all over it.'

'I agree, but we must wait for SOCO to come up with any fingerprints or anything that puts Chambers in the frame.'

'We have Mrs Melissa Ward and Colin Sapsford, Peachy's neighbours looking through mug shots, so hopefully they may pick out the villain who walked down the garden path.'

DC Facer called over. 'I have Oscar Keylock on the phone, Sir.'

'Switch the call through. Hallo, Oscar, what can I do for you?'

'Just to let you know I received a telephone call from Billy Chambers; he is delivering three photos for the passports; he wants to pick them up on Sunday, and deliver a further six photos for passports to be ready for the following Friday.'

'Well done, Oscar, keep up the good work and make sure you carry out your daily routine just in case some smart ass is watching.'

'Yes, Inspector.'

Superintendent Parker sat in his comfortable leather high backed chair, looking through the evidence from the different divisions when he received a call from the Deputy Commissioner. 'Parker, I watched the television news last night, is this murder of Terry Peachy connected with our ongoing case.'

'We believe so, Sir, at the moment we have Mrs Ward and Mr Sapsford, neighbours of Terry Peachy, looking at mug shots hoping they may be able to identify the villain seen walking down Mr Peachy's garden path. We have reason to believe it has something to do with Billy Chambers. Who has already been charged with the cleaning company robbery.

'We had him bailed hoping that he leads us to Costa Esteve and Andres Lara along with the big six who are planning this armed robbery. Our mol inside a flat in Norwood road is processing the passports for next Sunday, which should put us in the position of identifying all of the villains concerned.'

'Very good, Parker. I'm looking for a good result.'

Inspector Brown and Ward where checking their agenda. 'We need more officers if we are going to tail Billy Chambers as he already knows myself, Hirani and Smithy.'

'Who have we left?'

'Williamson, Beasley, Falcao, Illingsworth, Carter, and Samuels,' replied Ward.

All the named officers were assembled in the conference room; the video was turned on showing Billy Chambers. 'We are going to tail Mr Chambers twenty four-seven, and want photographs of everybody he meets. We are all well aware that a very large robbery is going to take place, but as yet we have no idea where, or the names of those criminals taking part in this robbery.

'However, we now know Chambers is collecting passport photos from an unknown person, which could quite possible by Costa Esteve or even Andres

Lara. The photos will be delivered to our man, Oscar Keylock, so we don't have to worry about the photos. As soon as our man has them, we'll know.'

Inspector Brown mentioned that it is imperative to catch these criminals before anymore murders take place.

Bob Warden called Ben Clark asking if it was possible to have a meet inside the hour at the usual place. As they arrived, Bob Warden was already sitting at the corner table by the window with three pints on the table.

'What's up, Bob,' asked Ben Clark.

'I've decided to go on holiday to Greece. I'm absolutely pissed off that Billy Chambers got bail after being charged with the Days Cleaning Company robbery and the other poor bastards on the robbery get remand.'

'Unfortunately, the Serious Crime Squad dealt with Chambers and the robberies, many of us are very unhappy with the result and situation.

'By the way, Bob, that supergrass the Serious Crime Squad have mentioned that there is a fourth person involved in the murder of Alonzo Ortuno. Have you heard anything?'

'Nothing, Ben.'

'Have a pleasant holiday and don't forget to give us a call on your return.'

After Clark and Quirk left, Bob sat at his table ordered another pint and thought matters through. At least the old bill were not looking for him as part of the murder of Alonzo Ortuno. It was now imperative that he made sure as many people as possible thought he was on holiday in Greece.

He already had another apartment ready for possession and a new passport in the name of Richard Moss. He would purchase a one way ticket to Greece and his mate, Sam Russell, who looked similar to Bob would use Bob's passport for the visit.

Bob travelled home and hatched his plan, calling Joe Bolt, telling him that he had taken his advice and was going on holiday to Greece.

'Bob, you are making the right decision, have a good time.'

After receiving Bob Warden's call, Joe sat wondering if he should also go on holiday, as it wouldn't be long before the Serious Crime Squad checked on who might have worked with Jeff Mitchell on the Mallards robbery.

The whole mess was getting bigger and bigger, Derrick Smallwood was no longer any help and should be extremely careful just in case this Liam Murphy had any information on the forthcoming robbery that Derrick was involved in.

Ben Clark and Alex Quirk sat at their desks. 'Ben, do you think Bob Warden was the fourth person on that murder of Ortuno?'

'Alex, I'm sure Warden is involved somewhere down the line, but where is the question, maybe this court case next Monday will shed some light on the whole investigation.'

Inspector Ward had been given the duty of looking through the statements and facts of Jeff Mitchell, a number of Mitchell's associates who had been involved with Mitchell on previous safe blowing robberies had to be looked at. There was Ralf Graham who had been on a number of robberies with Mitchell and had been sentenced to prison on three separate occasions. Then there was George Lopez who had been caught with Mitchell and served prison sentences twice.

There was Joe Bolt who had gone down once with Mitchell for safe blowing. Then there were a number of small time criminals who had been involved with Mitchell on a number of crimes. Thinking it over Inspector Ward decided to pass the investigation over to the CID at Kilburn.

'Sergeant Clark, I have faxed over all the reports on Jeff Mitchell along with his associates, perhaps you would start pulling in his associates for questioning, and see who drops in line with Mitchell on the Mallards robbery.'

'Are we now acknowledging Inspector Ward that Horn and Prince were not involved?'

'No Clark, not officially but it's pointing in that direction, my whole squad are completely tied up on this so called big robbery, so we would appreciate your teams assistance.'

'That's not a problem.'

Bob Warden met up with Sam Russell at the Swan in the Elephant and Castle, sitting down at a back corner table where they could speak freely. 'Here's your ticket to Greece Sam and three grand spending money which should be enough to have a good time for a month.'

'More than enough, Bob. Greece is so cheap.'

'Stay in the hotel that I have reserved for you under my name for a couple of weeks then move on to another area and book into a hotel in your own name. I'll leave it up to you how long you want to stay. But whatever you do, keep out of trouble.

‘When you arrive back in the UK, post my passport to my sister’s address,’ passing over the address. Finishing their beers Bob made his way to his new apartment.

Ben Clark and Reg More stood looking at the list of names that the Serious Crime Squad had faxed them. ‘These names are a bit ancient Ralf Graham, Joe Bolt, George Lopez, Peter O’Hara and Ted Doe. If I remember Ted Doe is doing seven in Dartmoor, and Joe Bolt I think we have already pulled him in, as he was on holiday in Cornwall.’

‘That’s right I remember.’ Checking the computer it appeared that all the named people except for Ted Doe were about when the Mallards robbery was pulled. It was agreed that Ben and Alex would pull in Joe Bolt and Peter O’Hara and Reg and Rod would pull in George Lopez and Ralf Graham.

Reg and Rod made their way to Ralf Grahams flat. Mrs Maggie Graham had been looking out of her window through the curtains when she noticed Reg and Rod pull up. ‘Ralf, it’s the old bill,’ she shouted. Ralf picked up his coat and made his way down the back staircase and out to the side road. Reg pressed the flat button and asked to speak with Mr Graham.

‘Who’s speaking?’

‘Sergeant Reg More from Kilburn CID’

‘Unfortunately, Mr More, Ralf’s gone up to Nottingham to see his brother.’

‘I see. I would be obliged if you ask Ralf to contact me on his return. I’ll leave my card near your phone button.

Rod turned to Reg saying, ‘I wouldn’t believe that cock and bull story if it was from a comedian let alone from a criminal’s wife.’

‘Put a call through to the station and see if Ralf Graham has any brothers living in the Nottingham area.’ The information came back over the car radio; Ralf Graham has no known brothers alive. ‘Ok Rod, let’s have walkabouts.’ Making their way down the street to the local pub. They had only walked about hundred yards when Reg received a tap on his shoulder, looking around he saw a slim young lady in her thirties with blond hair about 5’6.

‘Yes Madam, how can I help you’

‘I am one of the Grahams neighbours, I saw Ralf Graham running down the backstairs when you pulled up.’

‘Are you sure it was Ralf Graham, Madam?’

‘Yes that bastard stole my sisters handbag three weeks ago, my sister recognised him after visiting our block of flats. We confronted Ralf Graham and his wife and that bitch just slapped my sister around the face and told us all to piss off.'

'Did your sister make a complaint about the Grahams?'

'No, but she did report to the local police saying she had been mugged.'

'Why on earth didn't your sister tell the truth?'

'My sister and my husband and I were down at the Roast Hen pub when we were threatened by Billy Chambers, who told us if we persisted in giving the Grahams grief, something very nasty would happen to us all.'

'That's interesting Mrs…

'Mrs Roberts.'

'Ok, Mrs Roberts.'

'Let's sit in the car and have a good chat.'

'No way Mrs Graham sits all day looking out the window watching and writing down all the car numbers that pull up outside the flats, just in case they are old bill. I'm not making any statements as we are all frightened enough.'

'Rod, drive the car up the road out of the way.'

'Come on, Mrs Roberts take a walk with me as Mrs Graham cannot see this far up the street.' Reaching Reg's car, he opened the back door and Mrs Roberts climbed in, making an unofficial statement.

'If we get half a chance, Mrs Roberts, we will be putting Billy Chambers behind bars. Now if we need some more help would you be prepared to help us.'

'Yes I would and so would my sister, and probably my husband too.'

'That's great, Mrs Roberts, thanks for your help.' She got out of the car and made her way back to her flat. 'This bloody Billy Chambers is everywhere you look, now we know he's involved with Ralf.'

'Graham, it's another bit of the puzzle. We are just missing something that puts the puzzle together.' They waited in their car for another hour and were just about to leave when they noticed Ralf Graham on the corner of the street looking up and down.

'Rod, looky, looky, it's Ralf Graham.' They waited for Ralf Graham to satisfy himself that nobody was about and started to walk towards his flat. Reg and Rod got out of their car, making their move catching Ralf before he could run,

'Just back from Nottingham are we, Ralf? Now be a good lad and get into the back of the car, as we are off for a ride to Kilburn.'

'I haven't done anything.'

'You'll have plenty of time to get your story right.'

Next stop was to see George Lopez.

'Cor look at this house, Rod, it must be worth a million, and who says crime doesn't pay,' knocking on the front door.

'Yes can I help you?' Reg and Rod produced their warrant cards.

'Mr Lopez, can you tell us when you last saw Jeffrey Mitchell.'

Lopez sat back in his chair and put his hands through his hair. 'Now let me think. Yes it was probable nearly two years ago.'

'Mr Lopez, we are looking into the Mallards robbery as we have received information that Jeffrey Mitchell was involved.'

'I must stop you there gentleman, I'm afraid our conversation has just terminated. If you wish to contact me any further, this is my lawyers name and number.' Lopez got up from his chair and pointed towards the way out.

'Thank you for your time, Mr Lopez,' as the door closed behind them. Lopez looked through the curtained window to make sure the officers had gone, picked up the telephone and called his lawyer Joseph Silver letting him know that Detectives More and Muir from Kilburn CID had tried to interview him.

Ben Clark and Alex Quirk had drawn a blank at Peter O'Hara's flat as he was extremely unwell and had been for some time and therefore, couldn't have been involved in any robberies for the last three years.

Arriving at Joe Bolt's flat, the door was opened by Joe's sister. 'Can I help you?'

'Yes we would like to speak with Mr Joe Bolt,' showing their warrant cards. Joe made his way to the front door.

'We must ask you to accompany us to Kilburn CID.'

'What for. I've done nothing.'

'We've a number of questions that we need answering especially your relationship with Jeffrey Mitchell, so get your coat, Joe'. In the car, Joe Bolt was protesting his innocence to any crime that may have taken place.

Reg and Rod interviewed Ralf Graham, 'When was the last time you saw Jeffrey Mitchell.'

'I haven't seen Jeff for some time.'

'That's very interesting, isn't Rod.'

'You can say that again, Reg.'

'You see, Ralf, you have probably read the article in the newspaper, the Serious Crime Squad have a supergrass and guess what, he's given up your name with Billy Chambers and Jeff Mitchell as being on the Mallards robbery.'

'Not me, Mr More.'

'O dear, Ralf, you're not being very helpful. I've told you we have already received information, so it looks like we'll have to charge you.'

'I'm not saying another word until I get a lawyer.'

'That's fine, Ralf, we'll put you back in the cells, as we've got another couple of CID officers bringing in Billy Chambers, and I am sure he will be extremely happy to know that in the next cell is Ralf Graham.'

'You pair of bastards, I'm not getting fitted up.'

'Constable, take Mr Graham back to the cells.'

'Wait a minute, Mr More. I had nothing to do with Billy Chambers and the Mallards robbery.'

'Ralf, we are not going to waste our time listening to this, we've got Billy Chambers to interview'

'I can't make this out I thought your lot had already charged Ted Horn and Tommy Prince with the Mallards robbery.'

'Constable, take him to the cells.'

'No, no wait, Mr More. I have only heard names I swear.'

'Ok whose names have you heard mentioned?'

'Jeff Mitchell, Joe Bolt and Derick Smallwood.'

'That's a little better, Ralf; now tell us about your connection with Billy Chambers.'

'Look if I talk, I'm dead,' said Ralf. 'Please Mr More, you must help me.'

'How can we help you, if you can't be bothered to help us with information on Chambers?'

Ralf Graham put his head in his hands, 'Alright but I want protection.'

'That's not a problem, Ralf Graham.'

'Chambers is involved with some foreign guys and some big robbery which is coming off soon. Six heavy guys are carrying out the robbery, the same foreigners where mixed up in the Mallards safe blowing and employed Jeff Mitchell to blow the safe, but apparently Mitchell got greedy and they had him fed to the pigs. The plan is the foreigners are going to do the dirty on the gang of six.

'Billy Chambers has already recruited one of the six heavies and receives all the information. Once the robbery is pulled Billy Chambers, me and another two mates of ours are going to steel the money from the other gang. The foreigners will then tip off the police so the heavies will be captured.'

'When is this robbery taking place?'

'In the next two weeks' but I have no idea where as Billy Chambers keeps that information close to his chest.'

'Ok Ralf, I'm going to have to contact the Serious Crime Squad as they will without doubt want to interview you and place you in a safe location for your own safety. Rod have some coffee and sandwiches sent up.'. Reg left the interview room telephoning both Chief Inspector Bleasdale and Inspector Brown who immediately intimated that he was on his way to Kilburn. Ben Clark and Alex Quirk were coming down the corridor towards interview room 5, when they bumped into Reg More.

'Ben, I need a quick word please, it's urgent.'

'Alex, you take Mr Bolt into the interview room, I'll be with you in a minute.' After listening to the outcome of Reg More's interview with Ralf Graham, Ben pointed out he would use some of the information on Joe Bolt.

Ben entered the interview room sitting down next to Alex, tapping his fingers on the table 'Joe, you already know that the Serious Crime Squad have a supergrass. This guy has given up so many names and crimes and many villains have been arrested and charged.

'Now your name has come up along with Jeff Mitchell and Derrick Smallwood for carrying out the safe blowing at Mallards.'

Joe was startled at this information how did they know about Smallwood, Jeff must have told somebody before he was killed.

'Joe, when was the last time you saw Jeff Mitchell.'

'Mr Clark, I'm sorry, but I need a lawyer present.'

'Fine, Mr Bolt, have you anybody in mind'

'Yes Mr Joseph Silver.'

Ben and Alex walked back to the CID office where Ben was able to explain Reg More's interview with Ralf Graham; it appears Billy Chambers is playing a major roll, in all these crimes.

The telephone rang. 'Alex, it's Dia Robinson from Gatwick airport.'

'Hallo, Dia, how's it going?'

‘Just had your man Bob Warden pass through security and fly out to Greece, he left about fifteen minutes ago.’

‘Thanks Dia.

‘Ben, Bob Warden has flown out to Greece.’

‘That’s good news, Alex, another villain out the way; let’s go and get ourselves a coffee.’

Billy Chambers was at home sitting down in his easy chair pondering on the day’s events when his telephone rang.

‘Hallo, Billy, it’s Maggie Graham. Ralf has been pulled by two CID officers from Kilburn.

‘What for’

‘I don’t know, they picked him up in the street according to a lady I know across the road.’

‘Ok Maggie, leave it to me, I’ll find out what’s going on.’ Billy thought for a minute that bloody supergrass, he must be giving up more names. I better get myself down to the Duck and Hound opposite Kilburn Police station, once Ralf comes out I’ll pick him up. Billy drove down past Kilburn police station parking two streets back, walking the three minutes back to the pub.

Billy had disguised himself with dark glasses and an old floppy hat. He ordered a beer and sat in the corner so he could see the entrance of the police station. The pub door opened and two young police officers came in ordering two pints of beer. ‘Hallo, Tom, busy over there tonight?’

‘You bet, Mick, CID have pulled in two villains one of them is spilling his guts. The Serious Crime Squad are on their way.’

‘It’s the Mallards robbery and some murders and something about a big robbery going down shortly.’

‘That’s going to keep your lot busy then, Tom.’ Finishing their beers they left.

Billy sat still listening to the conversation and thinking the CID have Ralf, who’s the other one. Billy looked through the window as two cars screeched to a halt in the police yard and out jumped Inspector Brown and Ward. Brown stepped up to the second car giving some instructions and the car sped off.

Billy thought I’ve got problems if it’s Ralf talking his head off, I’ll stick around and see what happens.

Inspector’s Brown and Ward made for the CID office, where Chief Inspector Bleasdale was congratulating everybody on a wonderful job, after a short brief on the happenings and listening to the tape. Inspector Brown suggested that he and Inspector Ward would interview Ralf Graham first and then Joe Bolt.

Sitting in interview room No 1 with Ralf Graham, they had delivered hot coffee and sandwiches.

Inspector Brown started, 'Ralf, I've listened to your interview with Sergeant More and DC Muir, are you sure Joe Bolt and Derick Smallwood were with Jeff Mitchell?'

'Yes Inspector, it was those three for sure Billy Chambers told me.'

'Now you've also mentioned this big robbery going down shortly. Have you any idea where the robbery is taking place?'

'No Inspector, Billy Chambers has kept that information to himself.'

'What about these six villains who are carrying out the robbery, have you any idea who they are?'

'Again, Inspector, Chambers kept that info all to himself.'

'Ralf, it may be best if we put you up at a safe house until this business is finalised.'

'What about my wife?'

'Unfortunately, she will not be told of your whereabouts.'

'She'll not stand for that, Inspector, she'll be calling lawyers and all sorts.' Inspector Brown turned and looked at Inspector Ward. Ward shrugged his shoulders and said it would be potentially dangerous if Ralf went home.

'Listen if you want to go home, we'll have a police officer watching the flats. When you get home tell your wife that it was something to do with a mugging and a lady having her handbag stolen. Say we couldn't hold you as there was no evidence,' passing a card with a telephone number over to Ralf. 'This is a special number 24 hours a day, give us a call as soon as you receive information on this big robbery.'

Taking the card and putting it into his pocket 'I will, Inspector Brown, you can count on me.'

Inspector Brown held a meeting with Chief Inspector Bleasdale. It was decided that Constable Salem Sing would cover for days and Julia Carter would cover nights watching Ralf Grahams flat. Constable Sing brought his car around to the front of the police station.

Ten minutes later, Ralf Graham walked down the steps of the police station making his way to the bus stop. Billy Chambers watched carefully from the pub window noticing Chief Inspector Bleasdale walk towards Constable Sing's car tapping on the window and pointing towards Ralf Graham. Billy Chambers finished his drink walked out of the pub and towards where he had parked his car.

Constable Sing parked thirty yards up the road from where the bus would stop. Looking in his car side mirror and watching Ralf Graham standing at the bus stop waiting for Bus number 13 to come along the road.

Billy knew the Indian police office couldn't possibly see Ralf Graham once the bus had stopped.

He jumped out of his car walked across the road behind the bus calling out to Ralf Graham, 'Quick over here.'

Ralf hesitated for a moment, but then crossed the road and got into Billy Chambers car.

'What are you doing here,' asked Ralf.

'Your misses telephoned saying she was worried sick and you had been pulled by Kilburn CID.'

The bus pulled away and started to travel down the road. the Indian police Officer pulled in after the bus and followed. Billy Chambers in the meantime turned his car around and travelled in the opposite direction. 'What did the old bill want you for,' asked Billy.

'They asked me about Jeff Mitchell, I told them I hadn't seen Jeff for at least eighteen months, they also asked me if I had heard anything about a big job going down again. I told them that I had no idea what they were talking about. And lastly they asked me about a mugging which had taken place in my area when a lady had lost her handbag.'

Billy seemed to be happy with the answers that Ralf had given him, until Billy asked who was the other villain being interviewed and as soon as Ralf told Billy it was Joe Bolt, Billy knew Ralf Graham had been the one doing the grassing as Joe Bolt was well known for not saying a word when captured.

'We'll have a drink at the Cricketers,' said Billy turning his car into the car park and pulling in as far as he could to the back of the carpark. Ralf Graham jumped out of the car and started to walk to the entrance of the pub, as he turned towards Billy, he heard two muffled sounds.

Clutching his side as Ralf fell to the ground looking at Billy and saying, 'Why?'

'Because you are a fucking grass, you bastard,' as Billy pulled the trigger and put another bullet into Ralf's head. Billy smartly put the gun away looked around in case anybody was looking. Seeing nobody he walked smartly to his car and drove off.

The number 13 bus pulled up just down the road from Ralf Grahams flat's, Salem Sing watched through his car mirror, but Ralf never got off the bus. Salem thought perhaps Ralf uses the next bus stop. The bus stopped at the next stop but Ralf Graham never appeared.

Constable Sing jumped out of his car pulled out his warrant card and preceded towards the bus holding out his arm so the bus wouldn't move. Jumping onto the bus running up and down the bus, but there was no sign of Ralf Graham. Constable Sing found a telephone box and called into the CID office at Kilburn explaining what had happened.

When Inspector Brown was told that Ralf Graham was missing, he stood pushing his hands through his hair, how on earth is that possible, what the bloody hell has gone wrong.

The telephone rang in the CID Office.

'I want to report a dead body in my car-park.'

'What car-park, Sir.'

'The Cricketers public house. My name is Trevor Miles, my telephone number is 127.'

'We'll be on our way, Sir.'

Inspector Brown and Ward were interrupted by Ben Clark, 'There's been another murder in a car-park of the Cricketers pub.'

Brown looked at Ward thinking, no not Graham.

'Ok, Clark, you are coming with us,' Arriving at the pub in eight minutes. The local squad car was already there with an ambulance. The three detectives jumped out of their car making their way to the body. Inspector Brown immediately recognised Ralf Graham.

'How the fuck did this happen.' The local squad were already cordoning off the area and SOCO had been called. The landlord came towards the Inspector introducing himself as Mr Trevor Miles, the publican.

'Who actually found the body, Mr Miles?' Lifting his hand he pointed over towards a tall guy with blue overalls holding a pint glass in his hand

'I understand you found the body Mr…'

'Bennett.'

'Right, Mr Bennett, can you run us through what happened.'

'I drove my car into the carpark and noticed a guy lying on the floor. At first I thought he was drunk. I parked my car over there,' pointing, 'and walked back towards the chap on the floor. I noticed that on his cream cardigan there was blood.'

'Did you notice any other people in the car-park?'

'Nobody whatsoever.'

'Where there any other cars parked.'

'Yes those three cars parked over there.'

'Would you go with this constable who will take your statement.'

'Mr Miles, have you any idea who these three cars belong to?'

Three chaps came forward giving their names, but mentioned that they had no further information as they had arrived in the carpark before Mr Bennett, and at that time there was nobody around in the carpark.

SOCO arrived and Inspector Brown told the Sergeant that they would be at Kilburn CID office, so all information could be sent there.

Chief Inspector Bleasdale was waiting at the front entrance as Inspector Brown and Ward walked into the police station with Ben Clark.

'Inspector Brown, Mr Joseph Silver, Joe Bolts solicitor, is waiting to see his client.'

'Thank you, Chief Inspector, if you can have Mr Bolt brought up to interview room 5, Sergeant Clark and I will sit in on the interview, while Inspector Ward could interview Constable Salem Sing with you, Sir.'

Inspector Ward was focusing on how constable Sing could possibly have lost Ralf Graham.

'Sir, I parked my car in the bus lane just down the road from our station. Ralf Graham was standing at the bus stop and I could clearly see him in my wing-mirror. The number 13 bus came along and I noticed all the people at the bus stop getting onto the bus, as the bus moved off I drove off knowing where Mr Graham lived.'

'Why on earth didn't you follow the bus instead of driving in front of it?'

'I'm sorry, Sir, but knowing that Mr Graham was on our side now, I thought he would get off the bus as planned near his home.'

'Because you thought he was on our side now, he's been murdered, Constable.' Inspector Ward left the interview room.

Joe Bolt sat in the interview room No 5 with his solicitor, Joseph Silver; until Mr Silver was satisfied that Joe Bolt had all his answers. Inspector Brown and

Sergeant Ben Clark were called and entered the interview room taking their seats opposite.

'Mr Bolt, we have information that you, Jeffrey Mitchell and Derek Smallwood carried out the safe blowing at Mallards Publication House.'

'I have no idea where you may have received your information Inspector Brown, but I can assure you that I was not present at any robbery with these other men you have mentioned.'

'Inspector Brown, as Mr Bolt's solicitor I would like to see some written information regarding my client, or Mr Bolt and myself will be walking out of this interview.'

'Thank you, Mr Silver, we only wished to clear Mr Bolt's name from our inquirers. I am satisfied with his answers and you may leave with your client walking out into the street.'

Joseph Silver turned to Joe Bolt saying 'it would be very wise to take a little holiday, as I received a call from George Lopez this morning saying this police supergrass appears to be giving a lot of information.' They crossed the road and into the local pub sitting far away from the bar at a small table with their gin and tonics.

'Joe, I do not believe this Inspector Brown is finished with you and may come back for you in the next few days.'

'I am sure you are right, Mr Silver, maybe it would be best if I slipped away for a few weeks.' On the way Home in the taxi. Joe was deep in thought, how could Derek Smallwood have been connected with Jeff Mitchell and himself. Up until Derek had started working with Joe, he had been unknown and where did this supergrass fit in.

Constable Shelia Ross and Tina Cord visited Mrs Graham giving her the bad news about the death of her husband.

'How can my Ralf have been murdered while he was in custody?'

'Mrs Graham, your husband was not in custody. He had left Kilburn police station and was travelling home on the number 13 bus.'

'I just can't bloody believe, you lot, you haven't heard the last of this, now get out of my home and leave me alone.' Once the police had been shown the door, Mrs Graham picked up the telephone and spoke with Billy Chambers

'Billy they've had my Ralf murdered.'

'Murdered when, how? I thought he was in custody at Kilburn.'

'Yes he was but they are saying Ralf left the police station and jumped onto the No 13 bus home.'

'That's unbelievable, I'll have this looked into and get back to you.'

'I knew I could count on you Billy, thanks love.' Billy wanted to laugh out loud but decided to go to the local and have a few pints. As he walked into the street he never noticed a mini car following him which parked on the other side of the street when Billy entered the Crown public house, and unknown to Billy the car had followed him all day.

Inspector Brown and Ward bad been talking about the day's events and were sure that Ted Horn and Tommy Prince were not the villains who pulled off the safe blowing at Mallards. If we are to believe that Prince's car was stolen in Manchester, and is connected to these foreigners, it's a massive setup.

Sergeant Glyn Setting from SOCO arrived at Kilburn with his report from the Cricketers, 'Anything out of the normal, Sergeant?'

'Not as I can see, Inspector Brown, a thorough search has taken place running back to the next streets, but nobody witnessed or heard anything. Whoever shot Mr Graham must have brought him in their car. It's very difficult to get tyre tracks because of the gravel, but we are looking.'

Chief Inspector Bleasdale walked into the office being used by Inspector Brown. 'I must say I hold you responsible for letting Ralf Graham go home in the first place. I will be speaking with Superintendent Parker regarding your attitude.'

Bleasdale turned on his toes walking out of the room. Inspector Brown shrugged his shoulders and carried on reading through the statements received by Sergeant Glyn Setting, there was nothing outstanding to be seen.

Reg More and Rod Muir were in the CID office on Saturday morning; bloody good having to work Saturdays and still on these blasted murders. 'What about Inspector Brown letting Ralf Graham go home knowing the information he held. Somebody close by must have known about Ralf Graham and murdered him dumping him in the Cricketers carpark.'

'Yeah, Reg, that's got to be a bloomer, then we have Chief Inspector Bleasdale having Constable Salem Sing following Graham and driving in front of the bus instead of following the bloody bus, that's really going to go down well for us in the CID here, when Superintendent Parker hears of it.'

Billy Chambers made his way to Chelsea football club for his arranged meeting with Costa Esteve and Andres Lara in the Chelsea Arms pub, sitting at a table at the back, virtually in darkness sat Bob Warden.

Costa Esteve handed the photos for the passports to Billy Chambers.

'It's imperative that we have the passports for Friday, no matter what the cost.'

'Leave it to me, Costa.'

'We'll be seeing Big Sam tomorrow, so we need to meet you again either tomorrow night or Tuesday morning so our final plans are prepared and in place, make sure all your people are ready, Billy.'

'That's not a problem, Costa.'

Bob Warden was listening to the whole conversation and thinking so this is Costa Esteve and Andres Lara.

Bob knew where Billy Chambers was going so there was no need to follow him, he decided to follow Costa Esteve and Andres Lara.

Bob left by the side entrance watching Esteve and Lara walk down the road turning left two streets down, fortunate as it may be. Bob's car was parked on the corner of the road. He followed Esteve's car at a good safe distance towards Heathrow Airport when Esteve's car turned left towards Heston, Bob followed.

Esteves car pulled into Macan Street, Bob slowed down at the corner of the street, watching as Esteve's car pulled up at number 23. He drove past the block of flats stopping a little down the street, where he could observe Esteve and Lara in the living room of their flat.

To Bob this information of where Costa Esteve lived, was worth a small fortune. It was time to return to watch Billy Chambers, so he made his way back to London.

Billy Chambers telephoned Oscar Keylock.

'Oscar, I have the required photos for the passports, meet me at the Cock and Hen at Norwood in an hour.'

'No problem, Billy.'

Inspector Brown was told of the telephone call and immediately made arrangements for Sergeant Jessup to be present at the Cock and Hen as he was unknown to both Chambers and Keylock. The special telephone rang in Inspector Brown's office.

'I've just received a call from Billy Chambers asking me to meet him at the Cock and Hen at Norwood.'

'Very good, Oscar. Go to the meeting we'll be watching.'

Inspector Brown dropped off Sergeant Jessup at the pub, and then parked his car around the corner sitting with D.C.s Grant and Stanley.

Billy Chambers arrived having a good look around the carpark before entering the pub. Sergeant Jessup was sitting at a small table at the side of the bar reading his newspaper and watched Billy Chambers buy his pint and a gin and tonic sitting down at a table near the window so that he could monitor Keylock when he arrived. Oscar Keylock pulled into the car park and entered the pub.

'Oscar, over here said Billy, here's your G and T.'

'Thanks, Mr Chambers.'

'Now it's very important that these passports are ready for next Friday and its possible that there may be more than I anticipated.'

'That's no problem, Mr Chambers, I have already prepared a couple of dozen passports'

'You have been a busy boy, Oscar, you'll receive a nice bonus, and I will probably see you tomorrow night with the other passport photos.'

Billy Chambers left the pub walking across the road, standing in the shade of a garden watching to see that Oscar Keylock wasn't being followed. Keylock came out the pub and drove away, nobody following the little runt. Sergeant Jessup watched as Billy Chambers drove away, making his own way back to Inspector Browns car.

'All went well. Billy Chambers passed over the photographs and arranged to call Oscar Keylock for another meeting, possibly tomorrow with the other photographs. He requires the first lot of passports ready for this coming Friday.'

'Ok let's pop around and get copies of the photos that Keylock picked up.

'Here are the first lot of photos,' looking at them Brown pointed, 'so this is Costa Esteve and this one Andres Lara and we know this is Billy Chambers. Great, Oscar, we'll get these back to you today just in case some bright spark wants to see a copy of a passport.'

Costa Esteve and Andres Lara met with Big Sam at Heathrow terminal 2 where Sam passed over the six passport photographs.

'Are we still on target for our robbery, Sam?'

'Absolutely, Costa, our main problem was the bridge and I am happy to say we have sorted and overcome that problem.'

'Have you given any more thought to having Andres as a spare driver?'

'I will let you know by our next meeting as it will be a collective vote by the lads.'

Costa Esteve's next journey was to meet up with Billy Chambers and hand over the last of the photographs which had been arranged for 18.00, time to have lunch and a rest Andres.

Arriving back at Scotland Yard, Inspector Brown faxed through the photos of Costa Esteve and Andres Lara to Captain Sifre at the Headquarters of the Guardia Civil in Madrid for validity. Within the hour, Captain Sifre had verified that the two photographs were certainly Costa Esteve and Andres Lara. Inspector Brown popped along to see Superintendent Parker letting him know the results of the first photographs for the passports, which had been verified by Captain Sifre.

'So this is the face of Costa Esteve and this one is Andres Lara,' said the Superintendent, 'and tonight we should be in possession of the other six photos of the robbery team, at last we are moving forward. Very good news Inspector Brown let me know as soon as we have the other photos.'

Chief Inspector Bleasdale called Sergeants Ben Clark and Reg More along with D.C.s Alex Quirk and Rod Muir to a meeting over the surveillance of the Red Lion. It was agreed to continue with the surveillance for a further week, as all the evidence gathered from their snouts pointed to the big robbery taking place in the next two weeks'

Billy Chambers met once again at the Chelsea Arms with Costa Esteve and Andres Lara, they passed over the last six photos to Billy and the extra ten grand so they received the passports on time.

'That's fine, Costa, did the meeting go well with Big Sam?'

'Yes indeed he has told me he's on schedule.'

'That's great news, Costa, my team will be ready.'

Bob Warden who had followed Billy Chambers sat once again listening to their conversation. He had already decided to follow Billy Chambers as there was no point driving to Heston just to watch them travel home.

Billy Chambers called Oscar Keylock from a call box on the corner of Chelsea way 'Hallo, Oscar, can you meet me tonight as I have the other photographs.'

'Yes, Mr Chambers, no problem it makes it easier for me to get everything ready for you by Friday.'

'That's magic, Oscar, we'll meet in the same pub say 20.30.

DC Facer informed Inspector Brown that a call had been received at the Norwood road flat from Billy Chambers.

'It's ok D.C. Facer, I've already had Oscar Keylock on the telephone.' Sergeant Jessup and Inspector Ward entered the office,

'We need to move fast. Chambers is meeting with Keylock at 20.30, so Sergeant we'll drop you at the pub and then we will disappear up one of the side roads.'

Sergeant Jessup was fortunate to be able to get the same table as before; he sat there with his pint and a pie along with the evening news to read. Fifteen minutes later, Billy Chambers arrived and carried out the same surveillance on the car park entered the pub purchasing his drinks and finding a table again by the window. Oscar Keylock arrived a little after ten minutes.

Billy had seen him drive into the car park and was sure Oscar wasn't followed. Billy waved to Oscar as he entered the bar. 'Here's your drink, Oscar.' Billy passed an envelope to Oscar containing the last six photographs for the passports.

'No problem, Mr Chambers all will be ready for you on Friday. Will I be getting a bonus?'

'Oscar, you'll be getting a big bonus, I will make sure of it.'

Bob Warden had spotted Inspector Brown's car and managed to find a spot to park. There was no way he was going to go into the pub, he wanted to watch and then make up his mind on his next move. Thirty minutes later, a chap walked out of the pub and got his car and drove off.

Billy Chambers in the meantime had stood watching the car pull away; being satisfied, he walked into the car park got his car and drove off. Bob couldn't see anybody following Chambers, so he started his car and pulled away following Chambers at a safe distance. Sergeant Jessup came out of the pub, Inspector Brown pulled up at the curb and Jessup got into the back seat.

They drove off to meet up with Oscar keylock, after collecting the six photographs and passing the other three back to Oscar Keylock they made for Scotland Yard. Sergeant Jessup took copies of the photos and made for the identification room.

Inspector Brown and Ward looked at the mug shots, 'I've seen most of these guys before except for these two,' pointing at the two photographs. 'This one is Jimmy Simmons, these two are John and Peter Shephard and this one is Paul Jack Daniel.' Sergeant Jessup walked back into the office.

'Sir, this photo here is Samuel Davidson, who escaped from a prison van while being transferred, and this one is a small time villain Derek Smallwood, he carried out a six month sentence for stealing vehicles.'

'So at last we have our famous six heavy robbers, all we need now is where this robbery is taking place and where this bloody Costa Esteve is hiding.'. Inspector Brown went along to see Superintendent Parker giving him the up-to-date news.

While Inspector Brown was with the Superintendent, the telephone rang, 'Hallo Chief Inspector, what can I do for you?'

'We have the whereabouts of Ken Delanny, he's been trying to find a way to travel to France.'

'Arrest him immediately and have him brought to Scotland Yard Chief Inspector.'

'I'll contact you when we have Delanny in custody, Superintendent.'

Chief Inspector Greedy with ten other detectives and a dozen uniformed officers surrounded a farmhouse just outside Maidstone; four of the police officers were armed.

The telephone in the farmhouse rang. 'Mr Kenneth Delanny, this is the police. Your farmhouse is surrounded with armed police officers. I suggest you all come out of the house with your hands in the air, that way nobody will be hurt.'

The telephone went dead. Chief Inspector Greedy gave the word to move in, a shot came out of one of the windows, and everybody took cover. Chief Inspector Greedy called in asking for another dozen armed officers.

Inspector Mace made his way towards the farm house throwing tear gas through the open window. Twenty minutes later, Inspector Ronald Smith arrived with his team of response armed officers. After a short discussion, three of his team shot further tear gas through the windows, there was much coughing and spitting going on in the farmhouse.

Inspector Ronald Smith with six of his officers moved towards the farmhouse. Another shot rang out and Inspector Ronald Smith fell to the ground. Six armed officers burst through the door, Ken Delanny seeing the armed officers immediately dropped his gun to the floor putting his hands up above his head. One of the police officers taking no chances hit Delanny on the chin with his gun sending him flying to the floor, another officer picked up Delanny's gun putting it into a plastic carrier.

Other armed police officers started a room to room search. Delanny was half carried out of the farmhouse handcuffed and bundled into a waiting police car and whisked off to Scotland Yard.

Two other suspects were found hiding in upstairs bedrooms they were handcuffed and brought outside of the farmhouse. Where they were told they would be charged with murder of Inspector Ronald Smith and whisked off to Maidstone police station.

Chief Inspector Greedy telephoned Superintendent Parker, letting him know that Ken Delanny was on his way to Scotland Yard, but at the cost of one of his Inspectors being shot dead by Delanny. Two other suspects had been arrested and were being taken to Maidstone police station to be interviewed'

'I'm sorry to hear that we have lost another officer in the line of duty, Chief Inspector, this whole case has been one murder after another.'

Superintendent Parker called the Deputy Commissioner giving him the sad news's and the up-to-date findings of the case so far.

Inspector Brown called Inspector Ward and Sergeant Jessup saying that Ken Delanny was being brought to Scotland Yard and that unfortunately, he had shot and killed an Inspector of the Kent Police.

Chief Inspector Greedy and Inspector Winehouse interviewed Mr Terrance Bond and Mr Barry McDonald who both looked a little beaten up but probably had fallen down the stairs of the farmhouse. After being told they were accessories to the murder of Inspector Ronald Smith. Both Bond and McDonald made a statement saying they were only looking after the farm for Ken Delanny and never knew he had a gun.

Chief Inspector Greedy charged both men with the murder of Inspector Ronald Smith.

Inspector Brown and Inspector Ward waited as Ken Delanny was processed.

Ken Delanny was lead to interview room 5, where Inspectors Brown and Ward interviewed him. 'I have no comment, Inspector.'

'Mr Delanny, you're going to be charged with murder of not only Inspector Ronald Smith of the Kent police force, but also for the murder of Jeffrey Mitchell among others. We have received information that you were involved in feeding a number of people to your pigs. I'm also led to believe that you were paid by Costa Esteve, Andres Lara, Liam Murphy and Billy Chambers.'

'I have no idea of any of these people you have mentioned, Inspector.'

'Really we have Liam Murphy already in custody and he has made a statement to that fact that you were involved.'

'He may have but I haven't the slightest idea of any of these people you are talking about, Inspector,' smiling all over his face.

'Mr Kenneth Delanny, you are charged with the murder of Police Inspector Ronald Smith of the Kent police force, and Mr Jeffrey Mitchell.

'We have so much time for further inquirers, your farm will be searched by SOCO experts for evidence of other body parts you've murdered, and believe me there will be many villains inside prison who certainly will help us as you have been involved with murdering their friends and family for money.'

Ken Delanny shrugged his shoulders but never said a word as he was led away to the cells. 'What a cold blooded murderer Ken Delanny is, how on earth can some of these villains live with themselves?'

'I have no idea, Inspector Ward.'

Inspector Brown called Chief Inspector Greedy letting him know that he had charged Ken Delanny with the murder of Inspector Ronald Smith and the conspiracy to murder Jeffrey Mitchell.

'I have a team from SOCO searching the farm so I really hope we find other evidence of body parts, Inspector.'

'That's great news, Chief Inspector, as I do not want to rely solely on Liam Murphy's evidence'

'Leave that to me, Inspector Brown, I'll make sure it is well turned over.'

Superintendent Parker and Inspector Brown stood at the head table in the conference room, in attendance were Inspector Ward, DC's Hirani, Smithy, Facer, Williamson, Beasley, Vincent, Illingsworth and Samuels.

'It's imperative we gather the information on this big robbery, now that we have their names and photographs of those taking part it should help us. We also have the photographs of the conspirators Costa Esteve, Andres Lara and of course Billy Chambers. Chambers we know is involved in the middle of this puzzle especially with the passport side, so it's been decided to follow him and hope he leads us to the robbery suspects.

'Car one will contain Inspector Ward and DC's Hirani and Smithy. Car two will contain D.C.s Facer and Williamson. Car three will contain Beasley and Vincent. Car four will contain DC's Illingsworth and Samuels. Each car will follow Chambers for no more than two miles and then interchange and so on, we will all be in radio contact. Is that clear everyone?'

'Yes, Sir.'

Inspector Ward in car one, was parked two streets away from Billy Chambers flat. Car two with Facer and Williamson were parked in Chambers road. Car three with Beasley and Vincent were parked two streets away to the south and car four with Illingsworth and Samuels were parked two streets to the North.

Inspector Ward radioed to his team, 'Message timed at 10.00, are all cars in position?' Affirmative was the reply.

A mini car driven by Bob Warden drove down the road spotting Inspector Wards car, driving on Bob circulated the nearby roads and streets spotting three more other undercover police cars. So they were trailing Billy Chambers, parking his car further up the road from Facer and Williamson, he tuned in his police radio frequency band.

Billy Chambers came out of his flat, the police radio clicked in 'Car one, I have the suspect leaving his flat at 11.10. Chambers drove down his road turning towards Brixton. Car three, we have the suspect in sight and will fall in behind car two, car four plot your course to the south towards Brixton'

'Affirmative.'

Bob Warden watched as Inspector Ward's car moved off with Bob following at a safe distance. After some thirty minutes, Chambers pulled in and parked his car, walking into the Red Lion.

Inspector Ward radioed telling his team to park up in different roads.

Sergeant Weber in the surveillance van, logged 'Billy Chambers entered the pub, five minutes later, Jimmy Simmons was logged as arriving at the pub.

Chambers and Simmons sat at a small table at the back of the bar.

'What's up, Jimmy,' asked Chambers'

'Big Sam has decided to pull the robbery next Wednesday.'

'That's fine, Jimmy, is there any other changes?'

'Not as I am aware of. Big Sam has called a meeting with the whole team tomorrow morning. So we will meet as planned tomorrow evening.' They waited several minutes finishing their beers and left separately.

Billy Chambers drove towards Streatham, car two reported that they had the suspect in sight and would follow, cars three and four pulled out into the main road and made their way towards car two. Inspector Ward also pulled out into the main road and followed at a distance to car four.

Bob Warden, who had listened to the police radio, also pulled out into the main road and followed Inspector Ward's car at a discreet distance.

Ten minutes later, Billy Chambers pulled up and parked his car in the car park of the Swan Public house walking into the pub, five minutes later George Lopez entered the pub.

Inspector Ward who had witnessed Lopez entering the pub said, 'that's a turn up for the books, where on earth does George Lopez fit into this robbery puzzle.'

Bob Warden who had also witnessed the episode, was also wondering what George Lopez was doing with Billy Chambers.

Billy Chambers put out his hand to greet George Lopez. Lopez completely ignored Chambers hand.

'You called me, Billy. What do you want?'

'There's no need for that kind of attitude, George, I've got a nice bit of work which will give you three hundred grand.'

'Billy, I'm legitimate these days. I'm not interested in robberies, and I remember the last time I worked with you ten years ago, I certainly have no wish to pick up where we left off.'

'George, we haven't got to get involved with a robbery, the robbery will have already taken place. All we are going to do is take the money from the robbers, easy as pie.'

'Billy, you are a shit. I want nothing to-do with you or your robbery.' Turning on his heals and walking out of the pub.

'Who the fuck does Lopez think he is, I don't need him anyway, the toffee-nosed shit.' Finishing his half pint and walking back to his car.

'Car one to all units, George Lopez who doesn't look too happy has left the pub and is being followed out by Billy Chambers.'

Billy Chambers drove back towards his flat with undercover police cars two, three and four following, Inspector Ward's car followed at a respectable distance.

Bob Warden drove towards George Lopez's home, passing Lopez walking on the pavement, stopping his car a further fifty yards down the road, he walked back towards Lopez 'Hallo, George.'

'Do I know you?'

'It's me Bob Warden.'

'Bloody hell, what have you done with yourself.'

'It's my beard.'

'Well it fooled me so I am sure nobody else would recognise you. What's it all about Bob, five minutes ago I met up with Billy Chambers and then I bump into you. Is it just a coincidence.'

'No George, I happened to drive by the swan pub when I saw Chambers and then you walk into the pub. Chambers is bad news and he's messing with some real hard villains, also the old bill are watching and following him, so I thought I better let you know.'

'Thanks for the tip, Bob; I already told Chambers I was not interested in any of his schemes. Chambers offered me three hundred grand to help snatch money from a gang who were pulling another robbery, what a shit that man is.'

Bob said his farewells, jumped back into his car turned on the police radio, listening to Inspector Ward telling his team to park their cars in different streets as Billy Chambers had returned to his flat.

Bob decided to drive over to Liam Murphy's flat and take a good look around for further information. Bob was thinking about the conversation he had with George Lopez. Chambers was putting together a team, planning to rob the robbers of the big job everybody was talking about. There's only one way Chambers would be able to take the money and that was with guns. What a bastard the man is.

Arriving at Liam Murphy's flat, he had a good look around the surrounding streets just in case the old bill were monitoring the flat. Bob made his way up the rear staircase to the third floor. Finding the electric cupboard, Liam had hidden the spare key under a stone in the far corner; lifting the stone he found the key and made his way to Liam's back door.

Looking through the window just in case the old bill were lurking about inside the flat, he carefully unlocked the door, locking the door behind him. Checking all the rooms finding nothing, it only left the bathroom. Bob pulled up the green carpet and found a floorboard which had been cut in half. Lifting the floorboard out of the way he found six grand in cash and two black notebooks.

Replacing the floorboards and the green carpet, Bob made his way back into the kitchen finding a small plastic bag, placing the money and the notebooks inside the bag. He then wiped all areas that he may have touched. Unlocking the back door looking out to see if anybody was about, he relocked the door, placing the key back under the stone in the electric cupboard.

Returning home he took a bottle of beer from the fridge and sat in his lazy-boy chair. Removed the notebooks from the plastic bag, and started reading through the notebooks. There was a list of telephone numbers including Ken Delanny and some guy called Juan Riminez who apparently had carried out business with Delanny. Then there was two bank account numbers and so much information on robberies and who carried them out. My God thought Bob, Liam is a grass. Bob pondered on this Juan Riminez guy, shall I bluff my way through, I have nothing to lose telephoning the number he had

'Hallo, Mr Riminez.'

'Who's calling?'

'That's of no importance at the moment, I believe I have some very valuable information that you require. 'I have the address of Costa Esteve and Andres Lara.' There was hush on the telephone for a minute.

'what do you want Mr'

'Ten grand.'

'You are out of your mind Mr'

'Ok, Mr Riminez, I'll post the information to the old bill, see you.'

'Hold on, don't be so hasty, let us meet and discuss the problem and the address of the gentleman we are speaking about.

'Mr Riminez, I've been about for a long time, I'll call you in the morning and you can let me know, speak soon,' putting down the telephone.

Juan Riminez turned to Miguel Melgar telling him about the strange call.

'It could be a trap by the police.'

'No Miguel, if it was the police they would have picked up Costa Esteve already as they want him as much as we do. We better call Madrid,' telephoning Carlos Moran, telling him about the information received.

'Pay him, Juan; it's cheap if we can get our hands on Costa Esteve and Andres Lara. The documents are worth a fortune.'

Inspector Ward decided they were wasting their time just sitting in their cars doing nothing.

'Car three unfortunately you've pulled the short straw and will have to hang around watching Chambers flat until midnight, we will all meet at Kilburn for breakfast at 7.30.'

The following morning, Cars two, three, and four started the observation of Chambers flat. DC Hirani was to pick up Inspector Ward. It had been arranged that if Chambers moved, radio conversation would take place.

The Deputy Commissioner, Superintendent Parker, and Inspectors Brown and Ward discussed the next moves; the Deputy Commissioner was pleased with the procedure so far, but was concerned about this big robbery going down in the next two weeks.

The conversation changed to the court appearance of Liam Murphy, McRight and McCathy. Parker had hoped that McRight and McCathy would have cracked by now. But as time went by, it was becoming very doubtful.

McRight and McCathy had realised that it was Murphy who had turned Queen's evidence. All the snouts in the Brixton remand wing were speaking openly that Murphy was the supergrass, shortly there's going to be a very big price on Murphy's head said Inspector Brown.

Inspector Ward made for the tube station and travelled back to Kilburn police station for a quick sandwich joining D.C.s Hirani and Smithy, they drove off to meet up with the others.

Bob Warden continued to read the notebook of Murphy's; he had the police radio on, nothing was happening at the present time. Checking and double checking the telephone numbers in the notebook. He came across Jeff Mitchell and Joe Bolt; there was also Jimmy Simmons, Peter and John Shephard. It was obvious that sooner or later, Liam Murphy was going to need these two notebooks if he was going to keep on grassing. Bob looked at his watch it was 11.30, picking up the telephone he called Juan Riminez. 'Have you made up your mind?'

'Yes I have been ordered to pay you ten grand for the address, but let me tell you if you are messing us around, you have picked the wrong people.'

'Of course, Juan,' speaking in a bored manner.

'You seem to know a lot about me and I know nothing about you.'

'That's correct, I feel much safer that way. Now how do you wish to carry out our business arrangement, Juan?'

'We will meet you at the address of Costa Esteve and pay you there.'

'I think I am wasting my time with you, Juan. I thought you were more intelligent after your stupid routine last night. I promise you this Mr Riminez, I won't be calling you back.'

'Ok, Ok, how do you wish to work our business transaction, said Juan.'

'We will meet at I4.00 at Hammersmith Broadway Station, you will have the ten grand with you. We'll drive to Costa Esteve's flat and once you are satisfied with the location, I will shoot off. One of you can drive with me and the other guy can follow in your own car.'

'One minute please.' Bob heard muffled voices.

'Ok we agree.'

Bob arrived early and sat in the coffee shop overlooking the train station. He noticed two foreign looking guys walk up and stand outside the station. Bob walked over to them saying, 'Juan Riminez, I presume.'

'That's me.'

'I'm Bob Smith.'

'Hallo, Mr Smith, my friend Miguel here will drive with you and I will follow in my car.'

'Ok, but first I would like to check my money, let's pop into the cafe and have a coffee or beer. While I count my money.' Juan Riminez asked him why he was informing on the whereabouts of Costa Esteve and Andres Lara.

'Both those gentleman have caused my friends many problems, and in one case, a really dear friend of mine was murdered.'

'So its revenge.' Bob nodded, he had also finished counting the money.

'Mr Smith, once we have Costa Esteve and his friend, you will forget all about our business meeting, we want no double-cross.'

'Mr Jiminez, what you do with those people is none of my business, I just couldn't care less.'

They made their way to Heston which took forty-five minutes, parking in Macan Street. 'Mr Smith, you go over and knock on Esteve's door.' Bob crossed the street knocking, there was no reply, he tried again but again there was no reply. He walked back to his car and got inside. 'There's no answer so perhaps they are having a late lunch or drink.'

'Then we will wait.'

'No problem to me, Juan.' Another hour passed when a car came around the corner pulling up outside number 23, the passenger side door opened and out stepped Costa Esteve.

'Bob, you have done well, please make yourself scarce.'

'Nice doing business with you, Juan.' Walking back to his car and driving off with his ten grand and thinking, thank you Liam, that's sixteen grand you've given me in two days.

Miguel walked to the back of his car, opened the boot pulling out two weapons both with silencers. Unbeknown to Riminez, one of the house owners across the street had noticed the two cars parked for some time and had called the police. A lone pander car arrived and observed the dark haired chap hand a gun to the driver of the Jag. He immediately called for backup, five minutes later, three armed police cars sped into Macan Street one pulling in front of the Jag and one behind and another pulled up at the side.

Before Melgar or Riminez could respond, they were surrounded by armed police who demanded that they drop their guns and lie flat on the ground with their arms outstretched. Another police van sped into the street, and both Riminez and Melgar were bundled handcuffed into the back, and transferred to Heathrow Police Station. Juan turned to Miguel saying that bloody Bob Smith must have been a cop. One hour later, their Jag was towed to Heathrow police pound.

Costa Esteve and Andres Lara were looking out of their window wondering what on earth was happening.

Bob Warden had listened to the police radio all the way home, all the chatter said Billy Chambers had walked from his flat to the local pub had stayed there for three hours and returned home.

Superintendent Parker was at home when he received a telephone call saying that two foreign chaps with firearms had been arrested at Heston and were being held at Heathrow Police Station. Their fingerprints had been taken and sent to the forensics department for verification. Parkers heart jumped believing it might be Costa Esteve and Andres Lara.

The Superintendent called Inspector Brown letting him know of the possible arrest of Esteve and Lara. D.C. Isles collected both Parker and Brown and made his way to Heathrow police Station. The talk all the way was that of anticipating the arrest of Costa Esteve and Andres Lara.

Inspector Charles Beagle was interviewing the two arrested foreign men, who refused to say a word 'You should help yourselves gentleman by giving your names. As you will be charged with being in possession of firearms and attempted burglary with intent to harm unknown persons, which carries a prison sentence of at least ten years.

Superintendent Parker and Inspector Brown arrived at Heathrow police Station and were greeted by Inspector Beagle; Superintendent Parker produced photographs both of Costa Esteve and Andres Lara. Inspector Beagle shook his head saying neither of these men resembles the two foreign men he had in custody'

'Blast it Brown, I thought we had them'

'While I'm here Inspector Beagle, we might as well interview these two chaps.

Superintendent Parker and Inspector Brown sat at the table asking a number of questions, which went unanswered. Parker then produced photographs of Costa Esteve and Andres Lara 'do you know these two men' there was no reply.

'Ok we know you are Spanish citizens and your fingerprints have been sent to the Guardia Civil in Madrid, 'we will have your identification within hours. The two men were taken away to the cells. Superintendent Parker deliberated whether to move them to Scotland Yard, but decided against the move.

The Courthouse was totally secured with armed police officers and security present. Mick McRight and Paul McCathy were in a secure glassed witness box with four armed officers guarding them. The courtroom door opened and another four armed police officers along with Liam Murphy entered and were lead to another specialised witness box. As Liam Murphy passed, McRight and McCathy banged on the glass shouting, 'You fucking grass Murphy you're dead.'

Jonathan Crisp lawyer for the Crown opened saying that Mr McRight and Mr McCathy were charged with murder of Alonzo Ortuno, along with six armed robberies with members of the public being extremely hurt. We also have a witness who has turned Queen's evidence and has given us precise dates of the robberies and the movements of McRight and McCathy. Fortunately we have another witness, 'Mr Alan Macman who was fishing at the time and witnessed the defendants throw the body of Alonzo Ortuno into the canal. Therefore the Crown would like Mr McRight and Mr McCathy committed to the Crown court.

Mr Willis Shawbum lawyer for both McRight and McCathy objected to the court. Saying the main suspect in the murder was actually Liam Murphy, who had turned Queen's evidence for a deal with the crown prosecution. 'My clients are innocent of the murder.

The crown wishes to call Mr Alan Macman, 'Mr Macman would you please tell the court what you witnessed on the 26 June.'

'I was looking for somewhere to fish, passing through the wooded area and bushes when I noticed those men carrying a body wrapped in plastic with concrete hanging down from the poor chap's waist and legs. They lifted the body up onto the rail of the bridge and pushed the body into the canal.'

Mr Shawbum rose asking, 'Mr Macman how on earth could you see my clients, throw what looked like a body wrapped in plastic into the canal?'

'I witnessed the police remove the body from the canal.'

'May I suggest that it might not have been the same body, because as you have mentioned you witnessed men throwing something wrapped in plastic into the canal, it could have been a roll of carpet.'

'I witnessed those men over there throw a body into the canal,' pointing at them.

'I suggest, Mr Macman, you're not really sure are you that it was a body.'

'I can only say that four men throw a body wrapped in plastic into the canal.'

'Four men, Mr Macman, that's interesting as the police are saying it was three men.'

'I'm sure it was four men.'

'But you're not certain are you, Mr Macman?'

Mr Shawbum turned to the bench, 'Your Honour, I cannot see my clients have a case to answer. First of all we are told there was three people involved in throwing something into the canal. Now the Crown has a witness who states that there were actually four people involved in throwing something wrapped in plastic into the canal. The Crown would like to call Mr Liam Murphy as our next witness.'

Liam Murphy remained behind his glassed witness box, giving evidence, focusing on the fact that he and both McRight and McCathy had held Alonzo Ortuno in a flat for a number of days without feeding him. Before moving Ortuno to a factory unit, where he was chained to the floor and didn't receive any water or food, as they wanted information from Ortuno.

'Would you like to tell the court what information you required?'

'We wanted to know who murdered Kenny Owen.'

'Did Mr Ortuno give you the information you required?'

'Yes he did, he told us that it was Billy Chambers who murdered Kenny Owen.'

'Now let's move onto these robberies; what part did you and Mr McRight and Mr McCathy play?'

'Mick McRight who was armed held up the different post offices while Paul McCathy and myself gathered all the cash putting it into bags. If somebody got out of hand Mick McRight would give them a slap.'

A slap?'

'He would hit them,' said Murphy.

'I see,' said Jonathon Crisp.

Mr Shawbum suggested to Liam Murphy that it was himself that dished out the slapping and not his client.

'No it was Mick McRight,' said Murphy.

The court hearing lasted another thirty minutes, when Michael McRight and Paul McCathy were both committed to the Crown Court, both held without bail, and both shouting and swearing at Liam Murphy 'you're fucking dead, you bastard!'

Superintendent Parker and Inspector Brown who were sitting at the back of the court walked over to Jonathon Crisp, a little worried about the information that four men throw the body into the canal.

Jonathon Crisp suggested that the Superintendent should question Liam Murphy on the counter ability of how many people were present at the murder.

After returning to Scotland Yard, Parker received a telephone call from Captain Sifre, confirming the two men in custody, were Miguel Melgar and Juan Riminez.

Both worked for notorious crime family headed by Carlos Moran in Madrid. It is known that Melgar had flown from Spain to London Heathrow and were obviously connected with the Peter Sainsbury business.

Inspector Brown asked the Superintendent what procedure we should adopt with Billy Chambers.

'We will allow Billy Chambers to collect the passports and hopefully with Inspector Ward and his team following Chambers, it will lead to arrest of Costa Esteve and Andres Lara and the Heavy gang.'

Big Sam met up with the others members of the gang at Watneys Brewery at Putney riverbank, suggesting that maybe it would be better if they had a further driver and vehicle.

'Hold on a minute, Sam, we've already agreed on the split,' said Scotch Jack.

'Yes I agree, however our backers have suggested Andres Lara as another driver that would cost us nothing. But we gain another four-wheel drive on the other side of the bridge; the chain would no longer be a problem to us. Derrick and John Shephard weren't keen on the idea, saying that we are a team and trust each other, we don't know this Andres Lara or even if he can drive.'

Jimmy Simmons pointed out that another driver would give us the edge.

'I agree,' said Big Sam, 'what's your opinion, Scotch Jack?'

'I'm not sure Sam, as none of us know this Andres guy, however I agree with Jimmy it would give us the edge if there is any trouble.'

'Ok let's take a vote.' All agreed with Derrick and John Shephard being a little reluctant.

'That settles the matter; we'll pull the robbery next Wednesday. I'll be meeting with our backers and finalising the plan of how we are getting out of the country, the passports will be with us before the weekend, so as usual keep out of the limelight.'

Finishing their meeting, they all headed off in different directions except Big Sam who pulled Derrick's arm. 'Let's have a drink in the Horse and Groom,' said Sam, they sat at a table near the front window with their beers.

'Derrick what will your Mrs do while you are away?'

'She'll be fine Sam we have already talked about the situation.'

'What's your take on the setup, as I got the impression you were a bit reluctant on taking this other driver.'

'Sam I worry about taking on last minute people, especially when we don't even know the guy.'

'What do you know about George Lopez?'

'I don't know him personally, but Joe Bolt worked with him a few times in the past with Jeff Mitchell, and I remember Joe saying Lopez was sound. Why do you ask?'

'Last night he called me telling me that Billy Chambers and some other known villains were planning to take our money once we had pulled the robbery.'

'Why didn't you tell the gang?'

'I didn't want to worry anybody, plus I didn't like the information about Jeff Mitchell being fed to the pigs and may have a connexion with Costa Esteve and Andres Lara. If anybody is going to grass on us, it must be one of our own. The way I see this problem, is when I meet up with Costa Esteve today, whoever Esteve suggests should be seated in the four-wheeler after the raid will be the grass.'

'Bloody hell Sam, they could give my name, and I'm no grass.'

'They won't be giving your name Derrick that's for sure. I have it all planned so don't worry; tomorrow we'll meet up with Scotch Jack and plan our escape.'

'What about the Shephard brothers?'

'Don't worry if they are not involved they will be secure and that goes for Jimmy Simmons as well.'

Big Sam met Costa Esteve and Andres Lara at Twickenham. 'How did you meeting go Sam?'

'All was agreed. Andres will be our extra driver.'

'Good news as I have already got the other vehicle for you, now let's get down to business once the robbery has taken place. You will have a two way radio one for Andres and the other for yourself. Once you are on your way to the bridge you radio Andres he backs the getaway vehicle onto the bridge we load the money into Andres vehicle and away to Denham airport. I would suggest that at least one other member of your team travels with Andres.'

'Ok Costa who have you in mind?'

'What about Jimmy Simmons?'

'That's ok with me, but perhaps we should have two members of the gang travelling with Andres.'

'Ok who have you in mind Sam?'

'Me.'

'I don't think that's a good idea as you are wanted to organise the getaway.'

'Now for the escape. We'll have the aircraft ready to move us all out as soon as we arrive at Denham.'

Jimmy Simmons made his way to meet up with Billy Chambers. Inspector Wards team had been following Chambers all day and the direction Chambers was making looked like he was headed for the Red Lion. Bob Warden was also following Inspector Wards team who parked their cars in different roads as did Bob Warden, who continued to listen to the police radio.

Sergeant Weber had on his surveillance tape Jimmy Simmons and Billy Chambers entering the Red Lion.

Jimmy Simmons and Billy Chambers sat at a table as far as possible from the bar discussing the getaway plan that Big Sam was going to use.

'That's good news Jimmy, are you sure that Big Sam's pulling the robbery next Wednesday?'

'Yes he made that quite clear to us all today.'

'One question Billy how are you going to tip off the Old Bill about the robbery without dropping us all init?'

'That's simple Jimmy, we know Sam Davidson will be making his way to Denham airport, your vehicle will be travelling to a safe house in Heston. The police will be waiting at Denham for Sam Davidson and his gang to arrive, they'll all be nicked before they even know it. We on the other hand will lay low for ten days then slip out of the country, very rich men.'

'Great planning Billy.'

Superintendent Parker and Inspector Brown once again arrived at Heathrow police station and were met by Inspector Beagle. 'I'm pleased to say Inspector we have identified the two suspects you have in custody.'

Waiting in the interview room were Juan Riminez and Miguel Melgar.

'Hallo again gentleman, I'm not going to mess around with you. We have your identifications and we know you both speak English. You are Miguel Melgar and you are Juan Riminez,' pointing at both as he mentioned their names.

Both Juan and Miguel looked at each other.

'We have all the information Mr Melgar as when you arrived from Spain and when Mr Riminez collected you from Heathrow Airport. You both work for Carlos Moran and now face a lifetime in prison for the murder of Peter Sainsbury, let alone being involved with firearms.

'Now's the time to make up your minds either start talking or face a really long time behind bars, it's your choice. We will separate you now and commence the interview.

'Mr Riminez you have been in Britain for a number of years and know our justice system, life imprisonment will mean twenty years. You are a little younger than Mr Melgar, but you still will not be getting out of prison until you are in your sixties.'

'What's in it for me Superintendent if I help you?'

'Let's say only five years maximum.'

'Alright but how will you help me when Miguel finds out I have grassed?'

'Mr Riminez that's our problem, we'll assist you but we want information first. Why is Carlos Moran so interested in having Costa Esteve and Andres Lara back in Spain?'

'Carlos couldn't care less if Esteve or Lara returns to Spain; he only wants the documents and maps.'

'What documents and maps?' asked Parker.

'The maps hold the whereabouts of the Knight Templar Treasure and possibly the Holy Grail.'

'So you're telling us that Peter Sainsbury had these valuable maps and documents in his safe at Mallards Publishing house?'

'Yes, because some of the secrets are here in the UK and it was his job to locate and discover the whereabouts of this great Treasure.'

'Ok say we believe your story, where did Costa Esteve and Andres Lara fit into this plot?'

'Costa was in Madrid and somehow overheard the information regarding Peter Sainsbury and the maps. Costa came to England conned Peter Sainsbury into believing he knew all about the Treasurer and maps from Carlos Moran, which wasn't true.'

'Where are Esteve and Lara hiding?'

'First Superintendent I want the deal in writing, once I've received the deal in writing, I will give you all the information you require.'

'It's going to take a little time Juan; I have to communicate with the Deputy Commissioner.'

'Superintendent it sounds like I have all the time in the world, and I would like some really good Spanish food.'

Superintendent Parker telephoned the Deputy Commissioner briefing him on the situation, saying the case has once again opened up in another direction, this time maybe involving the Freemasons, 'and he wants the deal in writing.'

'That's going to be difficult Superintendent because of his involvement in different murders; however I will consult with the Commissioner.' The Superintendent realised there was nothing to be achieved by staying at Heathrow and would return to Scotland Yard.

The Police force had received quotations for cleaning and catering, the catering contract had been awarded to the Police helpers Ltd. One of their employees was a Spanish lad named Jose Alfonso; Jose would transport the food from the factory unit to the Police Station, and assist in dispatching the food to the prisoners. Entering the cell block which was monitored by a police Sergeant and a Constable, Jose received his orders and would return to his kitchen area and prepare the food. Once prepared, the food was placed on a trolley and taken back to the Cell block. The Sergeant or Constable would unlock the cells and wait for Jose to give the prisoner their food and relock the cell. As Jose neared the cell of Miguel Melgar the little hatch was open.

'What's your name young fellow?' asked Melgar.

'Jose, Mr…'

'Are you Spanish?'

'Yes I am.'

'If you deliver this message for me I'll give you two hundred euro.'

'I cannot help you, I will lose my job,' said Jose.

'Jose my message is very important if you call this number in Madrid, I'll give you a further two hundred euro.'

'Ok give me the number in Madrid.'

Jose Alfonso called Mr Carlos Moran in Madrid and passed on the message which was in code. 'Jose you have done well if you help me I will make sure you receive another 1,000 euros.'

'I will help you,' said Jose.

'Ok this is what I want you to do.'

Returning later to the police station Jose was told that there was a special food requirement for the prisoner in cell number 20.

Jose looked at the menu, thinking indeed Mr Riminez will be receiving a very special menu this evening, he loaded his trolley and made his way to the cell. The Sergeant on duty was busy and really didn't want to be bothered with food requirements.

Passing the cell of Miguel Melgar Jose passed the message he had received from Carlos Moran, Miguel Melgar smiled as he read the message.

Juan Riminez sitting on his bunk bed, tucked into his fish soup, thinking 'I'll be able to receive special treatment for as long as he wanted.' Juan dipped his bread into the soup savouring every last drop, his hands grabbed his throat, he couldn't make a sound as he fell first sideways onto the corner of his bunk bed and slipped to the floor dead.

Twenty minutes later the cell Constable making his rounds looked through the hatch of Riminez cell door, seeing Riminez on the floor he opened the door, after checking the body he immediately pressed the alarm button.

Inspector Beagle was called and couldn't believe what had happened, calling the cell Sergeant asking why Riminez hadn't been checked on before. He just shrugged his shoulders saying, 'I carried out my orders correctly to the book.'

'When Scotland Yard finishes with us, let's hope you carry out your duties to the book when plodding around the streets!' The Inspector hurried along the corridor to call Scotland Yard.

Superintendent Parker was enjoying the company of the Deputy Commissioner, when his telephone rang answering on the second ring.

'How on earth has that happened Beagle, the importance of the investigation was in your hands.' Looking rather stunned, Parker told the Deputy Commissioner, 'Juan Riminez is dead, it is believed he was poisoned.'

'Damn Parker damn your investigation appears to keep failing, what on earth am I going to tell the Commissioner?' As he walked out of Parker's office.

Superintendent Parker called Captain Sifre who was stunned at the news of Juan Riminez' death. Parker briefed Captain Sifre on the information received thus far.

'The story is now making sense, we will explore this new information regards the Knight Templars here in Spain, lastly I did warn you Superintendent, Carlos Moran has hands like an octopus.

Billy Chambers and Jimmy Simmons departed the pub, Sergeant Weber turned to his constable, 'That's the first time they have left together, I'm pleased we have it on tape.'

Inspector Ward and his team followed Billy Chambers back to his flat and couldn't really see Chambers going out again. Car two you have the short straw tonight, we all meet again 7,30 Kilburn.

Bob Warden had driven part of the way, and had listened to the police chat; decided that he would head off home and summarise the day's events.

Big Sam called Derrick and Scotch Jack making an appointment to see them both at l am at the Barbican centre.

The Commissioner was horrified not only of another murder but of handling of the whole investigation. 'There has been one disaster after another what on earth is Parker playing at. I want an immediate inquiry into this unfortunate mess, the home Secretary is going to want a head cut off I'm sure,' picking up his telephone from the side desk, he called Commander Rose, after a briefing, Rose was informed to report directly to the Deputy Commissioner on all findings.

Commander Rose and Inspector Peter Baker made their way to Heathrow Police Station and were met by Inspector Beagle.

'First of all Inspector I would like to have a look at your cell area. Now let's go from the first moment to the last moment when the food is delivered to the prisoners.'

'Sir, we have a Cell Sergeant and Constable, whose duty it is to log all food requirements and the times when the food is given to the prisoners.'

'Is the duty cell Sergeant here?'

'I'll find out Sir, in the meantime please use my office as your base.' The Commander and Inspector Baker made their way to the second floor office of Inspector Beagle.

'It sounds like a rum do Inspector Baker.'

Inspector Beagle entered the office very flustered. 'Sir I afraid the Cell Sergeant has reported sick and gone home.'

'Really, we will need his address Inspector; now tell me about the situation when Superintendent Parker was here.'

'The Superintendent gave instructions to make sure that Mr Riminez had special arrangements for food.'

'Who did Mr Riminez give his special food order too?'

'The Duty Cell Sergeant or the Constable,' looking down at the cell log, the Commander looked up.

'Inspector it states here that Mr Riminez ordered fish soup to start with and roast chicken for his second course, so you are saying that Riminez would have given this order only to the Duty Sergeant or constable?'

'Yes Sir.'

'Is the Cell Block Constable still in the station?'

'Yes he is Sir.'

'We would like to see him now.'

Constable Dickinson walked into the office and saluted.

'When Mr Riminez passed on his special food order was it you who received it?'

'No Sir it was my Sergeant, he passed it to me to deal with. I make sure the order went to the kitchen; they in turn would prepare the food and have it delivered to the cells.'

'Are you saying the kitchen staff has access to the cells?'

'No Sir, the food would be brought down to the cells on a food trolley and either my Sergeant or I would then unlock the cell door. The food would be handed over and the cell door relocked.'

'So in your opinion Constable nobody could have passed anything other than the food to Mr Juan Riminez without an officer being present?'

'That's correct Sir.'

Commander Rose looked at the analyst report which had identified poison. 'Inspector Beagle, somehow somebody gave Mr Riminez poison, so it's murder for sure. What time are the prisoners next meals provided?'

Inspector Beagle checked his watch looked up at the Commander saying 'about now Sir.'

'Constable Dickinson, I would like you to sit out there and write out your statement. Inspector Beagle let's make a visit to the cell block.'

The cell block consisted of twenty-five cells each side of the corridor, the Commander and the two Inspectors made their way down the cell block turning left at the end. 'The duty Sergeant cannot see us from his position,' said the Commander; a door opened and the food trolley came along being pushed by a member of the kitchen staff, who opened the hatch on the cell door and passed the food to the prisoner. Inspector Beagle was horrified.

'Inspector Beagle I believe you have a very lax operation going on here,' mentioned the Commander. 'I want the names and addresses of all the kitchen staff and anybody else who may have access to the cells.'

The Commander and Inspector Baker returned to Beagle's office calling Constable Dickinson in.

'I have just visited the cellblock and witnessed the procedure taking place, no officer assisted the kitchen staff. They were allowed to open the hatch on the cell door and pass the food through. Now lad, start telling the truth or you're going to find yourself out of the police force.'

'Sir we are short staffed and therefore have allowed the kitchen staff to pass the food through the cell door hatches.'

'My God, lad you should have told me this in the beginning.'

'I couldn't Sir as the Inspector is aware of the procedure.'

'Now write out your statement and pass it to me before I leave.'

'Yes Sir.'

Looking through the cell log book, the name Jose Alfonso continued to appear.

'He's a member of the Kitchen staff,' replied Inspector Baker.

'Go and see if he's still around; if he is let's have a look at him.'

Inspector Beagle returned to his office apologising for the mistake in the cell block.

'Inspector it's not my job to worry about who did what in the cellblock, but it will go into my report. Now I'm having a chap called Jose Alfonso brought up, this Alfonso is in there every day.'

Inspector Baker brought Jose Alfonso in. Alfonso was about 5,6 receding hair, a little fat and he wore glasses.

'Mr Alfonso my name is Commander Rose and I need you to answer some questions, I notice from the cell log book that you are in and out of the cell block all the time.'

'That's correct Sir, I deliver the food to the prisoners.'

'How long have you worked here?'

'About four years.'

'How long have you been living in the UK?'

'About twelve years.'

'You are aware that there was a death in the cellblock.'

'Yes Sir.'

'So what part did you play in giving Mr Riminez poison?'

'Me, I didn't have anything to do with it.'

'Mr Alfonso you were in the cellblock three times before Mr Riminez was murdered, if you tell me the truth I will try and help you, now who gave the orders.'

'Please Inspector Beagle you know me I wouldn't have anything to do with murder.'

'Inspector Beagle cannot help you Jose, only I can; now tell me all you know.'

'Will I go to prison?'

'I have no idea Jose, but I will try and help you.'

'The man in cell 8 Miguel Melgar asked me to telephone and pass a message to a man in Madrid called Carlos Moran. When I spoke with Mr Moran, he told me to write a note to Melgar which I did and that another Spanish man would arrive and give me two thousand euros and some special food for Mr Riminez.'

'Didn't you realise that the food may have been poisoned?'

'No Sir.'

'Did you keep the telephone number that Miguel Melgar gave you for this Carlos Moran in Madrid?'

'I think so, would you like me to fetch it?'

'Yes, Inspector Beagle you go with Jose Alfonso.'

Constable Dickinson had finished his statement and brought it in to the Commander. 'Now listen to me carefully lad, from this day forward, if you are on duty in the cellblock, make sure the correct procedure are always carried out.'

'I will Sir, thank you.' As the Constable walked out, Inspector Baker commented, 'What chance has a young constable got if their Sergeants and Station Inspectors are unwilling to make sure the correct procedures are carried out.'

'I'm sure Inspector that will be dealt with pretty smartly once my report is received.'

The Alarm in the police station went off down in the canteen area; the telephone rang in Beagle's office. Picking up the telephone the Commander was told that Jose Alfonso had hung himself in the cold room. Commander Rose and Inspector Baker rushed down to the kitchen area where they found some of the kitchen ladies crying and some of the men sitting on the floor holding their head in their hands.

'Inspector Beagle how on earth did this happen, you were told to stay with Jose.'

'Sir, Jose told me the paper and the addresses were up in his locker, as I looked up at the locker, Jose ran into the cold room, locked the door. By the time we were able to reopen the door, he was hanging from the ham rail.'

Commander Rose and Inspector Baker interviewed Miguel Melgar, who appeared to be very uncooperative. After informing Melgar of the poisoning of Juan Riminez and that Jose Alfonso had already admitted taking instructions from him. Calling a telephone number in Madrid and speaking with Carlos Moran.

'I suggest Miguel you start talking.'

'They'll kill me.'

'I'm sure they will in time Mr Melgar, but you have a choice, it would be very simple for us to furnish details to the Guardia Civil in Madrid, saying how helpful you are becoming and I'm sure the Guardia Civil would be able to pass on that information to Carlos Moran.'

'You Bastards, they'll kill me for sure.'

'Then I suggest you help us, first of all I'll have you moved from here to Scotland Yard, where you will be safe.'

'Ok, I'll talk but I want a deal.'

'Inspector Beagle I want an armed police vehicle to transport Mr Melgar to Scotland Yard.'

Sergeant Cox and DC Thomas had made a complete search of Jose Alfonso's home and his work locker, finding hidden in a shoe, telephone numbers that corresponded to Madrid, they also found hidden under a pile of shirts 2000 euro.

Commander Rose called the Deputy Commissioner briefing him on the situation, 'I'll have a full report ready for your perusal.'

The Deputy Commissioner called Captain Sifre giving him the details of the telephone numbers found in the possession of Jose Alfonso. The Captain had the numbers put through the Guardia Civil computers, finding one number corresponded to Carlos Moran's home, another to his office, all other telephone numbers were to Alfonso's close relatives.

Captain Sifre, Sergeant Gillispe and Officer Gloria Egido pondered over the case so far. 'Gloria have you found anything interesting on this Knight Templar situation?'

'Sir the Knight Templar's here in Spain are under the name of Grand Encampment of Spain and Iberia and may have secrets of the Knight Templar Treasure and the Holy Grail. All the names of those involved in the Knight Templars appear to be men of high quality and have no criminal backgrounds.'

'So we are back to Peter Sainsbury and the contents of his safe documents, plans and possible maps pointing to the Knight Templar Treasure. That is the information given by Juan Riminez which points to all these murders are certainly connected to those documents and plans.'

'So who is in possession of the documents and plans now, it must be Costa Esteve and Andres Lara.'

Gloria piped up, 'That's why Miguel Melgar was sent to the UK by Carlos Moran to find both Esteve and Lara.'

'Ok next question, why if Costa Esteve has these documents in his possession would he get involved in a big robbery?'

'Again Sir,' spoke up Gloria, 'to finance the search of the Knight Templar Treasure.'

Sergeant Gillispe put one of our undercover units on surveillance of Carlos Moran and let's start monitoring Moran's telephone said the Captain. Picking up the telephone and calling his Commander, briefing him on their theory about the Treasure maps and crimes.

'That's some theory Captain, but I must say it is defiantly adding up to that collusion.'

Bob Warden had been pondering over the facts that Jimmy Simmons was in league with Billy Chambers and was obviously a traitor to Big Sam and his gang.

Big Sam, Derrick and Scotch Jack met at the Barbican. 'Jack I have come across a traitor within the gang.'

'Who is it Sam, I'll kill him.'

'Later Jack, let's first look at the plan we put in place the other day, the Robbery itself is not a problem we will just fine tune the getaway. We'll take a chance and cut the chain on the bridge the day before the robbery. When Andres backs onto the bridge, we'll load the money as planned onto his vehicle, but as we are loading. Derrick you will go around the side of the vehicle and jump into the driving seat Jack you will climb into the back seat, telling Jimmy Simmons to get into the other vehicle. Andres won't like the idea but I'll take care of him and if necessary I'll give him a smack and throw him in the back with you Jack. By this time the Shephard brothers would have slipped the chain completely allowing their vehicle to follow us.

'Now somewhere nearby will be Billy Chambers and his gang waiting for us, they will be armed that's for sure, but so will we, if shooting starts unfortunately Andres and Jimmy Simmons will be disposed of.'

'Bloody hell Sam that's going to cause us problems,' said Derrick.

'It's unfortunate Derrick but it's going to be all over in minutes.'

'Ok Sam but we will not be able to use Denham airport for our getaway so where are we going to disappear too with the money?' asked Scotch Jack.

'That my friends is the million dollar question; we only have six days to find a new bolt hole, it must be somewhere near. I've got an idea; I'll give George Lopez a call as I know he has his hands in the property market.'

'Can he be trusted?' asked Derrick.

'Derrick remember it was George who tipped me off about the treachery.'

'What about this Costa Esteve guy?' asked Scotch Jack.

'We'll take care of him another day said Big Sam'

'What about Peter and John Shephard; when are we going to tell them of the change?'

'We're not Jack as I do-not want any more pressure put on the robbery, they'll have to trust my judgment on the day. Obviously you two will have to start searching around Brentford area for somewhere we can hide up for a least two weeks, we'll meet again tonight at 20,00 at the PIG in the Stick at Hedley.'

Big Sam made his way back home, making a call to George Lopez explaining the problem.

'I must say Sam I've been worried for some time about this foreign mob being involved. There is something more sinister behind all these murders. Anyway enough on the telephone, why don't you pop across and we can speak in peace and quiet.'

'I'll be there in an hour George.'

'That's fine Sam; by the time you get here I'll have the solution solved.'

Derick and Jack drove first to Greenford, Ruislip and then to Brentford where they found a factory unit with a small office and flat above. Finding the owner and inquiring about the price for a two month letting. The owner laughed saying,

'What are you trying to do run a long firm; I'm not interested in getting involved in any criminal activities.'

'No mate, all we want to do is store some materials and then ship the same to France.'

'Ok the price is ten grand a month and I'll look the other way.'

'We'll get back to you in a couple of days.'

'What do you think Jack it's promising but I don't like the guy.'

Big Sam travelled by the underground arriving at George Lopez's house within the hour.

'Nice seeing you again Sam and this time in better surroundings, I will never forget you saved my life in prison and I owe you for that.'

'George you owe me nothing, however if you can help me I will be obliged. You were certainly correct about the treachery it is Jimmy Simmons.'

'I must say that does surprise me Sam, I always thought Jimmy was a stand-up guy, however I have good news for you. I've found a factory unit with accommodation that might interest you.'

'Where George?'

'Richmond.'

'That sounds ideal George, how much will it cost me?'

'What's the robbery worth?'

'Three to four million.'

'How's a hundred grand sound Sam?'

'You've got a deal George.'

'Tomorrow you can take a look, here's the keys and directions and if you like it, give me a call and I'll let the key holder know that I have rented the factory out for three months. Now let's sit down and have a drink.' Sitting down with their scotch in their hands, Sam asked George what he meant about there being something more sinister behind the crimes.

'Look at it this way Sam, Jeff Mitchell carried out the safe blowing at Mallards and I would bet it was Joe Bolt with him. Whatever Jeff pulled out of that safe got him fed to the pigs, that's not rocket science. We keep hearing about the documents, maps and plans, so who has these documents, maps and plans, I would bet it's this foreign firm headed by Costa Esteve.'

'Do you think Joe Bolt had any idea what was in the safe?'

'No Sam, I believe Jeff Mitchell was the one who had the inside information, but it's not going to take long before the Old bill put one and one together and pull Joe Bolt in for the safe blowing at Mallards.

'Again everybody knows that Ted Horn and Tommy Prince didn't pull the Mallards job and the only reason they are still on remand is because it suits the Old bill.

'George I have to go as I have another meeting with a couple of my boys this evening, I hope you're wrong about Joe Bolt, as I wouldn't want to see him go to prison at his age it would finish him. Don't forget to call me tomorrow if you're interested in the factory unit.'

'Thanks George I'll be in touch tomorrow and you'll have your money in the next three weeks.'

'Sam pay me when the heat's off and good luck on the robbery.'

Big Sam met with Derrick Smallwood and Scotch Jack in the Pig in the Stick Pub, they sat with their three large gins and tonics in the far corner of the room, Derrick and Jack explained about the factory unit they had looked at,

'No worries I've found one through George Lopez, the three of us will visit the factory in the morning at Richmond. It's going to cost a hundred grand but that's coming out of Jimmy Simmons' share. George also mentioned about the Mallards safe blowing. He is sure that Jeff Mitchell and Joe Bolt pulled the job, and reckons the top brass in the Old bill know so it's only a matter of time before Joe Bolt goes down for the job.'

'That will kill him; he couldn't carry out another stretch inside,' said Derrick.

Commander Rose held a meeting with Superintendent Parker and Inspector Brown. 'With the information we received from Juan Riminez before he was poisoned. There's no doubt in my mind that this Treasure theory is correct, being a Freemason I've already been along to the Grand Lodge here in England and Spoken with the Grand Master of the Knight Templars. He assures me that somewhere in the world the Holy Grail and the Treasure exists, whether it is in Scotland, France, Spain, Portugal or Switzerland, however the keepers hold the biggest secret of all time.'

'Commander, if these Knight Templars already know the whereabouts of this Treasure why are there maps and plans?'

'That Superintendent is another mystery which we must try and fathom out. Our next step gentleman is to interview Miguel Melgar and try and prise this information out of him as quickly as possible, preventing any further murders.'

‘Ok Commander, say we all agree with this theory about the Treasure, maps and plans, what has it to do with this big robbery going down?’

‘Again Superintendent that’s the million dollar question we must try and fit all the pieces into the puzzle as quickly as possible. I have looked at the report from Inspector Ward, it appears that Billy Chambers has only contacted two known villains George Lopez (once) and Jimmy Simmons (twice), whose photographs we have. Obviously they are keeping their heads down. We know that their passports will be ready this Friday, so let’s hope one or two of these villains put their heads up above the board.’

Commander Rose and Superintendent Parker sat at the metal table with Miguel Melgar in the interview room. ‘I trust you are being treated well Miguel?’

‘Yes very well thank you.’

‘Good, now have you given any more thought to our conversation at Heathrow?’

‘Yes of course, but I am still very worried that Carlos Moran will put out a contract on my head, he has hands like an octopus all over the world.’

‘Yes Miguel we are aware of Mr Moran, now these documents, maps and plans of the Treasure taken from Peter Sainsbury’s safe at Mallards, in your opinion who has them now?’

‘Costa Esteve and Andres Lara.’

‘Why was Peter Sainsbury murdered?’

‘On the orders of Carlos Moran.’

‘Did you actually play a part in the murder of Peter Sainsbury?’

‘I’ve told you; I want a deal in writing before I commit myself.’

Commander Rose rubbed his eyes. ‘Miguel I’m getting tired of this nonsense, you’ll get your deal but you must give us a lot more information so that my report is looked at favourably for your sake.’

‘I’m not saying another word until I have my deal, take me back to my cell.’

Inspector Brown poked his head into the interview room saying that both the Commander and the Superintendent were wanted.

Inspector Brown sat opposite Miguel Melgar. ‘You know Miguel the Commander is only trying to help you, he has lots of evidence in his possession regards Juan Riminez and yourself murdering Peter Sainsbury.’

‘Why are you telling me this Inspector?’

‘Because sometimes you are unaware of the situation when negotiating you are unable to think straight. Also be careful of the Commander, if he is unhappy with the evidence. He won't mess around, he'll just charge you with all sorts of murders and then my friend you are facing life inside prison. Where your friend from Madrid Carlos Moran would be able to have you killed.'

Miguel went pale. 'I would like to go back to my cell and think matters over.'

Inspector Brown walked next door where the Commander and Superintendent Parker had been listening to the whole conversation. 'Well done Inspector Mr Melgar is a very worried man now we'll let him stew for a day.'

'What about his deal?'

'Bugger his deal he's a bloody murderer.'

Sergeant Clark and DC Quirk watched the latest surveillance tape from the Red Lion. 'There,' Ben pointing, 'it's Chambers with Jimmy Simmons, do you think we should give Simmons a pull?'

'Not at this time Alex as the Serious Crime Squad are keeping a watchful eye on Chambers, but perhaps I'll drop a note to Bleasdale.'

Inspector Ward and his team had achieved nothing of interest, Chambers hadn't visited anywhere except the local pub. Ward was wondering if it was necessary to have four cars following Chambers.

Bob Warden also hadn't ventured out, remaining in his easy chair drinking beers and listening to the police radio just in case there was movement.

Superintendent Parker and Inspector Brown travelled to the safe house to re-interview Liam Murphy. 'Liam its necessary to give up some more information, we need to lift some more villains.'

'That's not a problem Superintendent, we only have to visit my flat and retrieve two of my books and you can have no end of known robberies and robbers.'

'Liam there's no way you can travel or return to your flat it's too dangerous.'

'You'll have to tell me where they are and I'll collect them for you.'

'Sure you will then I haven't got a bargaining point.'

'Liam you will have to learn to trust us.'

'No way Superintendent what I will do is this. I will write out a simple contract giving the location of the books and my money. You will both sign the contract pass it to my solicitor who will sign and keep the document for safe keeping, if you both agree we have a deal.'

'We both agree,' said Parker and Brown.

Liam Murphy was allowed to call his lawyer Terry Cornell letting him know of the arrangement, one stipulation was to be added said Terry Cornell. That if in any case the books or Murphy's money disappeared Superintendent Parker would be held responsible.

All was agreed and signed, as Superintendent Parker and Inspector Brown made their way back to Scotland Yard they agreed to visit Liam Murphy's flat the following morning.

Big Sam, Derrick and Scotch Jack made their way to 220 Wiltshire Street Richmond, opening the big doubled front door, the factory was clean but the furniture was sparse. They made their way looking into the different rooms, there was a room for each one, also the factory had three bathrooms with toilets and two separate toilets

'This has to be our bolt-hole Sam,' said Derrick.

Scotch Jack agreed. Big Sam wanted to explore further. Walking down the factory unit they found a further double door which lead to the back street, making their way down the street for fifty meters with buildings each side which they found empty. They found it lead into the main street they first entered.

'This is great just what we are looking for, we need to purchase six put-up beds, blankets, sheets, towels, mugs and a kettle and a fridge,' said Scotch Jack. Having a last look around before departing, they made a list of all the equipment they would need. Shutting the big double front door and agreeing it would be better to purchase all the equipment in Brixton as it would defiantly be cheaper.

'Let's have a celebration drink,' said Sam, sitting down in the bar of the Brown Cow public house, they drank two pints each. Derrick asked Sam if it was necessary to shoot Andres, Simmons and Chambers and any others that might get in the way.

'Derrick yesterday we spoke about Joe Bolt probably getting pulled and going to prison, that's the game we are in you live by the sword and you die by the sword.

'Chambers and his mob are going to try and take our robbery money. They won't be worried about shooting us, they will also grass us to the Old bill letting them know where we are going.'

'Ok Sam I get the message.'

Big Sam drank his beer thinking once this job is over it's goodbye Derrick, you'll be going your way and I'm certainly going my way.

'Ok lads don't forget our next meeting is at Putney, I'll drop off all the equipment tomorrow at the factory unit.'

Inspector Ward and his team were sitting waiting for Billy Chambers to make a move, Bob Warden was sitting in his car listening to the police radio.

Costa Esteve had called Billy Chambers that morning, just going over the final details of their agenda. 'Have you spoken with Oscar Keylock about picking up the passports?'

'Billy pointed out that it was on his work list for today. Chambers was thinking that he had to pop over and see Len Eland and could easily see Oscar Keylock at the same time But decided to telephone instead.'

'Oscar its Billy Chambers how's it all going are we on schedule?'

'No problem Mr Chambers I'm well on the way for completion.'

'Fabulous I'll see you tomorrow.'

Sergeant Jessup called Inspector Brown letting him know that Chambers had contacted Keylock and would be visiting the following day. Inspector Brown received the usual call from Keylock.

Inspector Brown made his way upstairs to Superintendent Parker's office briefing him on the schedule of Chambers.

'This is important Brown don't worry about travelling with me tomorrow, I will take a driver to visit Liam Murphy's flat and collect the books, that way you will be able to coordinate any problems that may arise here.'

'Don't you think it would be better if I accompanied you, as we have both signed that contract of Liam Murphy Superintendent?'

'Don't worry yourself Brown I'm not going to run off.'

Superintendent Parker was driven to Liam Murphy's flat by DC Richard Glennie, Parker told DC Glennie to park the car in the side turning and wait for him. Walking across the road Parker made his way towards Murphy's front door, finding the correct key and letting himself in. Turning on the lights as all the curtains had been drawn; he had a quick look around, making his way to the bathroom. He lifted the carpet finding the cut-in-half floorboard, lifting the floorboard he couldn't see anything in the floor area. Reaching inside his jacket pocket, Parker pulled out a touch which he shone between the floorboards there was nothing there.

Pulling the carpet up at all the edges, there wasn't another cut-in-half floorboard.

'So Mr Murphy you are playing us around. I'll have your guts for garters.' Replacing the carpet, he made for the front door, closed and locked the door, making his way to his car; somebody tapped him on the shoulder, as he turned.

'Hallo Parker what on earth are you doing in East London?'

'Paul fancy bumping into you.'

'I'm just off on my holiday, fancy a quick drink Parker?'

'Yes why not for old times' sake.' They walked across the road and into the Bulls head pub.

'What will you have Parker?'

'Scotch will be fine.' Collecting their drinks they walked on the carpet which stuck to their feet to a table by the window, the bar was very dark and dreary and smelt of beer.

'So where are you stationed now Parker?'

'Scotland Yard, I'm hoping to get early retirement shortly as I cannot see any further promotions.'

'You've come a long way since you were my Sergeant at Chelsea Parker.'

Finishing his scotch, Parker thanked Paul for the drink and wished him a pleasant holiday. As he walked away from Paul Gear thinking the bloody guy should be calling me Sir not Parker. He was only a bloody Inspector when he retired and I'm a Superintendent. Reaching his car and climbing into the back seat DC Richard Glennie could smell the drink on Parker's breath.

'Back to the yard Sir?'

'Yes,' looking around to see if Paul Gear was watching. As Parker made his way to the office he called Inspector Brown but found that he was out on surveillance. Sitting down in his nice leather chair, picking up files from Jonathan Crisp on the latest court trials and thinking, tomorrow Brown and I will visit Liam bloody Murphy and give him a piece of my mind.

Inspector Ward and his team had followed Billy Chambers to Crystal Palace where Chambers entered the Swan and Keeper pub, Car 2 where are you parked.

'To the south of the pub.'

'Give it five minutes and one of you pop inside and see who Chambers is meeting.' Williamson walked into the bar ordering a half pint of beer. The bar was half empty, but sitting on a bench seat at the rear of the bar was Billy Chambers and a dark skinned man, thin but tall with a crew cut wearing smart clothes. Williamson thought for a moment, then it clicked. 'I know him he's the gun supplier. So Chambers is buying guns for the big job.' Finishing his half of beer Williamson walked smartly out of the pub, making his way back to his car.

'Carl, the suspect is meeting with a gun supplier whose name has slipped my memory at the moment.'

Bob Warden was sitting listening to the police radio so Chambers is buying guns it has to be Len Eland in this part of London.

Billy Chambers left the pub at 15:10 with the tall thin man with a dark complexion, shaking hands as they made their separate ways. Chambers got into his car and drove towards Norwood Road. Inspector Ward and his team followed.

Inspector Brown was hiding behind two trees in Brockwell Park opposite the flat at Norwood Road.

Fifteen minutes later Billy Chambers walked around the corner from Croxted road, knocking on the door. The door was opened by Oscar Keylock who looked surprised to see Billy Chambers standing there. 'Hallo Mr Chambers I wasn't expecting you today, come on in would you like to see some of the merchandise?'

'That would be great Oscar.' Billy Chambers followed Oscar Keylock up the stairs to the first floor, where he sat until Keylock came back with four of the passports.

'They're superb Oscar and you will have them all ready for tomorrow?'

'You can count on it Mr Chambers.' Chambers shook Keylock's hand and walked down stairs and out of the front door, turning left back into Croxted road. Inspector Brown had taken a dozen photographs of Billy Chambers entering and leaving the flat in Norwood Road. Cars I-2 and 4 were all parked in Croxted road with car 3 parked in Norwood road facing towards Brixton. Bob Warden was parked further up Croxted Road watching the proceedings and listening to the police radio.

Billy Chambers smiled as he got into his car driving towards home, as far as he was concerned he'd had a great day. He had ordered the guns; the passports would be ready the following day. As he looked over into Brockwell park which looked so green, even the trees looked great. There were people lying about on the grass and others just walking along as if they didn't have a care in the world, yes it was a great day.

Arriving back at his flat, he telephoned Costa Esteve, briefing him on his days' work.

'I'll be collecting the merchandise tomorrow so we could either meet tomorrow evening or the following morning.'

'Very good Billy I look forward to a very successful week.'

Inspector Ward gave the job of monitoring Billy Chambers flat to car 4, explaining if Chambers starts to move in his car other than to the local pub, they were to call him, otherwise he would see everybody a Kilburn in the morning at 7:30.

Bob Warden laughed to himself, it's a wonder the Old bill ever catch any of the real villains unless they had been grassed, driving home thinking over his next move. At home he poured himself a large scotch, sat in his easy chair and thought that he had to hit Chambers either Friday or Saturday night, that would be the only times when the police had only one car shadowing Chambers.

Commander Rose popped his head around the door. 'I've just been informed that Miguel Melgar has requested a solicitor.'

'He must be mad Sir.'

'Yes I am sure he is but that's his privilege, it will leave me with little alternative but to charge Melgar with the Murder of Peter Sainsbury and the attempted armed robbery of persons unknown in Heston. Come on Inspector Brown accompany me to the cells.'

'Good evening Mr Melgar, I understand you have a solicitor you wish us to contact.'

'Yes that's correct, there is a Spanish Solicitor named Jose Puig he has an office in Soho.'

'Ok Mr Melgar we'll contact him for you.'

Commander Rose and Inspector Brown returned to his office calling Jose Puig. The telephone rang four times and then cut into an answer machine which was first in English and followed by Spanish. The Commander was hesitant to leave a message but thought it would be better doing so. 'Mr Puig this is Commander Rose from Scotland Yard, we have arrested Mr Miguel Melgar, who wishes to engage you as his solicitor. My telephone number is that of Scotland Yard. Inspector Brown suggested that Jose Puig wouldn't be able to contact the Commander until the following day.'

'O, what a pity Inspector I must have forgotten I was just off home.'

Inspector Ward and his team had finished breakfast at Kilburn police station canteen and taken up positions around the roads of Billy Chambers' block of flats. Bob Warden had been up early listening to the police radio. So Inspector Ward and his team are already on duty, they must be anticipating something is about to happen.

Inspector Brown was reading files in his office as Superintendent Parker poked his head around the door saying we will be leaving in twenty minutes to see bloody Liam Murphy (no good morning or anything), this is going to be a nice day thought Inspector Brown.

Superintendent Parker with his coat over his arm. 'Let's go Brown.' DC Rice was already waiting with the motor running as they approached. Parker gave DC Rice a piece of paper with the address he wanted to go to. DC Rice looked at the address and handed the piece of paper back to the Superintendent. There was very little conversation during the ride over to the safe house, just over the hour they reached their destination. Knocking on the door, which was opened by an armed police office.

'Morning Superintendent.'

'Morning DC Matthews.' As Superintendent turned into the room where Liam Murphy was sitting.

'What the fuck are you up to Murphy, there were no books or monies under the floorboards, now stop jerking us around I want information do you understand.'

'You bastard Parker you've fucking nicked my books and the ten grand, just as I thought you would, but you're not getting away with it as my Solicitor has yours and my signatures on the agreement. Inspector Brown I want to make an official complaint against Mr Parker regards my private books full of information and the missing ten grand.'

'Hold on; were you with Parker at my flat because if you were I need to speak with another senior police officer?'

'No Mr Murphy I was not at your flat.'

Parker shouted out, 'You little shit,' as he rushed forward towards Liam Murphy both DC Matthews and Inspector Brown jumped between Parker and Murphy.

'I want my Solicitor yelled Murphy that bastard has stitched me up,' pointing at Superintendent Parker. Both DC Matthews and Inspector Brown looked stunned.

'Mr Murphy I must ask you if you are sure that there was Ten thousand pounds stored under your floorboards.'

'Of cause there was it was my getting away money and that bastard there has nicked it,' again pointing at Superintendent Parker.

Inspector Brown looked at the Superintendent saying, 'Sir you will have to make a call to the Yard.' Parker never moved just looked at the ground. Inspector Brown left the room and made a call to Commander Rose briefing him on the serious complaint.

'That's all we need in the middle of this high-powered investigation,' said the Commander.

'I'll have to call you back in ten minutes as I need to speak with the Deputy Commissioner.'

Superintendent Parker shouted out to Inspector Brown, 'We can sort this problem out.'

'Sorry Sir, I need guidance on this serious complaint, you better sit down until I receive the telephone call,' said Inspector Brown. DC Matthews continued to hold Liam Murphy by the arm as once or twice Murphy had tried to move against Superintendent Parker.

'Liam you better sit down over there and make a written statement to DC Matthews,' pointed out Brown.

Superintendent Parker looked up at Inspector Brown saying, 'That's your career finished Inspector.'

'I'm sorry Sir but a serious complaint was just made and I am personally involved having signed the agreement, so it was my duty to report the matter.' The telephone rang and Inspector Brown picked up the call. 'I'm sending another armed vehicle to transport Liam Murphy back to Scotland Yard, you personally will escort Superintendent Parker back to the Yard.'

'Yes Sir.'

'Liam Commander Rose is sending another armed vehicle to collect you, as this house may have been compromised.'

'Superintendent Parker you will have to accompany me back to the yard.' Parker never said a word he just looked at the ground.

The armed police vehicle arrived and after Murphy's personal clothes had been gathered up, they left for the yard.

The Commissioner was devastated, that a senior officer had been so stupid. 'I will have to call one of the Chief Constables to investigate, as I want everybody cleared of this serious complaint.'

'The Chief Constable of Northumberland will head the investigation, in the meantime, I would like you to interview and take a statement from Parker on these missing books and cash from Mr Murphy's home, you will need to suspend Parker from duties and remove his warrant card.'

The Deputy Commissioner called Commander Rose informing him that he would have to take over the responsibility of all Superintendent Parker's cases immediately. 'As for Inspector Brown after he has been interviewed and cleared of any wrongdoing will remain with you as will Inspector Ward.'

'Yes Sir, it's been a nasty business altogether.'

Commander Rose radioed Inspector Ward, informing him, 'From today all dealings on the investigation would be dealt with by himself and not Superintendent Parker. Once you have completed your duties today, report to me.'

'Yes Sir.'

Liam Murphy arrived at Scotland Yard and was taken to the cell block. Inspector Brown had also arrived at the yard with Superintendent Parker, who was immediately taken to see the Deputy Commissioner and Commander Rose.

'Superintendent Parker I cannot imagine how you managed to get yourself into this position. Fancy with all your experience you ventured to an informers flat to collect valuable books and cash without having a witness with you. The Commissioner has called upon the Chief Constable of Northumberland to investigate the serious complaint made by Liam Murphy, now what have you got to say for yourself.'

'I have been framed, that's all I wish to say at this moment.'

'Your comment is duly noted Superintendent. Until the investigation has been completed, I am afraid you are suspended from all duties; I require your warrant card.'

Parker was escorted from the building; rumours fled throughout Scotland Yard and even reached Kilburn and Heathrow police stations, nobody could believe that Superintendent Parker had been on the take, except Chief Inspector Bleasdale.

The Deputy Commissioner and Commander Rose interviewed Inspector Brown, telling him that an official investigation was being headed by the Chief Constable of Northumberland. 'However if we are satisfied that you were not involved with Superintendent Parker, then you will be able to continue your duties, are you happy to give answers to our questions?'

'Most certainly Sir.'

'Did you enter Liam Murphy's flat with Superintendent Parker?'

'I did not Sir.'

'Were you not intrigued as why Superintendent Parker insisted that you remained, to carry out normal duties, while he visited Liam Murphy's flat to collect the valuable informers books and cash.'

'Yes Sir I was surprised, and informed Superintendent Parker, that I should go along with him as I had signed the contract.'

'Are you saying that Parker didn't want you to go with him?'

'That's correct Sir, he told me to get on with my normal duties.'

'Is there anything else you would like placed on record?'

'I'm very disappointed that the Superintendent placed me in this very difficult position.'

The Deputy Commissioner turned to Commander Rose who nodded. 'We are satisfied with your statement Inspector Brown and you may return to your duties on Commander Rose's team.'

'Thank you Sir.'

Inspector Brown radioed Inspector Ward letting him know the situation, which was relayed to each of the team. Bob Warden had been listening to the messages and was surprised that Parker had been caught on the 'take'. As he remembered when Parker was a Sergeant at Chelsea once or twice Parker had taken bribes from different villains.

Big Sam had been over to Richmond making sure all was well for the following Wednesday, he was still perturbed about certain members of his team; Scotch Jack was no problem when it came to guns. Derrick on the other hand was the weak link and possibly wouldn't be able to handle the shootings. The Shephard brothers would be no problem and Jimmy Simmons was a no go anyway. He also worried about where the double-cross would be taking place; he was completely sure in his mind how the robbery would proceed right up to the bridge caper, which was the second weak link.

Inspector Ward returned to Scotland Yard to see Commander Rose, after briefing the Commander on the day's advents. Both guessing on when Billy Chambers would collect the guns. They knew when Chambers would be collecting the passports. The Commander was hoping that once Chambers was in possession of the passports it would lead to the arrest of Costa Esteve and Andres Lara.

'What about this big robbery Sir?'

‘We know all the players, it’s just the dam robbery ‘every airport, train station, ferry port and all exit’s out of the country will be covered, but I am hoping we get the gang beforehand.’

Commander Rose sat in his office looking over at his chart on the wall, thinking over every scenario. His telephone rang which gave him a start.

‘I am Jose Puig representing Miguel Melgar, I would be grateful to come along today and interview Mr Melgar in an hour.’

‘That’s fine Mr Puig.’

The Commander contacted Inspector Brown, telling him to be available in one hour to assist in the interview of Mr Miguel Melgar.

Commander Rose and Inspector Brown walked along the corridor to the interview rooms where Jose Puig and Miguel Melgar sat at a metal table.

Jose Puig made a statement for his client saying that Mr Melgar had nothing to say whatsoever.

Commander Rose and Inspector Brown stood up. ‘Mr Miguel Melgar I am charging you with the murder of Peter Sainsbury, you are also being charged with attempted armed robbery on persons unknown at Macon Street, Heston, anything you may say, could be used against you at a future time.’ Miguel Melgar was led down to the cells.

As the Commander and Inspector Brown made their way back to his office they spoke about the nonsense that Parker had managed to get himself in.

Chief Constable Roger McBean entered Scotland Yard and was immediately collected by Miss Breda Chester, private secretary to the Commissioner of Police.

The Chief Constable was shown into the Commissioner’s large plush office. ‘Good morning Sir John.’

‘Hallo Roger, so pleased you could assist me at such short notice, we have a very sticky business hear. After briefing the Chief Constable on the case, he was shown to his temporary office. The Chief Constable had chosen Chief Inspector Ian Tolly to assist him on the Investigation of the serious complaint against a senior officer. After the Chief Constable and the Chief Inspector collated all the statements from Liam Murphy, Inspector Brown, DC’s Matthews and Rice, they agreed it would be best to interview Liam Murphy first. Then Inspector Brown, followed by DC’s Matthews and Rice. Once they were satisfied with the results they would Interview Superintendent Parker.

The Chief Constable introduced himself and Chief Inspector Tolly to Liam Murphy, telling Mr Murphy why they were called in.

'Before we start Mr McBean, I haven't been looked after as promised, I'm stuck in those awful cells.'

'Mr Murphy we understand your complaint of being in the police cells, but you are there for your own protection. Once we are satisfied over a number of points, you will be returned to another safe house unknown obviously to certain police officers.'

'I see. Ok then,' said Murphy.

'Mr Murphy you have made a very serious complaint against a Senior Police Officer, therefore we would like to clarify certain points of your statement.'

'You say in your statement you kept a large amount of money along with two valuable books containing precise details of robberies and those villains who were involved under a cut out floorboard in your bathroom.'

'That's correct.'

'How much cash was involved Mr Murphy?'

'Ten thousand pounds.'

'That's a large amount of money to have hidden under the floor, are you sure that there was ten thousand pounds.'

'Most certainly. I had only counted the money two days before I was arrested.'

'These books definitely contained information on robberies.'

'Absolutely.'

'Why did you keep such information?'

'For the simple fact, I didn't ever want to go to prison, knowing that with such information I would be valuable to the police and be able to cut myself a deal.'

'Did you have anybody living with you who might have known or noticed you counting your money or storing the books?'

'No Mr McBean I lived alone, not even girlfriends or my gang members had any idea that I kept money in the flat or kept books on robberies.'

'Now tell us about the time Superintendent Parker and Inspector Brown asked you for more information.'

'I explained all the information was contained in two books which were hidden I was prepared for them to accompany me to my flat and collect the books. Parker didn't want that saying I would be in too much danger.

'I told the two of them that I was reluctant to hand over the books and cash as once they were in there possession. I wasn't needed anymore. So I suggested that an agreement should be drawn up, with the three of us signing and a copy given to my solicitor. So that if anything happened to my books and cash. Superintendent Parker would be held responsible.'

'Yes I see that was a Mr Cornell.'

'That's correct.'

'So Mr Cornell has the copy signed by Superintendent Parker, Inspector Brown and yourself absolutely.'

'I believe that will be all for now Mr Murphy, we will have you transported to another safe house.'

After looking through the statement, both the Chief Constable and the Chief Inspector were happy with its contents.

Inspector Brown entered the office of the Chief Constable and was introduced, Inspector Brown was asked to read Liam Murphy's statement.

'Are you happy with Mr Murphy's statement in every part Inspector?'

'As far as I can see the statement is correct.'

'In your opinion, did Superintendent Parker say to Mr Murphy that he would be in danger if he went along to his flat?'

'That's correct Sir.'

'Was it your intention to travel with the Superintendent to Liam Murphy's flat to retrieve books and cash?'

'Yes Sir that's correct.'

'Why didn't you go with the Superintendent?'

'The Superintendent asked me to remain and carry out my duties, just in case something important came up.'

'Wasn't Mr Murphy's books important enough Inspector?'

'In my opinion Sir they were very important.'

'Are you positive in your own mind that you didn't suggest to the Superintendent that he should go to Murphy's flat on his own?'

'No Sir it was Superintendent Parkers idea and I just followed orders.'

'Were you surprised that the Superintendent travelled alone without you, even though you had both signed an agreement with Liam Murphy to enter his flat.'

'Yes Sir, I was very edgy about the idea, but he was the boss.'

'Did it ever cross your mind that there may be a problem, like a setup?'

'No Sir, I thought the Superintendent was so experienced and as he was taking a driver, I thought the driver would have been present on the entree into Mr Murphy's flat.'

'Did you believe Mr Murphy had cash and books hidden under the floorboards in the bathroom of his flat?'

'Yes Sir, because if Mr Murphy had sent us to his flat on a wild goose chase, Mr Murphy had no bargaining position.'

The Chief Constable nodded to the Chief Inspector. 'Fine Inspector Brown if we have any further questions we will call you, by the way good luck in finding these villains.'

DC Matthews appeared before the Chief Constable and the Chief Inspector, after introductions, Matthews was asked to check his statement.

'You are completely certain that Superintendent Parker tore into Mr Murphy?'

'Absolutely Sir, he told Murphy that he was messing the Yard around as there was no books or cash hidden under the floorboards. That is when Mr Murphy went berserk, saying he wanted to make an official complaint because he believed that Superintendent Parker had stolen the cash and books. When Inspector Brown was asked by Murphy if he had accompanied the Superintendent to the flat and replied he hadn't.'

'What happened?'

'I had to restrain Murphy from attacking the Superintendent,' he pointed at the Superintendent saying, 'I want to make a complaint. Inspector Brown walked into the other room and called the yard for further advice, after receiving that advice he returned to the room and asked the Superintendent to accompany him to Scotland Yard. He also informed Liam Murphy and myself that an armed escort would arrive and take Liam Murphy back to the Yard.'

'Thank you DC Matthews if we have any further questions we will call you.'

DC Rice was called and introduced to the Chief Constable and Chief Inspector.

DC Rice gave his statement saying that he drove Superintendent Parker to the address given to him. He was told to park the car and wait, after some time Superintendent Parker returned to the car smelling of drink. The Superintendent never spoke another word all the way back to the Yard.

'Did the Superintendent at any time on the way to Mr Murphy's flat ask you to assist him?'

'No Sir, I was just told to park the car and wait.'

'Thank your DC Rice; if we need to ask you any further questions we will call you.'

The Chief Constable asked Chief Inspector Tolly for his opinion. 'Listening to all the statements they all appear to be solid as rocks, and with Inspector Brown believing that Murphy had hidden books and cash. I would certainly believe the story myself and let's be fair. Villains have been known to hide their ill-gotten gains for that rainy day when they have to be on their toes.'

'Yes I agree with your theory.'

'We will make an appointment with Superintendent Parker for tomorrow, and then we can make judgement for ourselves if he did remove the monies and books for gain.'

Inspector Ward and his team followed Billy Chambers from place to place; Bob Warden's car was also following Inspector Wards listening to the police radio. Billy Chambers pulled up at a telephone box on the corner of the road, making three calls before getting back in his car and driving towards Tooting. Parking his car outside an Indian restaurant, Inspector Wards team took up their usual positions. Bob Warden parked his car so that he could monitor exactly Billy Chambers' capers. The Restaurant door opened and two men made their way to Billy Chambers' vehicle with a large black holdall putting it in the boot. One of the men turned and walked up to Chambers open car window, where Chambers passed him an envelope which he looked inside and nodded to Chambers.

Billy Chambers then proceeded towards Ealing with Inspector Ward and team following in their usual Patten, Bob Warden staying some way back.

Inspector Ward had already related the information of the Indian Restaurant to Commander Rose, who had a couple of local CID officers monitoring the Restaurant.

Billy Chambers pulled into a side street just off Ealing Broadway, parking his car, opening the boot and removing the large holdall. He crossed the path to a set of garages, putting the holdall on the floor and pulling out of his pocket a set of keys. Opening the green garage door and entering, shutting the garage door behind him.

Inspector Wards team had parked at different positions in the area.

Bob Warden had parked his car in the next street and was listening to the police chatter on the radio, the address of the garage was radioed through to Commander Rose, Bob thought what a load of idiots, they couldn't catch a cold.

Thirty minutes went by before Billy Chambers opened the green garage door, shutting and locking it behind him and driving his car back towards south London.

Inspector Ward called Commander Rose saying they were headed for Norwood Road to collect the passports and perhaps we might be lucky to get a glimpse of Costa Esteve and Andres Lara.

Commander Rose and Inspector Brown travelled to Brockwell Park, so that they could watch the flat from the park.

Bob Warden decided not to follow as there would be too much police presence and he didn't want to take a chance of being spotted, anyway in his opinion another meeting would have been laid on between Chambers and Costa Esteve for later that evening.

Billy Chambers parked his car in Croxted road, walking around the corner and knocking on the door of the flat; Commander Rose and Inspector Brown were situated by a clump of bushes where they could easily photograph Chambers entering, Oscar Keylock opened the door.

'Hallo Mr Chambers,' shutting the door and making their way up to the first floor, Billy sat while Oscar went to fetch the merchandise. Chambers had considered killing Keylock, but changed his mind after the last visit, Chambers wanted an emergency plan in case his own plans went haywire.

Keylock returned passing a large brown envelope to Chambers, after checking the contents. 'Wonderful job Oscar,' taking from his inside jacket pocket an envelope containing fifteen grand.

'Thanks Mr Chambers, if I can be of any further help please let me know.'

Walking back to Croxted road jumping into his car and driving back to his flat, thinking this time next week I'm going to be a very rich man.

Inspector Ward and his team followed Chambers in their usual pattern, Commander Rose and Inspector Brown made their way to their car and travelled towards Billy Chambers flat. Bob Warden was being extremely vigilant; knowing the police presence around Billy Chambers flat would be intense, so he parked a little further away.

Billy Chambers had changed, walking out of his front door holding a small briefcase, Bob Warden who had been listening to the police chatter realised that

Billy Chambers was not going to take his car, jumped out of his own vehicle and made his way towards the shopping centre.

Inspector Ward and his team had panicked a little, when Chambers had walked past Inspector Ward's car. 'Car three, Chambers is on foot, 'Williamson and Beasley follow Chambers and keep in touch at all times. Bob Warden noticed Billy Chambers with his briefcase and then noticed the two police officers one on one side of the street and the other on the opposite side. Billy Chambers entered the Tube station purchased his ticket and made his way to the station platform. Williamson called Inspector Ward letting him know the situation; Vincent and Illingsworth were also now following.

Bob Warden purchased his ticket making his way towards the platform. When DC Williamson passed him on the stairs, DC Beasley was still at the top of the stairs when the train pulled in. Chambers climbed in the first available open tube door. Bob Warden jumped in two carriages down with Williamson jumping aboard in the carriage before Warden. DC Beasley never made the train; turning and with his radio called Inspector Ward, letting him know that Chambers was travelling towards Heathrow.

Commander Rose turned saying to Inspector Brown, 'Of course, that's where Esteve and Lara are located in the Heathrow area.' The Commander quickly radioed Inspector Ward telling him to move all their cars but one, towards Heathrow and hoped DC Williamson would be able to continue contact. Car three would remain just in case Chambers returned suddenly.

The train stopped at Hounslow Central, where Chambers got off, Bob Warden got out of his carriage and mingled with other passengers as did DC Williamson, walking towards the main street. Bob Warden looked grubby and blended in and didn't look out of place in the area, while DC Williamson look liked an undercover police officer.

As Chambers reached the street, he noticed Costa Esteve wave from the corner of the road, he also noticed Andres Lara some fifty feet back. DC Williamson had made his way up the stairs in double quick time, passing Bob Warden on his way into the sunlight. Andres Lara had already noticed DC Williamson just lifting his radio towards his mouth. Before he could utter a word, Andres pushed Williamson into an alley pulled out his knife and stabbed him in the neck, letting Williamson fall to the floor, 'blood was pouring out of his neck. Andres had a quick look around just in case there were any other undercover police observing 'nothing. Andres made his way to the corner of the road where Costa Esteve and Billy Chambers were waiting.

'What was that all about Andres?'

'You had been followed Billy, the cop was just about to radio somebody.'

'We better get a taxi away from the area,' said Costa Esteve.

Bob Warden who had witnessed Andres Lara pushing DC Williamson into the alley, made a sharp turn towards the station, knowing in ten minutes or so there would be a hue and cry when the body of the officer had been found. The tube train came and Bob jumped on.

The taxi carrying Costa Esteve, Andres Lara and Billy Chambers drove towards Barnes dropping them off at the Goose and Duck Public House. Sitting at one of the outside tables overlooking the river bank, Billy Chambers wondered where the undercover cop had picked him up.

Costa Esteve pointed out that most probable Billy had been spotted on the underground and followed from there. 'I wouldn't let it worry you, next week we are going to be very rich men.' Billy Chambers passed the large envelope to Costa Esteve from his briefcase.

'Have you taken your passport Billy?'

'Yes of course.'

Andres looked over Costa shoulder nodding as he handed another envelope to Chambers.

'Have we got every angle covered for next Wednesday Billy?' asked Costa.

'Every angle has been considered and covered, I've already collected the artillery and now we have Andres driving the spare car with Jimmy Simmons at his side. I believe we have outmanoeuvred Big Sam completely.'

'When is you next meeting with Big Sam?' asked Billy.

'Tomorrow morning, I will issue the passports that way he'll believe all is well.'

'Have you organised your own escape from the robbery scene Billy?'

'Absolutely; once I jump in the car with Andres and Jimmy Simmons, Andres will drop Jimmy and myself off at Boston Manor, we'll catch the underground home and three weeks later we'll be on our flight to Spain very rich men.'

Hounslow Central tube station had been sealed off with local CID and SOCO searching everywhere. Commander Rose had been informed by the Chief Inspector from Hounslow Police of the dead body of one of his officers;

Inspector Brown radioed Inspector Ward letting him know of the murder of DC Williamson, all of Inspector Wards team were devastated.

It must have been Chambers; he somehow must have spotted DC Williamson and then stabbed him. Costa Esteve and Andres Lara caught a taxi back to Heston, Chambers also catching a taxi back to his flat.

Bob Warden was driving in his car listening to the police chatter and thinking that he had to make his move that evening; otherwise Chambers would be getting away with the lot.

Inspector Ward detailed one car to watch Billy Chambers flat, there was no shortage of volunteers as all the members of Inspector Wards team wanted to get the bastard.

Bob Warden waited thirty minutes and then made his way through the back streets to the rear of Billy Chambers flat's, tapping on Billy Chambers door.

'Who is it?'

'Terry Webb from upstairs.'

'What do you want I'm busy?'

'I had to sign for some mail for you.'

'Wait a minute, opening the door.' Bob Warden pushed into the flat knocking Billy Chambers to the floor, before Chambers could recover. Warden kicked him under the chin which made Chambers smash his head on the floor. Closing the door of the flat, he tied Chambers to a chair and then searched the flat. Finding the briefcase containing twenty grand; in another room Bob found a further fifteen grand, putting the new money into the briefcase. Bob sat down facing Billy Chambers with his gun in one hand and the silencer in the other hand as, Billy Chambers came around from his grogginess, he could see a figure sitting before him.

'You fucking dead, mate.'

'No Billy you're wrong, it's you who's going to die in a few minutes, but before you depart from this life, I want to let you know why.

'First of all you murdered a member of my family Kenny Owen and you have hurt so many nice people just for the fun of it. Bob screwed the silencer to the gun very slowly, letting Billy Chambers wriggle trying to get out of the ropes. By the way Billy you would have been picked up either tonight or tomorrow by the cops. They have been following you for the last two weeks. They followed you from Crystal Palace when you had your meeting with Len Eland to purchase your weapons for next week's big robbery, then onto Norwood road where you collected all the passports including your friends Costa Esteve and Andres Lara.

'Next there was the meeting you held with Jimmy Simmons and George Lopez, my God you are such a prat Chambers. You didn't even no they were following you, and today when four of the undercover cops followed you to the train station and one of them is stabbed to death at Hounslow central.'

'Look mate I'll give you twenty thousand pounds.'

'Billy I have already nicked thirty-five grand of you money, I'm afraid it's goodnight as three muffled shots came out of Bob's gun, two hitting Billy in the chest and one to the head. Billy's head and shoulders slumped to his chest. Bob unscrewed the silencer from the gun, placing both in the briefcase, having another look around just in case there was more money hidden.

Opening the front door, walking the way he had come through the back streets returning to his car and away home.

Commander Rose, Inspectors Brown and Ward attended a meeting with the Deputy Commissioner. 'It appears that matters are getting worse, rather than better. Gentleman, we have no idea where this Big Robbery is taking place or the whereabouts of Esteve and Lara. Now we have another murder of a police officer.'

Inspector Ward suggested that Billy Chambers should be arrested immediately so that the moral of his team would be lifted. I really cannot see us finding out from Chambers where the robbery is taking place unless we have him in custody and force the answers from him.

Inspector Brown agreed with the suggestion. The Deputy Commissioner thought about the situation and nodded his agreement. Warrants for Billy Chambers arrest were issued.

Inspectors Brown and Ward, Sergeant Jessup and DCs Vincent and Samuels would arrest Billy Chambers arrangements were made.

Roger McBean Chief Constable of Northumberland and Chief Inspector Ian Tolley after introductions, interviewed Superintendent Parker, they pointed out the seriousness of the complaint, asking Parker for his side of the facts.

Superintendent Parker pointed out that he had been driven to Liam Murphy's apartment by DC Rice. He asked DC Rice to park and remain in the car while he visited the apartment. On entering the block of flats and under Liam Murphy's instructions, I was unable to find any books or cash from under the floorboards in the bathroom.

'May I ask why you never asked DC Rice to accompany you as a witness?'

'I never gave it a thought.'

'Are you sure you never collected the books and cash for gain?'

'No I didn't.'

'Carry on Superintendent.'

'I left the apartment and as I was about to cross the road, I bumped into my old Inspector from my Chelsea days, Paul Gear, who invited me for a drink. We crossed the road and had a quick drink together as Paul was off on holiday. I returned to my police vehicle and was driven back to the yard.'

'Why did you not report the fact of the missing books and cash to anybody at the yard?'

'I didn't consider the matter through properly.'

'I see, please carry on.'

'The following day Inspector Brown and I travelled to visit Liam Murphy and sort out the problem of the missing books and cash.'

'But Superintendent at that point you hadn't consulted Inspector Brown about the missing books and cash, had you?'

'No, but I cannot remember if I did inform Brown.'

'Now you can't remember if you did or didn't mention to Inspector Brown that no books or cash were found at the apartment of Liam Murphy. I really find that incredible Superintendent; carry on.'

'When we arrived at the safe house and asked Murphy about the books and cash, Murphy tried to attack me and was held by DC Matthews.'

'Have you anything else to add or mention Superintendent?'

'No, not really, however I believe I was set up but have no further evidence.'

'We will have to interview ex-Inspector Paul Gear Superintendent.'

'I've already told you, he is on holiday.'

'Then we will wait for his return from holiday. In the meantime you will remain suspended from duties and if we have any further questions, we will call you.'

The Chief Constable turned towards Chief Inspector Tolly. 'How that man ever reached the position of Superintendent amazes me, I find his answers frustrating and will report that fact to the Commissioner. We will have to locate ex Inspector Paul Gear, as it's important to know the facts of when Paul Gear met Parker on the side pavement and was he carrying anything. The explanation of he couldn't remember if he had spoken to Inspector Brown about the books and cash is incredible, I can smell a rotten fish here Chief Inspector.'

'I agree Sir.'

Arriving at Billy Chambers flat in two cars, Inspectors Brown and Ward with Sergeant Jessup in one car and DCs Vincent and Samuel in the other, they knocked on Chambers door, there was no reply.

Inspector Brown had been informed that Billy Chambers had not left his flat. They knocked again there was no response, Inspector Brown with a word of caution, 'Be careful he may be armed. Ok knock the door down.' Two minutes later they were in the flat facing Billy Chambers tied to a chair with three bullet holes in him. A number of neighbours were clustering around the knock downed door trying to see into the flat DC Vincent went to the door holding his warrant card.

'Please this is a crime scene go back to your apartments.' SOCO were called. More assistance was required and DCs Clark and Quirk were told to report to Chambers flat.

Inspector Ward asked them to start a door to door. 'I want to know if anybody saw anybody or heard anything.' DCs Vincent and Samuel were asked if they had noticed anybody lurking around the street, they hadn't seen anybody whatsoever.

'Well somebody came calling that's for sure.'

Sergeant Jessup had searched the flat carefully without disturbing any furniture. Inspector Brown asked Sergeant Jessup to take DC Vincent and assist Ben Clark and Alex Quirk on the door to door.

Inspector Brown had found some notebooks in a side cabinet which he placed in a plastic evidence bag, he then called Commander Rose letting him know that Billy Chambers had been murdered. 'This bloody case gets worst every day Inspector.'

'It certainly does Sir.'

'We have a door to door search going on at the moment, so maybe something will turn up.'

'I won't hold my breath Inspector,' putting the telephone down.

Ben Clark and Alex Quirk were in No 29, talking with Mrs Sibly, who told Clark that earlier in the day she had seen Billy Chambers departing the flats with a briefcase in his hand, and also noticed him return in a taxi with the briefcase later in the afternoon.

‘Was Mr Chambers on his own?’

‘Yes he was, he actually looked up and saw me and he stuck two fingers up at me, awful man.’

‘Did you notice anybody entering the block in the next hour or so?’

‘Come to think of it, yes I saw a grubby looking man coming in through the back entrance; I was throwing out my rubbish at the time.’

‘Would you be able to recognise him again?’

‘I don’t think so, sorry.’

Ben Clark, made his way to the next flat, Mrs Roberts opened the door. ‘We are speaking with all the residents of the block asking if anybody noticed Mr Chambers coming or going from his flat today, and if anybody later entered Mr Chambers flat.’

‘I noticed Mr Chambers returning this afternoon with a briefcase.’

‘Did you see anybody later who is not a resident?’

‘Yes I noticed a grubby bearded man enter through the back about sixty minutes after Mr Chambers.’

‘Did you happen to see where this grubby man went?’

‘No sorry.’

‘Thanks for your time Mrs Roberts.’ They finished the door to door, meeting up with Sergeant Jessup and DC Vincent. They all made their way back to Inspector Brown. Ben Clark opened his notebook telling the Inspector that a couple of the residents had seen a grubby bearded man enter the flats about sixty minutes after Billy Chambers returned in a taxi holding his briefcase.

‘Inspector Ward did you notice a briefcase in Chambers flat?’

‘No, I didn’t. We better take another look around.’ After looking in cupboards under beds in the kitchen and bathroom, there was no briefcase to be seen.

Inspector Ward said, ‘Perhaps it’s a mugging.’

‘We cannot rule out the possibility of a mugging,’ replied Inspector Brown.

SOCO arrived. ‘You lot took your time,’ pointed out Inspector Brown.

‘This isn’t the only case we have had today Inspector.’

‘Sorry lads, this case is getting to me.’

Ben Clark pointed out that Billy Chambers was a real handful and he couldn’t really see Chambers letting anybody in he didn’t know.

One of the SOCO team came over saying, the struggle started at the front door. He was knocked to the floor and probably kicked as there is blood on the leg of the table and on the floor and wall.

'So Chambers couldn't have invited anybody in.'

'Thanks lads.'

'Ok there's nothing further for us here, well get back to the yard, if you two,' pointing to Clark and Quirk, 'remain here until the body has been removed and if anybody comes along with further information, give me a call.'

Big Sam met Costa Esteve and Andres Lara at Kew Gardens in the Deer public house. 'I'm sure you're going to be delighted with the passports Sam,' taking Sam's out of the large envelope and passing it to him.

'Excellent Costa.'

'Are we all set for our big day Sam?'

'Certainly we are ready to go, and you have the other spare vehicle Andres.'

'Yes it's a nice blue Range Rover.'

'Wonderful and how about the aircraft at Denham Costa?'

'All taken care of Sam,' looking around saying how beautiful Kew Gardens was, the beautiful flowers and plants are so peaceful. 'Well Sam we'll be off and see you next Wednesday.'

'You bet.' Sam drove away very disappointed that both Costa and Andres had lied and were about to carry out the double-cross on his gang. He had always hated treachery and would certainly teach Costa and his mate a big lesson. Arriving at Richmond he drove in through the big double doors, removing from his vehicle stocks of food and drinks which he put into the fridge, he had already installed two televisions so the lads wouldn't get to bored.

Commander Rose sat at his desk studying all the reports and statements. He had received written replies from security companies and aircraft companies that might have a huge consignment of cash, diamonds or gold being carried in the following week. His telephone rang.

'Hallo Chief Inspector Greedy how are you?'

'Better than I was Commander, I'm pleased to say we have some good news. My SOCO division have come up with evidence on the murder of Jeffrey Mitchell at Ken Delanny's farm; the package should be with you in the next hour or so.'

'Chief Inspector that's the best news I've had all-day, thank you so much.'

Inspectors Brown and Ward sat in the Commanders office and were briefed on the Jeff Mitchell case. 'Evidence had been found connecting Ken Delanny to the murder of Jeff Mitchell, so we are now in a better position to proceed against Delanny.'

'Jonathon Crisp will be delighted,' said Inspector Brown.

'What about the Horn and Prince case Sir?'

'I've been looking at the file. The more you look at the evidence it's so flimsy and without doubt would possibly get kicked out in the end. Unless Jonathon Crisp links both the detonators and safe blowing together then I would believe Mr Horn and Prince would go down.'

Jose Puig travelled to Brixton remand prison visiting his client Miguel Melgar. 'Carlos Moran has authorised the finance for the finest QC in the country to defend you, but he needs the following information. Where are Costa Esteve and Andres Lara Living?'

'I have that information Jose but first of all I want bail.'

'Miguel that's going to be very difficult; you are charged with the murder of a high profile person in Peter Sainsbury.'

'Mr Puig that's my deal, please convey my thoughts to Carlos.'

'Carlos is not going to be very happy with you Miguel.'

Commander Rose was in deep conversation with Jonathon Crisp on a number of cases Jonathon was delighted that evidence was now available to prove Ken Delanny murdered Jeffrey Mitchell, which should put Delanny away for a very long time. With the Horn and Prince case I have spoken at length with Chief Inspector Bleasdale and he promised more evidence which unfortunately hasn't appeared. 'I would believe Jonathon that if you could somehow put the knowledge that Horn and Prince are known safe Blowers and Prince was found with detonators in the boot of his car, it should be enough.'

'Maybe Commander but Miss Kerry Dickson is a QC, it's going to be difficult but I'll give it my best shot.'

'By the way Commander, it has come to my attention that Superintendent Parker is in trouble and has told the investigation Officer Roger McBean. That ex-Inspector Paul Gear will be able to substantiate and help the Superintendent. I'm afraid that will not be the case as Gear detested Parker, Parker was an awful Sergeant to Paul Gear and played some very nasty tricks when he was at Chelsea. One time he wrote a number of poison pen letters against Paul Gear. Another time he gave false accounts for his expenses it was one of Parker's colleagues that gave Parker away, it could never be proved but Parker was transferred to Hendon.'

'I see, I can only say the Chief Constable of Northumberland will leave no stone unturned.'

'I hope so too Commander.'

Inspectors Brown and Ward were discussing the missing briefcase of Billy Chambers when the Commander entered their office. 'Sit down gentleman and carry on. We were discussing this missing briefcase of Chambers.'

'Yes it is a mystery. Checking your reports and statements of the residents. This grubby bearded man that has cropped up is either a mugger which I doubt or a member of Chambers gang. And was disgruntled about payments and may have removed the briefcase which contained money. Or lastly a contract was placed on Billy Chambers and the grubby man carried it out, I will leave you two to ponder on which it was.'

Captain Sifre received a telephone call from Commander Rose 'briefing him on the situation of Miguel Melgar, suggesting if it would be possible to put pressure on Carlos Moran.

Captain Sifre accompanied by Sergeant Moratal arrived at Carlos Moran's plush apartment in the middle of Madrid.

'How can I help you Captain Sifre, we have been contacted by Scotland Yard who have in custody a chap named Miguel Melgar who has been charged with the Murder of Peter Sainsbury and has apparently mentioned your name.'

'I am surprised Captain as I cannot recollect a chap called Miguel Melgar so why should he mention my name.'

'The investigation which is taking place in London continues to bring your name to the front of a number of murders.'

'Are you accusing me Captain, if so I'll have my lawyers present.'

'Mr Moran the Guardia Civil is only here on a friendly visit.'

'Have you anything else Captain as I'm very busy?'

'Perhaps Mr Moran if anything crosses your mind regards Miguel Melgar you would give me a call.'

'Yes Captain of course.' Moran watched Captain Sifre and his Sergeant from the window walking out of the building to their car.

Carlos Moran picked up his telephone calling Jose Puig in England, pointing out that he had just received a visit from the Guardia Civil asking questions about Miguel Melgar.

'I cannot see Miguel giving information to the English Police; I have already emailed you with Miguel's requests.'

'Jose what can you do to get Miguel out on bail?'

'Carlos it's very difficult as Miguel has been charged with the murder of Peter Sainsbury and it's going to be a very high profile case, I'll do my best and contact the Crown prosecution.'

Carlos was wondering if it wouldn't be better just to take out another contract this time on Miguel Melgar, but it was imperative that he received the address of Costa Esteve and his friend.

Captain Sifre emailed Commander Rose with the results of the interview with Carlos Moran, reminding the Commander that Moran was a very dangerous character.

Bob Warden had called in to see George Lopez. 'I was wondering when you would turn up Bob, there are so many rumours circulating regards Billy Chambers murder and this grubby bearded chap that had been seen by a number of his neighbours. And there's the Superintendent Parker suspension who's been accused of removing cash and certain books containing robberies and who carried them out.'

'You never fail to amaze me George with your knowledge.'

'Bob, I'm sure you know all about the Chambers murder, so I won't bore you with the details, I would suggest you get cleaned up. I'm not sure about the Parker business Bob, but I would hope that those books of Murphy's never fall into the wrong hands; by the way a £l00,000 contract has been taken out on Liam Murphy's head.'

Bob drove back to his flat happy with himself, knowing Liam Murphy's books were safe at the moment, and maybe at some future time, they would save him from prosecution or would at least become a bargaining chip.

Jose Puig called Jonathon Crisp, 'I wonder if I could make an appointment with you to speak about Miguel Melgar situation.'

'Mr Puig there is nothing to discuss, Mr Melgar has already been charged with Murder of Peter Sainsbury.'

'Yes, yes of course Mr Crisp, but I wondered if you would consider a petition for bail.'

'Bail, you must be joking Mr Puig, the first thing Mr Melgar would do is travel to South America, sorry Mr Puig, goodbye.'

Jonathan Crisp called Commander Rose briefing him regards Jose Puig conversation.

'That's very interesting Jonathon it would appear that my call to Captain Sifre is already paying off. Commander Rose made another call; to Captain Sifre letting him know that Jose Puig had called Jonathan Crisp on the pretext of getting bail for Miguel Melgar.

'Commander I am concerned that the next step for Carlos Moran would be to take out a contract on Miguel Melgar, this did concern the Commander.'

The death of Billy Chambers had not made the press which was incredible; Bob Warden was puzzled how George Lopez gathered his information. He must have a policeman in his pocket somewhere down the line.

Big Sam held his final meeting with his team, letting them know they would all be moving to a new base in Richmond in one hour, some of the guys objected especially Jimmy Simmons.

'However,' Sam insisted, 'I have information that the Old bill are already pulling in informers for any snippets of information on this big Robbery, so it's imperative that you all disappear. Once the robbery has taken place the Old bill would be pulling in everybody, but they wouldn't be unable to say anything about you guys because you hadn't been around.'

Sam passed around the new passports. Jimmy Simmons was obviously aggravated as there was no way he could contact Billy Chambers. Derrick congratulated Sam on the quality of decorations and fixing up the factory with televisions and beds and more importantly enough food and drinks to last a month, the toilet facilities would suffice so all was well.

Jimmy Simmons asked why they wanted enough food for a month if they were flying out of Denham airport on Wednesday.

Big Sam pointed out that it is just cautionary so enjoy yourselves until Wednesday. Scotch Jack realised who the traitor was and really wanted to pop him here and now, but Sam just glared at Jack.

Costa Esteve telephoned Big Sam but there was no reply.

'Don't worry Costa in a few days we'll have the money, we have the documents, maps and plans safely in our hands,' said Andres.

Carlos Moran sent Antonio Ballester to the UK, as information had been received that Costa Esteve and Andres Lara were hidden in the Heathrow area, they must be found at any price. Other orders given to Antonio Ballester was to find a contract killer that could be trusted to murder Miguel Melgar, finance had been set up for whatever contracts needed to be carried out.

The Commissioner of Police Sir John Bacon held a breakfast meeting with the Deputy Commissioner and Roger McBean Chief Constable of Northumberland. McBean explained the evidence so far wasn't favourable for Superintendent Parker, he was unhappy with the answers given by Parker. Especially Parkers remarks that he couldn't remember if he had mentioned to Inspector Brown that he had not found any books or cash in Liam Murphy's flat.

'It is imperative that we interview Paul Gear ex-Inspector of Parker's at Chelsea, as according to Parker he bumped into Gear as he left Murphy's flat. We really want information from Gear if Parker was carrying anything when he bumped into him. In my opinion Parker became overwhelmed with the sight of ten thousand pounds and most importantly the incriminating evidence that those books contained.'

The Commissioner pointed out that a man of such experience as Parker entering a informers premise without a witness was rather odd. They all agreed that the way the evidence was pointing for Parker it didn't look good.

Inspector Brown accompanied by Sergeant Jessup and DC's Hirani and Smithy knocked on the door of Len Elands house.

Opening the door Eland just sneered, 'What do you lot want?'

'Mr Eland we have a warrant to search your property.' After searching the whole house from top to bottom, they found one handgun and a shotgun.

'Mr Lenard Eland we are arresting you for holding unlawful weapons, whatever you may say will be taken down and could be used in a court of Law.'

Len Eland was taken to Scotland Yard where he was interviewed by Commander Rose and Inspector Brown. 'We are aware that you supplied weapons to a known villain in the person of Mr William Chambers.'

'I've never heard of him.'

'Perhaps these photographs of you and Mr Chambers will refresh your memory.'

'O, that chap. I didn't realise his name was William Chambers and I certainly never supplied guns to this person.'

'Perhaps once again Mr Eland we can refresh your mind with these photographs of weapons being given to Mr Chambers at an Indian Restaurant in Tooting.'

'What's that got to do with me?'

'Mr Eland you are connected with the Indian Restaurant as the owner of the establishment.'

'O, yes I remember I gave my name to some Indians who wanted to start a business.'

'Mr Eland we have already arrested a number of people from the restaurant who have identified you as the owner.'

'So is it a crime to be associated with a restaurant?'

'Fine Mr Eland we already have you in possession of a handgun and a shotgun, with your form you'll be going down for six or seven years, we'll also let the lads from the Indian restaurant know you are being very helpful.'

'Hold on a minute don't let's be too hasty here, I'll help you if I can.'

'Really Mr Eland, tell us about the weapons you supplied to Billy Chambers.'

'Chambers wanted some firepower for some robbery next week.'

'Have you any idea where this robbery is taking place?'

'Somewhere in the Heathrow area but he didn't confide in me. Commander what about my deal?'

'What else can you tell me Mr Eland?'

'My restaurant is a cover; we supply weapons to those who require firepower. You must understand I am only the middle man, I do not want to go to prison for six or seven years, I'll tell you everything I know.'

'I realise that Mr Eland, but unfortunately, unlawful weapons are an automatic five years prison sentence, take him down.'

Commander Rose turned to Inspector Brown; at least we have closed an illegal weapon factory. We must obtain warrants to search the homes of all those who either work their or those who are associated with the restaurant.

Now Inspector Brown we are going to concentrate all our manpower towards the Heathrow area where Costa Esteve and Andres Lara are hiding. 'All we have is that this big robbery is taking place in that area. I'll have a quick word with the Deputy Commissioner and if he agrees we will move all our units to the Heathrow area leaving only a skeleton staff to take care of minor crimes.'

The Commissioner called the Deputy Commissioner and Commander Rose to his office. 'Your proposal Commander Rose to move all available units to the Heathrow area for a few days is very risky indeed. I'm not sure that I care for the idea so I propose to give you half the manpower for the Heathrow enterprise.'

Commander Rose had already drawn up a task force of Serious Crime Squad officers, Flying Squad Officers and CID officers from Kilburn. 'It certainly leaves us thin on the ground Commander if anything big happens in London.'

'I'm aware of that Deputy Commissioner, but if we miss the chance of catching these villains and this blasted man Costa Esteve before the robbery we'll be kicking ourselves.'

A further meeting took place with Chief Inspectors Bleasdale and Morrison of the flying squad, Inspectors Brown, Ward and Beagle, Sergeants Jessup and Ben Clark. After outlining his plan of moving all possible units to the Heathrow area for the next few days, Inspector Beagle thought that his own CID and armed units would be able to contain any robbery taking place around his area.

'Inspector Beagle at this present time we are unsure of the size of this robbery, we are fully aware of the danger that these robbers are armed and will shoot to kill rather than be taken.'

There have been so many murders connected with Mr Costa Esteve and Andres Lara, that we are taking no chances whatsoever. All units will be meeting at Heathrow police station at 20.00 hours. 'Inspector Beagle your duties will be to accommodate everybody as we will require round the clock canteen facilities.

'Chief Inspector Bleasdale I will require four of your CID officers, Ben Clark, Reg More and DC's Alex Quirk and Rod Muir. Altogether there will be a total of thirty-two officers.

'Lastly I have already contacted Heathrow Airport and other major companies as such, requesting details of any knowledge of payrolls, shipments of gold or diamonds, they may be taking place in the next few days.'

Chief Inspector Morrison suggested that maybe they should widen their search to nearby towns, just in case there were any large shipments happening.

'Very good Morrison I'll leave that for you to arrange.'

'Inspector Brown you will coordinate the accommodation with Inspector Beagle.'

'Yes Sir.'

'Ok Gentlemen, see you at 20,00 at Heathrow Police Station, good luck.'

Chief Inspector Bleasdale and Sergeant Clark returned to Kilburn where all the CID officers were assembled, Bleasdale pointed out that Sergeants Clark and More along with DC's Quirk and Muir would be joining a special task force headed by Commander Rose for the next few days.

By 18:00 all thirty-two officers were assembled at the Heathrow Police station, extra canteen facilities and hotel accommodation had been arranged and all had signed in.

At 20:00 the meeting commenced with Commander Rose addressing the officers of the task force. Pointing out how dangerous these villains were especially Costa Esteve and Andres Lara who had been involved with many of the murders associated with this case so far.

'Many of you officers will be armed to protect yourselves and the public. We are still unsure where these villains will strike; I was hoping to have all the information of any large movements of money or jewels being delivered in the next few days, so until then you will be briefed by your individual Inspectors.'

Antonio Ballester had contacted a number of known Spanish and South American mafia living around the London area, a meeting had been set up. Antonio greeted everybody thanking them for attending. 'We have a problem my friends as you know the police have a supergrass in the name of Liam Murphy. But first Carlos Moran would be very grateful if we could remove this annoying stone in his shoe Miguel Melgar 'who is on remand at Brixton remand centre.'

Rafael Miranda suggested that he had just the man, who was also on remand at Brixton.

'What will be the cost Rafael?'

'Thirty thousand.'

'That's fine you have the contract.'

'My man Joao Carvanho will complete the contract this week.'

Jorge Pereira pointed out that information received was that Liam Murphy was in a safe house at 468 Croydon Road, Mitcham Common. Liam Murphy had two damaging books containing the names of criminals who had carried out different robberies through the years, it is very important that this contract is carried out quickly, therefore I Antonio Ballester will carry out the contract.

'Hallo George your contract offer has been accepted and will be executed.'

George Lopez poured himself another large scotch sitting in his favourite chair smiling to himself, all we need to know who has Murphy's books, and I would imagine it's Superintendent Parker.

Finishing his scotch George made another call to a mobile number. 'Hallo Jessup have you any more information on the missing books and Parker?'

'George the Chief Constable of Northumberland held a meeting with the Commissioner and his Deputy, what has been related back to us is that Parker would not survive. Chief Inspector Tolly is waiting to interview Paul Gear when he returns from holiday, as they want to know if Parker was carrying anything when he left Liam Murphy's flat. Once this take place everybody believes Parker will cough.'

'Good Jessup, make sure those books make their way to me, there's fifty grand in the pot for you.'

'I'll find the books George.'

Inspector Beagle rushed into see Commander Rose. 'I have just heard there is an aircraft arriving tomorrow at Terminal 4, carrying five million in diamonds.'

'Anything else of interest?'

'One armoured vehicle carrying two hundred thousand to the bank in terminal 2.'

'This mob wouldn't be interested in two hundred thousand that's for sure. If anything it's the diamond shipment. Ok let's take a look at the cargo area.' Inspectors Brown and Ward accompanied the Commander and Inspector Beagle.

Miguel Melgar was in the showers with all the other remand prisoners, he didn't notice Joao Carvanho creep up beside him until it was far too late. The knife entered Miguel's ribcage and into his heart, Miguel slipped to the floor. Carvanho was out of the showers walking back to his cell when the alarm went off. Guards rushed everywhere but nobody witnessed anything, prisoners were shifted back to their cells.

The Governor of Brixton remand prison put through a call to Scotland Yard, the message was passed onto the Deputy Commissioner, who delegated the investigation to be carried out by Brixton CID. A further call was made to Commander Rose on his mobile.

'Thank you Sir,' putting down his mobile and putting it back in his pocket. Turning to the other Inspectors. 'Miguel Melgar had been murdered in Brixton Prison,' showing Captain Sifre was totally correct in his assumption that Carlos Moran had hands like octopuses.

After checking the cargo area and finding out exactly where the aircraft would park, Commander Rose suggested that twenty officers should be placed in and around the area.

Chief Inspector Morrison was waiting for the Commander to return, there are three other security vehicles all carrying four to eight hundred thousand pounds, Heston, Hounslow and Hayes.

'Ok let's have four men teams in those areas, the biggest is most certainly Terminal 2 cargo area, something still bothered the Commander but he couldn't put his finger on it.'

Big Sam and his team had finished breakfast. 'Let's run over the robbery again lads, is everybody one hundred percent sure of their positions. Jimmy you'll be with me, Scotch Jack and Derrick you'll take the second car and John and Peter you'll take one car apiece. Peter your job is to follow the armoured van and to keep radioing letting us know how long the vehicle is away from the scheduled point. Once you are at the factory units you will pull in right up his arse. John and I will block his front movement, Scotch Jack and Derrick you'll pull in ramming the side of the van. Derrick you jump onto the roof of the van and cut the three aerials. Scotch Jack you've got the teargas ready and Jimmy and I will do the windows, Peter you've got the getaway vehicle, all clear lads?'

'You bet,' was the reply.

'Once we have the cash we'll make for the bridge, Andres will be waiting for us. We load the money onto his vehicle, Derrick, Jimmy, Scotch Jack and myself will travel in that vehicle. John and Peter will travel in the spare car leaving the BMW blocking the bridge.'

Jimmy asked why there is a change of plan; I thought I was the only one travelling with Andres. 'Yeah that was right but we changed our minds. The other change is we head back here to Richmond instead of going to Denham Airfield.'

Jimmy immediately pointed out, 'But that's where we are flying out from.'

'No we have changed our minds.'

'But Andres and Costa Esteve have the getaway planned.'

'Have they, or are we being taken for fools?'

'I don't understand Sam what you mean.'

'Somebody does,' looking away from Jimmy.

'Ok lads it's 9:30, let's make a move we want to be in position at 11:15.' They all drove towards Hayes in the stolen vehicles, the mood was clear and not subdued they were all focused on their jobs they had to carry out.

Commander Rose and twenty officers making themselves blend into the background of the cargo terminal, Harani, Smithy, Facer and Jessup were driving around Hounslow. Ben Clark, Alex Quirk, Reg More and Rod Muir were in Hayes, four flying squad officers had been located to Heston, all was covered.

Big Sam had all his vehicles in position; Peter was parked, waiting for the security van, which arrived ten minutes early. 'First Car to base, my client is ten minutes early.'

'Received, let me know when you are about to leave.' The security guards loaded a number of large bags into the side door of the security van, and climbed back into the van.

'First Car to base we are leaving now.'

'Received.'

Ben Clark's squad car was cruising around Hayes high street knowing they had ten to fifteen minutes before the security van arrived in Hayes High Street. He pulled up just down the road from Woolworths waiting for the security van, they were all chatting away about the amount of Police officers involved in the strike force, fifteen minutes went by and no security van.

'Where was the last pick up point for the security van?' asked Reg More.

Ben looked at the schedule. 'Knells Petrol Station, another fifteen minutes from here.'

'Let's take a ride to the petrol station, surely we couldn't have missed the van.' They drove back arriving at Knells Petrol Station twelve minutes later, Clark and Quirk rushed into the petrol station holding there warrant cards, 'Has the security van turned up yet?'

'Yes sergeant they left here fifteen minutes ago.' They rushed back to their car relating the news to Reg and Rod. Reg looked at the schedule, 'they should be at the bank.'

'Where's their stop after the bank?'

'EMI factory.'

'Ok we take another look at the bank, maybe they stopped for coffee.'

'That's a possibility, if we go charging into the bank and the bank is being watched that's it game over.' They made their way back towards the bank.

'First Car to base my client is turning into the area now.' Peter was behind the security van, Big Sam's car came straight at the front of the van as did John's, Scotch Jack came from nowhere and rammed the van from the side. Derrick jumped up onto the roof of Jacks car and then onto the roof of the security van, cutting the three aerials. Big Sam had electric battery glass cutters which he immediately smacked against the driver's window.

'If you don't open the van doors we are going to pour teargas inside.' Peter ran across to the other factory unit collecting their getaway vehicle and driving it ready for their escape. The security guards in the front could see there was no point in being shot and ordered the guards in the back to open their doors. As the back doors opened the guards jumped out with batons in their hands. Jimmy who had arrived at the back of the van pulled his gun; both security guards dropped their batons. Jimmy whacked both guards who fell to the floor, jumping over the guards he started pulling the sacks of money out towards the back of the van.

Derrick and Big Sam joined him passing the sacks to John and scotch Jack who loaded them into the getaway vehicle. Sam shouted to Jimmy, 'Leave the bloody coins; how many sacks is there left in the van?'

'Maybe ten.'

'Let's hurry.' They finished loading the getaway car, jumped in themselves and away towards the bridge.

Ben Clark's squad car had travelled back to the bank, not seeing the security van; they made their way to the EMI factory. 'Where the dickens is the bloody security van, let's backtrack in case they have stopped for coffee.'

Big Sam's car arrived at the bridge; Andres noticing them pull up, reversed his vehicle back towards the BMW, the sacks of money were transferred quickly. Derrick had moved around towards the driver's side, Andres looking in his side mirror, watched as Derrick approached his door. What's going on here thought Andres before Andres could move, Big Sam opened the passenger side door jumped in pulling Andres out of vehicle, at the same time smashing his gun butt twice on the side of Andres' head. Derrick was in the driving seat, Peter and John made for the other car. Costa who had parked his car in a side turning jumped out of his car and started running at Big Sam shouting, 'What are you doing?'

Sam shouted, 'You bastard, I'll be in touch with your share!' Andres was recovering, pulling out his gun, which fortunately was spotted by Scotch Jack who levelled his own gun and shot Andres in the shoulder. Big Sam was sitting in the passenger seat, Jimmy Simmons was looking around for Billy Chambers wondering where he had gotten too. Jimmy looked at Sam in the passenger seat half turned with the door open.

'It wasn't my fault Sam,' knowing what was coming at the same time trying to pull his own gun. Scotch Jack shot Jimmy in the head, who fell to the floor as Scotch Jack jumped into the back of Big Sam's car and sped away, with John and Peter following.

People started coming out of the door of the small pub after hearing the entire racket. Costa who was running back towards his car started firing his gun at anybody coming out of the pub door, hitting one poor fellow in the leg. Others scattered either back through the pub door or lying on the floor. Andres was in agony, nearby was the body of Jimmy Simmons dead on the floor.

Ben Clark's squad car screamed around the corner of the factory units nearly hitting a security guard with blood running down the side of his face, Reg More radioed Commander Rose.

'We've been hit at Hayes, the security van has been robbed,' giving the address. 'We will continue following the villains,' as they drove around the road they came to a bridge which was blocked by a BMW. They noticed two men on the floor, one holding a gun in his hand.

Clark and Quirk made their way up one side of the bridge, Reg More and Rod Muir moved up the other side making their way to the centre of the bridge.

One of the people crouching down behind a large stonewall, shouted, 'Be careful he's got a gun!'

Rod Muir shouted at the person on the floor with the gun, 'Police put down your gun.'

Andres could see both police officers and opened fire hitting both, Rod Muir who fell clutching his heart and then Reg More went down. Ben Clark didn't mess around running up over the bridge and shooting Andres in the shoulder, he continued running towards Andre's body kicking the gun out of his hand. Alex Quirk was over with Rod Muir and Reg More both were dead.

Alex Quirk shouted into his radio, 'Officers down backup and ambulances required urgent.'

The pub landlord had also called the police; one police car was with the security van, two other police cars raced by through the factory units 'driving towards the bridge. Fifteen minutes later squad cars were pulling up from all directions, Commander Rose arrived with Inspectors Brown and Ward.

Ben Clark and Alex Quirk had removed their jackets which lay over the bodies of Reg More and Rod Muir. Ben Clark looked up with tears in his eyes at Commander Rose. 'Both Reg More and Rod Muir are dead Sir, shot by that person over there,' pointing towards Andres. 'I had no choice Sir; I shot the villain in the shoulder.'

'Who's the other character on the floor and who shot him?'

'I have no idea Sir.'

'Inspector Brown and Ward take three of these officers and start receiving statements from those people in the pub.'

Chief Inspector Morrison arrived at the factory units and started taking statements from the security guards, as you never know if one of them was involved in the robbery as the inside man.

Derrick drove the getaway car towards Richmond with John and Peter following, they were all excited that the robbery had been such a big success. Big Sam thanked Scotch Jack for his quick thinking over shooting Jimmy Simmons, Scotch Jack just replied by saying, 'I never liked traitors, so it was my pleasure.' Five minutes later they drove into Wiltshire Street. Scotch Jack jumped out of the vehicle opening the big double doors, the two vehicles drove into the factory unit. Scotch Jack shut and locked the double doors; with more excitement as they unloaded the moneybags.

'How much do you think we have Sam?' asked Derrick.

'Maybe three or four million, maybe a bit more,' shrugging his big shoulders.

Big Sam poured out five glasses of scotch, sitting down he told the Shephard Brothers the story of Jimmy Simmons. Peter was disappointed that Big Sam hadn't confided in them before.

'So what happened to Billy Chambers and his gang?'

'I have no idea Peter, but I must say I'm pleased he never showed up, otherwise there would have been more killings.'

Scotch Jack piped up, 'And it could have been anyone of us lying on the floor dead, if Chambers had his way.'

Costa Esteve drove into Macon Street, Heston, not believing that his plan had gone terribly wrong and what happened to Billy Chambers the bastard with his gang.

Commander Rose searched through Andres' pockets looking for identification. 'Wait a minute Brown have you got those photographs of the passports in the car?'

'Yes Sir,' collecting the file and passing the photographs to the Commander.

'Well look who we have here, Andres Lara Ferrer,' who looked up at the Commander saying, 'help me, my shoulder.' The Commander looking around and seeing nobody looking accidentally kicked Andres in the shoulder. 'Shut up you bastard you murdered two of my officers, I really couldn't care a shit about your shoulder.'

Two ambulances arrived; Andres Lara was loaded into one ambulance with Inspector Ward and an armed police officer as security, the bodies of Reg More and Rod Muir were loaded onto the other ambulance and driven away.

Commander Rose walked over to Ben Clark and Alex Quirk asking how they both felt. 'Absolutely sick Sir.'

'Ok I'll call Chief Inspector Bleasdale letting him know the bad news.'

Chief Inspector Morrison arrived back at the murder scene. 'I received all the statements from the security guards Commander, I have sent two of my lads to the local police station to run the names through the computer in case any of them have any form.'

'Very good Morrison. Have we any idea how much has been stolen?'

'Not as yet but the security company should be able to let us know shortly.'

Inspector Brown walked over to the Commander and Chief Inspector Morrison. 'The other body is that of Jimmy Simmons; why on earth was he shot in the head?'

'I'm not sure, it's all a bit funny Sir, there was also two people shot outside the pub but they seem to be OK.'

'Thank God for that Brown,' said the Commander.

Commander Rose called over a uniformed Inspector, 'Which Police Station are you from Inspector?'

'Hayes Sir.'

'Good so you have local knowledge, I would like you and a number of your officers to start a house to house, asking if anybody noticed any strange cars or people in the area in the last month.'

'Yes Sir.'

Commander Rose, with Chief Inspector Morrison and Inspector Brown along with Sergeant Ben Clark and Alex Quirk made their way to Heathrow police station.

The television news broke the story:

'A daring daylight Robbery took place in Hayes today, with four million pounds being stolen it is thought. Unfortunately there is a death toll of two CID officers, one robber, with another robber injured. Two bystanders were also shot by a man running for his car, who has yet to be identified. The police have not disclosed the names of those killed.'

The Deputy Commissioner called Commander Rose, saying the Commissioner was upset with another two police officers killed in the line of duty.

'That's the understatement of the year Sir, we are all sick as parrots,' said the Commander, 'nobody could have guessed which security van or aircraft was the target. The information given to us by the security companies were that none of their vehicles were carrying any more than eight hundred thousand pounds. The aircraft however which was due to land was carrying six million in diamonds, so which do you go for a security van carrying eight hundred thousand or a cargo of six million.'

Commander Rose held a meeting with all senior officers. 'We must now move quickly, pulling in all known villains associated with those in the enclosed photographs. We will also analyse the surveillance tapes from the Red Lion, as two of the villains who frequent the Red Lion pub are now dead, Billy Chambers and Jimmy Simmons. Also get onto all your snouts and receive as much information as you can on the robbery and its robbers, any clue will be investigated, we want results yesterday Gentlemen.'

Andres Lara had two armed police officers guarding his hospital room, Antonio Ballester had been given the information that Andres Lara had been caught and was in hospital. He was also fully aware that the police would be searching for those who had carried out the robbery at Hayes, so now would probably be the ideal time to visit Liam Murphy.

Driving towards Mitcham Common and finding 468 Croydon Road, Antonio surveyed the area; there was no security camera which again was ideal. He decided to wait until it was dark. Lights appeared in the downstairs rooms, he made his way to the back of the house. Looking through windows as he passed, in one of the rooms sat three men watching the television, noticing one of the three was Liam Murphy, so the other two must be police officers. After five minutes one of the officers walked out of the room and re-entered with three plates of food. The television was all about the daring daylight robbery at Hayes. The two police officers killed in action were named as Sergeant Reginald More and DC Rodney Muir, also the name of the dead robber was named as Jimmy Simmons.

'Did you know Jimmy Simmons Liam?'

'I met him once or twice.'

One of the officers asked why Simmons would have been shot.

'Perhaps it had been a mistake,' said Murphy.

The food being finished, one of the officers removed the dirty plates, taking them into the kitchen. Emptying the waste into a black plastic bag, opening the back door and putting the plastic bag in the dustbin, as he turned to return he was hit over the head knocking him to the ground, he was out cold. Antonio walked into the house screwing the silencer onto his gun reaching the living room he shot the police officer twice, turning towards Liam Murphy saying, 'Sorry it's only business,' putting three bullets into his head. Antonio unscrewed the silencer from his gun walking back through the back door stepping over the police officer on the floor saying, 'This was your lucky day, officer,' he walked back to his car and away.

Thirty minutes later the police officer came around from the knock on the head, he felt dizzy staggering towards the back door which he noticed was open, after reaching the inside of the kitchen using his arms to lean on the wall he shouted for help. There was no reply making his way further into the house he found both Liam Murphy and officer Kent dead on the floor from gunshot wounds.

'Bloody hell, what a mess,' picking up the telephone and reporting the incident to Scotland Yard.

The Deputy Commissioner couldn't believe what was happening, quickly calling Commander Rose.

'How on earth could that happen, we must have a spy within,' said the Commander. 'I'm waiting for the Commissioner to call back as special branch are now involved.'

Commander Rose looked shocked putting his hand to his mouth, 'I'm afraid I have further bad news, Gentlemen, our supergrass and one of the armed officers have been killed in a safe house.'

'What is our next move Commander?'

'We have the photographs of all those villains who have received dodgy passports, so I believe we should circulate those photographs to the media, asking for those persons to come forward to eliminate themselves from our enquires.'

Chief Inspector Bleasdale was devastated to learn from the Commander, that both Reg More and Rod Muir had been killed in the line of duty; I have the unpleasant duty of facing their widows. The whole of the Police Station is in mourning.

Antonio Ballester arrived at the General Hospital, finding out what time the police guard changed shifts noticing one of the police officers was a similar size to himself, he decided he would follow him home.

After Constable Crockford had reached his home, turning on the lights, it was obvious to Antonio that the officer lived alone. He knocked on the door and as it was opened by Constable Crockford. Antonio shot him twice moving quickly inside the house, shutting the door behind him and finding his way to the bedroom. Looking inside a wardrobe he found the police officer's spare uniform which he quickly put on, placing his own clothes into a black bag. Making his way back to the hospital he noticed another police officer just arriving, calling him over Antonio explained that he had noticed some suspicious people lurking around in the basement area. He followed the police officer into the basement; clubbing him on the head with his gun and tying him up with duct tape. Antonio made his way back to the hospital ward where Andres Lara was being held. Walking down the corridor, he waved at the other police officer sitting on a chair.

'You're bloody late, mate, I'm off to the canteen,' as he got up from his chair and walked down the corridor the other way without looking up at Antonio, who quickly opened the door of Andres Lara's room.

Andres was laying on the bed with drips running from his arm. 'I'm sorry about this but it's business. I need to know the address of Costa Esteve.'

Andres shook his head.

'Andres don't make this too hard on yourself if you don't give me the address I'm going to kill you,' putting out his hand and stopping the drip.

'Please don't kill me.'

'Give me Esteve's address now.'

'23 Macon Street, Heston.'

'Now that's wasn't too difficult, was it? Goodbye Andres and best wishes from Carlos Moran,' placing the pillow over Andres' face until he was still. Antonio walked out of the room down the corridor and out to the car park and drove away.

Inspector Brown arrived at the hospital to interview Andres Lara; speaking with the ward sister they both walked down towards Andres Lara's room.

'Where on earth are the two officers guarding our suspect?' Brown pushed past the sister into the room. 'Bloody hell he's been murdered.'

The sister tried to help Andres breathing but failed.

Police constable Millow walked slowly back down the corridor after returning from the canteen.

'Where the hell have you been?' asked Inspector Brown in an aggressive manner. 'Our suspect is dead.'

'But Constable Crockford was here,' replied Millow.

'Well he's not here now is he,' shouted Inspector Brown, 'there's going to be hell to pay when the Commander receives the news.'

Inspector Brown asked the sister if he could use her telephone.

'Commander Rose, I'm at the hospital, Andres Lara has been murdered.'

'But we have two police officers guarding his room,' replied Commander Rose.

'Unfortunately, it appears neither of them were here, one was in the canteen and the other I have no idea where he is.'

Hounslow CID travelled to Constable Crockford's house, where they found him dead on the floor having been shot twice. Constable Richards was found tied up in the basement of the hospital after a search was made. Constable Richards was unable to give a description of the man who attacked him.

The Deputy Commissioner gave permission for the photos to be given to the media, with a caption please come forward to assist us in our inquires.

The Serious Crime Squad had started to interview different villains for the Hayes robbery; many of the villains were pleased to be associated and have their names in the newspapers, showing how important they were.

Big Sam had walked down Wiltshire Street to the local tobacconist shop, purchasing three of the daily newspapers. He was completely surprised to notice photographs of all the lads on the front page staring at him, looking around in case he had been recognised. He pulled up his coat around his chin, walking briskly back to the factory. As Sam walked into the factory, all the lads shouted, 'We're on the television news, how on earth did they get our photographs?'

'Wherever Costa Esteve had our passports made is obviously the leak, it's too late now to-do anything about it, all it means is that we are holed up hear for two or three weeks until our appearances alter. Our passports will hold up if we are careful about getting out of the country, if we use a private aircraft or the train service to France, the downside is we will not be able to venture out.'

Antonio had also read the newspapers and was ready to pay Costa Esteve a visit, with his photograph plastered on the front page; he knew Costa wouldn't venture out especially now that he had lost his hard man Andres Lara to protect him.

Driving out to Heston and finding Macon Street, he parked his car watching no 23; there was no visible movement in the flat as far as he could see. Antonio walked around the block of flats into a small wooded area; he could see Costa Esteve looking into a filing cabinet. He walked back to the front of the flats, walking up to the front door and knocking there was no answer, he knocked again. He heard movement a voice came from the inside, 'Who is it please?'

'My name is Antonio Ballester, I have some documents from Mr Billy Chambers.'

'I'm sorry Mr Ballester one moment,' unlocking the front door and finding himself face to face with this large man pushing himself into the hallway Costa thought for a moment but it was too late.

Antonio pushed Costa to the floor; pulling Costa up by the arm he pushed him into the living room.

'Ok Costa I'm here for the documents, plans and maps you stole from Carlos Moran. Your mate Andres Lara is dead, I killed him yesterday in hospital, so unless you want the same treatment, hand all the documents over now.'

'Ok, Ok I'll fetch them,' making his way back to his little office, opening the filing cabinet and pulling out a gun. But before Costa could turn around, Antonio rammed a knife into Costa's shoulder. Costa let out a cry slamming the cabinet shut.

'Now this is your last chance, silly man, give me the documents,' poking the knife into Costa's face and cutting a small cut on his cheek. 'Do you want me to start cutting?'

'No, No please, the documents are in the fourth file,' opening the cabinet and removing the file.

'Are they all here Costa?'

'Yes, yes.'

Antonio picked up the telephone calling Carlos Moran. 'I have the documents in my hand,' after answering Carlos's questions, he passed the telephone to Costa Esteve.

'You have caused me many problems Costa and a lot of money. I was going to have you killed but now that you have the police on your back for murder and robberies. I shall leave you alone. But if you ever get in my way again, you'll be joining you friend Andres Lara.'

Antonio received the telephone from Costa Esteve. 'When you get away from his home, telephone the police letting them know where he is.' Putting the phone down, Antonio said, 'You are a lucky man today Costa.'

Antonio stopped just outside Heathrow Airport, making the call and tipping off the police as the whereabouts of Costa Esteve, the police officer asked for his name, which he gave as Kenneth Morris. 'I'm known informer, so I will pop into your station tonight and claim my reward.'

'Very good Mr Morris.'

Inspector Beagle didn't bother calling Commander Rose, thinking I'll show that fancy fool who's a good copper; two squad cars arrived at 23 Macon Street, six officers ran up the path knocking down the front door, finding Costa Esteve lying on his bed trying to bandage the stab wound.

'Mr Costa Esteve I am arresting you for the murder of Peter Sainsbury, anything you might say will be written down and could be used in evidence against you. 'Beagle picked up the telephone calling Commander Rose, 'I've arrested Costa Esteve for the murder of Peter Sainsbury.'

'That will do for the start; have Mr Esteve transferred to the yard.'

'Yes Sir.'

Commander Rose immediately contacted the Deputy Commissioner informing him of the good news. 'Excellent news Commander, perhaps Esteve will now enlighten us on the murders and robberies.'

Derrick Smallwood wanted to see his wife as did Peter Shephard, Big Sam was totally against the idea of anybody going out on the streets, but understood their feelings.

'Ok but be bloody careful, as you will have every police snout and villains who are jealous of your success ready to tip off the police. You better take some money with you as I'm sure your old Ladies will be in need of cash.' John Shephard suggested that he would go along to help his brother.

'Ok John be careful as you leave and return as we do not want any people outside becoming suspicious.'

Derrick parked his car two roads away from his house, looking around he couldn't see any unwelcome visitors. Making his way to his house he slipped up the pathway to the back entrance as he put his key in the door, six police officers appeared handcuffed him and led Derrick away to Scotland Yard.

Peter and John Shephard had travelled by underground and then caught the bus to where Peter lived, as they turned the corner of Peter's road, Peter's wife shouted, 'Run Peter the Old bill are everywhere.' They both turned and started running down the road towards the shopping centre. John yelled at Peter to run through the old alleys into the park area where they could meet by the old pinworks. John turned one way and Peter the other.

As Peter turned into one of the alleys it was blocked at the other end by two police officers, as he turned to run back out of the alley three other police officers appeared and brought him down to the floor, where he was handcuffed and led off to the yard.

John Shephard kept running through another alley and into the park area which had many trees and bushes, he could use as cover. Making for the old pinworks and the disused wastepipe where he knew he could hide out for at least a day.

The police presence was heavy, they searched through the park and alleys running off the park, the shopping centre and roads nearby, Inspector Ward was convinced John Shephard had got out of the area, making sure that any of the nearby train stations where covered by police.

Big Sam and Scotch Jack watched the television news, which reported that three fugitives had been apprehended Costa Esteve, Derrick Smallwood and Peter Shephard.

'Bloody hell Jack I knew they shouldn't have gone.'

'Will any of them grass on us Sam?'

'No Jack, don't forget we have the money, and if they want their share they have to keep their mouths shut and Costa Esteve hasn't a clue where we are.'

Commander Rose interviewed Costa Esteve letting him know that he had already been charged with the murder of Peter Sainsbury and would later today be charged with the robbery at Hayes, so he would be going to prison for a long time. 'However we may be in a position to help you, but we need information.'

'I have nothing to say Commander.'

'Who killed Andres Lara?'

'I would imagine it was a contract hit from Spain replied Costa.'

'Are you telling me that all these killings and robberies are all down to these treasure maps and plans?'

'That's for you to decide Commander, I have nothing more to say.'

Commander Rose interviewed Derrick Smallwood next.

'Before these robberies took place, you were unknown to us. Now you are in the big league, but at what cost? Your wife is young and you are thirty-three so when you come out of prison you'll be in your late fifties, if you want my help, I need information. Where are Samuel Davidson and Scotch Jack Daniel?'

'I have no idea, they went up north somewhere.'

'What about the Mallards robbery?'

‘Commander I know nothing of any robberies whatsoever.’

‘Derrick Smallwood I am charging you with a robbery of a security van at Hayes with a number of other people to be named at a later time, anything you may say will be recorded and could be used against you.’

Peter Shephard came next and wouldn’t even say a word; he was duly charged with the Hayes Security Van Robbery. Both Smallwood and Peter Shephard were transferred to Brixton.

Commander Rose telephoned Captain Sifre briefing him on the capture of Costa Esteve and the murder of Andres Lara. ‘It would appear you were right about the contract killings; I can only imagine your Carlos Moran has retrieved the treasure maps and documents.’

‘Commander we in Madrid will not rest until we have Carlos Moran behind bars. We’ll be in touch Captain.’

The Surbiton area had been searched for Samuel Davidson, Scotch Jack Daniels and John Shephard without success.

Former Inspector Paul Gear returned from holiday and was met by Chief Inspector Ian Tolly, the conversation on the way to Scotland Yard was very interesting. After introductions to Chief Constable Roger McBean, Paul Gear was officially told of the very serious complaint against Superintendent Parker, who was involved with the missing ten thousand pounds and some valuable books.

Paul Gear said that he met Parker outside a block of flats, after speaking with him he invited Parker for a drink in a pub opposite. He may have had something in his coat pockets. It became obvious that Parker was not interested in speaking and only mentioned that he hoped to be retiring shortly, five minutes later he was gone.

‘I understand that Parker was quite difficult to work with when he was in your charge at Chelsea?’

‘Unfortunately Chief Constable, Parker was always a problem he had been a suspect when some monies disappeared from a robbery, but it was never proved, then there was pilfering of petrol and overcharging of expenses. Some of that was proved and I had him transferred. However being one of the boys, he was promoted to Inspector and transferred to the flying squad. After some more unfortunate ventures Parker rode on the back of another Inspector who didn’t receive accolade and Parker was promoted to Chief Inspector. Then a terrible mistake was really made, he kept his head down for three years and because he was one of the boys freemason, he was promoted to Superintendent, God knows who was behind that mistake.' Finishing his statement which he signed, Paul Gear was thanked for his time.

Chief Constable Roger Bean turned to Chief Inspector Tolly saying, 'I'm convinced now knowing Parker's background that he obviously pocketed the money and books, it wouldn't surprise me one day, somebody will pay Parker a lot of money for the contents of those books.'

I suggest we complete the report for the Commissioner, as our next duty is the investigation into the murder of Liam Murphy, which sounds to me as an inside job.

'I totally agree Chief Constable,' replied Ian Tolly.

Big Sam and Scotch Jack were dismayed to receive the news on the television that Derrick Smallwood and Peter Shephard had been charged with the robbery of a security van heist at Hayes.

'I wonder where John Shephard is hiding, John will make his way back here when he's ready. It's time to bank our monies, I've a good friend at an international bank that for a fee, will open five accounts for us.'

'Will the money be safe Sam?'

'Without doubt Jack, I will take you to meet the manager.'

'How much will we receive each Sam?'

'Looking at the whole picture I00,000 for the factory, a possible million for opening the bank accounts we should all receive about 580,000 each.'

After a long discussion with the bank manager, Jack was convinced he could remove his money at any time he wished. Five accounts were set up under the names of Samuel Davidson, Jack Daniel, John Shephard, Peter Shephard and Derrick Smallwood, pass books were issued to Sam except Jack who took his own book. Another item was added that if any of those named accounts were reported dead, their money would be transferred back to Sam Davidson's account.

After returning to the factory, Sam decided he was going to move out, but he wanted first to turn over Costa Esteves flat at Heston, Jack decided he would like to go along for the ride.

Arriving at 23 Macon Street, parking their car they walked down the street towards no 23. There was no police presence, the front door of number 23 was still damaged and was easy to get inside. Jack wanted to know why Sam wanted to search the flat.

'With all the information we have now accumulated, something must be hidden here.' They searched every room, returning to the little office. All the files had been ransacked by the police. Looking around Sam noticed that the filing cabinet had been moved recently as the colour of the floor and carpet was a little lighter. After moving the cabinet they found a large envelope containing drawings and documents.

'Sam those drawings look like maps to me.'

'You could be right Jack,' putting the envelope into his inside pocket of his brown jacket. As they returned to the factory, sitting in a chair watching television was John Shephard. 'Bloody hell John we thought you had been caught.'

'No but Peter and Derrick are in Brixton remand prison.'

'We know John, but I'm pleased you made it back, I've opened bank accounts for us all so hear is yours and Peters pass books. As you can see you have deposited in your name 580,000 each. I've decided John that I'm going away to Cornwall as I have a couple of good friends down there that will look after me. You are welcome to come along, or like Jack you can remain here for a couple of months.'

'I'll stay here, Sam if you don't mind, just in case I can help Peter out.'

'Ok that reminds me,' picking up the telephone Sam called Willis Shawbum.

'Hi Willis it's Big Sam, I want you to represent Derrick Smallwood and Peter Shephard they are both in Brixton remand, please pass on the following message. Accounts have been opened in their names.'

Both Jack and John remarked how great Big Sam was not only did he make sure they kept their monies but also to arrange a solicitor for them.

'That's the secret lads always make sure your gang is looked after even when they get caught.'

Willis Shawbum made appointments to visit Derrick Smallwood and Peter Shephard, passing on the message from Big Sam. Although they were delighted with the news they were alarmed at the prospect of facing prison for fifteen years. Willis Shawbum encouraged them by saying the police had a lot to do, as they have no witnesses placing them at the site of the crime at Hayes. And he would be doing all he could to get them out of prison.

Big Sam caught the coach from Victoria Coach Station to Plymouth, catching the train from Plymouth to Looe, a lovely little fishing village. As the train came along the river bed, he looked out of the window, watching the ducks, swans, pheasants and other wildlife, what a place to live he thought.

Big Sam had already made arrangements to meet his friend Derik Major, who was owner of a number of small boats that were hired out to tourists in the holiday periods.

'Hi Sam, nice to see you again, is it a holiday or just hiding out?'

'Derik I'm looking for somewhere nice and quiet and I need a car.'

'I have just the place for you and nobody will disturb you, you'll be perfectly safe. With a car one of my mates has a Volkswagen for sale about four grand, but it's clean and in good working order.'

'That will do me Derik.'

'Come on then I'll drive you up to the cottage, it's in West Looe.'

Derik drove over Looe Bridge and into West Looe, turning right into a small road and left and right and stopped outside this wonderful cottage.

'What do you think Sam?'

'Derik it's superb,' walking inside it had two bedrooms a living room, kitchen and small office, two televisions and a telephone, the kitchen had all the mod cons.

'I'll bring the car up tomorrow if that's ok Sam?'

'No problem Derik, here's six grand that should cover the car and the rent.'

'How long do you want the cottage for Sam?'

'Maybe three months or less I'm not sure at the moment, my plans are to travel to France and into Spain when the time comes.'

Jonathan Crisp was sitting in the Crown Court with Chief Inspector Bleasdale talking about the case. 'I believe we will be in for a hard time Chief Inspector, as Miss Kerry Dickson will be out for our blood.'

The Crown Court opened with Judge Peter Samuels presiding. Jonathan Crisp put forward the Crowns case against Edward Horn and Tomas Prince.

Miss Dickson ripped the evidence apart. But the juries were unconvinced that two professional criminals drove a car with detonators hidden in the boot, and hadn't a clue they were there.

Jonathan Crisp summed up saying that it was unusual for well-known personalities in crime such as Edward Horn and Thomas Prince to have cars stolen at just the time when the Mallards robbery was taking place. Miss Kerry Dickson submitted her summing up that even though Mr Horn and Mr Prince were as Jonathan Crisp suggested were well known personalities, even personalities have vehicles stolen from time to time. And one must be fair; it is very unlikely that Mr Prince would drive around with detonators in the boot of his car. Therefore I would suggest to the jury that Mr Horn and Mr Prince be found not guilty, as there is clearly not enough evidence to place either of them at the Mallards Publishing house safe blowing.

The Jury went out to deliberate, on their return they gave their verdict of Guilty for the Mallards safe blowing and carrying dangerous substances in their vehicle.

Judge Peter Samuels sentenced both Edward Horn and Thomas Prince to five years prison. Jonathan Crisp turned to Chief Inspector Bleasdale saying, 'We got a good result that I would have never imagined.'

Miss Kerry Dickson walked over to Jonathan Crisp saying, 'You are very lucky today Jonathan, but you will not be so lucky on the appeal.'

The sentence of Horn and Prince came as a big surprise to the CID at Kilburn and the Serious Crime Squad at Scotland Yard.

Joe Bolt, who was holidaying in Greece and had followed the news in the newspapers, was sorry that Derrick Smallwood had been charged with the robbery at Hayes, but there was little he could do. Now that Ted Horn and Tommy Prince had been sentenced for the Mallards safe blowing. That appeared to be the end of the saga. Joe just wondered if the police would continue looking for him, so he decided to stay in Greece for the time being.

Big Sam Davidson drove from Cornwall to Richmond to collect his belongings; his new car had never travelled outside Looe. The previous owner had only driven from West to East Looe twice a day. As Sam opened the large doors of the factory driving inside Jack and John walked down from the upstairs office. 'Nice car Sam.'

'Yes it runs like a dream. What have you two decided?'

'We are going to stay here for six weeks or so, then probably travel to France or Spain.' Shaking hands and wishing them all the best, Sam drove out of the large double doors and back to Cornwall.

Sergeant Jessup called George Lopez letting him know that Chief Constable Roger McBean had interviewed Paul Gear and was now writing his report for the Commissioner.

'It was wildly believed that Superintendent Parker had actually taken the money and the books.'

'When will you know for sure about the report?'

'I would imagine a few days.'

'Let me know as it is very important.'

George Lopez sat down in his easy chair pondering over the situation, if Parker actually had the books he must be either killed or hurt until the books were recovered.

Scotch Jack had been talking with John Shephard about going out to the West-End for a night out. John turned down the idea saying it may be a bit early to go out clubbing when the police were still looking for them. Jack caught the underground train to Leicester square; there were enough people about so he didn't believe he would be noticed. He found a nice girl, Jean she was about 5, 7 black hair, sweet face, dressed well and she was clean, he handed over £-four hundred for the night and a dinner.

Jack spent the evening in a top class Chinese restaurant, drank two bottles of champagne, a few gin and tonics, finding a local hotel where Jack ordered another bottle of champagne. The following morning they had a bath together and drank more champagne.

'Are you married Jack?'

'No Jean I'm divorced, would you like to go out again tomorrow night?'

'Ok if you are sure Jack it will be another four hundred.'

'That's fine Jean, I'll meet you here at the station at 8:00 pm.' They kissed goodbye, Jack walked down the stairs of the tube station and caught the underground train back to Richmond.

Jean telephoned her pimp Ray Collins, letting him know that she spent the night with a punter.

'How much did you get?'

'Three hundred.'

'Well you better get yourself over here as I need more drugs.' Jean hated Ray, all her money went on drugs for him, she had tried to leave him twice. Only to be found and beaten badly, he had threatened her the next time she ran off, he would have her legs broken.

Reaching Brixton Jean told Ray that she had another date with Jack the following night for the same price.

'I better come along and take a look at this guy your meeting, he may be married and then we can put the squeeze on him, if he has six hundred to splash about in a week, he must have plenty of money.'

Scotch Jack was telling John Shephard about Jean. 'I'm thinking of asking her to go abroad with me John.'

'Jack you hardly know her and if as you say she has a boyfriend, and he finds out who you are he could grass you out to the Old bill.'

'I'm in love John; I'm going to chance it with her.'

'Ok, it's your life, but be careful Jack.'

Bob Warden had also followed all the newspaper stories about the Hayes robbery he was disappointed that Derrick Smallwood hadn't listened to Joe Bolt, as now he was down for at least ten years.

Scotch Jack travelled to Leicester Square, thinking more and more about asking Jean to go away with him. Walking up the stairs at the tube station Jean was waiting at the entrance.

'Hallo Jean,' putting his arms around her waist and kissing her on the lips.

'Where would you like to go tonight?'

'I thought the restaurant we went to last night was great.'

Finding a table in the corner, Jack ordered a bottle of champagne and the best meal on the menu, holding hands Jack said, 'I thought of you all day, now what about this boyfriend of yours?'

'Jack, I'm very unhappy being with him, it was alright in the beginning, but Ray lost his job and started using drugs. We nearly lost our home and was in financial difficulties, so I went out on the game.'

'Why on earth don't you leave him?'

'I tried twice but he beat me up and said if I ever try and run off again, he would have my legs broken.'

'Nice guy you have. Listen I'm thinking of going abroad for a few months, how about coming with me?'

'Jack we hardly know each other, what happens if you get fed up with me in a week, I would be right up the creek.'

'That wouldn't happen Jean, let's play it cool and see how the night turns out.' They made their way to a pub in the Square and ordered two gin and tonics, chatting and laughing together.

Ray Collins was outside the window looking in at them, there was nothing he could do, as he needed the money from Jean to purchase drugs. Jack suggested that they book into a hotel and have drinks in their room; after making love three times, Jean asked Jack if he was serious about taking her away.

'Jean I want to go to France, Spain and Mexico.'

'Ok Jack but I haven't got many clothes.'

'Don't worry about that we can purchase new clothes.'

'Alright Jack when do you want to go?'

'Next Monday, have you a passport?'

'Yes Jack, but how will I get away from Ray?'

'Don't say a word to your boyfriend just make your way here next Monday.'

Jean kissed Jack warmly saying she couldn't believe this was happening. 'I'm so happy.'

The following morning, Jack gave Jean four hundred pounds as they walked towards the underground station. Jean turned to Jack saying, 'You won't let me down will you?'

'I'll be here sweetheart don't you worry about that.'

The Chief Constable of Northumberland had completed his report saying potentially all the evidence received in the statements point to Superintendent Parker having actually taken the ten thousand pounds and the valuable books from Liam Murphy's flat. I also believe Parker will sell those books at a later time for a considerable amount of money. My opinion Parker should be dismissed from the service.

The Commissioner and his deputy read the report in detail, and came to the conclusion that Parker had to go.

Superintendent Parker was summoned to Scotland Yard, when he was told that after receiving the Chief Constables report and the evidence, they had come to the conclusion that Parker had two choices:

1. To go before a disciplinary committee
2. To retire on medical grounds

Parker opted for the second suggestion and was escorted from the building.

Rumours of Superintendent Parker being fired from Police Station to Police Station inside the MET.

Sergeant Jessup called George Lopez letting him know of the findings. 'Thank you I'll be in touch.'

George sat down in his favourite chair with a whisky in his hand, pondering on how to deal with Parker and hopefully retrieve the books. Picking up the telephone, he called Jorge Pereira, 'I have another contract to carry out.'

'No problem George. Who is the target?'

'An ex-police Superintendent, name of Parker, he has some books that I want to retrieve.'

'George that's going to cost you fifty thousand.'

'We have a deal Jorge.'

The following day Parker was followed down his street, as a large white van pulled up beside him, three men jumped out from the side door, grabbed Parker and pulled him into the back of the van, driving off.

'What's going on?' shouted Parker.

'We want the books you stole from Liam Murphy's flat.'

'There were no books.' Parker was smashed in the mouth breaking the front lower tooth.

'We'll start again, where are the books you stole?'

'I haven't got them,' another smack this time cutting open Parker's lower lip.

'Parker you have an hour and a half; if we haven't retrieved the books in that time, nobody will care anymore as you'll be dead.'

'I'm telling you I never found the books, somebody else must have stolen them.'

'You are a silly fucker Parker,' smacking him so hard that it knocked Parker out.

Parker came around feeling absolutely groggy, finding himself tied to a chair with his feet in a bucket of cement and surrounded by at least six or seven men. 'Parker, you have already been warned; we want the books you stole from Liam Murphy's flat.'

'Don't you realise that half the MET police will be looking for you when they find out one of their Superintendents is missing?'

'Parker you are a prat, you were sacked yesterday, the MET aren't worried what happens to you. Now for the last time where have you hidden the books?'

'I haven't hidden any books,' replied Parker.

'Give the liar an electric shock.'

'No, no please I haven't got the books… Ahhhhhhhhh!' as the shock ran through him.

'Now are you going to tell us about the books?'

'Ahhhhhhhhh!' as another shock ran through Parker.

'He's not going to tell us anything, take him out for that fishing trip.'

'Look, please, I haven't a clue where the books are.'

'Parker you've always been a liar as long as I have known you.'

Parker strained his eyes trying to see who had spoken to him. 'Ahhhhhhhhh,' as another shock ran through him.

‘Take the lying bastard away and feed him to the fish.’ Parker was thrown in the back of the large white van and transported to small factory that lead onto the Thames at Nine Elms.

‘You’ll never get away with this,’ as he was pulled struggling from the van to the factory.

‘Have a good look around, you bent copper, as this is the last sight you are ever going to see.’ Parker could hear the trains going past, he tried to shout for help, but the traffic noise stifled his shouts.

‘Look I can give you money, I have plenty stashed away in Spain, and also I own two villas.’

‘Well Parker, dream on, as you won’t be seeing them again you bent bastard.’ More cement was poured into a small dustbin that Parker was standing in.

‘Don’t worry Parker we are not going to feed you to the fishes, we have a better place just for you,’ pointing to an alcove. The seven large men pushed the dustbin that Parker was standing in into the alcove, one of the men picked up a brick looking at it saying looks good to me and laughing as he put the brick down on the floor. Two of the others started bricking up the wall around the alcove.

Parker shouted for the last time, ‘You’ll never get away…’ as the last brick was put in place and nobody could hear Parker’s voice again.

Scotch Jack had worked out in his mind his escape plan, he and Jean would travel to Dover, purchase a cheap day return ticket to France. Once there, catch a train to Paris spend a week, then fly out to Mexico. Packing his suitcase he slipped his handgun inside, and would dump it at Dover. Jack had already made arrangements with the bank manager; so that he could collect money from different banks with the gold card he had been given. Looking around the factory and shaking hands with John Shephard, they hugged each other.

‘Good luck Jack, I really hope it works out for you both.’

‘Thanks John and good luck to you, I hope you also find peace.’ John closed the big double door behind Jack. Jack made his way to the underground station walking up the street with the two up and two down houses on either side of the street with their basket of flowers on the window sills.

The train journey was fast, as Jack walked up the stairs towards Leicester Square he hoped all would go well for Jean and himself. Looking at his watch he found he was early, it was barely ten-thirty and he had told Jean eleven. Sitting down at an outside table of a cafe, Jack ordered a coffee. Thirty minutes went by, no Jean. I'll give her another thirty minutes then I'm away. Crossing Jack's mind was did Jean really want to leave this prat Ray or had he hurt her, either way he knew he had to leave the country. Eleven-twenty that's it, I'm off, walking towards the underground station disappointed when he heard a cry, 'Jack.' Turning around Jean was running towards him. 'O, Jack I thought I was going to miss you.'

'I was just about ready to leave; I thought you had changed your mind Jean.'

'Never Jack,' kissing him, 'I've got my passport,' waving it at Jack.

'Ok let's make a move.' Arriving at Dover, where Jean went shopping while Jack purchased the tickets, looking around making sure all was clear.

The ferry passengers were called, Jack had two passports, one in his own name Jack Paul Daniel or the new dodgy passport in the name of Paul Jack Williamson, Jack watched the security encase they were checking passports two customs officers really didn't observe anybody, just stood inside the corridor that lead to the ferry. Jack and Jean walked through arm in arm chatting onto the ferry.

As they disembarked in France, again nobody seemed that interested, they walked into the shops casually looking around; Jack noticed the sign pointing to the train station, catching the next train to Paris.

Mrs Helga Parker reported her husband missing at the local police station, after a series of questions, the station Inspector noticed that Superintendent Parker had a red flag against his name, calling the Serious Crime Squad.

Inspector Brown who had known the Parkers for some time, visited Mrs Parker at home, explaining the problem of the missing ten thousand and valuable books. Mrs Parker was totally unaware of the situation. Inspector Brown asked Helga if she thought he had flown to Spain.

'I really wouldn't know Inspector, you know what he's like always keeping his cards to his chest, plus we hadn't been getting on too well.'

'Was there somebody else in his life?'

'Again, I'm really unsure.'

Inspector Brown reported the disappearance of Parker to Commander Rose and in turn to the Deputy Commissioner. They all agreed that Parker must have travelled to Spain with the money and would probably sell the books to the highest bidder; the file on Parker was closed, other than if the books came to light.

Alex Quirk named the big day for his wedding to Gloria Egido in Madrid, Ben Clark had been named best man and Captain Sifre would be giving the bride away. Gloria didn't have a large family; only one brother and two aunties along with their children and a dozen or so friends.

Alex would have his uncle from Palmer along with two cousins. Captain Sifre had made all the arrangements at a local restaurant Ben and Alex landed at Madrid airport and were collected by Sergeant Gillispe; the conversation towards Madrid centre was jovial. Sergeant Gillispe dropped Ben and Alex off at the Intercontinental Hotel, telling them that Captain Sifre along with a few friends were coming over later to take them out to dinner and a few drinks, as it is your last night of freedom.

Ben laughed, no matter where you are in the world nothing changes when it comes to getting married.

Captain Sifre brought Gloria down the aisle of the Church, happiness was the order of the day, at the restaurant everybody congratulated the wonderful couple. When it came to opening the wedding presents Alex was amazed when one present was from Bob Warden. The happy couple left the reception and drove off for their honeymoon.

Alex's uncle was very pleased that Alex had decided to retire from the police force and would be living in Palmer and working for the company.

As Ben Clark arrived back in the UK, he wondered how Bob Warden had known about Alex Quirk's wedding.

Jonathon Crisp had a meeting with the Deputy Commissioner and Commander Rose, the conversation was on the forthcoming trial of Derrick Smallwood, Peter Shephard and Costa Esteve, all had been charged with robbery of the Security Van at Hayes, Costa Esteve was also charged with murder of Peter Sainsbury and Jeffrey Mitchell.

Willis Shawbum was representing Derrick Smallwood and Peter Shephard.

Malcolm T Bruton was representing Costa Esteve.

The QCs were Toby English representing Derrick Smallwood, Michael Gardener representing Peter Shephard and Albert W Smith representing Costa Esteve.

'The whole of this conspiracy is about murder and robberies, after all the evidence had been produced and the witnesses called, I am sure you will agree they are all guilty.'

Judge Sir Michael Leon called for the end of proceedings for the day, the prisoners were removed to the cells.

The following day after Crown court had opened, Mr Albert W Smith rose saying that his client wished to make a full confession of the crimes.

Judge Leon asked Jonathon Crisp if he objected to Mr Esteve making a full confession.

'My Lord I would ask for a short recess to confer with Mr Smith.'

Judge Leon knocked; there would be a short recess of one hour. The prisoners were removed to the cells. Albert W Smith sat with his client Costa Esteve, while Jonathon Crisp sat opposite at the metal table.

After hearing Costa Esteve's version, Jonathon Crisp agreed.

Judge Leon called on the Crown Court. Both Toby English and Michael Gardener complained that they hadn't been invited to this special meeting with Mr Crisp, Mr Smith and Costa Esteve.

Judge Leon inquired of Jonathan Crisp if any deals had taken place regarding Mr Costa Esteve.

'No My Lord, there were no deals to be made.'

Judge Leon turned to Toby English and Michael Gardener. 'Your complaint is duly noted, Gentlemen.'

Costa Esteve took the witness stand saying that he had been involved in the hunt for the Knight Templar Treasure and the Holy Grail. 'Maps of the Treasure and documents confirming the whereabouts of the hidden Treasure were hidden in Peter Sainsbury's safe at Mallards Publishing House. Mr Sainsbury's job was to locate the site according to the Maps where the Treasure was hidden. I did not kill Peter Sainsbury; his assignation was ordered by the Mafia in Madrid and carried out by hitmen.

'After trying to find suitable safe blowers, I was given the names of Jeffrey Mitchell, Ted Horn and Tommy Prince, I met with those gentlemen and agreements were made, that I was only interested in the documents, maps and plans. Whatever money was in the safe they could keep. Once the safe had been blown Jeffrey Mitchell tried to blackmail me into giving him more monies, he wanted a further thirty-thousand pounds. I retrieved the documents, maps and plans after giving Mr Mitchell his money. However, he tried to flee the country with the thirty thousand, the last I heard of Mr Mitchell was that he was taken to a farm and fed to the pigs.

'The robbery of the security van at Hayes was put up to me by persons unknown; I was given a list of names, I contacted one of those named Mr Samuel Davidson, who recruited other men for that robbery, they were Scotch Jack, Jimmy Simmons, Peter Shephard, John Shephard and Derrick Smallwood. At the same time I was approached by Mr William Chambers who told me that once the robbery had been carried out, the villains named would run off with the money.

'However, he had an associate in the gang who would help making sure we got our share of the money. That person was Jimmy Simmons. I must point out here that the villains named did run off with the money and Jimmy Simmons was shot dead. Derrick Smallwood was the guy who pushed Andres Lara out of the vehicle, and was consequently shot,' pointing at Derrick Smallwood and Peter Simmons, 'I am sure in my mind that those two villains also killed Mr William Chambers in his apartment.

'The documents, maps and plans were taken from me by force at my apartment in Macon Street, Heston, again by Carlos Moran who is connected with the Mafia in Madrid. They were also responsible for killing my friend Andres Lara in the hospital. I am guilty and will be sent to prison but my life is in terrible danger from a number of people, that's all I have to say.'

Both QCs Toby English and Michael Gardener argued for their clients saying that Costa Esteve who without doubt was the mastermind of murders and both robberies at Mallards and Hayes and was trying to put blame on their clients because he was bitter of being caught.

Jonathan Crisp for the Crown summed up by saying that without a shadow of doubt Mr Costa Esteve had masterminded the Mallards safe blowing robbery and the security van heist at Hayes. He was also involved with the murders of Peter Sainsbury and Jeffrey Mitchell.

Derrick Smallwood as you have been told played a large part in the Security Van Heist at Hayes. 'I cannot say if it was Smallwood who shot Andres Lara Ferrer or Jimmy Simmons, that's for the jury to consider.

'Peter Shephard was on the robbery of the security van at Hayes, as witnessed by Mr Carter of the Boars Head public House and many other witness's. Again I cannot say if Peter Shephard shot Andres Lara Ferrer or Mr Jimmy Simmons, again that's for the jury to consider.

'We have been informed by the police, that no monies have been recovered from the Hayes heist, one can only believe the monies have been hidden for a rainy day. The evidence is overwhelming against Costa Esteve, Derrick Smallwood and Peter Shephard and I hope that justice will prevail today.'

Toby English for Derrick Smallwood pointed out that his client was innocent of the security van heist at Hayes, there is no evidence that Mr Smallwood was anywhere near Hayes at the time of the robbery.

'We have heard from Mr Carter of the Boars Head Public House that he recognised Mr Smallwood. But I ask you if you were standing outside a pub at some distance away from a nasty fight would you be able to look through a vehicle window screen, and definitely say I recognised that man, I can assure you that you cannot. My client is innocent.'

Michael Gardener for Peter Shephard suggested that his client had no idea about a robbery at Hayes, until he read about it in the newspaper, as he was on holiday in Kent at the time.

Albert W Smith pointed out that his client was fearful for his life; he had stood up and told the truth because he was hurt and sorry that people had been murdered. Yes he has admitted taking part in both robberies, first at Mallards Publishing House and second the Security Van Heist at Hayes. Mr Esteve denies having played any part of the murder of Jeffrey Mitchell and Peter Sainsbury, as it was a contract hit by Mafia in Spain run by a Mr Carlos Moran.

Judge Sir Michael Leon requested that the jurors withdraw and consider their decisions of whether the prisoners were guilty or not guilty of the crimes committed. There will now be a recess until the jurors return with their verdict. As the prisoners were escorted from the dock and lead to the cells, both Peter Shephard and Derrick Smallwood tried to attack Cost Esteve.

But were held back by security guards, they were able to shout and threaten Costa Esteve with death threats.

Judge Leon was informed the jurors had their verdict and reopened the trial.

The foreman of the jurors rose.

Judge Leon asked, 'Have you a wholehearted verdict?'

'We do, Your Honour.'

'Do you find Mr Derrick Smallwood guilty or not guilty of the security van robbery at Hayes?'

'We the jury find Mr Derrick Smallwood guilty.'

'Do you find Mr Peter Shephard guilty or not guilty of the security van robbery at Hayes?'

'We find Mr Peter Shephard guilty.'

'Do you find Mr Costa Esteve guilty or not guilty of the Mallards Publish House safe blowing?'

'We find Mr Costa Esteve guilty.'

'Do you find Mr Costa Esteve guilty of not guilty of the security van robbery at Hayes?'

'We find Mr Costa Esteve guilty.'

'Do you find Mr Costa Esteve guilty or not guilty of the murder of Peter Sainsbury?'

'We find Mr Costa Esteve guilty.'

'Do you find Mr Costa Esteve guilty or not guilty of the murder of Jeffrey Mitchell?'

'We find Mr Costa Esteve not guilty.'

'I would like to thank the jury for their diligent work in this very difficult trial, you are now dismissed. Sentencing will be given tomorrow morning at 11 am; the court is now in recess.'

The Crown court was reopened by Judge Sir Michael Leon.

'The prisoners will stand. Mr Derrick Smallwood, you played a large part in the conspiracy of these robberies, and it is difficult to wonder if you played any part in the shootings of Andres Lara Ferrer or Jimmy Simmons, you did however push Mr Lara Ferrer out of the vehicle, where he was shot. I therefore sentence you to fourteen years imprisonment. Take him down.

'Mr Peter Shephard, it has been proved that you were in the gang that robbed the security Van at Hayes. I therefore sentence you to eleven years imprisonment.

'Mr Costa Esteve, although you have mentioned your guilt in the robberies of both Mallards Publishing House and the security van heist at Hayes, there is no doubt in my mind that you were involved with the murder of Peter Sainsbury. I therefore sentence you to life imprisonment.'

The trial having ended, Commander Rose thanked Jonathan Crisp for his hard work and dedication in putting these villains away.

The newspapers were full of the reports, George Lopez was very interested in the report of hidden monies that could be in his factory, he would visit the factory when Big Sam had gone in three months' time.

Joe Bolt had followed the trial and read the reports, and was very concerned for Derrick Smallwood's health, now serving fourteen years, he didn't know if he would make it.

Scotch Jack had also followed with interest the trial and was disappointed and sorry for the lads who got prison sentences; they should have listened to Big Sam and not ventured out.

Jonathan Crisp successfully had Kenneth Delanny found guilty of the murder of Jeff Mitchell and was sentenced to life imprisonment. Ken Harvey, Michael Staler and Paul Bailey were found guilty of the Days Cleaning Company robbery and each received a sentence of six years. Mick McRight and Paul McCathy were found guilty of the murder of Alonzo Ortuno and received twenty-year sentences.

Big Sam had followed the trial with interest, after finding the documents and maps inside his jacket pocket and listening to Costa Esteve's statement. He realised that the maps were in fact those pointing to the hidden Knight Templars Treasure. He thought about the situation and realised he must put together another gang and search for the lost Knight Templar Treasure.

Picking up the telephone he called the factory.

'Hallo.'

'John it's Big Sam, sorry to hear about Peter's result. I'm onto something new, would you be interested?'

'Sam count me in.'

'Is Jack about, John?'

'No he's found himself a young lady and has travelled to France and Mexico, but you'll be able to get in touch with him, with the agreed advertisement he has given me for you.'

'I'll be in touch soon John, first I'll have to find another safe property for us to stay.'

Sam was certainly the lonely man.

The Lonely Man will return in The Hunt for the knight Templar's Treasure